THE WEST HAVEN UNDEAD BOOK 4

A VAMPIRE NAMED ALLISON

NICK SAVAGE

4 Horsemen
Publications, Inc.

A Vampire Named Allison

NICK SAVAGE

DEDICATION

To my wife, Kris.
She puts up with my insanity.

TABLE OF CONTENTS

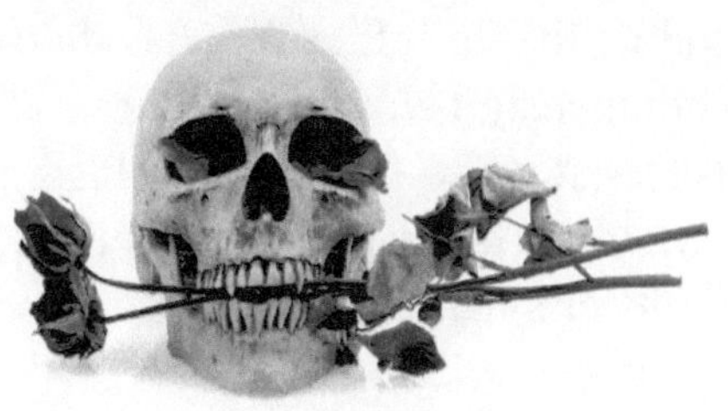

CHAPTER 1

"We fight and we fight…mainly against ourselves."
~L. Taylor~

ow much worse can things get? That thought runs through Allison Petrovsky's mind as she stands, hands cuffed behind her back, with her pixie-cut, pink hair disheveled and mascara dried in extended drips down her face. She struggles against the urge to break down in tears as a cop grips her arm. She watches the lobby television trying not to cry, but her attention turns from the newscaster rattling on about the World Health Organization's search for a location to build a new facility to the doors of the West Haven police station parting ways for her father, Vistrus. His ice-cold stare pierces his daughter, freezing her in some reverted state to when she was a young girl, learning right from wrong. Right now, at this moment, she already knows she was wrong, even before his stone-cold stare impaled her. At least his paternal ability to inflict fear has distracted the hysterics simmering below the surface.

Vistrus steps to her, turning his attention to the officer holding her arm. Vistrus notices old scarring on the officer's hands and a familiar undertone to the color of his eyes. "Are you in?"

The officer nods his head. His whispers are quiet enough that most would think he is mumbling to himself. "I am in as they put out the star-light."

Vistrus's smile relaxes to one far more comfortable for such an uncomfortable situation.

The officer unlocks the cuffs binding Allison. With her hands freed, she gives her wrists an obligatory, soothing rub.

"Are you hurt?" His parental concern shines through.

Allison lowers her eyes to the ground, shaking her head.

That one word, "hurt," rings through her mind, tearing her back to the hole she dug—frantic conversations with a deceased friend and how it can't be. No. It can't. The tears well back up.

"Is my car in one piece?" His tone grows sterner with the knowledge his daughter came through the event unharmed.

Reluctance to answer overtakes her, sinking her head lower. She knows he has no idea what transpired. To her father, her action indicates another sign of rebellious youth. Decisions made by someone not as mature as she should be. Little does he know there is so much more to it. The tears push their way closer to the surface.

Vistrus turns back to the officer, hoping for a response.

"Mostly. It'll need some repairs. Looks like she hit a boulder or swiped a tree," the officer fills him in. "Must've hit a patch of black ice."

Vistrus places his index finger under his daughter's chin, raising her head. "What did you hit? Ice?"

She does not answer, instead pulling her head away from his finger and turning her stare to the terrazzo floor below. "Can we talk in the car?" Her tone rings meek and apologetic. Her blurred gaze fixates on tears that broke past the surface and are falling, wetting the floor below.

Vistrus takes a deep breath in. "Of course. I am just glad you are not hurt." He turns to the bench behind him. "Take a seat. I need to speak with the officer."

Allison trudges to the bench as her tears continue to well up and fall. The weight of her actions slows her down.

"My car?" Vistrus's words are short and to the point.

The officer pulls out a pocket notebook and tears off a page. "All the information is on there: the tow lot, her charges, fines, etc. All payable through the town website."

Vistrus notices the letters "DUI" were crossed off and replaced with "diabetic reaction to low blood sugar." He eyes the officer with a raised brow.

"No one was injured. Just your car and some bushes she trimmed. I felt no need to further affect her future more than the punishment she will inevitably dole out herself." The officer nods in recognition of the favor he did for both Petrovskys.

"Thank you." Vistrus turns to gather his child.

Allison rises from the bench. Eying a spot on the bench dampened by her tears, the phrase once again runs through her mind. *How much worse can this get?*

The officer whispers as they head to the door, "Are you in?"

Vistrus stops for a moment to whisper back, "I am in a night chilly and dark."

In the parking lot of the West Haven police station, Allison opens the passenger door to her father's Porsche, kicking sludge off her shoes as she enters. A rare moment that she gets to ride in it. However, she feels this occasion will not be one she holds dear.

Shutting the door as he swings his feet in, he turns to his daughter. "I am glad you are not hurt."

Again, Allison's reluctance prevents her from saying anything. She knows his words might be baited, so she gives an acknowledging nod as she fails to hold back tears.

"Have I ever given you a reason to think you could not come to me?" His voice struggles to remain calm.

She shakes her head, avoiding eye contact.

"No head shaking. You made adult decisions with adult consequences; use adult words. You are not a child anymore." Irritation rises in his voice.

"What do you want to hear?" Allison swings her head to her father, searching for answers. He completely misses or ignores the agitation in her voice.

"What is my first rule?" A simple response in calmer words.

"That I come home safe," she replies without hesitation. "But…"

"But nothing. And my second?" he continues his pop quiz.

"Dad, you're not…" she tries to interrupt.

"And my second?" He ignores her pleas.

"That I don't get a scratch on me or the car." She tries to hold her head up as the words, the guilt, and the tears weigh her down. "It's not that simple, Dad. There's so much you don't understand."

Her tears take over as she starts sobbing. The weight in her chest with each heave makes her feel like she can't stop. The pressure and force behind each cry weigh her down like an elephant stepping down onto her. She rubs the snot, tears, and smeared mascara from her face.

"I am trying to understand. Help me understand how drinking and driving play into not breaking the second rule." He takes a deep breath. That last question concludes his pop quiz.

Allison's mind races. Her eyes shift as she searches her thoughts for the words that won't sound defensive. "It's not that simple. It's not like it was some act of teenage rebellion!"

"You did not drink, then drive?" Vistrus's eyes grow in paternal anger.

"Yes! I did! Fine. Your little girl drank, then drove." It finally spills forth. A truth she has long denied doing on previous occasions, all culminating in tonight's events. "I drank, but it's not why I hit him—" Allison cuts off her words.

"So, it is not *what* you hit, but *who*?" A tint of red stains his face. The restraint in his voice keeps him from shouting. "Who did you hit?"

"Dad." The only word she can muster as her hysterics take over all actions. Tears fall into her hands as snot drips from her nose.

The sounds of despair fill the car as her mind tries to grasp the reality of the night's events.

Vistrus's signature restraint has abandoned him. His voice booms, "Who did you hit?!"

Allison's tears stream down her mascara-mottled face. She buries her face in her hands even as her nose drips through her fingers.

A realization washes over Vistrus. The officer said she hit a boulder or tree. There must have been nobody there—no body at the scene.

He slows his breathing. An exercise that, to him, always seemed much easier to control when transitioning in and out of his Legendary form versus this instance of dealing with his daughter.

"Allison, why did the police not find a body? Did you hide it somewhere?" All anger has left his tone. Now, concern dominates his emotion.

"Not *his* body." Simple words uttered by a confused, hysterical young woman. But simple words can mean so much more.

A meaning not lost on her father. "Who is he that you hit and whose body did you hide if not his? What's going on?"

Caught in ever-growing hysteria, Allison pulls her hands away from her face. She sees the faded, black mascara smudged onto her palms like some metaphor. A metaphor that does nothing to calm her down. Sobbing, she turns to her father. "Scarlett and Connor! I was going to visit Scarlett at the cemetery. I saw Connor leaving and found her dead at her parents' grave. She was dead. I didn't know what to do. I freaked out. Remembered a dream I had where I buried her, so I buried her. But then, driving back to find you or Connor or someone to talk to, I hit him. I don't know how. I was speeding down Osceola or Monitor or some street, and he was just there. I veered into the bushes, and he was gone. Gone. Daddy, I don't know what to do. Scarlett is lying in a ditch I dug in some forest preserve, and I may have mortally wounded my boyfriend, who may have killed his own cousin."

She returns to burying her head in her hands, continuing to sob. The events replay in her mind. She sees it again in the slow motion of her mind's memory—the sight of Connor flipping over the hood of her car, panic filling his eyes, as he glimpses her behind the driver's seat. She saw the panic in his eyes turn to confusion upon seeing her. The sound of his body thudding simultaneously against the car, bush, and concrete echoes in her mind. Nausea pulls her from her thoughts as the scene repeats. Instead of thinking about her boyfriend, who may or may not be lying in a ditch somewhere dying, she gets to stare at the grave disappointment and worry etched on her father's face.

Vistrus, in all his centuries, has never been in a situation like this. He has never had a twenty-year-old daughter, and definitely not a daughter in this predicament. Now he has to figure out how to deal with these wounds.

Vistrus starts the car, having sat in the police parking lot for far longer than anticipated. He drives away, listening to the worry in his daughter's cries.

With the events of the past three years, Vistrus must figure out what led Connor to such an extreme measure, how to help Scarlett, and make sure his daughter survives all this. For now, home to help get Allison cleaned up. Then, he can worry about Scarlett. A plan of action sprouts in his head. In Allison's head, however, that same phrase plays on loop in her mind. *How much worse can things get?*

Eleanor's tears break the heavy silence surrounding her. Her house, normally filled with the joy of loved ones, now sits empty, drowning in sadness and sorrow.

She stares at the blood covering her hands. The blood of her beloved Nick, her confidant and best friend for more days than anyone can count, covers her as she cradles him. The years that became centuries of bonding and being lifelong partners all led to this.

Eleanor strokes his hair, crying for him to stay with her. She rocks him, attempting some sort of comfort or solace. Legends die and resurrect, an occurrence every Legend experiences at least once in their lifetime. A car accident bringing about freckles or a deep tan they did not have before. A fire leaving their eyes changed when they return. With each new return, a new name. An act symbolizing a new family member took their place in the community. A cover, a story to keep them and their conditions hidden. A Legend resurrecting is not a matter of if in The Nation, but a matter of when. The certainty of the situation does not make it much easier when it does happen. But something in this moment does not sit right with Eleanor—a violence that was not opportunistic. She sees intense anger and hatred when looking at her husband's wounds—an intentional overkill.

She rocks his body back and forth. The distant sounds of sirens bring no solace to her ears. The wall behind her—broken and torn. His 21-gram vial lies open; hers stands unopened and untouched. This final end to his life while she continues on. No more shall he rise up a little older, a little wiser. No more shall she wake up to his smile or hear him tell her how much he still loves her after all these years.

His last words echo through her mind. "Connor. Not what you think." Connor did this to him. He told her. The last four words Nick spoke are lost on her. Connor did this. Her own grandson killed his own grandfather. In her husband's final act, he leaves the world with a smile on his face as the last glimmer of life fades from his eyes.

Now, of her last two grandchildren, she will never be able to look at the only male heir the same. No matter the circumstances behind his decision to take a life, she will only see this moment in her mind when she looks at Connor. The sight of him will always remind her of her husband's dying words and, in her mind, will be motion pictures of how she envisions the struggle played out.

EMTs rush through the door, medic bags in hand. They pause for a moment at the carnage before them before collecting themselves. Turning to see Nick, they set down their bags near his body.

"Ma'am, we need to tend to him. Please. We need room," an EMT pleads with her.

Eleanor holds him against her chest, reluctant to let go.

"Please, ma'am, if you want us to try to help." He again tries using his words to get her to move.

Finally, Eleanor sets Nick down and steps aside. She reaches for her amulet, smearing it with blood as she strokes it, trying to find some sense of calm. An amulet that has been a reminder to her for far too long about the choices she made. Eleanor can't help but wonder if they have all led up to this moment—if she harbors some responsibility for the blood on her hands.

Eleanor watches the EMTs trying in vain to resuscitate Nick. After numerous futile attempts at cardiac compressions and several jolts with a defibrillator, the EMTs unroll the inevitable end to their visit—the body bag.

A tear runs down her cheek as Nick disappears behind the zipper closing over his face … forever gone to the other side. She can't help but wonder why Connor did such a thing. Nick's final words, the message he tried to tell her as he passed away, replay over and over in her mind. How can Connor not be who she thinks? Now, she is left alone to ponder if it matters why Connor did this. But when the why is all that remains, it matters very much.

Brianna and Duncan squeeze next to each other in an otherwise empty booth at Manic Monday's, the local, over-priced, 300-grams-of-fat-per-entrée-fried-food chain restaurant. A mix of half-eaten appetizers and scribbled-on paper cover their table. Their jackets lie next to them on the booth seat.

Duncan feeds Brianna a mozzarella stick. "We have time, ya know. We don't have to plan our entire wedding shower and wedding in one night."

Bri swallows the cheese stick. "But I'm so excited! Aren't you excited? It's a very … exciting time. Don't cha think?" An ear-to-ear smile breaks out.

With a smile to join hers, Duncan shakes his head in agreement. Taking a drink of his soda, he adds, "We need to prioritize. Everything we need to plan is scattered." He gestures at the mess in front of him. "We need to make a to-do list."

"Well, like, what's the first thing we check off?" Bri starts gathering the mess of papers.

Duncan grabs her hand, stopping her. "Besides breaking the news to our friends? How about a date?"

"A date? Aren't we on a date?" Bri misses the meaning.

Duncan sets her hand free, a chuckle escaping him. "I mean a date for the wedding. Nothing to plan if we don't know it's gonna happen."

"A date, huh? Summer." Her excitement swells, "A June wedding. Ooh, no! Christmas! No. New Year's." Her voice finds resolution.

"Eve or Day?" Duncan swallows a fried green bean.

"Eve," she squeaks. "Day. No Eve. No Day."

"Very decisive." Duncan switches to a nacho.

"Let's decide on that later. But New Year's for sure." Bri beams with joy.

"Great. This year or next? I mean, this year will be very fast. Might come off as rushed. If we wait 'til next year, we'll have plenty of time to get all the details sorted out. Give you the wedding you deserve. The one you always wanted." Duncan washes down his food.

Bri pauses all motion. The reality of what they are planning starts setting in. "This is really happening, isn't it?"

Duncan takes pause in her words. "Only if you want it to."

A hint of uncertainty creeps out in her smile. "It's just all so surreal."

She continues to smile, watching Duncan toss down another bite of food. As fast as the excitement of the idea of being married lifted her to the clouds, she finds herself suddenly slammed onto the ground. An impact not unnoticed by Duncan.

He gathers all their scribblings before turning to her. He grabs her hand, cradling it between his. "Love, I can see something is written all over your face. It's there. Just not sure what it says."

Bri's smile widens while looking at everything around her. She searches for the words to say, but nothing comes to mind.

"Wanna tell me what it says, or you gonna look at everything but me while I guess?" Duncan's demeanor turns to worry.

She turns to him, forcing herself to keep eye contact. "Everything's changing. I'm barely into my college years. Well, would-be college years. It's been a crazy past couple of years. And all I can think about is all the years ahead. Everything is different. Everything will be different. And I want it. I want you. It's just a lot to take in. Sometimes, it's a bit overwhelming."

Duncan nods in understanding. "Let's put this on hold for the night. We can plan all this out as slow or as fast as we want. It's our wedding. Our life. Our future. Our plans to do on our time."

She hears his words, but each time he says "our," her mind feels nails being driven in by some proverbial hammer into some proverbial coffin of her freedom and individuality. With each "our" he speaks, the hammer hits harder and harder in her mind—a feeling causing her to fidget in her seat. As her mind urges her to run as far as she can, she stays in the booth but pushes on the table, sliding a few inches away from him.

"I do want this. But it's a lot. I don't understand what it all means. I mean, I do, and I don't. Yes, there is this idea, this picture of what being married is that's pushed upon us from a young age. A happy marriage with a happy husband and wife and two-point-five kids surrounded by a white picket fence. A life where I make dinner while drinking martinis or wine, and you come home to freshly cooked meals and a bottle of beer, and it's this image of moments that they make kids focus on and obsess over. But home-cooked meals are moments. Not a marriage. And what do we expect of each other? I mean, I don't even know what changes. Does nothing change except for a ring on my finger and a piece of paper that says we are married? Will people look at us strangely for being so young and married? Once we're married, will everyone start badgering us about when I am going to pop out kids? Then what? I mean, it's so much, and I want my future to be with you, Duncan. But it's scary. Ya, know?" She calms her hysterics down to find Duncan smiling instead of jumping up and running away. "You're smiling."

He nods. "You aren't the only one in this relation-ship who has thought all those things. I'm in this, too, and I want to figure out all those things with you. They scare me a bit, sure. But they don't scare me off. They are the things life throws at us, and I want to figure them out with you. I want to figure out how to navigate this thing called life with you. Not with anyone else. But only if you want me by your side."

As his words were meant to help assure her and ease her mind, the nails that had been hammered into the proverbial coffin moments ago are clawed out. Bri leans into Duncan, resting her head on his shoulder. For the moment, she rests a little easier, a little more sure. But even though the nails have been removed from the proverbial coffin, the lid still rests on top.

Meanwhile, watching Bri and Duncan from the corner of her eye, December Childers sits at the bar near their booth. She feels the muscles in her cheeks try to pull a smile, but she withstands. Not out of a disdain for youth or the two young adults specifically, but out of ages trying to get over her own whimsy for more innocent times. She turns back to long-time confidant, Raymond Chandler, who sips a cold, pale yellow beer, enjoying a night of good food and simple pleasures. She continues staring past Raymond, who is too entrenched in his own thoughts that she doesn't want to disturb him. Across the bar, she spots Linda Espinoza, though she knows it is an impossibility. Linda Espinoza, teacher extraordinaire, who was killed by West Haven's own Allison Petrovsky, could not be sitting here while she lies buried somewhere else. And while she may have been someone the students thought was one helluva teacher, Jack Taylor and those she kidnapped and killed before him would have a very different opinion. But there she sits; December would swear her life on it.

She turns to Raymond, nudging his arm. "Hey, look across the bar. It's Linda Espinoza."

Her words whisper in his head, but it is the nudge that makes him spill a little beer. "Impossible." His words ring back into December's mind. He looks across the bar to where December nodded her head, but Linda is nowhere to be seen.

December turns her gaze back across the bar, also no longer seeing Linda. Seated where she was a moment ago is a face neither have seen in close to twenty years, that of Inessa Petrovsky. Both December and Raymond recognize her face, a face that should not be sitting there, either. A face that, much like Linda, has since passed away.

Before either of them can be a hundred percent sure of what sits before their eyes, the face they believe to be Inessa Petrovsky turns around to greet someone.

Both December and Raymond turn to each other in disbelief. In all their years, they have never seen the dead walk. They have met their fair share of those in the Tennyson Society who are called Undying, but none of them are actually dead. Both the faces that December saw, and the one face that Raymond saw, are deceased … passed on … crossed over. They should not be sitting at the bar across from them very much alive.

With no time to process their disbelief, the figure turns around from greeting the man, though it is neither Inessa nor Linda who sits across the bar from them. As if the universe revels in playing tricks on them or that they each have had one too many more than they thought, it is now a large man with broad shoulders standing in the spot. A man that could be a spokesperson for lumberjacking, if such professions had spokespersons. This new acquaintance seated between them obscures his face.

"Maybe we've had one too many," December whispers in Raymond's mind.

Raymond shakes his head. "Something isn't right," he whispers back in her mind. "There's a familiarity to him."

Both Raymond and December quiet their minds while they try to listen in. While it is not much, they do hear the word "Easpag" said a few times. Neither Raymond nor December is sure if Easpag is a title of someone based on its use or a name. From what they can hear, it sounds as if it is being used for a commanding rank in some organization. They put a pin in that note for a moment to listen for what else they can hear. Both Raymond and December keep hearing the two ask "who" over and over. As if both men across the bar are confused about who they are speaking of. The only other word they can clearly make out is the name Espinoza. December finds that interesting after swearing to have seen Linda seated there just moments ago. Also the words, The Nation, The Council, and Dryden Society, which the lumberjack of a man corrects himself to say Poe Society.

For the moment, Raymond and December forget about the tricks their minds and eyes played on them in order to focus on the more pressing matter apparently at hand. Figuring out what an Easpag is and who they are talking about that they keep confusing each other, as well as how this all relates back to The Nation, The Council, and the Poe Society all seem to be far more imminent concerns than them seeing the long-dead after possibly a few too many drinks.

December turns back to Bri and Duncan who are still snuggling up next to each other, oblivious to the world around them. A sense of calm washes over December. Something in the purity of the moment looking in from the outside. Neither of them seems to have a care in the world. But much like listening in on conversations not meant for them to hear, if she was listening to Brianna's thoughts right now, the moment's carefree innocence would not exist.

Connor rounds the corner of his block, keeping close to the bushes. He holds his head in his hands as he hobbles back to his house. Looking at the sky just above the roof line toward his grandmother's house about a block over, he sees flashing lights peeking up. He doesn't give it a second thought to the lights, as the impact from Allison's car stings fresh on his bruised and possibly injured body. When he has time to check, he'll examine the extent of any injuries, but for now, he has to get his cousin.

Opening the door to his house, he calls out, "Scarlett! Al's in trouble! Come on!"

No response.

He makes his way to her bedroom, calling for her once more. "Scar! Come on! We gotta help Allison!"

He opens the door to her bedroom and finds it empty. He peeks his head into the room a tad farther, as if she is hiding in a corner, but still finds no one.

"Scarlett?!"

Connor makes his way through the entire house but cannot find Scarlett. He checks out back on the off chance she has decided on a different spot to relax but finds an empty yard—no signs of life in the house.

Something inside his body starts ignoring the pain from the car crushing him. He knows he is injured, but the pain begins subsiding. A warmth washes over him despite the cold as his walk turns to a run toward his grandparents' house and the flashing lights. He stands a little taller, the tenderness from the blow lessens with each step.

The closer he gets to his destination, the brighter the lights. His mind stays occupied, trying to figure out why his pain diminished. He wants to know if this is a good thing—as if he somehow healed. Connor wonders if this could be part of his Legendary state. Or is this a bad thing, like when a body is about to give out and the nervous system stops working? Though, he figures if his body was about to let go of this life, he would not be running full speed.

All thoughts of pain, life, and death leave his head upon realizing the flashing lights are in front of his grandparents' house. He slows his run to a stroll, counting one ambulance, two squad cars, four police officers searching the area with one talking with his grandmother, Eleanor, and two paramedics loading a body bag on a gurney into the ambulance.

The conversation his ears pick up half a block away between his grandmother and an officer, as well as a news reporter on the scene getting her preliminary scoop, causes his pace to slow even further and duck behind a hedgerow.

"I came home and found him," Eleanor says, holding back hysterics.

"Do you have any idea who did this? Was there anyone else in the house at any point?" the officer questions her regarding possible suspects.

The officer notices Eleanor's hesitation to respond. Something in the far-away, squinted stare alerts the officer she may be holding something back.

"Ma'am, if you know something, not telling us will only make things worse," the officer adds, digging for a response.

Eleanor takes a deep breath to calm her nerves. "He said something to me. As he lay in my arms."

"What did he say, miss?" the officer urges.

"That Connor, my grandson, was … that something was wrong with him." She looks at the officer. "I don't know what that means."

The officer holds his pen to his notepad, ready to write. "What is Connor's last name?"

He writes "Connor DeSalvo" in his notepad as she answers his question.

"Was Mr. DeSalvo over tonight? Do you think he might be involved?" The officer scrawls more notes.

Eleanor's eyes light up for a moment at the thought of her grandson. "Connor, no. He wouldn't do such a thing."

The cop still waits on an answer. "But he was over?"

The light in her eyes fades as she finally responds. "Yes. He was helping with some cleaning and organizing. But I don't think Connor would do something like this. Oh, dear, I'll have to tell Scarlett now. This won't be easy."

"Ma'am," the police officer grabs back her attention, "where can I find this Connor?" He jots down Connor's address that she is reluctant to relinquish.

The officer clicks the CB mounted on his shoulder. "I need an APB on one Connor DeSalvo…"

The words fade from volume as the office rattles off his address over the CB radio. He watches two officers hop in a squad car and speed off in his direction. Connor ducks behind a bush before the headlights illuminate him. He realizes his home is no longer a place he can call a safe haven until he figures out what is happening. As the sound of squad cars fades, he watches and listens once more to the officer speaking with his grandmother.

The cop holds out a business card for her. "If you hear from him or remember anything else, please give me a call."

Eleanor takes the card and nods in understanding but doesn't say anymore as she heads back inside to face a world without her beloved Nick.

From his hiding spot in the bushes, Connor watches the ambulance and police cars drive away, the perfect shot for the reporter to begin her piece. "A brutal murder has shattered the quiet Chicago suburb of West Haven this evening. Little is known at this time about the victim or the circumstances surrounding the crime, but police have noted that one Connor DeSalvo is a person of interest. Whether he is a suspect or someone with knowledge has yet to be disclosed. More to come as details emerge. Back to the studio with an update on the World Health Organization versus Six Flags."

Wrapping up their broadcast and taking off, the news van leaves Connor alone in the bushes for no small amount of time to ponder all he's heard. The moon in the sky moves far past where it began, as the late-night silence weighs heavy in the air. He listens to the world around him but hears only nocturnal creatures skittering about. Finally taking a moment to check himself over, he sees wounds that, at first, should have seemed near mortal, if not mortal, have almost healed. A moment later, he climbs out from the bushes and takes cautious steps toward his grandparents' home.

He walks up the driveway, but before he can get to the door, his ears are filled with the sounds of his grandmother weeping. A sensed absence stops him from taking another step; no sounds from his grandfather. His mind flashes to the body bag being loaded onto the ambulance and what the news anchor said, and it all comes together.

His knees collapse under him, sending him to the ground once more tonight. Connor lies on the damp driveway, uncaring if anyone sees him, even after what he heard. All he can do is listen to his grandmother cry. His strength abandons him, leaving him to lie there thinking about all the memories he has to carry with him of his family and how little is left. He listens to the muffled sound of love, loss, and grief from inside, all pouring out from his grandmother.

After listening to his grandmother's sorrowful cries for long enough to make him feel like he is somehow invading her privacy, Connor acknowledges that he can't lie here forever, even though it seems the only option. He has to figure out how he somehow plays into all of this and sort it all out before anyone else gets killed.

CHAPTER 2

*"It's the unfortunate state of how things have
always been."*
~N. DeSalvo~

Vistrus speeds down the road toward Scarlett's
house, hands tapping the steering wheel in anxious worry. "Is her house okay?"

Allison stares out the window as the street flies
by, the events replay in her mind in vivid detail. She
doesn't hear her father's words.

"Is her house in order?" he repeats himself, turning
to her in frustration but noticing her distracted state.
"Allison," he barks.

She snaps out of her daytime nightmare.
"Yeah, sorry."

"Have you been to her home since you," he realizes
the next words may sit heavy and slows himself, "laid
her down?"

"No. Why?" Allison doesn't understand why he
asks what he asks.

Vistrus runs through the usual spots, like behind China cabinets, where Legends keep their 21-gram vials. Though, with everything that happened to Scarlett's parents when she was a baby, he thinks the go-to spot isn't where Ken and Tracy hid them. Perhaps it is behind the bathroom mirror or medicine cabinet. He realizes the thoughts that plague him at this moment are moot if the walls rest undisturbed. On a far more morbid note, the thoughts are moot if the vials have been opened. So, for now, he concentrates on driving.

It doesn't take long before his car stops outside the home. There are no lights on, and no cars sit in the driveway. Approaching the house, Vistrus finds a bit of comfort in that both the screen and front doors are closed and locked.

Seeing her dad jiggle the locked knob, she pulls out her set of keys. "I got a spare."

Vistrus stands aside so his daughter can let them inside.

They find the house undisturbed upon entry. A wave of relief swells up, but he stands reluctant to let the initial findings lull him into a false sense of security.

"What exactly are we looking for, Dad?" Allison searches for something out of place.

"You will know. A wall that has been punched through. Something big." Vistrus's words are vague but paint a proper picture for his daughter to follow.

A thorough search reveals nothing out of the ordinary. That wave of relief finally washes over Vistrus, a dim light in weary times.

"All quiet on the western front." Allison seems happy in their search efforts.

With a raised brow at his daughter, he notes, "I did not know you are familiar with that book."

"What book?" Allison's quick response causes him to smile at her colloquial yet uninformed knowledge.

"Never mind. This," he gestures to the undisturbed house, "is a good sign for Scarlett. Let us go."

"Where?"

He replies not with words but with steps out the door.

Connor watches, hidden in the shadows, as Allison and Vistrus leave his house. He wants to run to her and tell her he is alive. Seeing no signs the police have been by and not hearing any approaching cars, he wants to run to them and proclaim his innocence. But he knows charging out from the shadows while wanted for questioning in a murder would not be the brightest move. Instead, he listens, waiting for them to leave.

"So, she'll be all right, and I didn't kill my boy-friend. That's a couple of good things we got going for us. And, well, I guess for them as well. I mean, I don't know many people who would rather be dead," Allison stumbles through unsure thoughts.

Vistrus clicks the key fob to unlock the car door. "Yes, I guess you are correct. They are good things. After taking care of Scarlett, we shall find Connor."

A hushed cough from the bushes grabs their attention. A moment of tension for Allison. She knows that cough. She loves that cough—a small sound that fills her with mixed emotions. Love, relief, confusion, frustration, and too many more to list all flood her at that moment. Her father, on the other hand, remains calm and collected but does not miss the elation on Allison's face.

"Mr. DeSalvo," Vistrus whispers. "It is safe for the moment." His tone takes an air of defensiveness not usually reserved for those he knows. "But keep your distance."

Connor takes a few cautious steps out from behind the bushes. His eyes meet Allison's, and he is pulled back to the impact of his body versus the car—the look of abject horror on his girlfriend's face as he flipped over the car. But here he stands in the driveway, and he needs to explain what's happening as much as he needs things explained.

"I'm not sure what's going on," he starts at warp speed, talking to Allison. "I mean, I know Grandpa…" He slows for a split second but knows that he might not have the time to grieve. "Well, but I am not sure how they think I did it." He turns to Mr. Petrovsky. "You know me. I wouldn't do this. It wasn't me. I was walking home from watching a friend die."

Vistrus holds up his hand. "What happened to Nick? What friend did you watch die?"

"Rex?" Allison asks with wide eyes before Connor can respond.

Connor nods his head. "I got him there too late." He turns to Vistrus. "He was a friend. You probably never met him, but he was good. A Normal, as you say, but good. Grandpa … you haven't heard?"

"Heard what?" Vistrus's voice grows impatient.

"Dead. They think I killed him. But I didn't. I didn't kill my own grandpa or Rex. I don't know why this is happening."

"How do you know they think you killed him?" Vistrus is cautious with his words as flooding grief washes over him. "Start from the beginning."

"We got into a fight. A bad one. That guy, Ashby. He was trying to recruit kids, teens, whatever. Some organization to separate the men from the Men." Before Vistrus or Allison can respond, Connor clarifies. "Small M and big M. But things went south, fast. Rex was injured really bad. I took him to the hospital as they worked on him—"

Vistrus interrupts, "You took a Legend to the hospital?"

Connor shakes his head. "He is … was a Normal. I stayed with him. They stabilized him and everything. I was in his room, and something happened. I don't know. But the machines made noise, and the doctors pushed me out. After a few minutes, they walked out, heads hung low. They told me the news. Said they would contact his family."

"Then what?" Vistrus asks, indicating Connor needs to get to the current situation at hand.

"Then I was walking," Connor continues. "Thinking about how I just saw another person die right next to me. I watched through the window. Well, tried to, but the pull shade thing was drawn shut. But I was walking, thinking, all up in my head, and the next thing I know I'm flying over a car. It all went so fast; I didn't know what happened. After a moment, when I stopped seeing stars, I saw your car. Allison, you were still. You didn't look hurt, but not moving. I ran to find Scarlett, but she wasn't home. So I went to Grams to see if she was there, but before I got too close, I heard them. So, I hid. I heard Grams talking with the police. She said I was there helping them with some cleaning, except I wasn't. I was with Rex in the hospital."

"If it wasn't you I talked to at the cemetery with Scarlett, then who was it?" Allison's concern rises as she voices a thought that pops into her head.

Connor tilts his head at her words, unsure of what they could mean. "What did I say at the cemetery?"

Before she speaks, Vistrus clears his throat, grabbing their attention.

Raising a doubting eyebrow, Vistrus chimes in, "What you are implying is impossible. Everything you say implies the existence of shapeshifters, and those do not exist. They never have, except in myths and legends." Vistrus searches for an answer that will not only remove any suspicion from Connor but also deny the reality that Nick DeSalvo is no longer among the living.

"Myths and legends, Dad? Aren't you always telling me that we're Legends?" Allison snaps back.

Vistrus turns to his daughter. "Point taken. The more likely scenario is that Connor is losing his memory and ability to control himself while he transitions. It happens … rarely, but it happens. This is where the werewolf legends the Normals know of were born."

"Mr. Petrovsky, you are telling me that in all the Legend community, Nation, whatever, there are only fairies, vampires, werewolves, and Undying? Nothing else at all?"

"Each point of The Nation symbol stands for one of five Societies," Vistrus starts. "And we are not vampires and werewolves. I wish you would stop calling yourselves such names."

"That's only four, Daddy." Allison wastes no time in pointing out the inconsistency.

"The fifth is a Legend that died out long ago. It does not matter," Vistrus tells them. He checks his surroundings to make sure no one is around to hear their conversation.

"Are you sure they died out?" Connor pushes the subject.

Vistrus does not nod or respond.

"Then maybe it matters more than you think," Connor continues.

Vistrus nods. "The fifth point is for the Clochnawa—Stone Men. Near indestructible. Bones of steel and skin thicker than tanned leather. But they have not been seen for many years."

"And there is no other explanation?" Allison urges her dad to share more.

He squints his eyes. "I am working on that." He turns to Connor. "But I do believe that you would not do something like this of your own volition. I have to report this to The Council. I have to give your name."

Allison grabs her father's arms, tugging on them. "Help him, Dad! You can't turn him in!"

Vistrus squints, trying to find a coherent thought in the torrent of pain he feels for the loss of Nick. "I have an obligation to The Nation, an obligation to do what is right for all humankind."

A desperation seeps out of Connor. "Am I no longer part of humanity?"

Vistrus understands the multitude of meanings in Connor's words. "Grab your things." Vistrus motions to the house. "Find a safe place to hide. I mean, where no one will find you. Not myself, not Allison, not anyone. Do you understand?"

Connor nods and faces Allison. "I love you."

Allison smiles, unable to find the words to say it back. "I'm sorry I hit you with my car."

Vistrus clears his throat.

Allison corrects her words. "With my dad's car."

Vistrus finds a brief moment to smile, not in the death of loved ones or the tribulation that lies ahead for Connor, but that in this moment, his throat clearing was meant to hurry up, not correct Allison on the proper possessive of his car.

Connor shakes his head, waving it off. "I'll be fine."

Vistrus chimes in, "There is no time for this."

"How do we find him?" Allison's eager words cling to desperation.

"We do not." Vistrus dashes her hopes. "He stays hidden. If, and when, I can prove his innocence and guarantee his safety, I shall worry about finding him."

"What about The Council?" Connor brings up an unavoidable encounter.

"I will tell them I could not find you. I will think of something. That is my concern. Staying safe is yours. Until we can sort things out, you must stay away. Now go."

Connor plants a deep, passionate kiss on Allison's lips, a move he never would have dreamed of trying in front of her father a few months ago. Now, though, it seems that such things are trivial compared to what they face.

Vistrus smiles, knowing his daughter has turned into a woman and one that he is proud of, despite recent events.

As Connor turns to the house, Vistrus realizes one last thing that needs addressing. "Mr. DeSalvo, where is your car?"

"Hospital. I needed to walk afterward. Never made it back."

Vistrus nods. "I will have it taken care of before someone finds it." Vistrus gives one final warning as Connor again starts toward his home. "Connor." He waits until Connor turns back. "Trust no one."

Connor nods.

Inside his home, he keeps the lights off and his movements quiet in case anyone comes by looking for him. He gathers a few essentials that will keep him sane and healthy: a toothbrush and toothpaste, a few books to feed his mind, non-perishables and a can opener, and a few bags to pack it all. He checks Scarlett's room, but she is not there. Even knowing his time is limited in this house, he does not want to leave. This is his home. If he leaves, Scarlett will be alone, and he does not want that for her.

In his room, he lies down on his bed, looking at everything, memorizing everything he is about to leave behind. The temptation to fall asleep creeps into his mind, but he knows if he is to help himself and help solve his grandfather's death, he cannot wallow in pity.

He heads back to Scarlett's room to leave her a note. Grabbing a notebook from her desk, he writes,

Scarlett,

I'm not sure what is happening. Grandpa is dead, and they are saying I did it. I am not sure why or how. I don't know where you are, but I could use you right now. You'd know what to do. You always seem to know, but I can't find you, and I have to go. I've been told to go. So, I guess I'm leaving. I don't know where I'm going or when I'll be back, but I have to somehow prove it wasn't me. I don't understand the world around me anymore. Just a few years ago, everything seemed so easy. Like I knew it all. Now it all seems impossible to understand. Everything that was once so close to me is so far away. Like my life is slipping. I didn't get to properly say goodbye to anyone, and it's making me feel like I abandoned them. I know I'm not, or, well, at least not permanently, but it still feels like I am. So, please, please let Allison know I love her and am sorry I can't be there for her right now. Let her know that I'll be back. Scarlett, please look out for our home. You're the only one left to take care of it right now. Please, do what you all can to prove I am not the one who killed our grandfather. I love you all.

Connor

He sets the pen on the letter, grabs his bags, and exits his house, not knowing when or if he'll ever be back.

A young Rajmund and Dášenka, covered in dirt, blood, and badly injured, hike through the woods. Leaves and dirt cling to their bodies, plastered on by blood and pus. Smoke from their burning village clouds the distant horizon behind them. Ahead in the distance, the sights and sounds of another village tease their senses. A renewed flow of energy grips them, speeding their step as they hurry toward this new town.

While they approach the would-be savior of the village, the relief and joy fueling their tired bodies die as the villagers' laughter comes into clear focus. However, it was not laughter they hear but sounds of terror. Armored infantry and cavalry invade the city, slashing down anyone in their way, shattering the peace felt seconds ago. The invading forces slaughter the villagers, decapitating them and placing their heads on stakes. A warning to anyone who might fight back.

The destruction spanning before them tugs at their humanity. After the plague they lived through in their village and the slaughter of any who might have been infected, they cannot stand by watching as more innocent countrymen get slaughtered for no reason, other than where they live. Still unable to speak since drinking the concoction at the village hut, Rajmund and Dášenka turn to each other. They both think that they must do something. At that moment, they heard the other's voice in their mind. A simultaneous agreement of what must be done. Nodding to each other, they turn and rush into battle, still not wholly sure about what happened back home, but knowing that death can't be any worse. As the adrenaline of battle courses through their veins, an overwhelming pain pierces them from the inside. A pain they have only felt once—when they drank whatever it was that spared their lives. They pay no attention to their physical forms as they start thrashing the invaders. Snatching the cavalry off their steeds, breaking necks, even through their victim's armor. As swords, axes, and maces swing at them, they block the attacks, swiping the steel weapons aside as if they were bamboo. Rajmund leaves Dášenka to the cavalry, turning to the foot soldiers. Tearing them limb from limb and tossing them aside like trash, neither he nor Dášenka realizes the violence and atrocities they are committing. They rampage through the village, killing off any remaining invading forces and chasing out those choosing to flee. Even though Rajmund and Dášenka's rampage saves the villagers, all the villagers see are two disfigured bodies on a killing spree and how it coincides with the invasion—two acts the confused villagers do not realize are separate.

A correlation that Rajmund and Dášenka realize when the locals attack the would-be saviors. Unable to communicate their intentions, and not wanting to hurt any innocents, they hold their arms against their faces, protecting themselves. Running from the battle, they leave the dying village to its imminent demise. Perhaps their small contribution will leave a few spared to rebuild.

After sprinting deep into the forest for longer and farther than either thought humanly possible, they finally feel safe to stop and breathe. Upon catching their breath, they notice the sounds of violence have faded away. Nothing assaults their ears except the sounds of a sleeping forest. They hear no approaching footsteps or distant cries of anguish. Only the sounds of forest animals scurrying about and leaves falling. Both hope that they have run far enough to not hear them because the other option is that the entire village has been decimated. As the adrenaline from the events fades, they finally get a good look at each other and realize why the villagers thought Rajmund and Dášenka were not on their side. They stare at each other, eyes locked on the other's transparent skin. The veins, arteries, and capillaries are visible and flowing with blood. Their muscles look moist underneath the clear coating. Neither feels ill, though they look like nothing either has ever seen before. The muscles have grown over twice their size, as if the marathon through the woods favored them, though they know that is not the case. They turn their gaze from the other to themselves to examine the clear skin that covers them. They feel their muscles but cannot comprehend that they are theirs. Surely, these muscles are not their own. The strength granted to them to rend humans limb from limb could not have come from the body they are used to seeing. This new form cannot be true, so their eyes must be deceiving them. They examine themselves and each other, unable to understand this new reality they see. Fatigue catches up, causing them to collapse against a tree and slide down to the ground.

As their new reality starts to set in, and the horror of the moment settles down, their skin regains its usual color, and their muscles shrink down to what they know them to be, as does their strength. Their voices, however, seem to be lost forever. They try to speak, but only empty wind passes through their mouths. Anxiety builds as Dášenka tries in vain to shout over and over. Each time, her skin loses the color and opacity it regained moments ago. Rajmund grabs her arm to calm her down. They lock eyes, and he pulls a hand toward him as he takes a deep breath, then pushes his hand away as he exhales. Dášenka understands his efforts and follows along. Her skin again regains opacity. He pulls her in close, embracing her in an attempt to give her some sort of solace at this moment. She holds him back, and they lean against a tree, unsure of what comes next in their lives.

Countless minutes pass before either feels comfortable letting go. Once they do, they decide to set up camp for the night out of nothing more than fallen leaves for bedding and the tree canopy above them to protect them from any rain that may fall.

Before sleep comes for either, they both reach the same, sad conclusion—that whatever they have become will be nothing more than Legend. Dread and isolation fill them as they feel their existence will amount to nothing more than stories told to keep kids from misbehaving and campfire stories to scare one another. And too soon do both realize that to not be hunted, in order to stay safe and live a normal life, no one can know what they have become and what they are. They can already hear in their minds the stories that those poor villagers will tell others of the monsters who ransacked their town. The invading forces will be forgotten, or the villagers will confuse friend and foe, grouping the monsters with the invaders and never realizing the help that was trying to be given.

It is now just Rajmund and Dášenka—two people forever hiding who they are from the world. If, in the moment of needing a savior, the helpless turn them away, they know that in the calm of safety, no one will accept them for their difference. No one who is not the same as them will ever be able to know who they truly are. And they know, if this new reality is related to the plague and the potion, there is only one other who will understand. One other person who will know what they are and accept them—Pasha.

An utter sadness fills their souls. A hopelessness and desperation in knowing that they will never be who they thought they were. A melancholy fogs their sights that they may never feel at peace as long as they still live. They both stare skyward, peeking at the stars through the canopy, searching the expanse of the endless sky above for anything that might help them understand. But the uncaring universe offers nothing for their solace, leaving them to search the sky instead for sleep. A search that does not take long, finally calling them for the night.

Clouds polka-dot the sky as they float on the winds. The sun sits in the sky but refuses to shine down on anyone. Allison smiles at the cosmic acknowledgment of the day's task.

Staring out the car window, she thinks of the last time she saw her best friend as her father drones on about responsibility. Words she has heard before now sound out like white noise. She knows what she did was not right but knows the events of the night, while all interconnected, are not all her fault. She can't seem to connect the dots as to how Connor both stood in the cemetery and in the street when she hit him.

That thought sends the thud of his body smashing against the hood of the car, before smacking the ground, reverberating through her memory. The events of that night play on repeat in her mind, sending a tear rolling down her cheek.

Vistrus sees the tear fall. "I am sorry. It is never my intention to make you cry. You need to understand what it means to be a responsible adult." He looks back at the road, searching for a way to turn around his daughter's mood. She does not hear his words, her thoughts still focusing on the accident. A few moments of silence fill the car as he turns into the forest preserve parking lot. Their silence and the quiet of the forest-turned-makeshift-burial ground drown out any semblance of whatever mood they felt moments ago.

"You want to know what will happen?" Vistrus shifts into park, turning off the car.

Allison leaves the nightmare thoughts behind to join her father in his conversation and nods.

Exiting the car, he grabs two shovels from the trunk before Allison leads him to where she buried Scarlett.

Vistrus scans the woods for other people. "She will not be coming home with us today."

He sees all hope vanish from his child's face.

"It is not a bad thing. She needs time. It is called 'the Waiting.'" He attempts to reassure her.

"The Waiting?" Allison's patience wears thin.

"Each Legend must convalesce in order to return. They must be left undisturbed for however long it takes their body to heal. This period is called the Waiting," he explains.

Allison throws up her defenses. "Then why bring me here at all?" She stops walking and looks at her father. "Huh? What's the point of this—of any of this?! To teach me another lesson in responsibility and being Legendary? Who cares? If there's no helping us return from the dead and come back to life, why tell us? Why make us worry about what we can't control?"

"This is not about instilling worry or giving you undue anxiety about the things you cannot control. It is about understanding. Education to better know why our bodies act the way they do." Vistrus motions for her to continue walking. "Just because we are Legends does not mean we heal instantly. We are not Wolverine. We require help. Ironically, from the decomposer bacteria in the soil."

Allison shakes her head, leading the way. "That makes literally no sense. Not one bit of sense, and I say this knowing what you say we are. I still think all of this is some joke or prank or mass hysteria delusion. Can a whole community get that—mass hysteria? Cause I think that's what's happening here."

"It is not mass hysteria. I promise," he offers. "While the science behind Legends and the Waiting has never been fully understood, even with all the time we have existed, we believe that the decomposers have something to do with us coming back different."

Allison stops and turns to her father. "Different? Like what? She can come back a he? Or will she have a third eye on the back of her head?"

Vistrus motions for her to continue walking. "I think I tried explaining this to you before." He pauses, pondering if this fell on deaf ears once before and may again, but he cannot recall. "No. Not that different. A change in eye or hair color. Hair turns curly. Skin complexion, freckles. We age. Little things we utilize to help us stay hidden."

Allison continues onward to where she buried Scarlett. "So, every time I see her, I have a reminder of letting her killer walk away from me. Every time we hang out, I have to be reminded that the reason she doesn't look like she used to is because I let her die. Is that why we change? A constant reminder of everything I couldn't do right?"

Vistrus pulls his daughter close to him, holding her tight. "That is not why we change. Do not let that burden you. Physical appearances change for so many reasons. Do you think when Connor sees you, he assumes he is the reason you dyed your hair pink?"

He releases the hug, and they walk for a few moments. Every possible change that may occur runs through her head, adding to the guilt bogging her down and forcing her to relive finding Scarlett dying at the cemetery.

She points to the ground. "Here." The reality confronting Allison as she stares down at a pile of dirt weighs like an elephant on her shoulders. Her voice shakes. "She's under there." She turns once more to her father. "It's bad, Daddy. She's real bad."

Vistrus kneels down, hesitating before beginning to dig. "You do not have to relive this. I will look."

Allison stays standing, arms crossed, shaking her head. "She's my best friend. I'm staying. I need to see her."

Vistrus nods.

He digs in the dirt until the dirt he moves uncovers Scarlett's face. He continues brushing only as much dirt as needed to assess her injuries. Her wounds lie as still as her seemingly lifeless body, caked in dirt and dried blood. Her body lies warm and silent. Vistrus examines her wounds. Wounds that have stopped bleeding and have already begun scabbing over. He holds two fingers to what little area of her neck is unscathed, feeling for a pulse. Long after the standard six-second time elapses, a small smile upturns the corner of his lips.

He pulls away his fingers. "She will heal."

Allison scans the woods around them. "Don't wild animals ever get us? Birds, scavengers, carousels, things like that?"

Vistrus's head cocks a tad. "Carousels?"

"Yeah, carousels. Those things that rummage for dead things to eat?" Allison clarifies.

"Carrions," Vistrus corrects, stifling a laugh from the flickering moment of levity. "While I am sure there have been a few of us either lost to them or delayed, I have never read any reports. I suppose if the birds do not sense our demise, they leave us alone."

Allison shakes her head in disbelief. "I won't leave her to chance. I won't be the reason there's a written account of one of us dying because vultures didn't know she wasn't dead. I won't do it."

Vistrus holds his daughter again. "She will be fine."

"No, I already lost her. I won't make it permanent because no one wants to wait with her. Why can't we wait with her?" Allison stands firm in her idea.

Vistrus digs a deeper hole around Scarlett. "What would you say if an authority figure came through to find you standing next to a mound of dirt?"

Allison's response comes quick. "I'd think of something."

Vistrus imparts some learned wisdom to his daughter. "Part of that thinking is us digging a deeper hole and spreading the dirt so it does not mound up."

"Hiding her body more discreetly? Is that what we're doing? What are we, some sort of mafia wannabes rewriting a scene from some mob movie?" Allison's voice sounds in disbelief.

Vistrus shakes his head. "She will need time undisturbed. The better we hide her, the quicker she can heal. There is nothing about being a Legend that roots itself in the Hollywood lens or rose-tinted glasses. What we do, we do to survive. There is nothing glamorous about burying your friend. There is something noble, though, in that we get to see her again. Not everyone is so lucky."

Allison joins her father in digging to make a better spot for Scarlett to convalesce.

"Nothing about digging a deeper hole for your friend feels lucky. Quite the opposite," she observes. "So then what? When she's all healed and ready to be born again, or whatever, she just wakes up like nothing is wrong and hops out of the ground all hunky-dory?" Allison tosses dirt to the side.

Vistrus stops for a moment upon hearing Allison's question. His jaw clenches at the thought of himself having had to climb out of the ground many, many years ago. Memories he has never spoken of rise and play across the silver screen of his mind. Memories that he has not thought about in too many decades to count flicker to life, reminding him why he protects The Council and The Nation. He wraps his hands around the end of the shovel handle and grips it with white knuckles, trying to find words that will suffice in answering his daughter's questions but comes up with only one. "No."

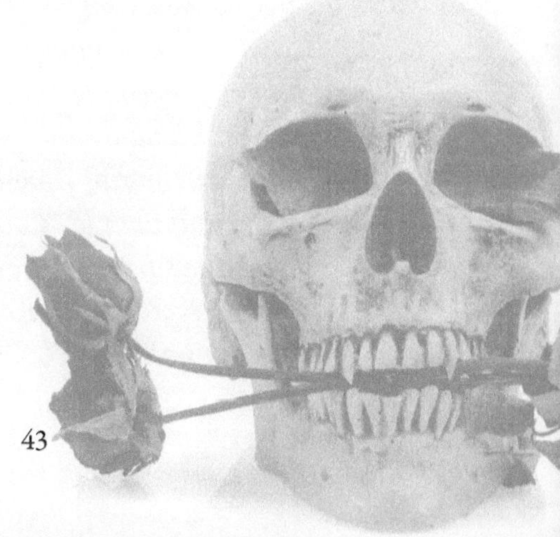

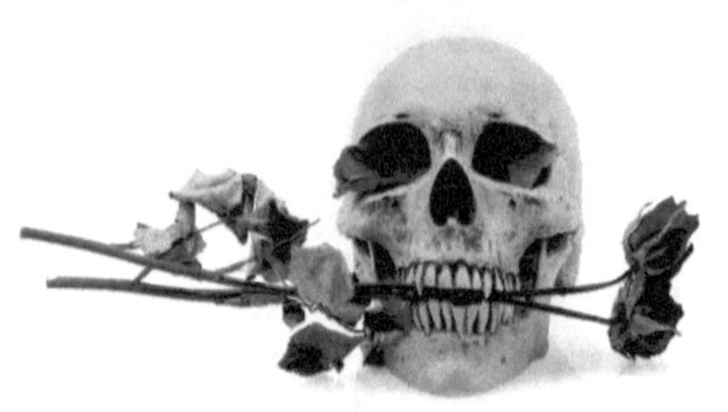

CHAPTER 3

"It doesn't mean it has to stay that way."
~L. Taylor~

I nessa stands at her bathroom sink, tugging at a wall-mounted mirror. She tugs at the mounting brackets, struggling to free it from their grasp. Behind her, propped against the wall, is another mirror, still wrapped in its protective cardboard corners and shrink-wrap.

"Ugg!" Inessa grunts.

Entering from around the corner of the bathroom as if summoned by her struggle, Vistrus offers assistance. "I can get that for you, dear."

She continues struggling with the mirror. "No. I got it. It's my project. Something I wanted to do."

"You do not want to ruin…" as he is about to finish his sentence, the mirror rips from the wall, carrying a large chunk of drywall with it. "…the drywall."

"Well…" Inessa starts. "I got it. And getting it off is half the battle. Now the other mirror goes up. Right up on the wall, and it's all better."

"We will have to repair the drywall first, my love," Vistrus observes.

Inessa shakes her head. "Easy access, in case you need to get inside. Sometimes the answers are hidden, and hidden is easier when exposed."

"What answers would I need to find inside a wall?" He pulls his wife close to him, embracing her in a big hug, knowing she means well—that Inessa wouldn't cause the chaos unless she thought it would create something beautiful. He holds her in his hug, remembering the years together before her change. No matter how many times he dwells on the cause or reason behind it, his feelings remain. She holds his heart and if she thinks the wall needed change, whether it be a new mirror or a hole behind a mirror, he looks forward to the final design.

Pulling back from him while staying embraced and looking him in the eye, she continues, "You never know. Pipes may leak. And pipes carry water. Pirates like water, and pirates bury treasure. There might be treasure inside. Treasure comes in all varieties, and people like variety and treasure. Double whammy there. No whammy, no whammy, stop!"

Vistrus shakes his head, chuckling. "You do like your old game shows." He releases her from his hug. "Let us check for some hidden treasure."

Vistrus peeks inside the sizeable hole in their bathroom wall, looking around for hidden gems. "Nothing but pipes. Maybe the pirates will bury some treasure another day."

Inessa nods. "Maybe. Maybe we will look again and find some doubloons."

A sad smile overtakes him. The clarity waxes and wanes, but even when she is lucid, her words do not always make sense—like her mind traps her inside some imagination, and she reacts and speaks to the images in her head instead of what's real. His smile fades as they gaze into each other's eyes. She awaits some response. "Perhaps. But in the meantime, let me make some calls."

As if she never saw the sadness in his eyes and knows nothing of the concern he feels, Inessa continues rambling on, "A treasure map and we can go on an adventure. Something that will lead us to a great discovery. But some discoveries, though great, are terrible. Terrible, great discoveries. That does not sound like fun anymore. No fun at all."

Vistrus pulls her to him again, staring into her eyes. She gazes back as if everything in the world is coming up roses. She smiles at him, curiosity about his worry seeping into her expression. "My love, my beautiful Inessa. Are you with me?"

Her gaze wanders about his face, inspecting him to find the source of his melancholy. "Of course, I am. Why wouldn't I be?" She turns, smacking his shoulder as if pulled from a deep thought. "I think the world needs to be more fancy-free. Whatever that means. Sounds good, though, don't it?"

"It means free of amorous attachment. Footloose."

"I know what it means. It was an expression, silly. The meaning of it all … it's all in the Mind." She smiles as the answer to life pours from her mouth on her words.

"So you have said. It is all in your mind." He plants a kiss on her cheek.

"Not my mind, silly. The Mind. You'll understand one day. I think I need to rest now."

Without hesitation or a reply from Vistrus, Inessa exits the bathroom and enters their bedroom. She climbs into bed *and pulls the covers over her neck, leaving only her head exposed, and closes her eyes.*

Approaching her in bed, Vistrus leans down and again plants a kiss on her, this time on her forehead. "Sleep well, Inessa."

Eleanor stands outside Connor's home, trying to sneak a peek through the windows, but the drawn curtains foil her attempts. She gives the door a good, hard knock and rings the bell.

"Scarlett!" she calls out. "If you're home, please answer the door. It's your grandmother!"

No one responds. She leans her ear to the door, listening for what her ears can detect below the whipping wind. Nothing. Concentrating a little more, her pupils dilate as the sound of the wind moves to the background but still no noises sound from inside the home.

"Where could she be?" she whispers. "No matter. I'm old. I can play the old card and stand here as long as I want. Stubborn we are." She laughs at her expense and turns to head out. "Well, I'll just have to try again later." She grabs her car keys, realizing she has a spare key to the house. "Maybe I'm not playing the old card. All good things, right?" She heads back to the house, jiggling the keys before opening the door.

Closing the door behind her, she calls out, "Deary? Anyone?" But again, no response. She heads to the kitchen, then the living room, looking for a piece of paper on which she can leave a note but finds nothing.

"Maybe she's taking a nap. Maybe I talk to myself too much. Eh, someone's gotta talk to me. Might as well be me."

She heads to Scarlett's room, finding it empty, though a notebook and pen await her. She sees the note left for Scarlett and takes a seat on the bed before reading it. Tears well in her eyes as she learns of the pain and uncertainty that her grandson feels. A wave of hope passes through her as she finishes the letter. For now, she knows, or at the very least truly believes, he did not kill her husband. The confusion in his words is enough to convince her of his innocence.

She pulls a clean sheet from under his note and scribbles one from her for Scarlett.

Dear Scarlett,

I'm sure you have read Connor's note first. If not, read it, then come back.

So, we need to have a chat. Please come over when you get this.

Grandma Eleanor

Vistrus closes the door to his basement studio behind him, locking it. He descends the same stairs he has countless times before, but this time, determined steps carry him as he is lost in thought.

He thumbs through his vinyl collection, searching for the perfect rise and fall for this day's endeavors. Skipping Bach, Beethoven, and Brahms, and blowing past Glass and his personal favorite, Holst, he even pushes the like of Mahler and Mussorgsky aside until he pulls out Igor Stravinsky's *Firebird Suite*. Resting it on the turntable's platter, he clicks the tonearm to the right, activating the motor and sending that unmistakable static click through the speakers. Upon resting the needle on the vinyl, the masterpiece comes to life.

He turns up the volume, drowning in the ballet's beauty and noise, to once again lose himself in the volumes of Inessa's journals. This time, a few of his own books join the fray.

He sets out all the diaries in front of him, fanned out chronologically. On his right sit the books from his personal collection that he feels may help him in this hunt. Starting at the beginning, he sifts through page after page of ramblings he has read time and time again. After a short while, he stops himself before spending too much time rereading what he has reread countless times. "I know what you wrote, Inessa, but the Adeirrig is not real. It cannot be."

He puts the books down on his lap. He lays back, taking in the orchestral sounds blaring out from the speaker. His eyes clench shut, attempting to reset his mind, his visuals, and this moment.

"The Clochnawa. The Adeirrig. Accounts of Legends experiencing memory loss in those who have already transitioned. This is where I must start. Inessa, my love, if there is a way to prove him innocent, I know you will be the one to have known, to have written something. I shall find it." He dives back into his research.

Thoughts flow through his mind, pondering the reasons Inessa never felt safe telling him what had her so scared. He wonders what may have had her so scared that she resorted to the volumes of diaries and strange speech patterns; a question he must find the answer to, for he feels it has more relevance now than it ever has since her passing. He thinks back to the Faoi Dhó Duine, how his wife decoded its relation to the prophecy of the Grey Fairy. A prophecy that The Council believes dead, but if his wife's journals were correct, is still alive. His mind stirs with how all these things could possibly be related, not only to each other but to her death; why, after all this time, all these years, it is happening again.

Flipping through page after page of Inessa's journals and his books, he comes across an entry about the Clochnawa. He finds nothing he hasn't read before: Legendary state abilities, solid steel bones, tough skin near impossible to cut, organs that withstand impact damage, and even being impervious to the effects of crush syndrome. He continues reading through the notes on a subject he has read about before—when the Clochnawa died out. Though something grips at him, shaking him in some cosmic wake-up call, leaving him to wonder why he never knew this before. The Clochnawa went into hiding, even within The Nation.

A kernel pushes itself into his mind. A kernel that brings him flipping through Inessa's journal, where she wrote about the bodies she was sent to investigate. The state of damage evident on the bodies at the morgue. The remarkable lack of damage on one. It was this lack of damage that was the last time he, or his wife, was to read about the Clochnawa again. And since his wife was the last one to see one, he can't help but wonder if this has something to do with her death. In some way, this Legend having to be the last put her in some sort of danger. He tries convincing himself that this has to be the only acceptable option because the other option, the unthinkable option, is one that he, even as a Legend, has never considered—that the Adeirrig is real. He does not want to chase a false flag but cannot help thinking that this might be connected somehow.

The rise and fall of the Firebird keep Vistrus submerged in the music of his listening room. Finding a moment to enjoy what he hears, he feels that he may have made some sort of breakthrough, even if he can't connect it all just yet. Leaning against the chair he would normally sit in to play an instrument, he relaxes, listening to the music surrounding him, flooding his ears.

He reaches for a blank sheet so he can take an inventory of the situation. No loose-leaf is to be found, so he grabs a blank notebook from his shelf. Not a schoolbook-style notebook. Not in this room. He grabs a yet unused musical notation book. While he anticipated the notebook would be used for some great musical score he has yet to compose, using it to figure out how everything from Inessa's investigation to her death and the current situation all connect sits fine with him. At least the lines of the staff provide a guide for his words.

Wasting no time, he jots down, "The Council, The Nation, Clochnawa, Adeirrig, Connor, Inessa, Nick, Sylvia, James, Lucretia," and the names of all the others that have passed in the last few years. He continues his slew of bullet points with "the old council" before crossing it off.

The old West Haven Council. Separate the old from the current. The Faoi Dhó Duine. The Mind in relation to the old West Haven Council. Everything in relation to everything else.

How is this all connected?

What am I missing?

What do not I see?

Why was she so afraid?

Why could she not trust me?

If not me, who?

Could this be connected to Linda and the blond man?

The boy I found in the alley?

Could all these things not be random?

What am I missing?

What did she see?

What did she find that got her killed?

What did she find that got her killed?

He writes that last sentence over and over again. The details and circumstances of his wife's death have been kept from his daughter. No child should have to bear the weight of a parent's murder. No child should have to live through that, especially at such a young age. So, Allison was told stories, a more palatable version of what actually happened.

Now, with everything happening, he fears the truth may not stay hidden much longer.

He continues writing in his notebook:

The five individual Societies under one collective Society—The Nation. The Faoi Dhó Duine—A dead prophecy. The Clochnawa—a long extinct Legend. The murders—then and now. The Adeirrig—A real myth?

He pauses. A forgotten moment shoots to the front of his mind. A moment when he sat in front of his computer searching for something. For what, he can't remember, but the search turned up old pictures of someone who looked like he did in a suit he told himself he never owned. A memory that strikes him because if he never owned that suit, but the man in the picture looked like him, then perhaps the Adeirrig might be more than a myth. Shaking his head, he convinces himself that the slight blur in the old photos only made the man in them look like him. Someone who was similar in height and stature who could be mistaken for Vistrus was in those photos. Someone other than himself. He puts the pen back to the paper.

> The Cure. The murders and the cure. Linda, the blond man, the Taylors. All connected. Recent events.
>
> The old West Haven Council. The old murders. Inessa. The Faoi Dhó Duine. The Mind. All connect. Past events.
>
> How are the past events and the recent events connected? If Inessa was murdered by a Legend connected to past events, then she is the key.

Vistrus collapses against the foot of his chair. The ground below him keeps him from sinking deeper into the earth under the weight of it all.

He suspects the rest of The Council know nothing of their predecessors. Though, confirming that suspicion may prove harder than asking them. *If they are unaware, then why hasn't the same person tried to kill them as well, or have they been lying in wait all these years? Have the past three years been just the beginning?* These questions circle around in his mind. He second-guesses everything he knows and everything he thinks he knows—unsure who on The Council he can trust. He tries to hatch a plan that will help him separate friend from foe. For now, though, he listens to Stravinsky.

Before he can get too engrossed in the rise and fall of the music, Vistrus recalls the journal Inessa hid in the track above the door, separated from the other journals. He pulls that out from the pile before him.

Thumbing through page after page, scanning for some word that isn't a retelling or paraphrase of the countless other entries she has scribed, he finds one.

Five. Five. Not six. Five alive. Not six. Not anymore. Six was once, now five. Why five? Why die? Why now? When was now? When now was then? When then was five? Five remain. Who will know? Vistrus knows. Five, not six. Six said dead. Only in our heads. Six alive. This is true. Not five. Five seems four. Symbolic fifth. Symbolic sixth. Sixth removed. Five remain, though only four alive. No. Five alive, six alive. All alive all still thrive. Numbers small. Six not five. Vistrus knows. If not now, he will. All in due time. Time is not on our side. Not any-more. All in due time. My time is due. His time is due. All in due time.

Vistrus grabs his pen to jot down more questions to be answered. To hopefully figure out what he missed in her writings. Perchance to see something right in front of his eyes that he can't see.

What five? What five that is really four that was once six? What did she mean? All in due time? What time? My time? Someone else's? I sound as crazy as she did. What does due time even mean? With the parchment locked away in The Mind, does it even matter? The glove and the Grey Fairy kept safe from all that haunted her. What haunted her? Why The Mind? Why so close? So many questions that need answering. Six to five to four. All the same. All still remain. All in due time. Where to start? The heart of it all in due time. The young boy there and the young here, but only was is true. How can he be both places at once? It cannot be the Adeirrig. It is not real. Inessa must have been wrong.

Inessa and Vistrus sit together on a park bench. No clouds line the sky; the sun shines down to warm the still air, yet, despite the beautiful weather, the swings lie still. There are no children shooting down the slide or crawling across the monkey bars. Pedestrians do not stroll by, nor are any birds in the air. It seems this moment was meant for just the two of them.

Inessa holds his hand, squeezing it. "I love you, Vistrus. I have always loved you."

He nods his head, unsure of her foreboding words. Her lucidity may wax and wane, but right now she can focus. Her mind knows what she says, though the reasons behind them are lost on him.

"I love you, too, Inessa. Since the first day we met." A meek smile breaks across his lips. "St. Petersburg. It was a cold evening in November."

"It's Russia. Most evenings are cold in winter."

He nods. "But this was especially cold. You were huddled by a fire."

Her eyes light up, remembering that evening. "And you walked in, needing to use the bathroom."

Vistrus shakes his head. "It had been a long day. I was passing by and saw the firelight. It seemed warm."

Inessa nods. "I invited you to share the warmth."

"The way you looked at me as I shivered … a sparkle in your eyes. You still have that sparkle. Something about it spoke to me. It showed me everything that we could have in this life, in this world."

She turns to her surroundings for a moment, scanning them for something, before turning back. "There is so much we have in this world. So many memories. I never want it to end."

"Nor do I." He waits for a reply that does not come. "I treasure every moment with you. Every moment." He stresses those last two words, hoping that she will give a clue to her cryptic mood.

She smiles, gazing into his eyes. "I know how I sound sometimes and know how it must sound to you, to those around us. I wish I could explain."

"But you can. There is no one here." He gestures to the emptiness around them. "It is just us two. You can tell me anything."

Uncertainty defeats her growing smile. Her eyes dart around the park, searching for anything that may lurk in the shadows before stopping back at him. "How do we tell such things?" Her stare grows long. All sense of wonder and nostalgia from moments ago fades, and an exhausted defeat takes over. "All in due time."

"I do not understand. What is going on—what has been going on—that you cannot tell even me? What has you so scared that you are overcome with paranoia and spell-like ravings?" Vistrus tries to cover the pleading in his voice, but it seeps through, bringing tears to Inessa's eyes.

She turns her stare toward the sky. "People always look for metaphors. Something easy to compare the situation to. The problem with metaphors is that they simplify a complicated situation."

"Perhaps, sometimes, a complex situation needs to be simplified before the complexities can be understood." He keeps his gaze on her, searching for some tell or sign that the Inessa he knew still fights to break through.

A knowing smile upturns her lips. Her gaze pans to the left like she is following the path of a shooting star, though none are in the sky. "Life moves forward. We see the things in front of us. The events that take place within our line of sight. We know that all around us, other, far more complex events take place."

His finger tugs her chin, trying to pull her back to him, but she resists, still looking at whatever her mind saw above them. "Inessa, what events?"

Finally, she turns back to him. "Pawns on the front line only move straight. We have to assume they can only move toward what they see. Thus why they can strike diagonally. But their sight is short, limited. Rooks, while they have sight that extends much farther, can only see in a straight line. But it is never the things coming straight toward you that get you. It is never the speeding train with the light that blinds. You see it and move off the track. It is all the things in the peripheral, the sideways, and the diagonals that people never see coming."

"Love, I am frightened. Please tell me." His normal, authoritative tone completely abandons him, replaced instead by soft and begging words.

"Even if we look to our sides, our line of sight is still straightforward. No matter where we look, that spot we look at is straightforward. We never see to our side because our eyes only look in one direction ... forward. There are things that will come to light ... sooner or later. All in due time, my love. All in due time."

The static from the record player needle spinning on the vinyl's edge fills the room as the *Firebird Suite* ends, drawing Vistrus out of his memory. He looks down at the open diary. A drawing he has seen only a few times, sketched in various ways throughout other volumes, catches his eye once more. In the past, he always thought this doodle helped Inessa think or work out some anxiety as she wrote, but now he wonders if it means something more. Everything she wrote in all her diaries and journals held meaning, so this, too, must mean something. Six wavy lines stacked and evenly spaced. A simple drawing, sometimes drawn only with lines and other times shaded to give it more depth, but six lines that start low, end high, and always crest twice—never more, never less. Like a mathematical similar-to sign stacked three high. Vistrus doesn't know what it means. The relevant importance of it dawns on him now, after having read the journals so many times since betraying the trust of the once-living. Yes, he knows his dearly departed wanted him to read the diaries, to follow the clues hidden within. How many times he has seen this symbol, he does not know, but something gnaws at his mind. The symbol has no clues written around it, and from his million-mile-per-hour-mindset, no clues anywhere within the pages.

His first instinct urges him to call upon the man who has always been there for him when he could not figure something out on his own—Nick DeSalvo. The instant he thinks of calling his long-time confidant, an emotional tsunami floods his mind, drowning out any notion of good memories and would-be phone calls, reminding him that Nick has passed. The ability to laugh while passing time with his friend is no more. With that reminder, he also thinks of James and Lucretia Taylor, Sylvia Waldgrave, James and Hillary McAllister, and every other Legend he has known who has gone before him. A reminder once again that time eventually abandons him of all friends he calls family. While remaining members of The Council do still sit around debating policy, he trusts none of them, nor would he rely on or confide in them about such important matters. There was one member he trusted … Ken DeSalvo. Gone, too, along with his wife, Tracy. Both taken before their time by possibly the same person or persons that still hunt them, that hunted Inessa. Then an idea hits him like the freight train his wife once spoke of: if no other council members have said anything about being hunted, could it be only Ken, not the entire council, was targeted? Assuming that was true, would Vistrus be next? If not, then what separated Ken from the rest of them?

So, he sits, contemplating those thoughts, letting them stew in his head while he listens to the static of the spinning record, surrounded by musical instruments, albums, and musical literature. He tries to figure out the mysteries left for him by his late Inessa. Alone, he sits, staring at the six wavy lines.

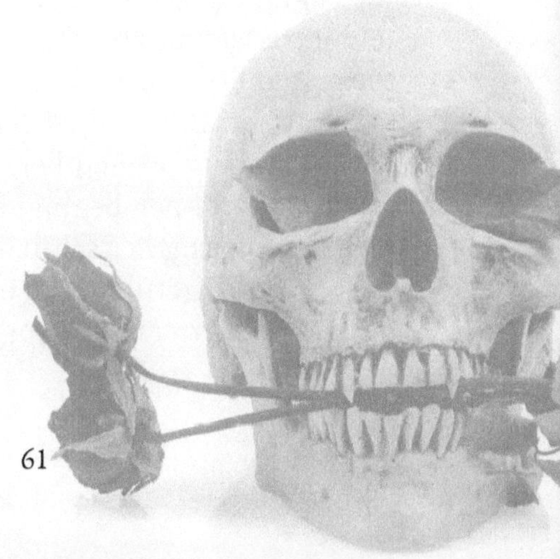

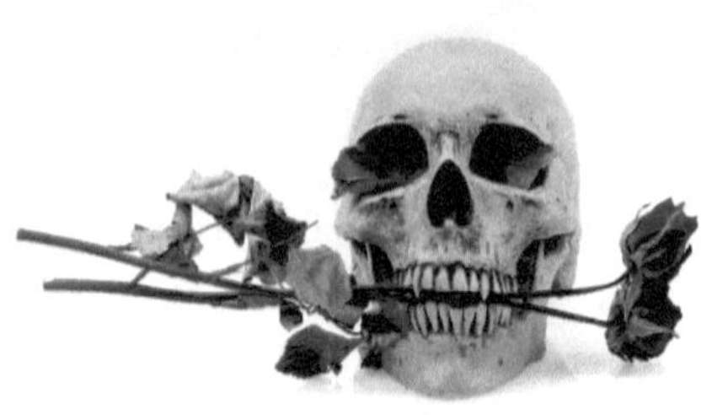

CHAPTER 4

Allison hits play on her iPod stationed in its dock, and the spooky organ intro opening up White Zombie's *Astro-Creep:2000* and the song "Electric Head, Pt. 1 (The Agony)" blares through her speakers, trying to drown out the world around her so she can hear the narrator telling her to start from the beginning. A sentiment that might play better to her ears if it suggested instead to start over, relive her life from the beginning and not simply retell it. That way she might possess the ability to affect something and have the possibility to make it end any other way than how it has so far. But as she falls onto her bed to drown out everything around her, the world, it seems, has other plans for her, beginning with the ringing doorbell interrupting her self-indulgence.

She huffs, getting back up. "Can't even enjoy the intro," she mutters. "Coming!" she shouts toward the front door.

She pulls the curtain aside to see Eleanor standing there.

"Hey, Grams. Dad's at work."

Eleanor motions in question to come inside.

"Sure, sure," Allison says, making a way for Eleanor.

"Do you know when he'll be back?" Eleanor wipes her shoes on the front door mat, more out of habit than necessity on this day, and closes the door behind her.

"No clue. Cop a squat." Allison motions to the house as she starts back to her bedroom.

Eleanor stands, unsure of the words she just heard. "Do what now?"

Allison responds as she continues back to her room, "Grab a seat."

"Cop a squat. What funny phrases the kids have." Eleanor chuckles, taking a seat on the couch.

A moment later, Allison returns, cell phone to her ear. "Hey, Dad. Grams is here, but you're not. So, call me, well, her. Don't call me. Call her. I mean, yeah, you can call me, but, yeah, you know what I mean." She hits the end button on the phone. "No answer."

"I gathered as much."

Allison sits on the couch with Eleanor. "How you holdin' up?"

"I've lived a long time. I'll survive."

"Survive? That's not the same as, well, anything good."

"It's hard, but we've had more time than most will ever get. And for that, I'm thankful." She forces out her words, choking back truer words not meant for young ears. "Arrangements are being made for a funeral."

"There've been a lot of those the past few years," Allison notes.

"Too many. None of which were needed."

"Are any?"

Eleanor huffs at Allison's observation. "Death is as natural a part of life as being born, but none of the deaths in the past few years were from natural causes. And those, my dear, are why they were not needed." She takes in the sights of the room around her, remembering what she can of her past visits here, while Allison sits in an awkward silence. "I needed to see if your father knew where Ms. McAllister is, but you would know better than he." She ponders that thought for a moment. "So, I guess I came here to see you. Huh, isn't that something?"

Allison's muscles tense up. Her jaw locks tight, clenching over and over. Her stare freezes on Eleanor, who awaits her response.

"What is it, dearie?" Eleanor leans forward a tad and pats Allison on the knee.

Allison holds back tears. "How has no one told you?"

Fear begins to overcome Eleanor, tightening her shoulders. "Told me what?"

"Something… I don't… Scar is … waiting."

"Waiting for what?" The word does nothing to calm her fears.

"My dad says she needs to wait."

Eleanor tosses the word around in her head for a few seconds before realizing what Allison is trying to say. It is a phrase that she has not heard in many years, but one that allows her to relax her shoulders some. "She's in the Waiting?"

Allison nods. "Yeah. That. Dad says it's something all of you must do. How has he not told you? How has anyone not told you?"

"There's no one left to tell me besides you and him. Everyone else is dead, and Connor has left."

The weight of that fact sinks Allison back into the couch. "Sorry, Grams. I didn't think."

"It's okay. Of all the things happening around here, a Legend in the Waiting is the least of my concerns. Though it saddens me that she won't be at the funeral."

"Can't you hold off until she's back alive, or whatever? Crawls out from her grave?"

"Crawls out of her grave?" Eleanor huffs. "It's not like a George Romero movie. Have you ever woken up from a sleep so deep, it takes you a moment to realize where you are at?"

Allison nods. "Sure, I guess."

"It's nothing like that." Eleanor shakes her head. "See, when you or I wake up and it takes a moment for us to orientate ourselves, we are in a bedroom or on a couch. Somewhere we are familiar with. The familiarity helps with the otherwise disorienting moment."

Allison furrows her brow, trying to see where Eleanor is taking this.

"When a Legend wakes from the Waiting, they do not get all the time they need to orientate themselves. They need to breathe, and that is something hard for them to do because of the dirt-covered cloths blocking their airways. So, before they can bat their eyes, stretch, and realize the dream was the worst part of it, in order to comfortably fall back asleep, they have to struggle against the weight of the dirt, taking in what little air makes its way through the loose pile on top of them. When you are buried and wake up in such a state, up and down are not directions you can tell, so you have to hope you don't turn yourself around and dig yourself deeper. Then, if you don't make it out, you fall back into the Waiting until you can come to again and try once more to dig yourself out. An experience that is never fun, never amusing, and never something I wish any of us had to experience." She watches as Allison tries to hide the horror plastered across her face.

While Eleanor knows she could stop where she's at, she feels the whole truth always provides better education and preparation than half-truths. So, she continues, "It will not be enjoyable when you have to do it; it never was for me. Not to mention, when you finally emerge from the ground, you are often in the middle of god-knows-where trying to find your way back to familiar territory so you can rejoin civilization as some long-lost relative or twin that no one knew about. Starting over is never easy, but it beats the alternative. To which Legends have no idea how long the Waiting is. Nick's body may not hold. So, unfortunately, Scarlett will miss the service…"

"Thanks … for the crash course … I guess." Allison's attempt at gratitude falls short in sounding sincere, but Eleanor takes it as it was meant.

"When your time comes, you will be better prepared than others. And that preparation can save you much anxiety."

Allison straightens herself up. While her belief in this whole Legend-Nation-Waiting-Vampire thing still has to solidify, her interest in it piques, at least for the moment. "What else can you tell me? Dad didn't say much."

"When you wake, most likely you will not remember dying. Obviously, you will not remember being buried. If you are buried by someone who has been through this before, they will use a cloth to ensure no dirt gets into your mouth. Don't suck in the cloth trying to take a deep breath. Keep your lips close together but open enough to breathe. If you can, remember to breathe through your nose, if possible."

"If they know you need dirt, but will wake up covered in it, struggling to breathe, why not put your head in a bag?"

Eleanor shakes her head, holding in an amused laugh. "I'm going to let you figure out why we don't do that specific idea. However, we don't put a gap in the airway because we need the dirt, the bacteria, and the organisms as close to us as possible. Otherwise, our changes have proven more drastic and disfiguring than when we have less air."

"That's a real doubled-edged coin there, Grams." Allison grasps the situation better than before.

"Sword. Coins don't have edges. There seems to be a bit on this that your father never told you."

Eleanor winks at Allison, but she misses it. Something has the gears turning inside Allison's head, dragging her down from the teachable moments of this situation to the moment she stood there, beside Scarlett, burying her best friend.

As Eleanor continues filling Allison in on aspects of the Waiting that Vistrus decidedly did not tell her about when he and his daughter were beside Scarlett, Allison slips further away, reliving the discovery of Scarlett's body, the drive to the woods, burying Scarlett, and hitting Connor. But she sits, listening to aspects that, as they hit her ears, she wishes she could unhear and never learn about. But she has and can't unhear them, which plants thoughts in her head of what her father and mother must have gone through. Images and imagined feelings of what Grams and every other Legend she knows must have gone through. The idea that takes her breath away is the idea and imagining of what she, herself, might have to go through at some point and what changes may come with that. The thought of the dirt and the claustrophobic spaces weighing down on top of her, the idea of swallowing dirt and bugs, and the disorientation all tense her already anxious nerves more and more, until it all comes out in uncontrollable sobs.

Eleanor realizes her final approach may have not been the most delicate or tactful and wraps an arm around Allison. "I didn't mean to. Once I got going, I guess I forgot how new all of this still is to you. I'm sorry." She exhales, bringing herself back to thoughts of Nick. "Nick and I may have had our time together … time that most never even fathom, but it makes the loss no easier. You didn't deserve what I said. I could have handled that differently."

Stuck on the crash course teachings of the Waiting, Allison misses Eleanor's last words on Nick. "But I don't want to do that. I don't want Scarlett to do that. Maybe I should wait with her so when she wakes up, I can dig her out. I told Dad that, but he said no."

Eleanor pats her on the back. "He's right. There's no telling when she might end the Waiting. It could be tomorrow, could be next year. You can't sit by her side, hoping to help. The unfortunate part of being who we are is that the hardest part we must go through alone."

Eleanor stands, giving Allison a goodbye hug. "All will be as best it can be."

While those parting words are meant to instill some sort of comfort in Allison, all she hears in her mind are the words before that … that the unfortunate part of being who we are is that the hardest part we must go through alone.

Later, Allison sits on her bed, staring past her pink sheets, black comforter, and all the posters hanging on her walls. The lessons learned from Eleanor sound in her mind, portending things to come. All comfort Eleanor tried bestowing on Allison loses out to the cycle of obsessing over it. No music blares from her MP3 player, no television drones in the background with nightly news or sitcom reruns. She stares at the unknown beyond: the abyss of the future and the uncertainty that she and her father will ever be able to exonerate Connor from his accused crimes. She stares at the grave of her best friend, still painted so fresh in her mind—the dark brown dirt piled on top of Scarlett's fair skin and red hair. The sounds of scurrying forest creatures while she dumped her friend into a hole still ring clearly in her ears. Allison stares into the ever-darkening fog of loneliness and isolation she feels enveloping her.

She pulls out the only friend she feels comfortable with right now—her flask. She stares at it, knowing the consequences she faced the last time she found comfort in this object. Right now, though, the temptation pulls it toward her while her logical mind pushes it away with the same force, causing her hand not to move either way. She searches her mind for every reason not to drink it and put it back down but comes up blank. Whispering in her mind is the only excuse either side can conceive at this moment, and it tells her she won't be driving tonight. So, she unscrews the top and takes a long swig. The translucent brown liquid burns as it cascades down her throat. The numbing as it continues its waterfall, glug after glug, working its way into her bloodstream, makes the torment she feels a little more tolerable.

Even realizing the counter-productivity of her actions—that her inebriation will inhibit any forward progress toward proving Connor's innocence, she can't help but take another swig, feeling the utter destitution and despair of the moment—of not fully trusting that her father knows what he does, of not fully believing all the evidence laid out in front of her over the past few years or what Grams had told her earlier.

One last swig to finish off the flask, drowning any remaining feelings thanks to the liquid therapy inside. Feeling more numb with each passing moment, she sits, staring past the veil of her surroundings, tears welling up before rolling down her cheeks. Slow at first, but they build. A slow trickle turns into a steady stream into a raging river of uncontrollable emotions pouring out.

Burying her face in her hands, Allison tries to hide her feelings from herself. Falling to her side, she continues crying. No more does she stare into the abyss. No. Every emotion she has ever felt, every time she has doubted herself, her existence, her purpose in life replaces the empty abyss. All those moments replay in her mind, seeing them each in vivid detail as they all overlap the next like some bad, multiple-exposed film playing out in some small, thirty-seat, old-timey, silver screen theater of her mind's eye. She feels the depression of life's uncertainty weighing her down. She feels the confusion of loving a man while, at the same time, feeling those same feelings for not just someone of the same sex, but someone she had sworn to be mortal enemies with. The aching in knowing she was wrong about hating someone as confused as herself.

As Allison focuses on her own confusion, all other feelings washing over her suddenly vanish. Only the confusion of every choice ever made remains. The self-inflicted pain, as well as the pain caused to others, stabs at her. Allison buries her face deeper into her hands, falling onto a pillow and crying harder than ever before. Her father sits a floor down, playing some sonata on the piano while his daughter weeps. Blissfully ignorant of the mental breakdown his daughter experiences at this moment. She cries and his fingers dance on ivory, supplying a beautiful soundtrack for her dark moment. As suddenly as it came, her confusion leaves for a moment, letting lone-liness take another round at kicking her.

This continues for a while—rotating emotions tag-teaming each other and draining her of what little happiness she found, kicking a dog while it's down, until she finally passes out, giving into the slumber of exhaustion.

Vistrus sits alone on the ground, surrounded by green-and-black walls of serpentine marble, his eyes puffy and red from recently fallen tears. Mourning lost ones never gets easier, no matter how many go before. Each loss reminds Vistrus that his loneliness grows; that one less person lives who understands his situation, and one less person whose situation he understands. The world holds one less life who shares this experience and can share it with him. This death hit him especially hard. Nick mentored him—his guiding light when all his years of experience weren't enough. Nick kept Vistrus's trademark sto-icism grounded in compassion. It also reminded him that no matter how long someone has lived, there is always more to learn and someone with the experi-ence to teach it.

The overhead lights begin flickering. A single bulb flashes one last bright flare before burning out. He turns his head to find the dimmed bulb, not that he would replace it. He just notates one more thing dying in this room. The mystery of such modern lighting in a room that predates its invention is a mystery he never solved. Though, he does not think that it is a mystery worth solving. Perhaps, a little something to ponder once everything else has been tended to. An afterthought for another day, not a distraction from the main focus. Though, the dying light bulb reminds him that this room, too, closes in on its final rest once more.

Looking around, Vistrus tries to imagine what once took place here. Imagining council meetings when, perhaps, The Council was trustworthy sets a smile on him. He imagines faceless people he's only read about from Inessa's diaries, laughing and sharing moments in here. Confiding in one another about secrets the world knows nothing about. A sad smile etches itself across his face for a moment upon realizing that no matter how different the world is now compared to his youth in late seventeenth-century Russia, nothing ever really changes. His thoughts turn to silent contemplation on the future of this once-honored room, thinking of ways it could be used, if not for The Nation, perhaps for the museum or his personal studies. A solitary office away from his home and work office. A man cave to contemplate The Nation, the world, and his future. Pulling his attention away from all those musings about this room is the parchment in his hands.

"How do we tell…?" He stops in his words to think about what he just said. "Who is 'we' anymore? James, Ken, Sylvia, gone. Lucretia, Tracy, gone. Now Nick. Gone. Am I next?"

When Sylvia was alive, he informed The Council of the parchment she could read. The one that said, "We know" in ultraviolet light. But they dismissed their concerns, and he was appeased. Now, though, he wonders if their appeasement wasn't an attempt to cover something much bigger than themselves. That thought brings back a scolding Nick gave him when he first approached him about the possibility of something more. But Nick bought into the idea, and he now lies six feet under. Vistrus knows all the pieces are there, floating around his mind. Putting them together is a different matter.

He looks around the room, recalling diary entries scribbled by his late wife. Entries that recall the deaths they sent her to investigate. Entries that he now knows were messages to him, had he only read them sooner. An idea crosses his mind like a speeding train crashing against a wall; was Inessa the first to die? A notion that lingers, and the weight bears too much to move from under.

"Could this all have started with you? With what they sent you here for? If so, what? What has been lying in wait for all these years? Too many to count. One year. Two years. Three decades. Into centuries. Why now?" He recalls the last words his betrothed ever spoke to him: "All in due time."

He turns back to the parchment, looking at the drawing sketched upon it. His brow furrows, trying to figure out how this could have been made; how this could be true. At first, his thoughts go to the Google search results where the pictures looked like they could have been him. The suit he never owned and the coincidence of it all. But those pictures were blurry. The similarities between the person in the pictures and himself were there, but the soft focus could have played into forcing the connection. This picture in his hands seems to be much more convincing. He has not doubted it since he first found it almost two years ago, and he dare not doubt it now. His jaw tightens, eyes fixated on the portrait, as words wisp past clenched teeth. "How do I tell her?"

After staring at the parchment for a few extended moments, still contemplating the impossibility of it, he sets it face down on the ground next to the white glove. As he stands up, another light bulb flickers its last light. Letting out a soft huff, he says, "For the best that everything in this place is laid to rest."

He opens the secret door to the secret hallway before shutting off the remaining bulbs for what he hopes is the last time. He stands in the darkness for a moment before shutting the door, leaving the items in their tomb.

Allison sits at her mother's feet, staring around an unfamiliar room. She looks down at herself to see hands and feet much tinier than her normal petite stature. She tries to stand, using the undeveloped muscles in her legs to support her weight, but she falls back down.

Inessa reaches down, picking the infant Allison up. "My little princess, come to Momma."

Allison stares at the familiar faces around her, though now she can't recall why she knows them. Everyone looks slightly younger than she feels they should look. Her mother lives and her father bears an expression that might be mistaken for joy or happiness, if one did not know the pain he would come to hold.

Allison looks around at all the adults in the room as Inessa holds her toward them. Their names all come back to her—James and Hillary McAllister, James and Lucretia Taylor, her father Vistrus, even Connor and Scarlett's grandparents Nick and Eleanor. Something about Nick looks a little different—his hairstyle, perhaps, or the color might not be as white. Something.

Inessa turns Allison to face her. "Who's my big girl? Huh?" A mile-wide smile crosses Inessa's face. "You are! That's who!"

Inessa passes Allison to Hillary, who coddles the infant in her arms, caressing little Allison's cheek. She talks in a baby voice, not at Allison but to the adults around her. "It's a shame, really. We all know the inevitable end, but we never admit it."

Hillary passes Allison to Lucretia, who looks at Allison while talking to everyone else. She does not use a baby voice. "Sad. She'll never know what could have been." A laugh escapes her as if this is all some sort of joke. "None of us will. Here's the rub, though. Most of us will never know who killed us."

Lucretia passes Allison to Eleanor, who bounces the baby on her knee. "That doesn't matter, Lucretia. What really irks my ear is that we still don't know the why behind their actions."

Vistrus puffs a cigar. "To cure us. We know that because the blond man tells Jack that while killing James and Lucretia. It all comes out eventually."

James nods. "That's right. They are looking for a cure. We are a disease, he said."

Vistrus continues, "And then the other man, Ashby. He spouted the same rhetoric."

Eleanor stops bouncing Allison. "Those are the reasons for their actions. Not the reasons for the emotion."

Sylvia Waldgrave floats in from the kitchen, appletini in hand. "What do you mean?"

Eleanor stands up, setting Allison on the floor. "I have to powder my nose. Nick, care to explain?"

Nick stands, holding his shirt as if it was the breasts of a suit coat, and he was about to give some great oration. "The actions we take, from killing those we hate to who we tell our secrets to, are all based on something deeper than trust in who we tell or someone's disdain over our differences, whether it be physical or philosophical. The ability to hate or lack trust, or whatever it may be, stems from somewhere. If you are going to kill off a group of people, something pretty bad must have happened. A traumatic event that damaged you. Officer Max Espinoza, for example."

As if summoned, Max appears and raises his hand. "Here."

Nick points to him. "You are a Legend, yet you sided with those trying to kill our kind."

Max nods.

Nick prods for more. "Care to elaborate?"

Max nods. "I hated myself. Hated what I believed. So, I believed lies. I believed they could make me someone I was not—someone I thought I should be. It's Linda's fault. She told me there was something wrong with me."

From an unseen corner, Linda strides in. "That's not true, Max. I only thought that you would be better off if you were just like everyone else. If we have nothing to hide, we have nothing to fear."

"And while I agree with the sentiment of the statement, we hide what we do not because we fear others but because others fear us," Max defends.

Nick turns back to the other adults. "That was his reason for following someone who turned him against us. But in order to be able to be turned, some event or events occurred that made Max able to be turned."

Max interjects, "He's right."

"Would you share those with us?" Nick asks.

Max opens his mouth but only a blaring siren sounds forth. Over and over, Allison stares as the siren repeats as Max's lips move. She reaches out, smacking him across the face. The alarm stops.

As she averts her gaze for a moment, she finds herself back in the abandoned school auditorium back room where Max and company had held Jack and his parents—the dilapidated room that caused as much pain as a room such as this could.

Allison sees no other company than Max in the room. The slap somehow landed a mortal blow—he lies dying on the ground.

He looks up at her, smiling. "Here's the funny thing, Allison. You understand why I did what I did. You understand why Linda stood by my side, kidnapping and killing our own kind."

Allison wants to tell him to shut up. She tries to open her mouth and form the words, but her lungs won't give breath. She can't look away. Her eyes stay locked on the man and his words. She tries over and over to part her lips and scream for him to stop talking, but only muffled whimpers usher forth.

Max continues, "Of all your friends, their families, and even your father, you are the only one who understands and feels that sort of self-hatred. That self-loathing that eats at you. That makes you feel like, just maybe, in the end, I was right. None of us are long for this world. After all, nobody lives forever; some just longer than others."

Allison continues to whimper when she wants to scream. Tears stream down her face, his words echoing in her ears.

A smile fades from his face. "It's only a matter of time for any of us."

Before he can say another word, the sound of an alarm bursts forth from his mouth, over and over until Allison's eyes shoot open wide. She springs up in bed, grabbing her head as the budding hangover takes its hold.

She tries to catch her breath, but the words from her dream sting in her mind with the pain of a thousand wasps. Reaching into her nightstand, she does what she always does after the initial shock of her dreams. She grabs her journal and begins jotting down the details her brain held onto.

CHAPTER 5

Allison struggles to hold her skirt down in the whipping wind. "My dad was right; I should have worn pants."

"A lesser man might crack a joke about the levity that could bring to such a somber situation, but not me," Duncan replies, watching Allison fight against the wind.

"I think you just did, Duncan. Sidestepped it but still made one." Allison wins the fight against nature for the moment and holds her skirt down.

"Perhaps, you're right. Apologies," Duncan offers, looking around the cemetery, watching friends and their family mourn the loss of a good man. He looks back down at her skirt, unsure of what to say at a moment like this. "I've never been to a funeral before. Not as an adult, anyhow."

Allison nods. "Where did Bri wander off to?"

Duncan scans the crowd but does not see his fiancée. "Paying her respects, I'm sure." He turns back to Allison. "How you holding up?"

The wind whips up again, causing the trees to clap their branches. A convenient excuse for Allison to avoid his question.

"You ever wonder what's next?" The distance in Allison's tone reflects her thoughts.

"Not sure." He stares in the distance at another funeral awaiting its person's burial. "We'll have to head over there. I should say bye to Rex. He was a good guy. Better than people realized."

Allison squints. She has to decide the worth of reiterating her thought or if she should let that sleeping dog die.

She decides to poke it. "There has to be, right?"

Duncan's eyes still scan for Bri, his ears picking up bits and pieces of Allison's words. "Sure. Something. We'll find out soon enough."

Allison's eyes grow big with concern. "I mean, some sooner than others, sure. But I never thought you thought about it."

The tone of her words pulls Duncan's full attention to their conversation. "Sure, I think about it all the time. I mean, Bri might need to become an important part of your world. Whatever comes next that you are all a part of, I'm sure, will be important."

A waning smile crosses Allison. She turns back to watching her friends and father say their final condolences to a man far older than he looks. A motionless sadness hovers in the air, weighing down their movements as they force themselves to step away from Nick's casket.

The surreal reality of it all has Allison wondering how real can this be. How old can one man have been that his deaths were not always permanent? The things she has been told about coming back and what it takes to stay dead make sense in small moments, but the more she thinks and dwells on it, the less sense it makes. The sheer impossibility of living for centuries at a time and never aging, never growing older unless you die and enter the convalescent period they call the Waiting, seems like nothing more than a fairy tale. But here she stands, watching as the people she knows here all believe he was as old as Grams says he was.

A tap on Allison's shoulder snaps her out of her existential despair, if only for the moment.

"Hey," Bri says, forcing a smile. "You okay?"

Allison doesn't answer. Not because she doesn't want to, but because she does not know how to. Telling the truth, she feels, may raise concern, and she doesn't feel right lying to someone she has come to care so much for. So, she stares, saying nothing as Bri steps beside her man. Allison wonders if this was a conscious choice to place him between them or something else. Either way, Allison notices the physical barrier between them, further silencing her.

"Well, all right. This silent-type demeanor is a new look. Not sure what to think. Mind telling me where Scarlett and Connor are? Haven't seen them all morning," Bri rattles off.

Duncan, noticing Allison's tense jaw and forming tears, puts his hand on Bri's shoulder to hush her.

"Perhaps this is too much for them. Or they are running late. But I'm sure they'll be here."

Tears cascade down Allison's face from behind their broken dams.

Unable to hold back her emotions, she cries out, "They're not coming, you bolts!"

"I think you meant to call us dolts," Duncan retorts, failing to relieve the tension.

"Whatever! No. You know what? I meant bolts, cause you're both being dense as steel right now," Allison fires back.

Duncan does not respond, knowing now is a good time to remain quiet. He replies with an impressed nod for her wordplay.

Bri, always one to poke a bear, asks, "Why aren't they coming?"

Through gritted teeth, Allison answers, "Because Scarlett's dead, and Connor's on the run! It's been, like, less than a week since Rex died, Gramps died, and Scarlett died, but you two have been so wrapped up in each other that you never reached out to me. And since you didn't know every one of our friends is either missing or dead, I assume you didn't reach out to them, either. What the hell could be so important, Duncan?"

Both Duncan and Bri stand, dumbfounded at the words they heard. With sunken faces and shoulders, both their gazes strike the ground.

Allison's eyes grow wide, shocked by their silence. "Like, I know I'm going through some shit right now, but seriously, how do you not check on a friend who was taken to the hospital?" Allison's scorn continues.

Duncan looks up, clenching his jaw. "I didn't know about Rex. When I went to check on him the next day, Connor was nowhere to be found, and the people at the hospital wouldn't tell me anything, and I couldn't track him. I figured if it was that big a deal, Connor or you would have called. You could have called either of us, too, ya know. So don't tell me that I don't check on my friends, like I'm the only one who failed at this. But yes, we have been busy. There was no reason to think that Connor went MIA. Don't scold me. So, what's kept you so busy that you couldn't reach out to us? And what do you mean Scarlett is…?" His anger gives way to grief, making him unable to say the word to finish that sentence.

Allison forces herself to take a few deep breaths before continuing, "Finding Scarlett dead, burying Scarlett, hitting Connor with my dad's car, getting arrested for drunk driving but not for hitting Connor with my dad's car because Connor left the scene. Finding Connor, who Dad thinks may have killed Nick, but Connor says he didn't do it, and now he's in hiding. But also that Scarlett will be all right. She just needs time to heal."

Both Duncan and Bri stand slack-jawed at what they hear.

Again, awaiting some sort of response or recognition of what was said but receiving nothing, Allison continues, "And as much as all that is clogging up my mind pipes, I can't help but think how unfair it is that neither Scarlett or Connor—nor Connor—whatever, will be able to be here today and won't ever get to see their grandpa again. Nor will they be able to say goodbye to Rex over there. Which we damn well should do. Oh, and to top it all off, that cop who killed your ma is back in town, but he seems regretful of his choices … as if that makes a difference." Allison sighs as if the weight of all she has been bearing lifts off her shoulders. "What's been keeping you so busy?"

Bri begins to shake. "Back in town? Officer Espinoza? Regretful? What the hell, Allison?"

Allison waves off her concerns. "He gave me some speech while I was in the back of the squad car and left the door unlocked in case I wanted to escape. I had a choice to make. At least, that's what he kept pressing on me."

"Impressing." Bri can't help herself in correcting Allison's slight.

Allison holds a breath, holding back choice words at the correction.

"Whatever. He said he was sorry, and damn well knew that apologies meant nothing. He didn't want to hurt us anymore. Doesn't." Allison throws down her hands in frustration.

"Too late for that, Al," Bri growls.

"I don't know what to tell you, Bri. Scar dead, Connor MIA, everyone else is pretty much dead. Officer Max is back. I've just been sitting here thinking, *How much worse can things get?* But at least you two are alive, of which you still haven't answered what's been keeping you both so unavailable."

Duncan and Bri look at each other, unsure if now is the right time to say anything. As the two of them silently try to figure out how to broach the subject at such a delicate time, an idea lights up Allison's mind, waylaying her frustration for a moment. "Don't tell me you're pregnant."

Neither of them responds to her statement.

"Oh, my God! You're pregnant!" Allison gasps, trying to force out an ounce of happiness.

"No! I'm not pregnant!" Bri defends, half-shocked at the accusation.

Duncan interjects with calm words. "We're engaged. We didn't want to tell you at a funeral. Seemed a bit … uncouth."

Duncan says the words that should be happy words, but Allison catches an ever-so-subtle expression on Bri of a scared, little girl trying to break free.

"Couth or not, you said it," Allison says as the weight that was just lifted off her drops back down from a hundred feet up.

"What do we do now?" Bri asks, throwing her hands into the air.

No one responds. All three stand in silence, turning to see Nick DeSalvo's casket lowering into the ground. As it comes to a rest, they watch people throw flowers on top—a final keepsake for the faithful departed.

They continue watching as, one by one, this part of the cemetery empties, leaving the three young adults to stare at someone their own age about to be lowered off in the distance. They begin walking to Rex's casket, so they, too, can say a final goodbye.

While they trek toward Rex, they think about the time spent with him. Allison spent little time with Rex, leaving her with little to understand about him except that he was like her: confused about life, what it means, and how or if he fit in. She knows that while she doesn't have countless memories to remember him by, the similarities between them, despite their first meeting, and the way he left this world is something she can hold on to for a while.

Bri searches her mind for a fond memory of Rex but only recalls the psychiatric ward at West Haven General, how creeped out she was and the crazy patient who attacked them—not a time anybody wants to be remembered for. She knows Rex looked up to Duncan, admired him in some role-model fashion. Something in the way Duncan always tried to help fills her with a sense of calm for the future. Not so much a memory of Duncan to hold on to and cherish, but the round-about way Rex made her feel about Duncan.

Duncan has memories of Rex dating back to junior high. The first time they met, shooting spit-balls at the ceiling of math class, there was an instant bond. They were both outsiders. No one else in school wore the old-school leather jackets with torn jeans and old school rap and hip-hop T-shirts. They were a perfect pairing of friends. Duncan knows Rex always felt like an outsider; Duncan did, too. But Duncan knew Rex felt uncomfortable with that more so than he ever did. Duncan embraced it and made it part of who he was, while Rex always felt like it was a part that needed fixing. Perhaps it was this that made Rex gravitate to Ashby when Duncan was a phone call away. Doesn't matter now.

All three stand next to Rex's casket, saying goodbye to someone who never got the chance to see what he could become.

The sun beats down on Vistrus as he hikes his way to West Haven General Hospital to get Connor's car. It has been sitting a few too many days, and he knows it won't be much longer until someone tows it, tickets it, or, worse, finds something inside it that implicates Connor.

The lone walk gives Vistrus time to think about the young DeSalvo and his presumed innocence. He knows that precious time has already elapsed in the need to take care of any arrangements Eleanor needed help with. It is seldom that a Legend needs to be buried in a cemetery, though in the past few years, the occurrence has become all too common.

His thoughts bounce back and forth between needing to find any evidence that Connor is innocent and knowing that Connor may have, albeit unknowingly, caused the death.

He can't help thinking about—borderline obsessing over—that all of this, dating back to when Sylvia first found the parchment on her front porch, must be connected to his wife. His mind can't wrap around the why of it being related to her being moved to the States and her death in the end.

Those thoughts pervade his mind longer than he realizes as he turns to walk up the parking garage stairs to where Connor said he parked his car. A parking garage can be a place of solitude, a place one takes a lone walk after a long day of work, taking a moment to unwind before the drive home. In the morning, it serves as a place to take one last breath before walking into the day's chaos, perhaps with the occasional hello to someone who walks in your direction. As Vistrus ascends the stairs, sounds start hitting his ears. He slows his walk to concentrate on the noise: running engines, hushed conversations, something plastic being stretched out. Many engines and many conversations. Walking closer and closer, the sounds form words: car, blood, murder, suspect, registered owner, DeSalvo. His pace quickens to the floor where Connor's car has sat one day too long.

He turns the corner out from the stairwell to see around a dozen officers, crime scene investigators, officials, and more working away at the scene, all sectioned off with yellow police tape. Vistrus blends into the few citizens who have nothing better to do than watch the police. A sight he welcomes right now as it gives him an opportunity to observe what has already been found and work his way into the investigation.

A quick scan to the other side of the tape, he sees a man out of uniform. No badged blues or even a button-up and tie. Just a guy in casual clothes standing about as inconspicuously as Vistrus stands. This strange individual just happens to be past the police tape.

"Excuse me, sir." Vistrus tries to catch the man's attention.

He turns, pauses, and a look of recognition washes over him upon seeing Vistrus standing there. A look that Vistrus recognizes, though he does not recognize this man.

This man strides a few paces to Vistrus. "May I help you?" Vistrus takes note as the man attempts to play off his recognition.

An attempt that Vistrus will allow for the moment. "That car. What … happened?"

The man smiles. "Just an abandoned car."

"Then there would be no need for the tape." Vistrus calls his bluff.

They both stand in silence for a moment, unsure of what move to make next. Vistrus thinks he recognizes the man from somewhere but can't place where. He budges. "Are you in?"

Quiet words from a quiet man.

The stranger nods his head. "I'm in because of his age and his cunning, Mr. Petrovsky."

Vistrus leans closer to the man. "How do you know my name? Do I know you?"

The stranger turns to the police working around him. "Know that I am a man who believes Connor is innocent. A man who will do what it takes to protect The Nation because I spent long enough doing irreparable harm to it."

"I have no idea why you are telling me this, but I need that car. It belongs to one of us," Vistrus pleads.

The stranger leans in closer to Vistrus. "It was stolen. Don't you know? Found here after it was already reported."

A vague memory flashes in Vistrus's mind. A memory that places this man's face, but the details are still blurred. He is sure he knows him. "When did we meet?" Vistrus asks again.

Before answering, the man turns to a passing policeman. "The car came back stolen, correct?"

The officer looks at his notepad. "Yes. A few days ago. Must'a been parked here shortly after. Town's going to pieces." He shuts his book closed. "I heard CSI say they're collecting blood samples and hair fibers to test. Makes no sense why those guys'd want their hands in this, but, hey, ain't my circus."

"Thank you, Officer." The stranger nods him away.

"Then you know hair fiber analysis and blood testing is not something we want done," Vistrus stresses.

"I know. I will make sure it never makes it to the lab," the stranger assures him.

"And why are you doing all this again?" Vistrus reiterates.

"Ask your daughter about me. She can tell you who I was, what I did, and the choice I gave her," he replies.

"And what shall I say your name is?" Vistrus asks.

"Espinoza. Max Espinoza."

"Max, the whirlwind of the past few years blurs from where I recognize your name. I shall ask my daughter. While I appreciate the help more than I can say, I must insist on knowing why this event? Why help us? There has to be a reason beyond your apparent need for a random act of kindness," Vistrus calls him out.

"I can't talk about it here, and I'm hungry. Meet me at Ducky's in half an hour. I'll explain what I can. Know though that this is not a random act for me and far from kind in comparison…" With that, Max turns back to the police and investigators on scene.

Vistrus stands, unable to make heads or tails of what just transpired. He notices two people standing away from the crowd as if trying not to be seen, but he sees them—Raymond and December taking in the events around them.

An old, familiar voice sounds within Vistrus's mind. "Long time, old friend."

Vistrus smiles, a hint of whimsy in his eyes. He speaks within his head, "Indeed. The Council misses their sentinels. Is everything all right?"

They smile before sending any internal voice back to him. "With the events on the forefront, we figured there was no need for subtly. That, and it seems you have more on your hands than a car."

"Always pleasant to hear your voice, December," Vistrus gives his non-answered reply.

"Same to you." She smiles. "Befriending the enemy, are we?"

"Not that I am aware of." He gives a straight answer, though the subtext did not pass him over. He looks around, trying to find Max, who seems to have vanished.

Raymond interjects, "Seems we may have kept one too many things to ourselves."

"You don't know who that was?" December asks.

Vistrus turns back to them, shaking his head once.

"He was the husband of she who killed Sylvia," Raymond whispers, as if someone else might intrude on their thoughts.

Vistrus's realization, his past actions, and how they all fit into the moment wash over him in a heavy wave. His shoulders slump in self-dejection.

After watching Vistrus recover, December chimes back into his mind. "To the subject of The Council…"

Vistrus shakes his head. "Please, keep them away from the DeSalvo boy. We do not know enough yet."

Both Raymond and December nod in understanding.

December chimes in her side note, "No one knows much anymore."

Raymond nods toward the scene around them. "Seems like things might get worse before they get better. We'll do what we can, but…" He lets his thought trail off.

Vistrus picks up Raymond's thought. "But you have your own needs to tend to as well."

December nods.

"Still will not tell us what you need, though," Vistrus adds.

"Not everyone is who they seem. When the time is right, we will," Raymond adds.

"Any hint as to who or when that may be?" Vistrus inquires.

"Be good, Vistrus." December smiles as both she and Raymond walk away.

Eleanor sits on the floor outside of the closet, next to a patch of dried blood, trying to tune out the news droning in the background about the land struggle between the amusement park and the World Health Organization. The closet's contents surround her.

Even the box of vacuum bags remains untouched. Tears that both mourn the loss of a love that was centuries old, as well as celebrate the time they shared, cascade down her cheeks. Most loves have a mere three or four decades together unless two people find one another young enough and live long enough. But the stories of couples having been together for eighty years are far fewer than those who lose one in half that time, whether it be from death or divorce. Eleanor knows how luck shined down on her with centuries of love, affection, joy, and countless memories of laughter and good times. But weighing what you have to hold on to never seems to help alleviate the loss of never telling that person you love them one more time. At least, not so soon. When a Legend lives as long as they do, even knowing death will one day come, all the preparation time is gracious enough to allow never seems to soften the blow.

She touches the dried blood, the last physical connection to her dearly departed. The last thing that was him—a part of him—dried up on the floor, intertwined and bonded with the carpet fibers. Nothing else remains of his physicality for her to hold on to except, perhaps, a toothbrush or comb hanging onto a few hairs. While trying to sift through the last moments of his life, a used toothbrush or comb simply does not hold the same emotion as what's beneath her right now.

She dries a tear with her hand before placing it back on the patch of blood. The moist tears on her hand infuse with the dried blood. One final moment of two souls intertwining. A solitary moment to hold on to before once again facing the reality of what no one wishes they ever have to face; that they are alone and that their soulmate has left this world, never to return.

She turns back to the mess still surrounding her from the closet cleaning: a "discard" pile to one side and a "keep" pile to the other. A few items sit between the two, most of which she makes quick work of. One item, the white glove, she holds for a moment, trying to figure out if this is something still worth holding onto.

A knock on her door makes her decide, consciously or not, that she wants to hold on to it. She stands up, making the subconscious glove-toss onto the "keep" pile, dries off her tears with the back of her hand, and straightens her clothes before answering the door. In Eleanor's mind, a matriarch must always present themselves properly, even if the current situation is anything but. She has a certain notion that when people feel pain, grief, loss, love, or whatever the emotion may be, it is not for everyone to see. Only those who can tell should know; everyone else gets the societal version of her. Not that she doesn't, or hasn't ever, shown emotion and external compassion. Just that opening a door while crying is not something to subject someone to without proper conversation first leading up to it.

After fully composing herself to her satisfaction, she opens the door to see Bishop standing on the other side. An unexpected face at a time like this, though it is far less surprising than, perhaps, it should be.

"Bishop," Eleanor feigns more surprise than she feels, "why are you here?"

Bishop motions his desire to enter her house.

Eleanor nods, though her gesture for him to enter is not wholly welcoming.

"I wanted to say my condolences, Eleanor." His words sound sincere.

"You could have come to the funeral. I think that would have been all right." She brushes off his words.

"I was. You didn't see me, though. I was trying not to disturb anyone." He moves toward the hallway. "I figured a personal word between two old friends was best left for private."

Eleanor steps back to the closet, returning to her cleaning. "Understandably. Thank you, Bishop. I do have much to do, though."

She sits down between the two piles, peering into the closet and at the rest of the work laid out before her. "This was supposed to be a small project. It's been days."

"I could help. Take out the trash. Of which," he points to the white glove, "you still have that. I hope that's not the discard pile."

Looking at the glove, she internally questions her choice to place it there before saying, "It's not." She turns to him, "While the offer is appreciated, I don't think so soon after Nick's passing is the best time to try this," Eleanor heeds.

He understands her warning. "That was not my intention; I just wanted to lend a hand. At one time, you would have said yes."

She gives a fading smile. "We're old, Bishop. But neither one of us are fools. It was your intention. Don't patronize me by pretending it wasn't. You're just kicking yourself because you hoped it wouldn't be so obvious." He does not respond, keeping a stoic expression and not revealing any else. "And yes, many lifetimes ago, Bishop, I may have said yes. We were different people then." Turning to the waiting piles, she concludes, "This is something I have to do alone."

Bishop forces a smile. "I understand. But you have held onto old relics for sentimental reasons. If those reasons are still sentimental, then it means something … or at least it can. And that's something to hold on to." He turns toward the door. "When you need me to help, I'll be around. Just because he's gone doesn't mean you have to shut yourself out from everyone who cares."

"And just because Nick's passed doesn't mean my feelings have changed. It's too soon, Bishop, if ever. Thank you for stopping by." Eleanor turns back to her cleaning, but the sound of Connor's name spoken on the news stops them.

They turn to the television to catch what they can. "…wanted for questioning in the murder of Nick DeSalvo. Sources revealed the deceased was the grandfather to the man wanted for questioning. While the police still have been unsuccessful in locating Mr. DeSalvo, they are looking, and any leads should be called to the West Haven non-emergency line…"

Shaking his head as the news reporter concludes her segment, Bishop turns back to Eleanor. "It's a shame, really."

"I don't believe it. My grandson would not do such things." Her tone hits Bishop like a fastball to the face.

"Has anyone heard from him? Has he come back trying to claim innocence?" Bishop steps toward her.

Eleanor shoots him a look, stopping him in his tracks. "No. We haven't heard from him since it happened."

"He didn't tell anyone where he was going?" He sneaks a few inches closer.

Eleanor shakes her head, trying not to watch the news. "Disappeared. No one knows anything. Why are you so curious?"

Bishop steps close enough to grab her hand, holding it with both of his. "Because someone needs to worry about you—look after you."

She yanks her hand away from his, keeping her eyes on his hands. "I can take care of myself. More than you think. And even so, I still have those who care. Those I call family."

Bishop looks around the empty house. "I see."

As anger simmers below the surface, she says her parting words, "It's time you go. That is not a request."

The light from the near full moon shines through the rooftop crack in the abandoned cabin Connor now calls home. Books are spread out across a makeshift bed and the floor, each lying open to various poems by various poets. Various stanzas in some poems are circled with notes scribbles next to them.

The farthest book from where Connor sits is open to Rudyard Kipling's *The Law of the Jungle*. A black ink circle encompasses the line, "Because of his age and his cunning, because of his gripe and his paw." Notes scribbled around that circled line read, "Why tell us it's called the Law of the Wolves when we are not werewolves? Why change the title? Is there a law for fairies or vampires? Why change what is already written?"

Next to that book is a smaller, older book whose discolored pages tell the passage of time and whose cracked spine betrays its improper storage. It lies open to a poem by Mary Elizabeth Frye titled *Do Not Stand at My Grave and Weep*. Circled are the lines, "I am in each lovely thing. Do not stand at my grave bereft. I am not there. I have not left." The notes beside it ask, "Why this version? Why Frye and not Harner? Why change? To adapt?"

A few other books lie open to various poems with lines either underlined or circled, but Connor buries his nose in a book filled solely with the works of T.S. Eliot. His current read is *The Hollow Men*. While the wind whistles outside and the nocturnal forest creatures forage for food, he pays them no mind, soaking in the words Eliot committed to the page.

He reads the rest of the poem uninterrupted by the outside world. Setting down the book, he grabs a notepad next to him and jots down a few thoughts.

"Why change titles or author attribution? Does it matter? Just misinformation? Why those poems? Does it matter this is happening now or is now happenstance? Who killed Grandpa Nick, and why frame me for it?"

He tosses the notepad down, sighing. *Is any of this even relevant to what's happening? Am I headed down the wrong path? How does all this relate to me, Al, Scar, Bri … everyone?*

He pushes out his breath as his chest sinks down. Sitting up, he leans against the wall at the corner of his bed. His eyes weigh heavy with thoughts and unanswerable questions about what lies ahead until sleep finally overtakes him.

"If you're gonna make a hot dog, it has to be Vienna Beef. Anything else is just an impostor." Max chomps down, neon-green relish and chopped onions falling out of the bun. "I mean, sure, dogs can be topped many ways. Ya got Coney dogs, Jersey dogs, New York, Cincinnati, and God knows how many others, but I tell ya, Chicago-style dogs are the best. Maybe it's cause I'm from here. Maybe it's the celery salt."

Vistrus sits across from this man who murdered his friends, attempting to calculate his next move. He tries to anticipate what Max might have up his sleeve and his intentions.

"I'm just saying I like the celery salt." Max chomps down again on the dog. He notices a subtle anger creeping across Vistrus's face. His chewing slows as he sprinkles in some words. "I can see you aren't a man who likes small talk, so I'll get down to the point."

Vistrus squints his eyes. "Brevity suits me."

"Are you at least going to eat your food? It's a crime to waste a dog from this place." Max gestures at Vistrus's tray.

Vistrus's stern face relaxes into something a bit more cordial. Keeping eye contact with Max, he takes a bite of his fully loaded dog.

"There are a lot of strange things going on, wouldn't you say?" Max tosses a fry into his mouth.

"Strange and terrible things. Many of which you partook in." Vistrus shows a proverbial card with his words.

Max's face falls. He sets down the next fry about to be chewed apart. The muscles in his cheeks tense, almost pulling them inward. Vistrus can hear Max's heart pound harder than a moment ago—frantic, almost irregular, in his fright.

"The question begs, Max Espinoza, what do you want with us?" Vistrus's question is more of a warning to heed than something to be answered.

Max looks around the restaurant, watching people go about their everyday lives as if there isn't a care in the world for them. Turning back to Vistrus, Max organizes his thoughts for a moment before speaking. "I regret my past actions and have not made amends for them. Hell, I don't know if I can. Some things are beyond redemption." He pauses for a moment to gauge Vistrus's reaction but comes up empty. "I was wrong. I know that now. The man that fooled me has fooled others. He had me thinking I could be cured. I could be Normal. That there is something fundamentally wrong with who I am. That who I am is something other than human. Less than to him. I know we are not. I turned against my own kind … our kind."

Vistrus holds up a hand to stop him. "There is no 'our kind.' We are all human. There is no separation. We are not a different species, alien from those you wanted to be like. None of us are any better, worse, or more special than any Normal who has no idea of our existence. Do not use that phrase … 'my own kind.' Definitely never say, 'our kind.'"

Max nods in understanding. "There is much I should have learned different. Much I learned that I know is wrong, but the actions I took while thinking I was right cannot be undone."

Vistrus swallows a bite of his hot dog. His interest in this conversation wanes. "Brevity is not your friend."

"The people that first started hunting you and your friends and family, the people that got me involved, they are not gone. My wife may have been killed. The blond man may have died. But they were not alone. There was another. Someone above them all. She gave the orders. She recruited Ashby, Linda, myself, the blond man, all of us."

"When did she return to West Haven?" Vistrus cleanses his throat with a sip of his cola.

He listens to Max's heart some more. The franticness seemed to calm, but the blood pressure still pounds his heart in fear. Vistrus can hear it.

"She never left." Max keeps his words simple. He scans the restaurant for prying eyes and any ears on the walls. Scouting for some minuscule detail that changed from moments ago.

A move not unnoticed by Vistrus, who joins the search. Both come up empty.

"We are still safe. Continue," Vistrus urges.

"She is gathering. Preparing for a storm. But I haven't found out any more yet," Max admits his current limits.

"How do you know this?" A kernel of suspicion arises in Vistrus.

"She still trusts me. She still thinks I am looking for a cure." Max finishes his hot dog.

"There is nothing to cure. We are not a disease to be fixed or eradicated. We are not contagious lepers." Vistrus's voice grows irritated at the thought.

"I know that now. But it's what I thought, so it's what I used coming back," Max explains.

"What is her name? Where do I find her?" Vistrus's blood flows faster. His heart starts to race.

Max shakes his head. "You don't. She finds you. I tried following her once. She turned a corner and was gone. Just some homeless guy who didn't even see her turn. Another time, she entered an elevator. I caught the door as it almost shut, but when it opened, she was gone. Just the attendant. I didn't even know any buildings still used elevator attendants."

Vistrus takes a deep breath to calm himself. "What you are implying is not real. Teleportation is not something Legends can do. Neither is invisibility. Either you are lying, or your recollection is wrong. For the moment, I am going to assume your memory betrays you."

"And as for her name, she never says it. I've never heard it. I've never heard anyone refer to her by a name. Their numbers were kept small within the cells." Max sounds defeated.

"What does this enigma look like? Give me something," Vistrus implores.

"Beautiful. Pale," he pauses on his choice of words, "fair-skinned for her race. Dark hair. High cheek bones with gray eyes that are sometimes blue. For as much fear as she can strike into someone when speaking, she has the most delicate jawline. Truly hauntingly beautiful."

"That is rather vague," Vistrus replies, finishing his soda.

"It's all I got." Max shrugs. "I'm not a sketch artist."

"Anything else?" Vistrus asks. Annoyance in his tone that Max could not have summed this up in the parking garage.

"Just a theory I am working on, but nothing yet. I figured you oughta know that a storm is brewing, and The Nation is going to be in the center of it once it hits. You said there's nothing wrong with us—nothing to cure. But some think there is. You been paying attention to the news? Timing's a little suspect for everything, isn't it? I thought you should have time to prepare." With that, Max stands, grabs his tray, and dumps it into the trash.

Before Max can walk away, Vistrus calls out, "Funny thing about that metaphor, the center of the storm is the eye."

"So?" Max upturns an eyebrow.

"The eye of the storm is always the most calm. Serene even," Vistrus informs him.

"And I plan to infiltrate said storm. But you get the point." Max's irritation forces a stern smile. He glances up at a television playing the nightly news, pointing to it as he walks away.

"I do," is all Vistrus responds with, watching the news clip discuss the World Health Organization's search for land to build their new research facility. It has been narrowed down to a spot in either California, New York, or Illinois. But Illinois may present a problem if Six Flags grabs the land first. Vistrus turns from the television at the mention of Six Flags, tossing his garbage on the way out of the restaurant.

Vistrus pulls a blue steak off the stove top griddle and puts it onto a plate next to some potatoes Vesuvio and balsamic-roasted Brussels sprouts.

"Are you sure you want medium?" Vistrus shouts to Allison.

Standing table-side, Allison pulls the wine bottle from her lips, using her hand to wipe a little that spilled. "Yeah. I think med well was a bit too much." She pours her father a glass of wine and sneaks another swig before corking and putting the bottle back.

"How my little girl has grown." He flips the steak one more time before pulling it off. "In that case, dinner is served."

Allison takes a seat at the table, placing the glass of wine in front of her father's chair. A can of cola sits in front of hers.

Vistrus brings the plates to the table and, serving the food, sees the wine. "Thank you."

"Figured I'd save you a step. You cook, I pour," she jokes.

"Only seems fair." Vistrus takes his seat. "I met someone the other day."

Allison stops cutting her steak. "Like a lady friend?"

Vistrus shakes his head. "Someone you know."

She resumes cutting into her steak. "While that does narrow it down, you'll have to be more specific than that."

Vistrus chomps down on a bite of his blue steak. "Max Espinoza."

Allison stops herself before biting the food off her fork.

Vistrus motions for her to continue. "Chew. Everything is fine."

Allison chomps the food off her fork, chewing like a hungry animal. "What happened? What did he say? What did he want?"

"A lot. Nothing." Vistrus remains unsure how to view his and Max's interaction.

"He said a lot of nothing?" Allison swallows some potatoes.

Vistrus chews his thoughts for a short moment. "It would appear." He brings his full attention to his daughter. "Are you all right? I know who his wife was. You are still dealing."

"I'm fine. I knew he was in town," she replies before he can say more.

"You knew?"

"When I got arrested, he hopped into the car and said a few words." She keeps her words surprisingly brief.

"A few words?"

"Yeah. Just that I have choices to make. That it is what we do while we're here that matters and to make it matter." She chews on a Brussels sprout. "It was all very strange. The whole night was. You still haven't said why he spoke to you."

"Something about a brewing storm." Vistrus sips his wine.

"He wanted to chat about the weather?" Allison sips her cola.

Vistrus's chest rises with a small laugh. "It would appear so."

"You know, a teacher told us once it's always storming somewhere. Like, every second of every day, somewhere on the planet, it's storming. Not like the eye on Jupiter; that's the same storm. Just that it's always storming somewhere." Allison adds a bit of subconscious wisdom to the moment.

"So it is." Vistrus cuts and chews a large bite of steak, letting the rest of the moment between them sit in silence. He watches his daughter eat, oblivious to the world around her right now, glad he can do the little things, like cook a good meal, to make her ever-stranging world a little more normal.

Allison eats a few more bites of steak, unsure what to say but thinking about the night of prom. The look in Linda's eyes as Allison pummeled the life out of her. She can feel her heart speed up. Her skin begins to itch and crawl as the memories stir inside her mind. Her face tightens.

Vistrus watches as his daughter's lips recede and her nose withers. "Breathe, Allison. Slow breaths."

His words fall on deaf ears as the blood-soaked memory of Linda's death covers her mind. The words Allison shouted as Linda lay helpless on the floor echo through her ears.

Allison's hair thins as her muscles expand, stretching and contorting her skin.

"Breathe. Slow breaths," Vistrus repeats. Again, his words are not heard. He watches tears stream down her face. Staying seated, he reaches out his hand to calm her down, but as he touches her shoulder, she lashes out.

Thickened nails slice across her father's face. Flesh rips and blood splashes across the dinner table. He winces, surprised his daughter has so little control over herself right now.

"Allison!" he shouts.

The boom pulls her from her thoughts. Still in transition but close to full Legendary form, she sees the wounds she has caused. "I didn't mean to do it, Daddy!"

Standing up, she pushes her chair backward, sweeping it off its legs. She runs to her room, slamming the door shut.

Reaching between her mattress and frame, she pulls out her flask but finds it empty. Throwing it down on the bed, she runs to her closet and pulls out a bottle from her hiding place. In a swift flick of her wrist, the entire cap unscrews, flinging to the ground.

She chugs enough to make a dent of what remained in the bottle. Pulling it away for a moment, she picks up the cap and closes it.

Startled by her father's knock on the door, she tosses the bottle back into the closet and closes the door.

"Come in." As she moves to open the door, Vistrus turns the knob himself.

She takes a seat on the bed, sliding the flask under her covers as Vistrus closes the door behind him. Her stare turns from his no-longer-bleeding face down at the floor.

"Ignorance is bliss." He looks next to her at the bed cover.

"I can't deal with metaphors or similes or whatever you're doing right now, Dad. Please, leave me be," she cries.

"No metaphors here." He laughs to himself while muttering, "Met a five here. Could that be six there? I saw what you did, dear, but that's something for another day." He lays out his observation.

"Sorry to further disappoint you, Father." The anger in her voice does nothing to calm her condition.

Vistrus lets that one go for a moment. "Take a deep breath. Slow your breathing. We've talked about this before." His thoughts pull him to his wife's diaries. "Be four. Be five. Be six."

Allison's breathing slows, but she is still in Legend form. His odd words are not lost on her ears. "What are you saying?"

"Words, my child. Words. Trying to figure out some things. Not everything is about the immediate."

Allison looks up from having stared at the floor long enough and sees the already healing wound on her father's face. "Did I do that?"

Vistrus wipes a little drying blood with his fingers. "Yes. You were in quite the state. I think the events over the past few years are weighing heavier on you than I thought."

"Sorry I did that. I don't remember … it's all a blur." She averts her eyes again.

"You said you did not mean to. I am not mad," he assures her. "Though I feel I may have failed at my duties."

"I'm a grown woman. You can't be there for every little thing that goes wrong," says Allison, her turn to assure him.

Vistrus watches as her muscles calm down, and her hair thickens to her Normal state.

"Perhaps, but Linda was no small incident. Nor is Max being back in town." While his tone rings gentle, the implications do not. "I have been too caught up in the affairs of The Nation and The Council to pay proper attention to my family's affairs." His words seem to calm Allison down. Her nose reforms and lips fill out again. The face in front of Vistrus is the one the world knows.

"You may have been, a little. But you can't blame my actions on yourself. Some people aren't as perfect as others."

"No one is perfect, Allison. Certainly not myself." He defends his imperfections.

"Sure, but some are less perfect than most." She sounds defeated. "Some less long for this world, so I've been told."

Vistrus takes a seat next to Allison and pulls her in close, holding her tight. "No one is less long than anyone else. Do not think such things."

"It's hard not to most times. There's nothing left. Not much of anything, anyhow."

Vistrus tightens his hold on her. He wants to respond, but with all the loss around them, he finds it hard to prove her wrong. Everyone around them who remains has lost more in the last few years than some lose in a lifetime. The silver lining is that they are still standing. Vistrus can't help but wonder how much more any of them can stand to lose. There is so little left of all the families.

Allison lifts her head to see the damage she caused her father. The irony of her actions is not lost on her. All the death that surrounds them she knows she holds responsibility, in some way, for some of that. The weight of her actions has not lessened nor lifted. It has only weighed her down more and more each time something reminds her of what she did. Now, she has to stare at the bloody, flesh-torn outcome of her action—on her father, nonetheless. All she can do at this moment, lying in her father's arms, is think that she wants Scarlett. She wants her best friend, so Scarlett can tell her that everything will be all right. But the reality is she can't because she is buried a few feet deep underground while supposedly regenerating her health—something that Allison cannot wrap her mind around. She knows that Connor would comfort her and outline it all in silver hues, but he is hiding because he might have killed his own grandfather. He could have also killed his cousin. But her mind will not relive that memory, nor entertain that possibility.

So, she rests in her father's arms, trying to figure out what will happen. She tries to imagine all the possibilities of how Connor will come running home with a bag full of evidence proving his innocence, but the motion picture playing out in her mind never finishes. The film cuts and repeats like a broken projector, slowing his run up the driveway before cutting away to white nothingness. She tries to believe that The Council and The Nation would do everything in their power to help a member, but his hiding tells her that his membership privileges have been revoked, even if temporarily.

Allison begins to cry again, burying her head in Vistrus's arms, leaving the thoughts of Connor behind and turning them to herself. The idea of never seeing Scarlett dominates her thoughts. Even with everything told to her by Eleanor and her father, the disconnect in her understanding the entirety of the Waiting only adds to her inability to imagine a future without her friends.

The mere idea of happiness and all the ambiguity that entails seems like such a foreign concept right now. The darkness surrounding her allows no light to shine through. Even now, in her father's arms, the darkness suffocates her.

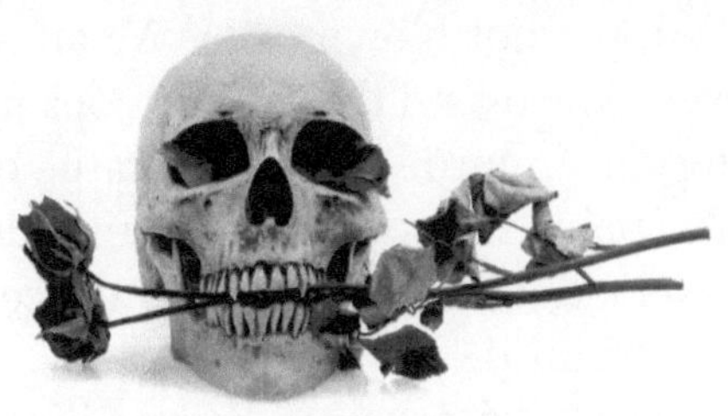

CHAPTER 6

"Let's not forget,
it also prevents any forward growth."
~J. Taylor~

"Thanks for seeing me," Bri begins. "I know things haven't been square between us for, well, a long time, but I needed to talk to you. Connor's not around, is he?"

A kaleidoscope of butterflies flutters through Allison's stomach, a feeling she tries to suppress in her words. "Still hiding. I don't think he'll be available anytime soon."

"Oh my God! I'm so sorry. I honestly thought, well, I don't know what I thought. Maybe that this would have blown over by now or that the fuzz or police or whatever would have stopped looking and he'd be back. I've never really had to deal with that before," Bri babbles.

As fast as Allison's annoyance with Bri washes over her, she knows that Bri's verbal diarrhea is a byproduct of nerves.

"Well, it's not blown over. We are not sure if it will ever blow over. I don't think cops just give up on looking for a murder suspect. Statue of limitations doesn't apply." Allison tries shutting down that line of conversation, taking a seat on the couch after welcoming Bri inside.

"Statute," Bri corrects her, smiling at the innocent misstep.

Allison shrugs. "Whatever. What did you need to talk about?"

Without saying a word, Bri breaks out into borderline frantic pacing, doing laps around the front room. Allison can see the wheels turning in Bri's head, but still, she doesn't speak. After an extended pause, Allison breaks the silence. "Wear a hole in the floor all you want. But you still haven't actually said anything."

Bri freezes before a quick turn to Allison. "I'm getting married!" Waves of hysterics drown out the sense of excitement in her voice.

Hysterics that are lost on Allison. "I know!" Allison feigns excitement to match what she thought she heard in Bri.

"No, Al." Bri's tone drops flat. "I'm getting married." The dread in her voice could be mistaken for nothing else.

Even Allison, in all her wishful thinking to hold the woman before her, can't pretend she doesn't hear Bri's cries for help. "See. I didn't hear *that* the first time. I thought you'd be excited. All elevated, wine-and-roses mindset."

Bri lets Al's word choice slip by. "I want to be elated. I do. Wine and roses would be a great feeling.

But all I want is vodka and cranberry without the cranberry," admits Bri. She collapses on the couch next to Allison. "Got any?"

Allison thinks for a moment before hopping up. "Burb."

"Did you just say BRB as a word? Burb?" Bri laughs.

"Sure did." Allison hurries out of the room. "It's my thing!" she shouts.

"What's your thing?"

"Saying acronyms as words."

Bri laughs. "That's not your thing."

Allison returns to the front room with a bottle of vodka. "Then what's my thing?"

"Like, never using the right word."

Allison shrugs off the comment. "Whatever. People know what I mean."

Bri laughs, eyeing the vodka. "Mr. P won't notice if we drink some?" Bri asks, taking the bottle from Allison.

"It's not his. Had this for a while," Allison confesses.

Bri stares at the half-empty bottle. "No wonder you got busted for a dewi."

Allison gives Bri a gentle slug on the arm. "Betty White up. We're gonna finish this puppy and make you happy."

"Cups? Glasses?" Bri waves an arm at the lack of drinking vessels.

"Nope." Allison mimes drinking out of the bottle. "Now drink up."

Bri presses the bottle to her lips, hesitant while she thinks it over.

Allison wastes no time reminding Bri why she came over. "Marriage."

Bri stops thinking it over and tilts the bottle back, feeling the sting of the alcohol trickle down her throat.

Shaking it off, tongue out, face contorted, she holds down the liquor that is trying to make its way back up. "That is so not good."

"Yeah, well, I take what I can get." Allison wants to talk about this, if for nothing more than to take her mind off Connor and Scarlett. "Wine and roses?"

Bri tilts the bottle back for another sip. This time it goes down a little smoother, though not much. "It should be wine and roses. And it is. Mostly. Like, there's nothing wrong with us. Duncan is great. He understands me, and, like, gets me. He loves me and accepts me for what I am."

Allison's interrupting words leap from her lips. "There's nothing about you that needs accepting. You are perfect just the way you are."

Allison realizes that sounded as if it could have been a come-on or some line said as a prelude to a move; it wasn't. At least, that's what she will convince herself of because she wouldn't want to be that person. Nothing more than a sincere moment between friends.

"I appreciate the words. But it's not Duncan. It's me." Bri gets lost in her thoughts, staring off into nothing.

"Do you not love him anymore?" Allison thinks a thought that should stay in her head. She doesn't want to say it, but the glimmer of hope in her mind urges her otherwise. "Did you ever love him?" It did not stay inside her head.

Bri turns to Allison. "Of course I love him, yes. He's everything I could ever want. Sure, we could both use a bit more money. But we're not even twenty-one yet. Well, I'm not."

"What does the ability to buy alcohol have to do with this?"

Bri shakes her head. "Nothing, you dork. I'm just saying we are young still. And I'll be that way for far longer than he will. Much longer? Doesn't matter. At least I'll look that way for longer."

"So, you won't love him as he grows up and you stay looking gorgeous?" Allison continues probing the problem at hand.

Bri furrows her brow, confused at the question. "No. I know I might be a little vain sometimes. I mean, who isn't vain every now and then? But I'm not that vain."

"Then what is it?" Allison snatches the bottle from Bri and takes a sip.

"The portrait of Dorian Gray," Bri says, falling back into the couch cushions.

"You lost me."

"It's a book about a guy named Dorian. He has a picture of himself. This picture is the bane of his existence. Mentally, anyhow. See, he never ages. He stays young forever, but this picture he is forced to see everyday ages. It shows him his true age, his true image."

"Visage," Allison interjects.

"What?"

Allison doles out a rapid apology. "Nothing. My bad. Go on."

"So, yeah, this picture ages, and he watches the world around him, everyone around him die, yet he lives on, forever beautiful." Bri snatches the bottle back, taking another sip.

"So, you don't want to stay beautiful forever?"

Bri huffs a laugh. "No. Duncan is the portrait, and I'm Dorian. That's the metaphor. And there's nothing I can do about it."

Allison slings a friendly arm around Bri's shoulders. "So what? He knows that being with you, that's what will happen. It's his choice to make."

"But he deserves to be with someone who will be the same as him," Bri responds.

Allison sits up, turning to face Bri. "Women always age more gracefully than men. Well, most do anyway. Here's the thing. They still want us, love us, whatever. You will be just way more beautiful throughout the ages. But as dense as I know I can be at times, I have a feeling your condition isn't the whole of your hesitantness."

Bri shakes her head. "Hesitation. But you sounded great until then."

Allison shrugs with a grin. "I try." She squares Bri with her. "At the end of the day, you can't make a decision for someone else. You can't tell them what is best for them because it makes you feel better about yourself. Only they can make that decision. Especially since the only person it affects is them. Enjoy what is happening, even if it is a little uncomfortable for you."

Allison sees Bri inching closer to her and does not let it pull her from her thoughts.

"Duncan is a good guy, and you deserve a good person. Love is a scary thing that makes you do scary things. I know. Been there, done them. But don't run. You won't be happy you did, and he won't be okay."

Bri smiles. "I'm going to do something now."

Grabbing Allison's face, Bri plants a kiss on her lips. Nothing hot and heavy. Nothing that, despite the wish in every fiber of her being, makes Allison believe Bri is switching teams. Just a kiss that says in many ways, "Thank you for the talk and for being a friend after everything that's happened." After a moment, Bri pulls away.

Bri stares at a shocked Allison before saying, "Thank you, Allison, for being a friend."

Allison nods over and over again. "We could travel down that road again anytime."

Bri laughs. "And back again, I'm sure." Bri embraces Allison, resting her head on Al's shoulder. "I needed to say thank you for what you did on prom night … for putting up with me after all I put you through in high school. I'm not great at being a friend."

Allison keeps nodding as she says, "No problem."

Bri lifts her head off Allison and hops up off the couch. Her mood flips a switch. "Don't think I'm leaving him for you or anything. It was just a thank-you for listening. But I have some thinking to do, and I think I need to be alone to do it."

"I'll walk you out." Allison starts to rise from the couch.

Before she can stand all the way up, Bri says, "Sit. Stay." Words that send Allison back on the couch cushion. "I can see myself out." She turns to walk away. "Sorry about the 'sit, stay.' Didn't mean to treat you like a puppy."

"No worries. I'm here if you need."

Bri exits, leaving a confused yet happy Allison to stew in the aftermath. She knows the kiss was nothing more than a friendly gesture, paid in a way that she would appreciate. If nothing more, it is a moment of levity in an otherwise dark time. But before she can bask in the warmth of momentary serenity, the phrase again runs through her head. *How much worse can things get?* She doesn't have an answer to that, and the impact of Bri's actions hasn't fully hit her. So, until it does, she will relish what remains of the moment.

Eleanor sits on her couch, staring at her empty living room. She sees the furniture and the shelves stacked with knick-knacks as she listens inside her head to the memories of past gatherings—friends and family laughing in the joy of a shared moment, stories of days gone by being told around the couch. But all those memories get pushed aside by the image of her deceased husband lying on the ground just around the corner. She tries to capture the happier times and hold on to them, but the blood keeps spilling before her eyes. The joyous laughter drowns beneath the flood of tears that streamed down her face only a few nights ago. Now, sitting on her couch, new tears join the memories. Her head falls into her hands, trying to stop the tears she fails to dam, sobbing at the thought of never seeing Nick again. Never seeing a new iteration of the same man he once was. She loved this man for many lifetimes, whether his name is Nick, Nioclás, or any other variation he was known as. But no matter what name the world knew him as, she loved him for who he was. She loved the man for everything he was, not just the parts he could show the world.

Each time before, the Waiting wasn't sad; she knew he would be back. The Waiting filled her with anticipation of what would inevitably change—his hair color, going from straight to wavy, the color of his eyes or complexion of skin turning a little more olive or pale, or a birthmark that wasn't there before. Something must always change, but, in change, the Legends live. This time, she holds no anticipation of anything to look forward to. No new Nick to trudge back through the door. No new smile to adorn his face upon seeing his love one more time that, in all the countless years, still made her smile back. So, she sits on the couch crying. She lets the tears fall and run down her hands and forearms because after the loss of someone so dear, after all others who were alive with you when you were young have passed on, all that remains are the tears to obscure the image of the inevitable end.

Her despair wants only to wallow in the wreckage of the current moments, but the unmistakable sound of knuckles hitting wood three times on her door pulls her from the moment. Drying her eyes, she peeks out the curtain to see Vistrus standing there. As she straightens her clothes to make herself more presentable, to present to Vistrus the version of herself she deems fit for the outside world, he speaks. "I can hear you. Please, Eleanor."

A meek smile buds but dies before happiness can sow its seed. She opens the door.

"You know you are always welcome, but the best of company I doubt I'll be," she warns, stepping aside so he can enter.

He nods at her warning and walks inside, looking around. He waits for the door to close but does not turn to her before saying, "You have been crying."

Eleanor nods. "We might be old, but the loss is never easy."

Vistrus shakes his head. "No, it is not. If you need anything—"

She interrupts. "I know. You needn't even say it." She walks to the kitchen. "Can I get you a glass of water? I think Nick has a couple of beers left. I don't think he'd mind."

Vistrus smiles out of courtesy. "Water, please."

Grabbing a glass from the cabinet and ice from the freezer, she turns to him. "What brings you by? Or is this merely a welfare check?"

Vistrus shakes his head. "A welfare check it may be, but you are a strong woman ... and an intuitive one. There is something that has been weighing on me."

Taking a seat at the kitchen table, she asks, "And this is the proper time to inquire?"

He pulls out his chair and sits before answering. "Nick knew. Nick was the head of The Council. But what I told him, The Council does not know."

"Then why are you about to tell me?" She pours their waters. "I think water will do me good."

"I do not think I can trust The Council." He keeps his words short.

"But you can trust me? Or are you testing the waters?"

"How about we add a glass of wine?" He motions to a bottle sitting atop the fridge. "I think you may need a glass."

She opens the bottle, pouring each of them a glass. "That serious, is it?"

"When I first approached him, I was unsure if I could trust him." He takes his glass from her. "Thank you," he says, before taking a sip. "He warned if what I told him did not sway him, The Council would be informed."

"And you would face charges," she adds.

He nods in affirmation. "As is the way."

"Does this have anything to do with Nick's murder? Is that why you are here?"

He shrugs. "Possibly, but not just Nick's."

Eleanor ruminates on his response. "The Taylors' and my Ken and Tracy's?"

He nods. "Possibly more."

Eleanor stops mid-sip; a name comes to mind. "Inessa?"

Again, he nods.

She gulps down the rest of the wine, taking in the seriousness of what he suggests.

"James and Hillary?"

Vistrus does not answer. He chews his thoughts while trying to piece them together in a layout that will make sense to Eleanor and provide structure for his argument.

"What do you think is going on?"

Raymond and December stand a few feet past the doorway in a darkened room. Dim light from the hallway's after-hours lights is more than enough illumination for the Legends seated in this room. A custom for council meetings dating back to their origins when light could have possibly drawn attention to their whereabouts. In the basement of the West Haven Historical Society building, the lights remain low more for carrying on tradition than anything else. The Council members sit at the table, listening to the words entering their minds. There are three empty seats at the table. One for Nick, the only member representative of all five Societies. One seat sits empty for Ken DeSalvo, who once represented the Kipling Society. It's the third vacant seat that leaves both the sentinels wondering about Vistrus.

"Whoever these people were, they kept repeating names and ranks." Raymond chimes into The Council. "We were not able to discern much."

December takes the reins. "The two seemed confused about the subject of their conversation. But we can confidently assume that everything happening is connected."

"I agree. The two men, the murders of the past few years, as well as that of Nick DeSalvo, are not random. We know this." Raymond's voice sounds through the heads of The Council members.

"Know may be a strong word," a Council member chimes in. "Do you have concrete evidence?"

"Know, feel, highly suspect, all but have concluded. Take your pick," Raymond retorts.

"We've all lived long enough to know sometimes evidence is not needed to know the truth," Decembers amends Raymond's words.

"That itmay be," a second member speaks out loud, pushing the conversation forward. "But we must protect The Nation as a whole. Any actions beyond what we have already done can lead to Normals knowing."

"So, your answer is to sit back and rest on the status quo?" December chimes inside their heads, sounding less than satisfied. "That would throw Connor under the bus and give no justice to the rest who passed before."

The third Council member exchanges furtive glances with the other two, unsure how to respond to such a leading statement. The silence filling the room begins drowning out any forward motion made this evening.

December begins pacing the small conference room situated below the West Haven Historical Society. The dark hallways beyond the room echo the emptiness of The Council's minds. "The dim lights to keep tradition tell more of your inane need to hold onto traditions for no other reason than tradition's sake. Here you sit, the leaders of The Nation, at least in West Haven." December pauses, letting her words sink into their consciousness. "We have come to you since your inception here, not as a means to simply help you keep status quo, nor as a means to only satisfy our ends, but to help each other in this symbiosis that we have forged."

She watches The Council members nod along with her words, causing a small smile to show.

"When we first started coming to you, it was with small things—a Legend in the beginnings of finding out who they were or when in the Waiting. These last few years, the events have not needed our messenger service, nor have you been able to help our ends of finding our 21-grams."

She turns to Raymond, who nods at her, giving her a go-ahead on whatever weighs on their minds.

"The deaths of James, Lucretia, and Jack Taylor … Sylvia Waldgrave, Ken and Tracy DeSalvo—Ken was one of your own. He was also on the city council. That should count for something. Now Nick DeSalvo, also one of yours … not to mention Scarlett McAllister in the Waiting." She scans their faces as all three wait with bated breath for her next words. "Yet nothing here has changed. You send in your cleaning services, making sure the media catches no wind of our Societies. You clean up mess after mess and all for the greater good. But in all our years, the usual course, the path most traveled by has made no difference. We still sit in the same dark basement, the same words exchanged. We no longer feel that our needs as acting sentinels are worth your time, let alone ours."

A Council member stands, his clenched jaw holding back harsh words, wanting to lash out. "We have always listened to your findings. Planned on courses of action to take. But we must protect ourselves from those who are," he pauses to chew his words for a brief moment, "not like us. We are not ignorant of the killings in our society. Nor are we ignorant of those who wish to cause us harm. We know about the teacher and the cop and his accomplice. This council is also short a few members. The death of our leader does not weigh lightly on us. It is a delicate situation, and careful steps must be prepared and plotted. One that is made more delicate without Nick and Ken and made no easier by the absence of Vistrus. So don't insinuate that we don't care. Do not place words in our mouths when we are also mourning losses."

Raymond stands, swaying into the dim light. "Point taken, but tell us then, what steps have you plotted out so far? What plan of action have you begun mapping while we sit back, continuing to watch our friends and loved ones die? There are young ones coming of age who see what is being done to them, to us, and have no one left to look up to. So, what is being done?"

The standing Councilmember turns to the other two members, reading them for any sign of objection, but they all sit stone-faced.

Turning from The Council members, he says, "We know that this, whoever is behind all the killings and attacks on our Societies, might go beyond West Haven. That Max Espinoza was working for someone, not just that man killed by Jack. But until we know the bigger picture, there is not much we can do. We must not go blindly into battle when we are not sure where the battle orders are being given from."

"And what are you doing to try to piece together the puzzle that is the bigger picture, this person above Max?" December whispers in their heads.

"First, we need to find Connor DeSalvo and deal with that. A Legend's death by a Legend is not something for the Normal world. We feel that he might be working with whoever Max works for."

December and Raymond turn to the other. A knowing glance of finalization on each of their faces form.

The Council member continues, "Once we have him, he will tell us, and it will be dealt with."

"And everything will go back to the way it was before any of this happened?" Raymond poses the obvious conclusion to their plan.

"That is the idea," The Council member finishes.

"Except it can't go back to the way things were because these things happened," December lashes out. "Do you not think that any of those children wouldn't kill a hundred Espinozas to get their parent back? To get things back to the way they were? But the thing these kids know, and perhaps it's because they lack the nostalgia of happier, more ignorant times, is that once things change, there is no going back; there is no back to the way things were. They know there is only forward and learning to deal. Time does not stand still because we are happy with the present, and your childish notion to try to preserve it only proves your inabilities as leaders. Do you now remember when you first transitioned? When you first felt the agony of knowing you had to keep a secret you so badly wanted to tell others? But you couldn't, not until you somehow found others like you.

"Remember, it was back in those beginning stages that you wanted to return to being a normal kid whose worst worries were what to wear and if you had enough money for Ducky's, or whatever the big deal of the moment was. But you had to move on, and you did. But now, you want no one else to move on, so you can try to recreate happier times from your youth that are long dead? There is no going home again; that place is gone. Your world is gone, and no amount of legislation will bring it back. It won't even create a simile of those times. At best, it will end up looking like a monstrous bastardization of what you thought you wanted."

Her words force The Council member back into his seat and he, along with the others, sit slack-jawed at her speech. They watch as Raymond stands next to December, intertwining his fingers through hers and attempting to calm her down without saying such words.

A Council member stands. His eyes shift around the room as if the words he wants to say are on some hidden teleprompter. "There is nothing wrong with wanting better times. There is something noble about the desire to make our world as happy as it once was. That is all we are trying to do."

Raymond's chest huffs up and down in silent laughter. "No. There is nothing wrong with wanting to make the world a better place. There is something wrong with wanting to recreate the past that you felt was so perfect when the only reason you felt that way was because you lacked responsibility then. You lacked the capacity to understand the conflicts of the world around you and, therefore, felt the world was a happier place. And it may have been for you, for your family, for people like you. But it sure as hell wasn't for people like us, for people who were different. And all you want to do, because you said so earlier, is look out for your own. That's why December is angry.

"All you want is this—these kids that are in danger, these kids that are watching their parents get killed off, in no small part due to your inaction, want the world to be better for everyone, not just The Nation. They don't care about The Nation because they haven't been in it long enough to care. What they do care about are their friends, their Normal friends. Their families, the people who need to be taken care of regardless of whether they are In or not. So, sit here with your status quo and futile attempts to recreate the past, all of which will do nothing to solve any current issues killing off West Haven Legends. We have better ways to utilize our time."

Raymond and December turn to exit, but a Council member speaks, "What of the DeSalvo boy?"

December does not turn back around while echoing, "We will find him and deal with him. Leave that worry to us. You concentrate your efforts on yourselves; it's what you do best."

"You have heard the tales of the Clochnawa, yes?"

Surprise paints Eleanor's face as Vistrus's words strike her ears.

"Long dead. Centuries ago, if not longer." Her response seems guarded and prepared.

Vistrus stares at her, trying to read between the words she chose. He sips his wine. "The Faoi Dhó Duine might not be as dead as we thought."

Her guarded body changes to concern. She tosses a playful yet warning glance around her living room. "Careful with the words you speak. Walls have been known to listen, even in safe spaces."

"I do not mean to burden you at such times." His words weigh heavier than they should.

She waves off his concern. "Such times take longer to pass than life allows. I have been lucky to have loved more than most ever will." She trails off her thought. "Bring this back around to the prophecy and the Clochnawa."

"I am stuck, and Nick was helping me. I read through my wife's diaries. I do not believe she was as crazy as she seemed." A tingle runs down his spine, planting a notion that they are not alone. "Perhaps the walls do have ears."

Eleanor leans toward him, dropping the volume of her voice low enough that only a Legend can hear. "You think her death is somehow connected to the events of the past few years?"

Vistrus's eyes shift around, searching for something that he cannot see. "She says it is a game of…" but he stops before saying the next word. "The Mind knows. Green and black and all below. The Mind knows." He nods a few times as if that will give Eleanor all she needs to know. He wants to tell her, to inform her, of all he has read and all he knows, hoping that she may hold a key to unlocking the answers to all the questions Inessa left behind. But the tingle in his spine stops him. The unnamed feeling that there is someone else who may hear, someone who might not want the secrets getting out, keeps him from telling her all that he knows. His glance darts around, looking as paranoid as he feels.

Her concern grows for his current state. "Perhaps you've been reading too many of her diaries."

"No. Not too many. Just right." His finger points dots in the air with each word he speaks. "She protected us. She did not know who she could trust." He brings his other hand up, waving them both as if conducting a slow orchestral piece. "And now Nick lies as she does. But why?"

She stands, stepping toward Vistrus, wrapping her arms around him in an attempt to calm him down. "Because Connor killed him." While she does not wholly believe her reply, she feels it's better and safer to lie than cause more harm by saying what she hopes is the truth.

"Ah." His finger shoots up again. "The premade response. Perhaps. Could he have not remembered? Could he have not been him? The Clochnawa may never have gone extinct. The Adeirrig may be real."

She pulls a chair close to him, sitting knees to knees. "The Clochnawa were stone men, unbreakable and indestructible, not shapeshifters. The Adeirrig, on the other hand…"

His finger again dots the air with his words. "But then, how did they die? Why five? Not six? I do not know these metaphors." He lets out a hearty laugh before dropping back down to a barely audible whisper. "Met a four. Met a five. I love my wife. Inessa was not crazy. She was a genius. Fine line, you know."

She takes his hand and leads him to the couch. "Lay down. Sleep. The company will be nice."

His head hits the pillow and, without missing a beat, he falls asleep.

"I know how they die, Vistrus. But that still does not explain why we have lost so many dear to us … or your behavior." She covers him with a blanket she drapes across the back of the couch. "Sleep well, child."

The screen door rattling catches her attention, causing her to freeze for a moment. The sound of footsteps scampering away urges her to the door. As she peers out the door's window, the figure turns a corner. She only caught a glimpse, but her pounding heart tells her Connor was listening … or at least someone who resembled Connor listened.

Standing outside the back entrance to The West Haven Historical Society, Raymond and December take deep, calming breaths. December stares at the night sky above, trying to find some peace and calm among the stars. She says to Raymond's mind, "They have no clue."

Raymond shakes his head in dejection. "They never listen and never learn."

"It seems that Vistrus might, though." December turns her gaze to Raymond. "We know better than to think Connor killed his grandfather."

"Never a question in my mind," Raymond assures.

"The question is who … and why." December lets out a heavy breath before stepping off into the night.

December turns to him. "Could there be another?"

"If not another, then what we seek may be closer than we know."

Raymond joins her as they walk away from the historical society and the remnants of The Council. The cool breeze hits a little cold for comfort, but the quiet streets and cloudless sky make it easier to bear.

"When we lost our voices," December begins, "we were the first."

"The firsts along with Pasha," Raymond adds.

She nods in affirmation. "But we are unique."

"In what way?"

"All Legends after us have a society, while we have been relegated to campfire tales and boogeymen."

Raymond's brow furrows. "And after these past centuries, it now bothers you?"

December smiles, huffing out a laugh. "No. But Connor didn't do it. Allison saw him at the cemetery as well."

Raymond stops walking. A car whizzes by, distracting him for a moment. "What are you trying to say?"

"While the Adeirrig may have become something of a fable, it is a possibility we considered and have not yet ruled out," December proposes.

"Who though? We know all the Legends that come in and out of West Haven."

"Do we? Knowing what we know about ourselves and what we choose to respond with, who else might not be so truthful with their response?"

Raymond takes a deep breath, realizing the hypocrisy of their past actions and the angered words at The Council earlier tonight. "The things we do to protect our own."

December nods. "Who could have seen the consequences?"

As they resume their walk into the night, Connor waits until they are a good distance ahead before emerging from the shadows. *Consequences, indeed.* He eyes the door from which they exited the building and stalks his way over, ensuring no one else can see him. He tries the handle, but it is locked. The keypad next to it offers no immediate help. He concentrates on the keys, thinking back to the first time his eyes turned for him in biology class, hoping that, perhaps, the answer is something only a Legend can see. But the more he tries to concentrate, the more he distracts himself with random thoughts, infuriating himself more and more. Though... the more he angers himself, the louder he can hear his heart and the louder his heart, the more his eyes concentrate and the light around him shifts to the spectrum he first thought was a trick of light. And in this spectrum, he sees the numbers 1,2,3,4,5,6, and 8 lit up. Which does him no good unless he knows the order, but before he can contemplate his next move, his ears pick up the soft buzzing of an elevator opening and closing its door and ascending up inside.

He scampers off into the shadows to see who emerges from the historical society. Not a moment after quieting himself down, he sees four people exit the building, all dressed in business-wear and all leaving work a little too late for government employees of a historical society. He watches as each enters a car and begins to drive away, but one car, in particular, catches his attention because of its plate—KIPLING.

Connor smiles, knowing he has found where The Council meets because who else but someone in a position of power would be bold enough to display a secret society on a license plate?

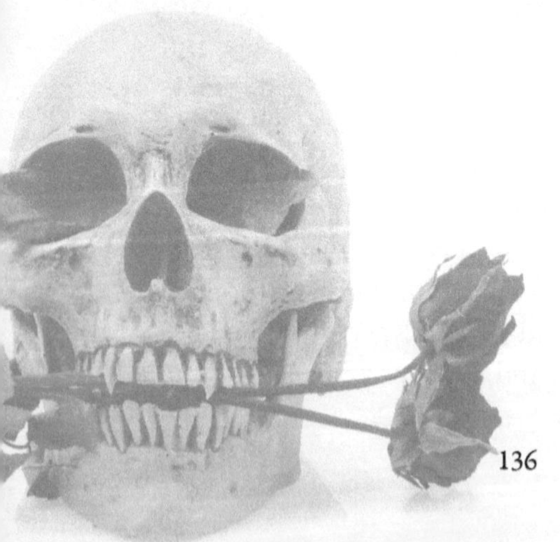

CHAPTER 7

Duncan and Brianna sit in her kitchen at the dinner table, magazines sprawled open. Each of them flips through the pages of a magazine, slapping a sticky note on everything catching their eye for the wedding.

"I didn't think this would be this much fun," Duncan says, sticking a note to a page showing black orchids wrapped in baby's breath.

"Oh, I did." Bri laughs. "I've been planning this day since I was old enough to know what marriage was."

"We have so much to do. We could use some help," Duncan admits. He sets the magazine on the table. "This is fun, don't get me wrong. I love picking out random things that will make the day that much more magical. But have you ever organized a wedding? Or picked out what food will be served? Will the appetizers be served table-side or butlered? What colors will the bridesmaids wea—"

Before he can finish the word, Bri interjects, "Easy cornflower blue with white trim and hints of pink."

Duncan gives an impressed nod. "What about the groomsmen?"

"Black, white, cornflower blue, and white highlights." A smile crosses her face that fades too soon for Duncan's comfort.

Duncan turns his attention from the magazines to his bride-to-be. "What's on your mind, love?"

"This seems, IDK, wrong?" Pouting and doubt overtakes her joy.

He stares at her, watching her eyes wander the kitchen floor for the right way to summarize her feelings.

"My love," he continues, "we still haven't set a date. Everything we're doing now is for when we do, and when we have the money to do it properly, we'll have all our ducks in a row."

A light bulb goes off above her head. "Oh, ducks would be so cute!"

He pulls her face to him. "Stay on track, love."

She nods a few times. "Sorry. I know all this. I think that with everything going on, our time could be better spent trying to help Connor or Scarlett or Allison. I mean Connor especially. Allison thinks he'll be on the lamb, as the fugitives call it, until he can prove himself or the fuzz catches him."

"On the lamb? Fuzz?" Duncan raises an eyebrow.

Bri's eyes light up as she nods. "Yeah, been brushin' up on crime slang. If we gonna associate, we gonna know the words, heard?"

"Heard." Getting his mind back on the task at hand, Duncan purses his lips, thinking. "I can't help but think it's not that our time couldn't be spent doing something else, so much as you feel guilty over the happiness you feel while you see your friends drowning in their situations."

Her eyes lock with his. "Exactly. And I don't feel comfortable being happy while everyone else is so … not happy."

"This is not the first time you've felt apprehensive about this. What would you have us do?"

Her eyebrows squish together in hard thought. Tapping her pursed lips with her index finger, a semblance of an idea forms. "IDK. We need to find a way to help Connor. We need to be there for Allison. She lost her best friend *and* her boyfriend. I mean, that sucks. Even if she is on the verge of switching teams, losing someone still sucks."

Duncan smiles at her concern. "First of all, honey, my love, my dear, my everything in this world, you have to stop saying things like becoming a lesbian or switching teams."

"Why? It's not offensive. I mean, she is becoming a lesbian, I think."

"That's just it. You think." He catches his last words. "Not that thinking is a bad thing. But she may not be becoming a lesbian. She might be bi, or she may just have mixed feelings about one woman, one wonderful woman who is awakening some set of feelings within her that makes her feel something she hasn't felt before."

"Yeah, lesbianism."

"No. Not lesbianism. Maybe. But not necessarily. We don't know. Hell, she doesn't know, or at least isn't ready to admit it if she does. I mean, just that her feelings may be in no way sexual in the end, just a new expression of compassion and love that, like lust, is confused at first for love, but unlike lust, ends with a mutual and platonic admiration for another in a way that is not felt for everyone."

The rest of Bri's face joins the squishiness of her eyebrows, skeptical of his words.

"Or," Bri counters. "She wants some of this." She points at herself.

Duncan relents, shaking his head. "Or she wants your hot bod. But either way, we can still plan the details of our wedding, ducks aside, and help our friends."

"Fine. We can do both. But we have to do it. Help them, I mean." She wags a stern finger at Duncan. "We can't half-ass helping them."

"I don't half-ass anything I feel is important. So, yeah, both. Definitely. But I started with first of all," he reminds her.

"So?"

"So, secondly. In order for you to give more energy to helping your friends, and so you don't feel like we are slacking on the wedding plans, I'll work out the details while I'm alone."

She lets out a laugh, crossed somewhere between adorable and evil rolled together. "You? Plan the wedding?"

"Sure, do you think I don't know how or that I don't know you?" He sets out the challenge.

"Let's start easy," she teases.

"Shoot."

"When's the date?"

"New Year's. Still haven't decided Eve or Day. Waiting until next year to not rush things." He beams with pride bordering on arrogance.

"Okay, do I want a live band or DJ?"

"For the reception, you want a DJ. For the wedding itself, you want that guy from TikTok who can make any pop song or movie theme into a wedding procession, Stephen Beerkens, and have him play 'Somewhere Over the Rainbow' as you walk down the aisle."

She gives an approving nod. "Okay. Colors?"

He goes to speak, but she stops him.

"Not of the wedding party. Of the wedding itself."

"Well…" He taps his temple. "The flower arrangement should be pink and as-close-as-we-can-get-to cornflower blue Stargazer lilies, filled in with baby breaths and finished with a sole black orchid rising from the center."

"That sounds beautiful."

He nods, having known that already.

"What else?" he taunts.

"Nothing." She leans in, planting a thankful kiss on his lips.

"Well, for now." He pushes himself away from the table, taking her hand in his as he walks away. "I know there are countless details you are obsessing over, thinking you are missing something. I'll give you a clue; you are missing something … many things. But that's all stuff I get to worry about now. As much as I would love to be your protector, I am very much aware that if push came to shove in some situation, you'd hold up just fine. So … let's forget about everything and see how comfortable your bed feels."

Allison jiggles the handle to the basement door. Locked. Her father's sanctuary of musical abundance defends itself against even the most well-meaning of people.

"Daddy?" she calls out.

But her ears pick up only a muffled response.

"Dad? Can we talk?" she shouts again.

This time, she hears his response. "I cannot right now. Must figure something out."

"But Dad!" Her pleading turns to whining petulance.

"Must figure out how four came from six. Not five, not anymore…" His words trail off as his thoughts turn back to the matter at hand.

Allison stands outside the basement, next to the locked door, dejected. Of all the things she thought her father capable of, not making time for her never made the list. She shuffles away, contemplating her next move.

She starts talking to herself. "I could call Scarlett. Oh wait. Can't do that. Maybe Jack would listen. Nope. He's gone. Connor. Nope. On the run."

Making her way to her room, she plops down on her bed. She pulls Bri's number up on her phone, staring at the send button. Their younger years as friends, the high school years lost to Bri's popularity, and everything that has happened since overwhelms Allison, stopping her from hitting that button. Taking a deep breath, she tries to steel her nerves, but the kiss from their last encounter painting itself fresh in her mind steals them away. Reaching for her flask, she unscrews the top but finds it empty. Only a few drops spill out. Not near enough to liquidize her courage.

She clears the number off her call screen and taps the photo album on her phone. Falling back on her bed, she scrolls through pictures of her, Scarlett, Jack, and Connor over the last few years. Times when they were happier … and two of them were still alive. These are the times she wishes she could hold on to, if only for just another moment. Something to take her away from the depths of despair she wades in. She swipes through her entire album, searching for a moment of solace but finding none.

A tear falls from her eye as her fruitless attempts to delude herself into happiness turn back to thoughts of Connor, Scarlett, Jack, and Bri. Even a few thoughts of Duncan, from when he stood up for Bri to all her old friends, bring a fleeting smile to her face. Fleeting her smile may be, but it cements in her that Bri is not the one to become her confidant in hard times.

Again, her yearning turns to Connor. The one who always stands by her side to help her understand the things about herself she cannot. She pulls up his number and hits send. In the moment it takes before connecting, she hopes his phone is turned on.

One ring.

Her heart starts racing at the thought of hearing his voice. It has been too long, and he knows the guilt she feels over the accident. He will pick up, she knows it.

Two rings.

It must be turned on, she figures. Otherwise, it would go straight to voicemail.

Three rings.

The butterflies in her stomach drop dead as they did in the hallway of her school when he was in college. Three rings then, and he did not answer. Why would he now? He would not abandon her at a time like this.

Four rings.

All hope abandons her of hearing his voice beyond a voicemail greeting. But a voicemail greeting she must settle for as it picks up to record her message. Beep.

"Hey, baby." She pauses, not wanting to sound desperate or cheesy. "I miss you. You know that, though. I just wanted to tell you again … in case you were forgetting … or already have." A sad huff escapes her lungs. "It sucks not knowing if you're okay. I assume you are. To assume anything else is too hard. I don't know what I would do if anything happened to you. It's hard enough as it is. I could really use you right now. Things around here aren't getting easier with less and less of us." Her words start quivering. "It's … my dad has become obsessed with something and … and I don't know. I assume it's something that will help you, but … he hasn't … he doesn't talk about it. He's locked himself up to do whatever it is he does. I just hope it brings you back to me. I can't do this by myself. And I definitely can't do this without you. I'm trying to hold on here. Trying to find some good in all this. That silver lining we're always told to look for in bad situations, but I'm just not finding any here. What's so silver about Scarlett having to wait or whatever or you hiding from society or your grandpa being dead? I just don't get it. So many people don't seem to care and the ones that do don't seem to be able to do anything about it. It's … Is that just the way it is? Those who care are powerless to do anything while the world around us crumbles? Is that life's great lesson?"

She doesn't hang up as her emotions overflow and her solemn tears turn to hysterics, but instead drops her phone to her side as it records her cries until reaching the end and disconnects, leaving her alone once again.

The florescent lights shine down the aisle of West Haven's Jewel Osco, a midwestern grocer and pharmacy, minimizing Connor's chances of staying hidden, but he needs supplies and food, and this is the place to get them. He keeps his hood up over his head to help conceal his identity. While the spring weather is warming, hoodies are commonplace most of the year in Chicagoland. Though he knows when trying not to draw attention to oneself, pulling a hood as far down as possible is probably not the best move. But short of wearing a Halloween mask, it keeps him as hidden as he can be in public. Still, his eyes dart around, looking for anyone who might know him and report him to The Council or anyone in The Nation.

He grabs a small notepad and a ninety-nine-cent pack of ball-point pens, tossing them in his basket. A grumble in his stomach tells him that a trip down the snack aisle is in order. Turning the corner to find some grub, he sees Duncan throwing a couple of granola bar packs into his cart. Connor tries keeping his head down as he turns around to walk away, but Duncan spots him.

"Psst. Dude." Duncan keeps his voice at a moderate indoor volume.

Damn. Connor stands still.

"Bro, come here." Duncan starts pushing his cart toward him.

Connor turns to him, checking the surrounding aisles for anyone he might recognize.

Duncan lowers his voice, catching up to Connor. "You all right, man? The girls are so worried about you."

Connor lifts his head a little.

"I am, too, but I figure you can take care of your-self, if any of us can." Duncan notices Connor's shift-iness. "You tweakin' on something?"

Connor shakes his head, unamused at what he assumes is either Duncan's attempt at humor or gen-uine concern. "Making sure no one sees me."

Duncan taps his temple. "Makes sense. Should have thought of that. Though constantly checking your sur-roundings for people is not the move of an innocent man," Duncan offers some advice. "Nevermind that. This engagement has my mind all muddled."

"This what?" A smile cracks across Connor.

"Shit. Yeah, I guess I never got a chance to tell you. She said, 'yes.'" Duncan bobs his head with pride.

"I'm missing out on some stuff. Congratulations. When did this happen?"

Duncan thinks for a moment. "We were in the city, walkin', window shoppin' outside Tiffany's. I thought there's no one I'd rather do that stuff with. A couple o' months ago. She looked so perfect."

Connor shakes his head at the thought of those two getting married.

"I've been gone so long. It sucks, bro."

Duncan bobs his head. "I bet."

Connor asks the big question. "How's Allison taking everything?"

Duncan realizes everything Connor still has to catch up on, and the joyous mood of telling Connor about the engagement turns somber.

"Not well, buddy, not well. She misses you. She can't talk to Scarlett or Bri about any of it." Duncan catches the words as they escape his lips. His gaze turns to the food on the shelves. "I think I need some chips, too."

A distraction that seems to have worked. Connor tosses a box of granola bars, a bag of rice cakes, and a bag of chips into his basket. "I feel so bad, but I can't contact any of them. I can't put any of them in danger. But I found something. I need to get in touch with Scarlett or Allison somehow."

"Try Bri. She can be quite the resourceful one," Duncan offers, again avoiding any talk of Scarlett and her current state.

Connor raises a brow at Duncan's comment. "You are gonna make her really happy, Duncs."

"I hope so. Should I tell her you're looking?"

"No. I don't want Allison to think I don't want to talk to her or anything." Connor's face drops, thinking of Allison.

"You miss her, huh?"

Connor nods. "More than I can say. I worry about her." Connor reflects on the current state of things for a moment. "Don't tell her we saw each other. This never happened. I'll find her when I can."

A shopping cart steered by a woman with pale skin for her heritage, a delicate jawline, prominent cheekbones, and medium-gray eyes, all shadowed by a look of eternal sadness turns into their aisle. Connor sneaks a glance at the woman, sending a tingle of familiarity down his spine, though he can't immediately recall why. Wanting more to protect his whereabouts and remain hidden than satisfy an itch to recall why she looks familiar, he starts off in the other direction toward the checkout lanes. Though as he puts distance between him and the stranger, he can't help combing his mind for why she haunts it right now.

Duncan maneuvers his cart to slow down whoever this new person might be, as he wants to protect his friends. He watches as Connor turns the corner, finally moving his cart, but this other person seems to be no one of consequence. Either way, Duncan is left with a cart half-filled with snacks and an encounter he can't mention to anyone he may want to.

Raymond's fingers tap away at his keyboard, as his desktop monitor illuminates an otherwise dark room. Before he can hit enter on his Google search, December's voice chimes in his head. "Have you tried Googling it?"

"I was about to hit the enter button." He presses his finger into his eye in annoyance. "We've come up with nothing in our paper research, so I figured this was next."

Turning his fingers back to the keyboard, he hits enter on the search bar. A list of results for "Eshpag" corrected to "Easpag" all show similar results—a chess piece more commonly known as a bishop.

"What do we know about chess?" Raymond asks her.

She abandons whatever she is doing and enters his room. She chimes back, "It's fun. I used to play a lot. But haven't in a while. My worldly knowledge of the sport ends with knowing Bobby Fischer was a chess grandmaster. Arguably the greatest player of all time. Why?"

"That rank we heard at Manic Mondays wasn't a rank. It's a chess piece."

"Easpag?"

"It's a bishop. A chess piece."

"What could this have to do with The Nation?"

Raymond shakes his head. "No idea. My knowledge of chess is take the king, even though the queen's more powerful."

"Hmm. You know what they say about what's behind every powerful man?" December offers.

Without missing a beat, Raymond answers, "A more powerful woman."

December taps her temple, turning to leave, but as she grabs the door handle with her other hand, a thought enters her mind. "Didn't Inessa talk a lot about chess?"

"That was many years ago, but if memory serves … yes, she did."

"Maybe this is something to ask Vistrus about. If anyone would know what she talked about, he would." With that, December leaves Raymond to his devices.

Raymond thinks, *As if that man doesn't have enough on his plate.*

Between sips of an extra thick malt and mouthfuls of a dipped Italian beef topped with hot giardiniera, Max Espinoza watches the people entering and leaving a Chicagoland grocery store. While he would have preferred to eat in the dining area of Portillo's, the filled parking lot and even fuller restaurant relegated him to the parking lot of the adjoining strip mall. Though car dinners are nothing he wasn't used to from his years in the West Haven Police Department, they are not his preferred dining spot. Not that his preference for indoor dining matters tonight. This evening, he is not on a stakeout. There are no perpetrators to keep an eye on or reckless drivers to ticket. Tonight, in his car, it is him and his beef. He watches a couple exit the store, pushing a cart full of groceries to a minivan. It makes him wonder how many kids they have. For a moment, he wonders if they are like him—if they harbor secrets they are too ashamed to tell anyone about or admit to themselves. Secrets he killed others in some futile attempt to deny what was real about himself. He stops himself from this train of thought, knowing that not wanting others to think this way starts with him not thinking those thoughts—not some karmic belief that his thoughts affect others but that his thoughts affect his speech and, therefore, how others will speak of him in the way he speaks of himself.

He swallows a large bite, pushing down the rising self-pity he feels, wanting nothing more than to enjoy his food in solitude. But solitude may have different plans this evening. He watches as a young man, about twenty-one and wearing a hoodie, exits the store, carrying three filled bags. Under the neon lights of the night, Max has a hard time seeing any details but recognizes a familiarity in the figure. A woman whose cheekbones reflect the streetlamps, accentuating their prominence and revealing her pale skin, exits right after the man, closing the distance between the two.

The young man pulls a hood up and over his face and heads toward Max's car. Max takes a sip as he notices the young man is not heading for his car, but only in his general direction. A semi-truck hauling a trailer drives through the parking lot, separating the hooded boy from the pale woman. As it passes, Max no longer sees the pale woman anywhere. The only person behind where the truck drove by is a man in a hooded red tracksuit with a white stripe down the sides, pumping his legs for his late-night run.

Max shifts his attention back to the boy headed his way. As the lights move from overhead to behind the young man, his face comes into better view for Max. A face that makes him stop chewing his food for a long moment. A face he knows as Connor DeSalvo.

His first instinct has him grabbing the handle of the door so he can open it and take Connor somewhere for questioning and safekeeping. He, much like the sentinels, knows Connor is innocent, or at least believes in his innocence enough to jeopardize his non-involvement in the situation. But years on the police force have him wondering why an innocent person would be a suspect for so long. And he wonders why an innocent person would hide away instead of prove his innocence. That thought shoots an instinct forward, one that has him hold back in favor of another idea. He watches Connor walk through the lot to the far end, where an old, abandoned miniature golf course sits, decaying.

Max starts his car and drives closer to Connor, finding a parking spot within eyesight. He shuts off the lights and the engine, opting for what little stealth this vehicle provides. Connor keeps walking, unaware that anyone might be following him.

Passing the old mini-golf course, Connor heads toward the road and sidewalk leading west to a forest preserve and nothing else until the next traffic light, more than a mile up the road. Max exits and locks his car, abandoning his meal to follow Connor on foot, hoping he stays far enough behind to remain unnoticed.

The man dressed in the hooded red tracksuit with white stripes bumps into Max while jogging.

"My fault," the man says, quickening his pace.

Max tries to ignore the distraction to keep his focus on Connor but can't shake the thought that he didn't hear someone jogging behind him while he trailed Connor. What bugs him even more is that Connor heard neither the man nor him.

The jogger does not take long to pass Connor as well.

The isolation this unlit stretch of road provides pedestrians with is not lost on Max. For now, he keeps an eye on Connor and the jogger, using the darkness as cover. Then again, if Max can see in low light because of his state, then he figures Connor may be able to as well. So, he slows his pace a little more.

The traffic light up the road provides minimal illumination as they stroll their way toward it. Max postulates where Connor might be staying: the cheap motel just on the other side of the railroad tracks running perpendicular to the street at the light, some vandalized spot in the public pool, or some other unknown spot. But before Connor makes it to the stoplight or anywhere that Max thought he might go, Connor ducks into the thick brush of the woods, with no paved path to follow or trail that is marked. He turns into the dense woods that run along the road, disappearing into the night.

Max catches up to where Connor vanished into the woods and notices the jogger turn around at the traffic light and head back toward him. But Max pays no more mind to the jogger. He sets his sights into the forest, trying to use what lowlight vision he possesses to spot Connor but cannot find him. He sees no trace in the wet ground of his footprints; no broken branches stick out that could lead him to where Connor stays.

Max contemplates for a moment about delving into the woods but forgoes that decision since the snapping of twigs and branches could raise alarms for Connor. That is not something he wants to do at the moment.

The jogger slows down as he approaches Max. "Scary woods. I wouldn't want to be in there this time of night. I don't suggest you try to brave them either."

Max turns to finally get a good look at the jogger to see a man far spryer than expected for his age. Also, a man far more broad-shouldered than he would normally attribute to a jogger. But before Max can respond, the jogger takes off toward the crumbling mini-golf course.

Max stands in place for a moment, caught between the strange encounter with the jogger and wanting to find out what he can about Connor's whereabouts. But the smart voice in his head reminds him about the sound snapping branches make, so he opts to walk back to his car, leaving the moment where it lies—somewhere on an isolated stretch of one of the main thoroughfares, Dempster Street, running along a random spot of forest.

Connor skulks through the forest preserve, trying not to disturb the nearby wildlife while avoiding the searching eyes and flashlights of Cook County deputies, who keep the preserves vagrant-free each night. Approaching a fork in the trail, he hears a branch snap close behind him. He halts his forward motion, whipping himself around to fend off whoever or whatever may be approaching.

Seeing no one there but hearing the cracking of a fallen branch sends his heart racing and adrenaline pumping, causing his hearing to amplify all surrounding sounds. Listening closely, he ignores the soft, whimpering snores of tiny chipmunks and squirrels, homing in on a more human-sounding breath a few yards off the trail.

"I can hear you and know you're there. I don't know what you want, but I have a very special set of skills…"

A small laugh escapes the would-be stalker as Connor gives his take on Liam Neeson's famous *Taken* quote.

Connor hears an unmistakable femininity in the laugh. "Allison?"

"No," a woman responds. "But I mean you no harm."

"Then what do you want?" Connor's adrenaline pumps harder.

A branch snaps behind Connor as her voice sounds from the same direction. "I want to show you what's out there."

Connor's heart races faster and harder as he turns toward the lady's voice.

A branch snaps from the side of him, causing him to turn in that direction. "I want to show you what The Nation really is. I want to show you what The Nation has been hiding from you, from your family, from all the councils in every city that holds Legendaries so sacred."

A female emerges from the tree line. The same cart-pushing woman from the grocery store, whose prominent cheekbones, pale skin, and gray eyes haunt Connor's mind as he searches for why he recognizes her.

She steps forward to him, letting the light of the moon fully illuminate her face. She continues, "I want to show you the truth."

Connor measures the weight of her words while deciding what to do next, and if he should and can trust her. He inhales a deep breath, holding it for a five count before asking, "Are you In?"

She pauses at his question, contemplating her answer. "I am in the existence between the essence."

Connor does not respond, though he recognizes her words as those of the poet T.S. Eliot. In all his preparation for his future on The Council, Connor has never heard that phrase referencing any Society. While he has been told the phrases and memorized the phrases, he has never heard that phrase before. The Kipling Society says, "I am in because of his age and his cunning." Responding back with, "Because of his gripe and his paw." The Tennyson Society says, "I am in true, whate'er befall." And they respond with, "I feel in, when I sorrow most." Of course, there's the Coleridge Society with their, "I am in a night chilly and dark," to which they reply, "The night may be chilly but not dark." Of course, there's the Poe Society taking from *Fairy-Land* by saying, "I am in as they put out the star-light," with his favorite response, "With the breath from their pale faces." And the now-extinct Frye Society, who once said, "I am in each lovely thing."

While their response was one he did not understand, Connor is not always one to question why, especially since he was told they have passed on, but, "Do not stand at my grave bereft. I am not there. I have not left," was also the longest reply. But for all that, and everything else Mr. Petrovsky taught him about etiquette between Legends, Vistrus always stressed the importance of never answering back if you do not feel comfortable. Never should he answer back if he does not know who else might be around. And never answer back with anything that is not true of the Kipling Society he is part of. But he has an urge to finish the line, to recite the remaining lines of the stanza. Not out of some suspended dissonance in his mind, but only because he knows. And perhaps, the desire to know why someone responded with something he had never been taught—with a response that, to his knowledge, should not exist. His studies of The Nation's Societies, and a newfound love for poetry, have taught him that the next line in the poems will be the response. One that can be faked if a lover of literature was so inclined. But he knows this may not end well no matter what action he takes, so youthful naïveté wins this round.

"And the descent falls the shadow." Connor watches the woman stand, stunned at his reply.

She stirs herself from the thoughts his response evokes and steps a few inches closer. "Why respond with a Society that is not yours?"

Connor's skin tingles more and more. He feels the blood race through his veins, feeding his muscles the energy needed to engorge at any given moment.

"Why use a reply that I assume you know I know isn't part of the current Societies? But, more importantly, why answer a question you know I would not recognize the answer to?"

A smile breaks on her. "This is why I must show you the truth that awaits. Perhaps even The Nation does not know of every existing Society. Or maybe it was a test."

Connor does not believe those last words. "Of my general literary knowledge, or specifically my love for T.S. Eliot? Either way, tests are stupid." He steps neither toward nor away from her. Opting instead to squint his eyes, searching for some tell as to who this pale woman might be. "Who are you?"

She does not answer.

Connor watches as the pale woman's smile grows. "Let me show you."

The evening moon shines through Connor's front room windows, fully illuminating the room as Eleanor opens the last closed shade and curtain. While the low evening light might be too dim for a Normal, it is more than enough for Eleanor to clearly see the surrounding mess. She smiles, knowing those she loved and loves spent countless hours enjoying this house and the memories it provided. As she straightens up the mess left by her grandchildren, Eleanor ponders the reasons young adults leave such clutter for later. She, too, was once their age and did such things. But years have abandoned her of the reasons why she once thought the same as the younger generation. In all her years, of the many things she has learned and forgotten, one has always stuck with her—procrastination provides nothing to lighten your load. At this moment, she cleans up what Scarlett and Connor left behind. Knowing Scarlett is in the Waiting gives her a reason to do so … gives her grandchild something to come home to.

The dizziness and disorientation of waking up covered in dirt prove most difficult anytime it happens, but the first time can be especially trying. While each Legend must come through on their own, since the time spent in the Waiting varies, what no one should have to come home to is a dirty home. It is a small thing, something that she wishes someone had done for her when she awoke. To Eleanor, it is not about doing what was done to her but making sure that the unnecessarily hard times don't get repeated when they can be spared.

While saddened by the current events still playing out in her life, she cleans. A small gesture to show someone she loves that they are not alone—that through her ordeal, there is someone who still thinks of the small things.

Making her way through the house and unplugging any appliances or devices that can be unplugged, and after a needlessly long struggle to turn off Connor's computer, she finds herself in Scarlett's room. She sets aside a clean change of clothes to bring to her house, in case Scarlett stops there first. Eyeing Scarlett's cell phone, she grabs that and the charger. After Scarlett's bed is made and the sheets are changed, she sees Scarlett's laptop on her desk. The green light blinks its message to the world that it is on and continues sucking up energy. Eleanor opens it and the screen lights up, catching her eye. While she wants to be the good grandmother and respect Scarlett's privacy, temptation wins this round.

She pulls out the desk chair, taking a seat. She reads Scarlett's notes on her parents and her thoughts about why they died and who might have been behind it. Grief creeps up as Eleanor continues reading. She realizes Scarlett has many theories behind her parents' deaths, and each theory varies far from the last. Everything from conspiracies to a car crash caused by her to newer entries that relate her parents' deaths to the current events surrounding them. After finishing her read, Eleanor scrolls up to the top to catch whatever came before her entering. But all that came before was the title of her document: *One Day.*

Eleanor taps the mouse over the shutdown button. She closes and unplugs the device from the wall. Resting her hand on the closed computer, she smiles, knowing that Scarlett holds a vested interest in her parents and yearns to know more about them. Eleanor smiles because it was her little intrusion into Scarlett's privacy that brings a shining light on her dark times. Not all hope is lost.

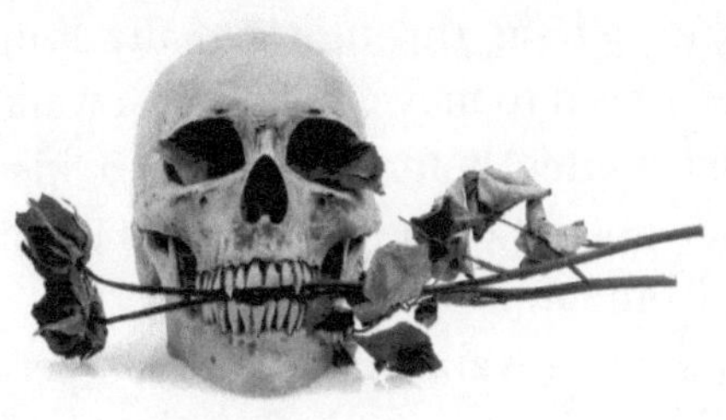

CHAPTER 8

The cool, spring breeze blows Brianna's hair while she and Duncan walk up to her front door. Clouds above float by on a starry night. The air breathes crisp and clean.

"I can't believe how awesome that movie was," Duncan says, laughing. "Way better than people are saying."

Bri nods in agreement. "For an action movie, it was good. I guess."

"Superhero, not action. And Zack is so underappreciated. He'll bring back DC, you'll see." Duncan finger-wags his last words.

Bri shrugs. "If you say so."

Duncan pulls Bri close to him. "Let's not go inside."

Bri pulls her head back, confused. "Why? Inside is nice."

"We just sat through a really long comic book movie. I need to move. Let's take a walk," he suggests.

Bri smiles before planting a kiss on his lips. "Sounds good. Let me just freshen up first." She pulls away from Duncan.

"It's just a walk. Plus, you look perfect." He tries to pull her close again, but she breaks free.

Bri chuckles. "Freshen up is code for gotta pee."

Duncan drops his hands. "Gotcha."

Stepping up to the door, she kicks something with her foot. Looking down, she sees a small flip pad opened to some writing. She picks it up to see what it says.

Bri, I need to talk. A birdie told me you were resourceful.

C

She turns to Duncan, holding out the pad. "What is this?"

He takes it from her, looking it over.

"I assume Connor wants to talk to you." He hands it back.

"How would you know?" Suspicion creeps out in her tone.

"It says 'C' at the end. Who else do we know with that initial?" Duncan offers.

"Why me? He has a girlfriend, ya know?"

Duncan shrugs his shoulders in an obvious cover-up. "Because he thinks you're resourceful?"

"Resourceful?" she asks with a raised eyebrow. "What birdie told him that?"

Duncan knows his cover is blown. "Connor asked me not to say anything. He says he can't face Allison right now and doesn't think he'd be able to leave her if he did."

"Yeah, and with Scarlett…" She lets her words trail off.

"He doesn't know. I didn't think it was my place to tell 'im."

"Well, what's he want?" Bri puts her hands on her hips.

"Dunno. Not my business. That's a you-and-him thing. Though, if I had to venture a guess, probably something about him being accused of murder."

"Is this why you want to take a walk? To see him?" Accusation grows in her tone.

Duncan shakes his head before looking up at the stars. "No. I just think it's a great night to do something … couple-y."

"I don't even know how to find him." She flips through the rest of the book, looking for a clue only to find it empty.

"He's been able to stay hidden this long. I think he'll find a way to find you."

"Well, I still have to … freshen up." She pecks Duncan on the cheek before turning to head in. "Be right back."

Duncan waves her off as she heads inside. Turning around to face away from the house, he returns his gaze to the skies. As he stares at the stars, he hears something tiny hitting the ground around him. He looks down and sees pebbles bouncing around. He looks out at the streets, scanning to find the source, but cannot.

The bouncing pebbles continue, and he feels the sting of a small rock pelting the top of his head. He looks up, shielding his eyes, spotting a few small pebbles flying from over the roof. Duncan starts around the side of the house when Bri comes back outside.

"You can't go for our walk by yourself," she teases.

Duncan waves for her to follow with one hand while holding a finger to his lips with the other.

Bri hears the pebbles raining down. "What's that sound?"

Duncan turns back, throwing his hands up and scrunching his face in a reminder to be quiet.

She throws up apologetic hands before he waves her his way again.

She double times her pace to catch up. Whispering, she asks, "What is going on?"

Duncan shrugs as they continue around back to find Connor standing in the shadows, holding a handful of pebbles, throwing them over the house. His scruffy face and unkempt hair show signs of his roughing it in the preserves, but otherwise, he looks healthy. Connor's ears pick up their muffled footsteps, stopping his tossing. He looks around and, while he can see in the dim light, misses their location.

Duncan clears his throat, revealing their positions.

"Dude!" Connor whispers.

"What the hell, Con?!" Bri's whispers border on loud talking.

"Shhh!" Connor urges. "I need help."

"More than I can offer," she jokes. "What do you need ... besides a bath? Are you doing okay out there?"

Connor waves her off before running his hand over his scruff. "What? You don't like the rough-and-tumble, rugged look on me?" Finishing with a laugh, he turns to Duncan, nodding in his direction. "Sup, Duncs?"

"Sup, Con." Duncan takes an air of cool collectiveness, sitting down in a patio chair.

Bri walks to Connor. "So, what's with the shadowy spy stuff? And to answer your question—on you, no. Definitely not a good look."

Connor leans in. "Here's the deal. I need to get inside the historical society. Duncan says you're resourceful."

She tosses Duncan a stink-eye. "So, I've heard. I can actually help with that."

"There's a code, keypad," Connor says as if it will prevent her from helping him.

She nods her head. "I know. I have the code written down." She turns to leave.

"Um, where are ya goin'?" Connor reaches out for her.

"To get the code, dummy. Can't get in without it."

Connor skulks to Duncan as if someone might be monitoring her backyard.

"So, Con, why not just go in during the day and hide until they close?"

"Noise. Look at you two trying to be all sneaky."

"You heard us?" Duncan's awe at Connor's keen sense of hearing frosts his words.

"You weren't exactly quiet as mice … at least she wasn't. But yeah, I heard."

"Point taken." Duncan sinks further into the patio chair.

Connor sits in a chair across from him. "I don't think entering a public facility in broad daylight that's staffed with government employees while I am a wanted criminal would be a wise move."

Duncan taps his temple. "Good point. Talk with your girl yet?"

Connor shakes his head. "No. I want to, but I have to figure this out. There has to be something out there that says it's not me. I still can't get a hold of Scarlett."

Duncan hops up. "Damn, I gotta pee." He starts off toward the house, avoiding a sensitive subject. "Too much soda at the movies."

Bri exits the house, passing Duncan as he enters. "Here." She hands Connor the code on a piece of paper, sitting in Duncan's vacant chair.

"Thanks," Connor says, taking it. "Any idea where I can find Scarlett? It's been a couple of months since I've been able to track her down, and she hasn't responded."

Bri tightens up. She looks down, trying to think of an answer. "Nope. Probably buried with work or something."

"At Manic Monday's? I haven't seen her there."

"Must be missing her then." She turns back to the house. "Gotta use the restroom again."

Connor senses the avoidance on the topic. "Too much soda?"

"Yeah! How d'ya know?" She hurries back into the house.

"I gotta jet. Thanks for the info." Connor shakes his head, trying to figure out what they are avoiding telling him as he trudges off alone into the night.

The light from Allison's laptop illuminates her face like a digital campfire as she leans against her headboard. She scrolls through scanned journal entry after journal entry, rereading her mother's words, adding to the countless times before, as she searches for some heretofore undiscovered wisdom waiting to be decoded.

"Come on, Mom. Give me something," she scolds the computer.

She skips down to a random entry, hoping this will be what she needs. Frustrated, she huffs and scrolls down farther. Again, she meets more frustration.

"Pointless. Didn't you write about anything else?" She shuts her monitor, setting it beside her. Reaching around the pillow behind her back, she pulls out her flask only to find it empty. She shoves it back behind her and unlocks her phone. The screen illuminates its electronic light while she stares at it, contemplating her next move. As it gets ready to go black, first fading a bit, she taps it to bring it back to life but still does not do anything more. Her head falls against her headboard as she runs her hand through her hair.

Succumbing to temptation, she pulls up Connor's number and hits send.

One ring passes, and her heart already knows how this will end.

A second ring tells her it will end the same way it ended before.

The third ring signals that she is right as it goes to voicemail.

Her heart sinks into her stomach, its weight sending pangs of nausea through her. Tears struggle to form in the dry wells of her eyes as she once again hears the recorded voice of the man she longs to speak with.

Beep.

"Hey, baby. I know you didn't do it. I hope you're getting these. It's been, like, I don't know … forever, and still no contact." She pauses for a quick thought. "Makes me miss your freshman year of college. You were easier to talk to then. I wish you would send me a signal. Something that lets me know you are still alive … that you still know I am waiting. That you still care." Her eyes tighten, trying to form tears. "I need something from you, anything that says there's a light at the end of this long, crappy tunnel. Something that says this isn't all for nothing. Some signal or sign that says I still matter to you. A text. I'd take a rock thrown at my window while I am sleeping." A sigh escapes her. "I guess the police could track you if you texted me. They are probably watching my house since Dad's on The Council. Whatever. This is all so stupid. God, I miss you. I have things I need to tell you … about Scarlett. I can't do it over the phone."

Tears finally break the surface and run down her cheek. She hits the end button and curls her knees to her chest, burying her head between her knees. The tension relaxes as the anxiety pours out of her eyes in chest-heaving sobs. Reaching again for her flask to help numb the pain, she is met with the immediate reminder of its emptiness and flings it across the room.

She picks up the phone with her finger wavering over the dial button to call Connor. After going back and forth, playing both the devil and the angel to her indecisiveness, she gives into the devil and dials him again. Not wanting to endure the disappointment of voicemail again, she pulls the phone from her ear to hang up, but before she can, his voice sounds through the phone's ear speaker.

"I can't talk. They can trace my location." He starts. No hello. No talk of how he misses her. Just facts.

"I … need you. I needed … to know … you aren't lying … in a ditch somewhere," she gets out in between sobs.

"Yes. I'm alive. I love you, Al, but you need to stop calling me. It's hard enough for me to do this knowing you're so close. I need to do this without you to keep you safe … so I can come back to you. If I am going to get dragged down in some conspiracy that I am not a part of, I can't have you being drug down, too, weighing on my conscience."

"But I need you, Connor. I need someone."

"I need you, too, Allison. But until I can figure out what is going on, you need to stop calling. I love you, but I have to go."

He hangs up, leaving her with his harsh but honest words. Words that sting her more than the sound of his voicemail ever did. A part of her understands why she can't call him. That logical part of her that understands wants to smack the emotionally wrecked part of her, telling it to Betty White up. But the emotional side is Hulk strong, strangling the logical side, leaving her to call the only other friend she feels safe talking with.

"Hey. Uh … can you come over?"

Raymond and December approach the front door to the Petrovsky residence. They knock on the front door, eyeing the Pontiac Solstice in the driveway, blocking any car that might be behind the doors from pulling out of the garage.

As December raises her hand to knock again, Vistrus opens the door wearing nice, dark denim jeans, finished with an Indian Motorcycle belt buckle, a black, casual button-down, and a sports coat. Cigar smoke twists in circles as it rises from the almost defeated Churchill in his right hand.

"You look spiffy, Mr. Petrovsky," December rings her voice in his mind.

He looks himself over before responding. "Thank you. I try." He turns his attention to the two people before him. "I am running late for a Council meeting and have already missed more than my fair share." He starts out the door.

Raymond sounds his internal voice, "Then one more should not make a difference."

Vistrus closes the door, leaving the three of them outside, but relaxes his stance, staying on the porch with them. "Make it quick?"

"Do you play chess?" December cuts to the chase.

Vistrus tightens up and steps away, saying, "I do not have time for this."

Raymond grabs his arm. "Please. We have been hearing things."

"Then a psychiatrist is in order. Not I," Vistrus jabs his words.

Raymond nods at the attack. "People talk, we listen; it's what we do. You know this."

Vistrus nods. "What does this have to do with me?"

"I am not sure how to say part of this, especially in light of your comment," Raymond begins with a defense.

"Just say it, Raymond." Vistrus's patience wears thinner.

December steps in. "There might be an Adeirrig in West Haven."

Vistrus nods. "So it seems. What does this have to do with my playing chess?"

"So, you do play?" she asks.

"I have not in a long time. But yes. I used to. Why?" Vistrus relaxes as his curiosity over their visit grows.

"We may have seen one. We are not sure. But we heard him talking with someone," she continues.

"Who?" Vistrus pries.

"We could not get a clear view and did not recognize the voices," December defends.

"But," Raymond chimes in, "we heard them mention the word Easpag a few times."

"Old Irish for the piece the English called a bishop. What else did you hear?" Vistrus's interest grows.

"Not much," December says. "But it got us thinking. When Inessa was alive … she mentioned the game on more than a few occasions to us, as if it should mean something. We thought it might mean something to you."

Vistrus squints his eyes, searching his memory for clues. "I will look into it. I remember such ramblings when she was fading." He chokes on his words as he now knows there was much more lucidity to them than people thought. "She talked about how people look ahead and to their sides."

December picks up his sentence as if from a book, "…but the things that kill us come from angles. Or something like that."

Vistrus smiles, feeling he might be able to trust them with this more than he initially thought. "Something, yes." He looks at them, trying to gauge their thoughts. "Where does this leave us?"

"We don't know. Until we can figure out who this Adeirrig might be and what it all has to do with the game of chess, I feel we're stalled." December admits the temporary defeat.

"And Connor?" Vistrus adds to the pile.

"We've staved off The Council for some time. We have some more. But it grows short," Raymond admits.

"Is he safe?" Vistrus's skepticism underlies his tone.

"We help from afar when able, but he does not know." December smiles.

"Good. I will deal with The Council as I figure out what all this means." Vistrus finalizes their brief meeting. "I think I shall study chess again."

Connor emerges from the shadows around The West Haven Historical Society, running on his tiptoes to the door, trying not to make noise even a Legend's ears might pick up. Pausing for a moment to ensure no one heard, he pulls out the paper and punches in the numbers to open the door.

Continuing his tiptoeing inside, he scans for any signs of life he needs to avoid but finds none. Remembering the sounds of an elevator from his last time here, he finds one at the end of the hall. He pushes the call button, and the doors open. Inside, he relaxes his third-rate ninja skills, looking at the floor options. He chooses "B" and heads down.

The chime of the arriving elevator negates any need for sneakiness, and he steps off the elevator with relaxed casualness. A pulsing sensation hits his ears, causing him to stop. He concentrates on the sound; it is three sets of beats. Heartbeats. Hopefully, he hears the hearts of those he seeks. They are calm and steady. He returns to his pace and treads light-footed down the hall, listening. They grow louder as he grows closer, but their soft voices remain calm. He knows they know someone is here.

"Mr. DeSalvo. Quite an unexpected arrival," a Councilman says.

Connor stops, still out of view of the door and The Council. "How did… I didn't… Yes. I am coming in."

Another voice speaks, "No one is stopping you."

Connor takes a few hesitant steps into the room. The light is dim, but to most of The Council, the light does not matter; to the one it does, they fare well enough. He sees them seated at a nondescript table in an otherwise underwhelming room. He notices a plainness that lends to their blending in, though Connor suspects this room provides other functions during the daytime.

A part of Connor is saddened at the lackluster ambiance. The ever-wishful boy in him wanted to walk into a candlelit room with Legends in their Legendary states. Perhaps with some incense burning or spooky music more reminiscent of a medieval video game or Halloween soundtrack than nothing at all. After seeing all the modern-classic movies like *Blade, Underworld, Interview With the Vampire*, and the likes, he wants something more from this reality than it offers.

The Council stares at Connor, waiting for him to speak. Though Connor stands, fidgeting, fighting himself to leave his wandering mind and focus on what to say that can help his cause, nothing useful comes to mind.

"I didn't do what you think I did," Connor spits out. He knows the irony in those words are that every innocent man says them with the same conviction every guilty man does. Now he knows he has never said more useless words.

The Council turn to each other, unsure who should respond first. One decides to take the floor. "Are you In?"

Connor takes a breath, remembering the proper response. "I am in because of his age and his cunning." A surge of adrenaline pumps through him. He has never spoken the words to strangers within The Nation before. He wants to run, fearing that this might somehow go awry, but he stands stalwart.

The man who asked returns an answer, "And if Ken were here, he'd say 'because of his gripe and his paw.' Alas, he is not. And for that, we offer our condolences."

As much as that response should have helped him relax, his heart pounds harder. The reality of the situation sets in. He starts wondering if coming here was the best choice or if this will end in any way that won't have him in captivity.

"I didn't kill my grandpa," Connor repeats with more concentrated conviction.

"The evidence says otherwise. Even your own grandmother, Eleanor, says it was you," a different member chimes in.

Confusion presses down on his shoulders, causing him to stumble back at the betrayal he feels. He knows what was said at the scene because he heard it, but to hear it now, after the chaos of the moment, hits harder than he thought it would. His eyes dart around the room, trying to take in the environment, weighing the possible ways this could go wrong and what he might be able to do to keep himself a free man.

"She's wrong," is all he can muster. He steadies himself. "I don't know why she would say it was me. I don't know why, but if someone somehow disguised themselves as me, then I was framed. I don't think Grandma would be so … malicious to say it was me without reason. But it wasn't me."

The member who answered on behalf of the Kipling Society speaks, "Why did you come here? To claim your innocence? We know that is your plea. Did you think you would make your case tonight?"

Connor takes a moment to think over his actions and reasons for coming but struggles to remember his original intent.

He looks toward the ground. "Right now, I can't remember. I had it all planned out, but now, standing here, I don't think it was my brightest idea."

"That it was not. The evidential testimony, your running from us, it does not bode well for you." The Councilman lays it out for him.

"Are you In?" Connor asks.

The Council members turn to each other, seeing if any will speak. But they falter among themselves.

Connor continues, "It's an easy question. Are … you … In? I am in because of his age and his cunning. Are you in a night chilly and dark? Are you in true whate'er befall or in as they put out the star-light? Or are you in each lovely thing?"

A member stands from his seat.

"Stay there. What do those phrases matter?" Connor conjectures.

The standing member replies, "As a way to identify oneself within The Nation. You know this already."

"I do." Connor shakes his head. "But what good are they when The Council, the almighty five who govern the likes of us, won't even give someone who is in the benefit of the doubt."

Another member goes to speak, but Connor cuts them off.

"It would seem the only function is to help you more easily decide who to throw under the bus and who to protect, regardless of if they are In or not. I do not know why you don't believe me. With all the history of Legends you have at your fingertips, it seems, to me at least, that you would rather take the easy way out and convict me of a crime I did not commit than do any real work and figure out how someone may have framed me to the point that Grams even thought it was me."

The rest of the members stand and step toward him.

"Stop." The two others stop. "Sit back down," Connor continues, but all three remain standing. "I'm not surrendering. The last thing I'll tell you right now is that I can figure it out. But I need time." The Council members remain standing, staring at him in the dim light. Light his eyes have adjusted to, perhaps because of his nature and the stress brought on by this encounter, or maybe he has really good eyes. But he can see them, and he sees each of them waiting for the opportunity to advance. His heart races, pounding harder with each beat. A panic-induced bargain ushers forth from him.

The member who greeted first breaks their silence. "Say we were to give you the benefit of the doubt ...

temporarily. How much time do you need? It's already been over two months, and all you've managed to do is stick a wedge between us and our Sentinels."

A raised eyebrow on Connor signals his cluelessness about who or what the Sentinels are or how he's done such a thing. "Whatever you think I've done in addition to what I've already been accused of, I've not. Whoever these Sentinels are is not my concern."

"Well, you are theirs. Raymond and December said they would find you. Though, since you are here, they can get back to other matters. It's not like you're leaving," The Council member says.

Connor shakes his head. "I am not staying here. I only came to tell you I am not running because I am guilty. I am running to prove I am not."

"Again, what makes you think you are leaving? You can't beat us all in a fight," the man says, smirking.

"I'm more lover than fighter, but I do think I can outrun you long enough to get outside. And the last thing you or The Nation want is a werewolf, or whatever you call us, running around being chased by another werewolf, a vampire, and whatever the hell the others are. I think a monster squad running amuck in the streets will do a lot more damage to your cause than letting me walk out of here."

The Councilman smiles at Connor's bravado. "How long do we give you? How long until we put effort into finding out where you are hiding?"

"I'll need less time at home." Connor throws a hail Mary.

The man shakes his head. "The other police are still looking for you. While not actively, they have an eye on your house. That would not be safe for you and worse for The Nation." Information that was not thought about by Connor. "So, how long?"

"I don't know. But if I can't figure it out on my own, I'll turn myself in."

"That is not a timeline."

Connor backs toward the doorway. "You'll have to take my word on it. Otherwise, we can have our monster marathon right now."

Three members still stand, ready to pursue, but the man that spoke for Ken extends an arm, motioning to stand down.

"It was not me. And I see you do not care about truth or justice, only saving face. I find it funny that for a society forced into an existence of hiding because of where you come from, that you've been reduced to this. But, as I said, I need time." Connor looks at each of them, studying the intent in their eyes. "While I do what I need, perhaps you need to look at yourselves and figure out if what you are doing is still relevant or if you are just relics of a time gone by."

As The Council starts to rabble at the audacity of Connor's words, a different member quiets them down. "Young man, you have no idea who put us in our positions or why. No idea about the formation of The Council or what came before. If you knew that, you would understand why we do what we do. But you do not. Tread lightly, speak softer, and carry a bigger stick if you wish to survive in this world."

"Thanks for the advice." Connor salutes them as he turns, dashing for the stairwell, not wanting to chance waiting for the elevator.

The time between Allison's phone call and now seems infinite, lying in bed, still struggling against the never-ending storm of tears. A text alert dings as a beacon of hope in her weary world. She reads the one word she has been waiting for—

[Here]

She replies.

[One minute]

She pulls herself out of bed, heads to her mirror, and wipes away the tears and ruined makeup before heading downstairs to the front door. She opens it, expecting to find two people but sees only Brianna holding a brown paper bag.

"Where's Duncan?"

"It's a girl's kinda night."

Allison forces out a smile before stepping aside for Bri to enter. While the smile may have been forced, her appreciation for Bri leaving Duncan elsewhere rings sincere.

"Where's Mr. P?" Bri looks around, not seeing him.

"I musta been in my room for longer than I thought." Allison looks around, too, realizing her father's not home. "Dunno. Work, probably."

"Good," Bri says, pulling a bottle of Moscato out of the bag. "Then this won't be a problem."

"I'm almost legal. It's all good," Allison mutters under her breath as she heads to her bedroom.

Though not under her breath enough. "I am so sorry I missed your birthday." Bri extends the bottle in Allison's direction.

"Almost legal," Allison repeats louder. "Missed nothing yet. Though, with the ways things are going, I don't expect much this year."

Bri ignores the self-pity prevalent in Allison's tone and presses the bottle further toward her. "This is for you."

Allison shakes her head. "Thanks?"

"And let me be the first to say, happy early birthday," Bri adds with a forced laugh.

"Really early. No worries, I promise. With everything going on, I think making a big deal about it might make things worse. Don't think it will matter much, anyway."

Bri slaps Allison on the arm. "Hey, birthdays always matter. It's a reason to have fun with friends."

Allison shrugs. "Sure." Allison enters her room, taking her seat again against the headboard.

"You gonna get glasses or save that for later?" Bri asks, unsure why she was called over.

Allison responds with a third option by twisting the cap off and swigging straight from the bottle.

"That serious, huh? What happened now?" Allison hears the word "now," and it stings more than Bri intended. She downs another long swig. Bri grabs it from her. "Hey, I'd like some, too." Bri follows suit and drinks from the bottle. "Still can't get a hold of him?"

Allison shakes her head, extending out her hand for the bottle back. Bri relinquishes it. "That's just it, Bri. He answered. He answered, and it's senior year all over again when he pushed me away. Well, mostly. But it still sucks."

"That's a good thing." Quickly qualifying, she adds, "Not the repeat of senior year but … well, he hasn't answered since … you know."

Allison raises her eyebrows at the irony of the whole thing. "Yeah. That's just it. He answered to tell me not to call him again. Do you know what a knife in the front that is?"

"Knife in the back," Bri corrects Al.

Shaking her head, Al says, "No. Knife in the front. A knife in the back would have been him telling you to tell me. At least he told me, but it doesn't matter."

"Why?"

"Getting stabbed by a knife hurts. Doesn't matter if it's in the front or the back."

"I'm sure he didn't mean don't call him, like, *forever*." Bri takes the bottle back for another swig. "This shit is so sweet. Sorry."

Allison grabs it back to take another sample. "It's all good, Boo. Does the job."

"Well?" Bri nudges Allison.

"Of course, he didn't mean forever. But not until this all settles. He's been hiding god-knows-where for months and no one knows if he's safe. I don't even think he knows Scarlett is dead or waiting or whatever. And it sucks, ya know."

Bri moves to Allison, putting her arm around her for comfort. "I know I'm not your first choice, but I'm here when you need."

Allison chuckles at Bri's choice of words, causing her to scratch the back of her head. "I'm not sure you mean those words the way they sounded." Allison turns to Bri. Their gaze is a little closer than either finds comfortable, but neither moves.

Bri breaks the stare. "I just meant that you hated me for so long. But that's all in the past." She takes a long glug to shut herself up before handing it back to Allison.

"Long, distant past." She holds the bottle, unsure if she should take a drink or do something she might regret.

"Connor is a lucky man, and he knows how good he's got it with you," Bri offers up.

"And Duncan, too, as well, you know. Lucky." Allison breaks her unsure hold and swigs the bottle. She wipes her mouth as she pulls the bottle away. "How's the planning comin' along?"

Bri sits, lost on Allison's words.

"The wedding?" Allison reminds her.

Bri shakes free of her lost thoughts. "Yeah. Good. Duncan's taking care of most of it, so I can try to help you. Connor. Help you and Connor." Bri huffs at herself. "This is strange."

Allison reads what she can in Bri's face. "What's strange?"

"The Moscato. Hitting stronger than I thought it would."

"Maybe it's not the Moscato." Allison plays her hand.

Bri scooches away from Allison a bit. "Duncan's good. He loves me, and Connor loves you."

The crushing weight of defeat and realization weigh down on Allison, suffocating the life out of the moment.

"Yeah. He is good. He'd do anything for you."

Bri nods. "He would. I don't want to ruin that."

"But there could be something, ya know." Allison waves her hand, motioning between the two of them. "Just saying."

"Yeah, there could be. But there can't be. I'm making a choice. One that's good for me. One that I'm happy with and makes me happy. I don't want to jeopardize that for a moment of whatever this alcohol is making me feel."

Allison sits back, dejected. "Well, there you have it. The perfect man. I am sorry I let my thoughts get to me."

Bri takes Al's words with a bit of skepticism. "I can't do this again." This time it's Bri who waves a hand between the two of them. "I love being friends and am beyond grateful to have you back in my life. But this is not okay for me."

"I had to shoot my shot."

"You did. Twice now. And I am sorry your boy-friend is playing Harrison Ford right now."

"What?"

Bri shakes her head at herself. "I've been around Duncan too long. From *The Fugitive*. The movie. That he's not around. It sucks, and I can be there to bend an ear and help make you feel happy."

Allison smiles a dog-sly smile.

"Not in that way," Bri adds. "But that's it. You have to stop looking at me like that. If you want some strange, I can find you someone. I wouldn't do that to Connor, but that's not my call."

Allison scrunches her face. "It's not about strange; it's about you. Hell if I wanted to feel this. Hell if I wanted to feel this for someone that spent the better part of high school ignoring me or worse. But here I am, pouring my drunk, little heart out and having it get stepped on. But whatever. I am glad you are happy. I really am. Seeing you and Duncan and me and Connor makes me realize they aren't the same picture. Sure, I want to be happy with him, but there's this side of me that wants something … different … or more."

"And that's something you will have to decide on your own what you want to do. I can't help with that stuff. Not in the way you want me to. Have you even ever talked with him about it?"

Allison nods. "Yeah. And he said to do what makes me happy. And that didn't help any because that only made me love him more. But I don't know what will make me happy cause nothing seems to make me happy. Like, if I think of something that might make me happy, like kissing you."

Bri tilts her head, a motion Allison notices.

"Don't worry, Bri. I'm done trying. But when I think of that and how happy it would make me, all I can think of is the pain it would cause him and Duncan if they found out."

Bri chuckles.

Allison pushes herself further into the headboard. "What?!"

"The thought of two guys getting upset over two girls kissing." Bri laughs.

"You know what I mean. Because I know that it's not about who I kiss or want to do more with, but that I did it. Which is why you won't do it. I get that. And it makes sense. But then, I'm back to being unhappy because the happy thought I had had unhappy outcomes or consequences or whatever. And every thought is like that. Like, no matter what I do or what I want, I will end up hurting someone or making someone upset in the process. I don't like it, and I have no one to talk with about it because one is playing fugitive, as you say, and the other is playing dead, and it sucks really bad." Allison's frantic ranting finally relents to the temptation in her hand and takes a long swig that is only stopped by Bri lowering it down from her.

Bri sets the bottle down and moves in to hold Allison in her arms. Allison cries into Bri's shoulder as they sit, hugging each other over Al's revelations.

Vistrus pulls into the back of The West Haven Historical Society, hoping to catch the last of the meeting and recap the discussed topics. While a part of him recognizes that his entrance may have to be on a bit of bended knee, he is not sure if he cares or if it matters much. Closing the door to his car, he turns to the building to see Connor exiting, catching them both by surprise.

"Mr. DeSalvo, what are you doing here? Why are you not elsewhere?"

Connor looks around, slowing down but not stopping. "Buying time. Or, at least, trying to." He steps toward Vistrus. "How's Grandma Eleanor?"

Vistrus nods at his selflessness. "Best she can be. Did The Council speak? What did they say?"

Connor shakes his head. "They want my head to present to the media. I won't give it."

"It is the wrong head to give." Vistrus puts a hand on Connor's shoulder. "I will do what I can. I am working on some … ideas … vague leads. Vaguely led ideas."

"Vague seems to be the mood of the evening," Connor jests.

"What do you mean?" Vistrus's attention snaps into place, knowing something deeper hides in Connor's words.

Connor shakes his head. "What came first?"

"As in the chicken or the egg?" Vistrus is not amused.

"No." Connor's tone takes on a sarcastic note. "They said I knew nothing of who placed them or what came before The Council." He ends his sarcastic impression. "It's weird. He said I'd understand why they do what they do if I did."

Vistrus's lack of amusement turns to worried thoughts about the Mind, the Body, and everything else his late wife was sending cryptic messages about. He no longer holds any doubts as to his distrust in The Council, the connection of everything to the murders, and that something bigger is going on than he ever knew about. Bended knee be damned.

He puts his hands on Connor's shoulders. "Are you safe where you are staying? Safety first."

"I think so. I've not seen anyone follow me."

"Pay more attention. Feel confident enough to know and not think. Thinking can be bad. Knowing is good."

"It's half the battle," Connor jokes, missing the severity of Vistrus's words.

Vistrus ignores Connor's attempt at levity. "I will help figure all of this out. We will get through this, though I do not think they," he motions to the room inside the building, "will be of any more assistance. If anything happens, find me. But more importantly, stay out of sight. If you need to find me, stay out of sight while finding me."

Adrenaline again starts pumping through Connor. Survival instincts course through him, pressing into him the reality of his demise if they can't prove him innocent and figure out why he was framed. All he can do is nod at Vistrus's words.

"Now go. Be safe."

"Please tell Allison I am sorry. She'll know what I mean."

Vistrus nods, then pushes him off, watching him run into the safety of the shadows.

He turns his stare to the door, knowing the people he trusted for so long are not who they say. He feels that his place in West Haven comes from different roots than theirs, that they are no longer trustworthy or confidants in The Nation's issues. Any thoughts he had of entering on bended knee dissipate. Instead of going in and playing double agent or subverting them for his needs, he gets back in his car and drives away, smiling as he does, knowing this final act of abandonment is one he may never be able to turn back from.

Connor turns a corner down a side street. Rows of brick townhouses line the left side of the street while single-family homes line his right side. As he passes a house whose front yard hosts a giant weeping willow, a voice whispers to him, "Are you ready now?"

He stops, turning toward the shadow cast by the tree. The pale woman steps out. "Do you think The Council will find you innocent? Or are your thoughts screaming to you that they don't care?"

Connor chews her words, thinking before speaking. "I don't know. Haven't had much time to think about it."

"Then let me show you what lies ahead. There is a world beyond West Haven. A world much larger than the happenings in this town." Her words seem sweet, but Connor thinks he tastes a saccharin coating.

"I still don't know your name. What little you have shown hasn't been the appetite- whetting tease you intended it to be."

She steps further out from the shadow. "A werewolf under any other name would smell as musky. So, what's in my name? What is it you want from me?"

Connor scrunches his eyes, debating the first words to enter his mind. "A reason to trust you."

"I can give you no other reason than those I offered before. Let me show you what The Nation really is. All it encompasses and the future it holds for you. A future where you no longer have to worry about hiding. One where you may find yourself at the head of the table instead of hiding under it."

Connor further licks the sweetness of her words, testing for the artificial sweetener but unsure if he tastes any. "And what do you expect in return?"

"That you listen to me. Trust what I say without question, and I will show you everything you have not been told; answer all the questions you haven't thought to ask … show you the meaning of life itself." She motions for him to follow her as she heads off toward the back of the house with the weeping willow.

Connor weighs his options for a moment, taking extra caution in her last words but decides to follow with hesitation before she disappears into the shadows, fearing he might not see her, even with his night vision. He knows to tread carefully, to be cautious of those willing to offer everything. Never has the meaning of life been offered by someone who wants nothing in exchange. Now, he must figure out what she truly wants from him and why.

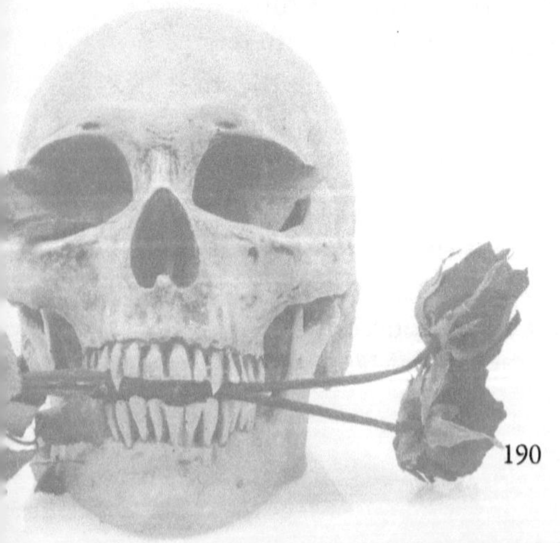

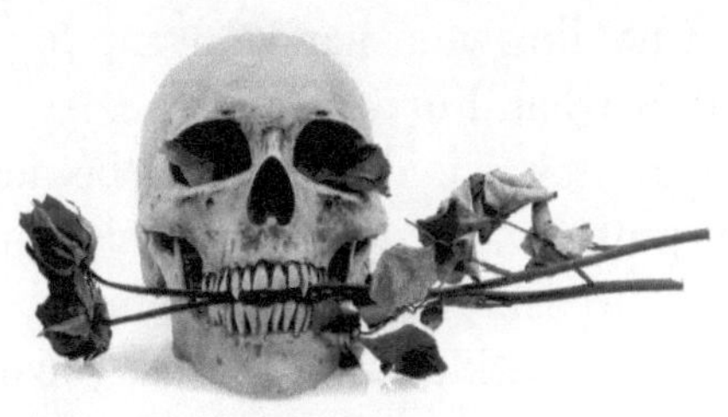

CHAPTER 9

*"All these adults tell me tigers can't change their
stripes. Well, I say, good thing we're not tigers."*
~B. Waldgrave~

Bri and Duncan walk down a busy Chicago street
on a sunny spring day, feeling the breeze from
the cars they watch whiz by while window-shopping. "I love days like this," Bri says, a wistful frost
on her words.

"Days like what?" Duncan laughs, looking around
at the crowded streets and the architecture.

"Me and you … window-shopping," she says,
pulling him in for a hug. "When it's just me and you
out and about, I feel like all my problems and stuff
just slip away."

Duncan tightens his hug before looking her in the
eye. "That's what I want for you. To be a reprieve
from this world that beats us down. This world that
never understood me, so I know it will never understand you. You've already been through so much, and
I don't know what lies ahead, but whatever it is, I want

to do it holding your hand. I want you to know that no matter what, I understand you. As best as I can, I will always try to understand you because you do me."

Bri pulls away from the extended hug. "Because I *do* you?" Bri asks, missing his point.

Duncan chuckles. "Not because you *do* me. Because you do understand me. But, yeah, I mean that too, sure."

Realizing her misunderstanding, she playfully slaps him on the arm.

"This," Duncan gestures around him, "is our world. Ain't no one gonna take it away from either of us, not as long as we do it hand in hand."

A smile crosses Bri's face as she continues walking. "I'm all for hand-holding, but sometimes I need both hands."

Duncan tilts his head, holding back a small laugh with his smile. "It's a metaphor, my love. We won't always be literally holding hands."

A proverbial light bulb goes off over Bri's head. "Gotcha." But as quickly as the light bulb lit up, the news segment flashing a picture of Connor DeSalvo on the giant electronic billboard mounted to a nearby building burns the bulb out.

"Police are still hunting for murder suspect Connor DeSalvo, wanted for the killing of his grandfather, Nick DeSalvo. Anyone with news of his whereabouts is urged to call the West Haven Police Department tip hotline at 888-555-0714. If spotted, he is considered dangerous, though unarmed. Anyone seeing the suspect should keep their distance and call the authorities. Do not approach. I repeat, do not approach."

The grim news segment juxtaposed with his smiling senior yearbook photo holds a harsh parallel to the commencement memorial for her mother and Linda Espinoza. Duncan stares at his fiancée, watching the news plaster their friend's face for all of Chicago to see. He grimaces, knowing their plans for the day will have to take a rain check.

"Hey," he says, nudging her from her thoughts, "I know we were gonna do all the marriage stuff, but…" He watches the wheels turn in her head. "Why don't you do what you need for," he lowers his voice below a whisper, "The Nation, and I'll take care of the wedding stuff?"

Bri's eyes turn downward in longing. "This is my wedding, too. This isn't fair!"

Duncan lifts her chin. "Sometimes things're not fair. We're a couple and we deal. It's what we do." He turns to the buildings, checking their present location, and thinks for a moment. "I'm pretty sure the Harold Washington is only a short train ride from here. If you're gonna find answers by yourself anywhere, it'll be there."

Bri nods in reluctant agreement. "I know you're right. I was just hoping, like, today would be a day off from this."

Duncan reroutes their walk, beginning the short trek to the train station. "Hey, there's always tomorrow. Plus, doing the right thing is always attractive." He winks, causing her to smile.

Brianna sits in a remote corner in the back of the Harold Washington Public Library, surrounded by open books covering subjects from various mythologies to medical journals covering genetic mutations. She thinks about her life and what has become of her. Thinking about how she wants a day off, she realizes that days off from life do not happen. The realization that every day has the possibility of turning into something bad saddens her. A feeling that the innocence of popularity and high school can never be recaptured. That those memories are a place she can't ever return to. But, sitting here, knowing what she knows about herself, her mother, and her friends, she is not sure if she ever wants to relive those days. Sure, innocent they were, but they were also naïve. And though naiveté has its blessings in blissful ignorance, she is unsure if that blind-leading-the-blind, popular clique is something she would ever revisit given the chance.

Leaning against a dusty shelf, knees curled against her chest between thoughts of who she was versus who she's become, she flips through old tomes of Native American, Babylonian, Celtic, and various other mythologies, scanning the pages for anything that might help her help Allison help her father. She skims passages about Hotoru, Tobadzistsini, Hastseltsi, Nergal, Ramman, Lugh, noticing the similarities between these and many other gods—their ability to shapeshift. She flips back and forth between the entries, paying special attention to all the gods' abilities to take on different forms to appease or to avoid frightening off their worshipers. But an entry about the Celtic god, Lugh, makes her drop all the other books she's been fumbling through. She reads about Lugh's ability to manifest any singular aspect of anyone he's come into contact with. While Brianna can't put her finger on why this is sticking out in her mind as important, she feels it is.

She scans the surrounding area to ensure no one is watching her before snapping pictures of the passage with her phone. Fumbling through the piles of books, she pulls out a notebook and begins jotting down some thoughts.

So, all these gods can appear how they want, and this Lugh guy can steal someone's abilities, or just ability. But all these gods look like men, well, humans. Could it be that they were nothing more than Legends? But...

How does that help Connor?

Turning back to the mythos and medical books, she flips through articles about bone density diseases such as osteoporosis and osteopetrosis. The articles tell of autosomal dominance, the mutations of the IKBKG gene, its relation to inhibition of nuclear factor kappa B kinase subunit gamma, and more, all of which draw memories from the back of her mind. Conversations with her mother about the diseases that cause their conditions. She scribbles down the medical information into her notebook before her concentration is broken by the grating sound of a throat clearing.

She looks up to see a vaguely familiar face staring down at her. A man whose face she can't place has his arms on his hips as if he's about to embark on a lecture, but his face, half-successfully trying to hold back a smile, tells her otherwise.

"If you need to, like, get something from behind me, I can move. Figured the back of this place would be private," Bri offers.

He shakes his head. "Interesting studies you have going on there."

"Yeah," Bri starts, thinking of what she can say to cover this up. "Interesting topic for a term paper. How the old gods of different mythos might have been human."

A soft chuckle escapes him. "Are you sure you aren't looking for answers more closely related to why you once carried your eye in a thermos of milk?"

Her emotions are shoved back to that night and the feelings of helplessness that enveloped her. She places his face, the man on The Council also in the Tennyson Society.

"Are you In?" Her words are silent, having chosen to mouth them instead.

"I am in true, whate'er befall."

Bri struggles to remember her response, taking a moment longer than either would like. "I am In, when I sorrow most."

He nods. "Glad to see your memory doesn't falter even if it lags." He waves a finger at the books. "You'll be hard-pressed to find new answers in old books."

She nods in defeat. "I've found a few things, but I don't know how they all relate, or what I am supposed to do with this information, or how it will help Connor, or really, what any of it means."

"Let's narrow things down. Why are you drowning in a sea of old and unrelated books?"

"I need to prove Connor's not a murdering psychopath," Bri lets slip, lifting the weight of it off her shoulders.

"This is quite the roundabout way to find evidence proving his innocence."

"Not sure where to start."

"Start with admitting he may be guilty."

Every muscle in Bri's body tightens up at his words. "Why would I ever assume such a thing? And why would you make such heinous accusations?"

"Just one accusation. But I didn't make any. I asked if you ever thought he could be guilty. People we love can be capable of despicable actions. The possibility he may have done it needs to be considered. Especially when all the evidence points to him."

"So, you've already made up your mind. Why waste time with the likes of me looking for new answers in old books if you're so certain he's a killer? How do you know I haven't found something already?"

He steps back from her sharp words. "Have you?"

"Lugh."

"That's not a word I'm familiar with." He motions to a spot near her where he can squat. "May I?"

She waves her hand to proceed.

"He's an Irish god, Celtic god. Is there a difference?"

"To Scottish and Irish people, very much a difference. But let's stay on track." He urges.

"Lugh can take on an aspect of anyone he touches. What if he's here? Or what if there's a Legend who has that ability? Or what if Lugh is a Legend?"

The Councilman cuts her off. "What if all the old gods were Legends? What if Joan Osbourne was right, and God was one of us?"

"Who's Joan Osbourne? Is she in The Nation? What are you talking about?"

He laughs, shaking his head. "Singer from more years ago than I thought. Never mind the reference." He stands, searching the shelf behind her for a moment before pulling out a book. "In The Nation, answers are never as simple as two plus two being four." He peers down at her notebooks and the medical texts open to osteoporosis, osteopetrosis, and osteogenica imperfecta. "While you are on the right track, you are missing your mark. Excuse the mixed expressions."

"What is my mark?"

"If I had those answers, your friend wouldn't be running from The Council, and you wouldn't be trying to prove his innocence. But if Lugh can take on aspects of people and other gods can shapeshift, then Ehlers-Danlos might be a better start. The elastic properties of the skin lend to some of our abilities."

He tosses her the book he pulled from the stacks. "This might help."

She reads the title, *Beyond Folklore: Societies, Fables, and Creatures from a Forgotten Time.* "Thanks, I guess."

He nods and turns to leave.

"Hey." She grabs his attention one more time. "If you're so convinced he's guilty, why do this?"

"I'm not convinced he's guilty. But while you have to prove one man's innocence, I have to protect The Nation. My duty and my personal feelings are not always directly related."

"So, what is this? I save him if I'm right or you save The Nation from exposure if I'm wrong?"

He nods. "Something like that."

She turns back to the book he pulled out and starts flipping through it, losing herself in another rabbit hole.

Allison sits upright at the kitchen table with notebooks, dream journals, printouts from her mother's diaries, and books spread out before her. The sounds of her father playing some piano concerto float up from his basement studio.

She knows she has time before he comes up. Her mother's writings are not something she wants to argue about, but she does not care. She needs to figure out the fact from fiction in the strange days that have become her life.

Reading over and over about the five, not four, and six still alive that she has read about in the past and of the Mind and the green and black, she is reminded of all the things she has yet to decipher with help from her father … if she can subtly weave in all she knows to her father without upsetting him.

Frustrated, she shoves her chair away from the table. Opening the refrigerator door over and over, hoping that each time brings something new, she relents, walking away in further tantrums. Pacing the kitchen provides no relaxation or realization to her plight.

She expands her pacing into the living room and dining room. She goes over everything told to her about the five Societies, that she isn't a vampire, despite common colloquialisms, and that yes, all of this is real. Her mind replays her assault on Linda, the unwanted, surprising feelings for Bri, hitting Connor with her dad's car, and Scarlett slumped against her parents' tombstones.

Her pacing quickens as the thoughts in her head tumble over each other, narrowing her field of vision in angry, blinding emotions, clouding any ability to reason, think through, and slow down her accelerating thoughts.

Five, not four. What the hell, Mom? What does that mean? And six still alive? What six? What are you talking about?

Over and over, these words race through her mind, unable to form a new train of thought that could make forward progress.

Okay, Al, calm down. Five what?

Her pacing comes to a dead stop by the chime of the doorbell. In her distracted state, she opens the door before checking who is there but finds a pleasant surprise in the form of Brianna standing there with her backpack.

"I think I have something." Bri's voice sounds somewhere between undecided and excited.

"Like syphilis?" Allison goes straight to the worst-case scenario.

Brianna cocks her head, confused. "What?! No, not syphilis. Something about the everything that's been going on for, like, three years."

Allison's brain catches up to the moment and the metaphorical light bulb flickers to life over her head. "Oh, yeah, that. Woo, glad you don't have herpes."

"I thought it was syphilis."

"Yeah, or that." Allison motions for Bri to enter. "So, now that STDs are out of the picture, what you got?"

"Something called the Add-E-Ear-Ig or Ader-Rig. I don't know how to say it," Bri says, kicking off her shoes. Reaching into her backpack, she continues, "I was at the library and ran into someone. He said to check out this book."

"What book?" Allison interrupts.

"Not important. What is important is what I found in it."

"So, what did you find in it?" Allison leads them to her bedroom, stopping as her hand turns the knob but does not open the door. "Look, I know things have been said … mainly by me. Things that might make you and I alone in my room uncomfortable, but that's not why we are going inside."

An uncomfortable smile escapes Bri. "Wasn't even thinking anything like that until you said it."

A pinkish blush overtakes Allison. "Well, then. Pretend I didn't say any of that."

Bri nods. "Any of what?"

"Of the whole thing I said about me—" Allison starts to recap, but Brianna interrupts.

"I know. It's a bit." She waves for Allison to enter her room. "Let's just move this forward."

The girls enter Allison's bedroom and take a seat on her black comforter.

"Back to what you found."

"Yes." Bri unzips her backpack and pulls out the library book, *Beyond Folklore: Societies, Fables, and Creatures from a Forgotten Time.* "As I said, the Addy-thing."

"What about it?" Allison urges.

"That's just it. It's like a campfire tale known only to our people or whatever."

"West Haveners?" Allison denies Brianna's implication.

"No, not West Haveners, Al, vampires, or whatever we are called. The Societies." She waits a moment for some verbal response from Al but continues before she can formulate one. "I think this might be what we are looking for."

"A campfire tale?" Allison moves to her nightstand, grabbing her laptop. She opens it, hits the space bar to wake it up, and starts scrolling down an open PDF. "I am caught on this passage." She stops and points to a scanned entry from Inessa's diary.

> I can say it all day. There were six then five now four, but no one understands that four we see doesn't mean six.

Bri points to the scan after the word "six." "What does that say?"

"Can't make it out." Allison closes her laptop.

"What else is there?"

"Psychobabble, or so it seems. See, I think that she was trying to tell someone something. I can't figure out what, though." Allison turns back to Bri. "I'm thirsty. You want water or a soda or something?"

"Cherry something if you have any." Bri hops off the bed as they head to the kitchen.

As they head down the hallway, Allison stops as the carved symbol on top of her father's humidor catches her eye. They both stand, staring at the wooden box Allison has seen countless times in her twenty years. A wooden box with its carved and burned symbol for The Nation. Five points. Five Societies. Five, not four.

"Hey, Bri."

"Yeah, Al?"

"What do we know of, for, whatever, about the freak parade?"

"That's not a nice thing to say. You've seen me when I do my thing. I've seen you." Bri crosses her arms.

"I've never done anything, Bri." Allison denies the truth. "But paint the picture any way you want. We're freaks."

"Whatever." Bri drops her arms. "What do we know about The Nation?"

Allison wags her finger. "I asked you."

"Vampires, werewolves, fairies, and undying, except we aren't supposed to call them vampires or werewolves or—"

Allison cuts in. "Yeah, yeah, but if I can count correctly, that's four." She holds up a finger as she recounts each vampire, werewolf, undying, and fairy.

Bri nods. "Yeah, so?"

"So? How many points are on that star?"

"Five."

"And what do they stand for, according to our crazy-ass parents?"

"One for each Society of The Nation." Bri catches up with Allison's revelation. "Ah, so what's the fifth?"

"What's the fifth, indeed?" Allison turns her gaze toward the kitchen. "Just grab yourself whatever you want, and grab me something, too." Realizing her manners, she adds a quick, "Please."

Bri shakes her head, starting into the kitchen.

"Daddy!" Allison cries out at a volume that could wake the dead.

His piano-playing halts, replaced by the sound of frantic feet climbing the stairs.

"Allison! Are you hurt?!" he responds. Before she can answer, he stops beside her. They both stare at the symbol—the five points and the house in the middle, all surrounding the equal sign.

"What happened, Allison? You sounded hurt." His eyes stare at the symbol, trying to figure out what she sees. "Is something wrong?"

She turns to her father. "Don't be mad, Daddy."

He inhales a calming breath. "If you want to try a cigar, we can do it together."

She scrunches her face. "Thanks, maybe, and not why I scrame, screamed, whatever."

"Then what will I be mad about?" He remains calm.

"Five, not four." She lays down a proverbial card to see if he picks it up.

"I see you are still reading your mother's diaries."

She smiles, knowing he understood.

"You told me that each point stood for a Society." She begins her hypothesis.

"Yes," he confirms. "In no particular order, Tennyson, Poe, Kipling, Coleridge, and Frye."

"Yeah, but fairies, vampires, werewolves, and zombies make four. Not five." She counts on her fingers as she rattles them off.

Bri emerges from the kitchen, sodas in hand. "Here. And he's just going to say not to call us that."

Vistrus's restraint frays. "She is right. I said not to call us those things. And Undying, not zombies."

"And not the point," she interrupts. "What is the fifth?"

"A legend, even among Legends."

The girls each raise a confused eyebrow.

"Lowercase L and capital L," he clarifies.

"Well, I don't think so. Or at least, I don't think Mom thought so. So, what was the fifth?" Allison prods her father for information.

"The Clochnawa. Stone-men. Thought to be unbreakable, impervious to injury. Yet somehow they died off. That is why they are nothing more than myths among Legends." His words ring final, yet uncertain. A boundary Allison contemplates pushing. "If they were ever alive, no one has seen them for longer than I can remember. Their Legendary form has never been written about."

"But that doesn't mean they do not exist or didn't or still don't. Dad, Mom wouldn't have written over and over about five, not four, if it didn't mean anything. I think this is all much more simple than we've been thinking … simpler?"

Her words strike something within him, and Vistrus sighs in relent.

"It is possible. I could be wrong. But it does not make sense. This Clochnawa could not imitate another. I have said it before: shapeshifters do not exist."

"They could have, though. Like the clock-men did at one time, maybe there was a sixth. Maybe that's what Mom was trying to tell us. That six are alive, not four or five. She wasn't crazy."

Vistrus chews his words, figuring out what to say at such a delicate moment. A moment like this, fathers do not play out in their heads. Moments like this do not happen, except for right now.

"I'm tellin' you, Dad. This is what she meant. I've read through her diaries more times than I ever studied anything in school. Everything she wrote meant something. No words wasted… well, yeah. No words. She was trying to tell us something without telling us. There had to be a sixth."

"So, it seems," he says. The uncertainty cements a finalization into his words.

Vistrus knows, though, that there was a sixth. He remembers the tales of the boogeyman called The Adeirrig. A story that sends chills up his spine even after all these centuries, perhaps because the thought of something such as the Adeirrig lends some understanding to the mistrust and prejudice Normals feel for Legends. He feels chills, not because of some inherent discrimination but because if Inessa was right, such a thing does exist and has stayed hidden for so long. All reasons why remain unfathomable to him.

Whether or not he can fathom the reasons a Legend would stay hidden within their community,

CHAPTER 9

Vistrus faces a bigger issue: admitting the boogeyman
under the bed exists.

"We need to talk," Vistrus says matter-of-factly, rub-
bing his hands together outside Eleanor's door. The
chill in the wind does not mask the urgency behind
his words.

"Nice to see you, too, Vistrus. I've been well.
Thanks for asking. Why, sure. Come on in." Eleanor
moves aside, extending her arm as an invitation to
enter but does not let the jab in her words go unnoticed. "What has you in such a mood?"

"Apologies." He takes off and sets his shoes in an
entryway cubby. "It seems that there is some truth to
our Legends."

"Of course there is. The kernels of truth that
make up the myths never fall far from the tree." She
smiles at her inclination at the coming conversation.

She guides him to the living room, offering him a
seat on the couch.

He sits opposite her on the couch. "It seems my
little Allison is not so little anymore." He scans the
room, looking for any proverbial flies on the wall.

"We are alone. No one has been here since you last
stopped by," Eleanor assures him. "Feeling better, too,
it looks like."

Vistrus nods his head. "Much." Vistrus takes one
of his trademark moments to choose his words. "It
seems The Nation was wrong."

Eleanor holds back a smile. "They've been wrong about a great many things. Governing bodies often are." She waits for a reaction, but he does not give one. "How is this related to what you started saying about Allison?"

His eyebrows draw together, almost touching. "Inessa kept writing about five, not four. And Allison pointed out…" Hesitance holds back the rest of his thoughts.

"The Clochnawa is still alive." She finishes the inevitable conclusion to his words with sounding confidence.

"But how? Every record has them having died off. Why would they have gone into hiding even within The Nation?" His words pour out like a child's inquisition—questions formed from half-thoughts clouded by the discovery of ignorance needing to be cured.

"For the same reason the Kipling, the Poe, the Coleridge, and the Tennyson Societies stay hidden from Normals." She keeps her answer short and vague. "It is the same reason that even The Nation changes the names of the Societies. Don't forget, young man, that Kipling was once the Dach Society as Coleridge was the Ramdas Society as so on and so forth."

"But we know. There is nothing to hide from us." His centuries of experience fall away in the moment's naiveté. "How can you be so sure? This whole thing must be a mistake."

Eleanor shakes her head. "It is no mistake. Inessa made no mistake. She knew something. But what? Was it as simple as remembering the importance of change? That change makes the history books vary, and thus any inquiry from a Normal into our societies looks as if they stumbled upon different, new, or incorrect information when all we did was change a label? Or could she have known something more?"

Vistrus shakes his head. "Her diaries are filled with riddles and hidden meanings in nonsense. I cannot figure it out. Allison seems to make more headway with these things than anyone."

Eleanor tilts her head. "Who and what else?"

He waves off her concern. "When Jack was missing, it was Allison who figured out the code."

Eleanor huffs in respect. "And again, she figured at least one Clochnawa is still alive. You should be proud."

"I am," Vistrus says, stopping for a moment to bask in the immense pride over this; an emotion he didn't realize he felt. Shaking himself from the moment, he continues, "But that is not the point. I have been on The Council for some time now and have never heard reports, rumors... anything." His eyes dart as his mind searches for answers.

Eleanor grabs him by the shoulders to steady his attention. "How could so many people not have seen us when we are so many?" She answers her question before giving him a chance to do so. "Because we take careful measures to stay that unseen. And we have our reasons."

"And what reason would the Frye Society have?" Vistrus's frustration grows.

"Over three hundred years you've lived and yet the words you speak take away all that experience." Eleanor stands from the couch but motions for

Vistrus to stay seated. "I'm getting wine. Would you like a glass?"

Without hesitation, he responds, "Red, please."

"Of course." She shakes her head.

She leaves Vistrus so she can pour the wine, and he can stew in his thoughts. A few minutes later, she returns with two glasses in hand.

Handing him one, she says, "At the end of it all, what does it matter if the Clochnawa is real? The only thing their Legendary state ever gave them was the inability to appear injured."

He sips his wine with her words. "What about their strength? Their perceptions?"

"Strength is something all Legends possess; that should not even factor in. Neither should their increased perception since some others possess that as well." She finalizes her argument with a sip of wine.

Vistrus thinks for a moment, keeping his eyes glued to his wineglass, only managing to respond back with an affirmative nod.

"So, Vistrus, what is the problem here? Their ability to show no injury? They could still be injured and killed like any other Legend. They still have to go through the Waiting like every other Legend." She pries him for more on his thoughts, but he does not budge. "Or is it something else you are not ready to admit? Something bigger than the Frye Society?"

He whips his gaze to her. "Of course, there is something more! After three hundred twenty-four years, there is something more! And that is a fear that does not diminish knowing the weight of the years behind it. No! It only compounds the fears. Fears that the Adeirrig is real! Fears that knowing my wife, my beautiful, wonderful Inessa, was not crazy. She was not going insane. No. She was scared. She was my age! Three hundred five years old and she was afraid. In all our centuries together, I had never seen her so afraid!"

Eleanor sips her wine, formulating her response. "Fear is a natural response to the things we do not understand."

"I know this. And I also know that learning to understand the Adeirrig can alleviate that fear. But that is not the worst. The fact that either Inessa was right, making me the worst husband since Henry the VIII and we have bigger problems than my failures as a spouse, or Connor DeSalvo really is a cold-blooded killer."

"Neither are good options."

"No, they are not." Eleanor debates leaning into his comparison to Henry the VIII but decides to leave it alone. "If the Adeirrig is real, what do I tell my daughter? What do I tell her that she can bring to her friends? How does this prove Connor's innocence? Is there physical evidence we can find to do so?"

Eleanor flashes a fading smile. Swirling the remains of her wine in the glass, she watches the legs fall down the sides, then get swept up again with each passing swirl. "It is funny how things in West Haven got worse when the kids started transitioning."

"We cannot blame the kids for this," Vistrus defends.

Eleanor shakes her head. "I never said it was their fault. But they uncovered the teacher and the cop. They uncovered the drugs used to transition Legends against their will. They have uncovered more secrets in this town than I can remember anyone else doing."

"It was not for lack of trying." Vistrus's meek words tumble from his mouth.

"No, it was not. But these kids, well, young adults now, have found a way to accept the truths, no matter how dark, and try to do some good. That is something we were never taught to do."

The right corner of Vistrus's mouth begins to upturn, but a huff pulls it back down. "No. We were taught to follow the leader. Keep the status quo that was set for us."

"So, proving Connor's innocence, finding evidence, and figuring out what to tell our kids may not be the right question to ask," Eleanor offers.

"Then what is the right question?" His eyes plead for a concrete response.

"If I knew that, I'd be out there fixing things instead of sitting in my house drinking wine with you. But how much worse are things going to get knowing that an Adeirrig is in West Haven?"

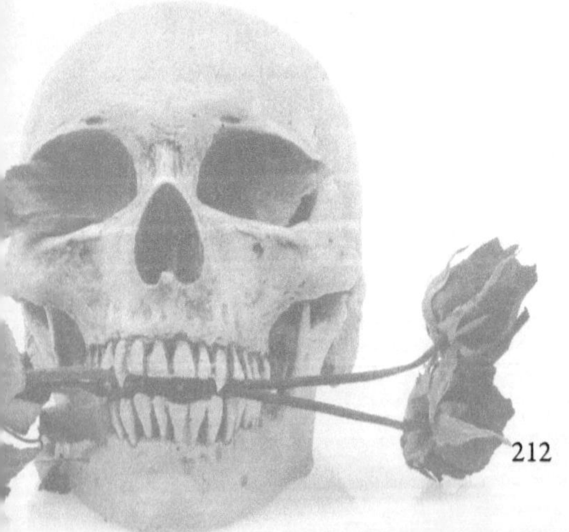

CHAPTER 10

I nessa leans on the bathroom sink, pen in hand, staring at the hole she made in the drywall above it last week. She looks down at her journal for a moment before turning to the mirror and repair materials stacked against the wall behind her. A sad, knowing smile tries digging its way to the surface, but she squashes it, finding nothing joyous in this moment. Putting her pen to the last entry in this journal, she writes.

I put it away. Kept it safe. Not in a safe. Safe place. No one will know where it went.

Inessa stops writing and turns to lean against the sink and cabinet, lowering herself to the floor. Losing herself in her reflection in the mirror propped against the wall, she pays no attention to the soft knock at the door, instead pushing on her forming crow's feet she could have sworn weren't there

213

before. She tugs at them, making them disappear. A smile crosses her face for a moment as she remembers younger days. The soft knock on the door grows louder with a toddler's impatience, pulling her back to the moment.

"Mommy? I in?" *a toddler-voiced Allison whispers.*

"A few more minutes, dear. I am finishing up."

Young Allison plops down to wait outside the door. "Okay."

Inessa returns to writing in her journal.

Am I chicken? Keep safe out of sight out of Mind. He created the prophecy. Manifest destiny. No savior shall come. Except. They were drawn. Drawn then created or created then drawn. There's the rub. What came first the chicken or the egg? Pretend to be paranoid long enough and the act is no longer acting. Chicken. Egg. One glove, one portrait. Why one glove? Why one portrait? Why one? Egg. Chicken. It was never real. It was ever real. Words hurt sometimes. Is the drawing the egg?

Pausing to take a deep breath that finishes with a shiver, she forces the pen back on the paper.

Unknown, but I know. I know, I know, I know, but they know I know, and I know they know I know they know. Too many knows. I can't do this much longer. Something must be done, so no one has to know, and those that know won't be in the crosshairs anymore.

A tear falls, landing on the page.

It must be me. It must be stopped. I can pretend no more. If everyone is to be kept safe, I must deal with the Adeirrig. I must stop him. I must know he knows I know he knows no one knows. But how? Will I ever know?

She stops once more, inhaling more air than she has ever done in her life. Her lungs fill with air and resolve.

A soft knock at the door again breaks Inessa into tears. "Just another moment, Alli." She collects herself to bring her pen back to the journal one last time.

I love you, Vistrus. I always have. More than words can ever say. I love you and our little Alli.

She continues writing a final sentence after her declaration for her husband and daughter as she stares past the door to the small child waiting on the other side. After finishing the final entry, she drops the journal into the hole in the wall. A thud as it hits the floor cues little Allison to call out.

"Mommy fall?"

Inessa chuckles to herself at her child's concern.

"I'm fine," she says, opening the door. She bends down to lift her baby girl. "I had a tiny slip and stubbed my toe." While lying to her child is not something she relishes in, a

small white lie to save an explanation lost on someone so tiny is a small price to pay.

Allison's eyes open. She stares at the ceiling while collecting her bearings. *That was strange,* she thinks. She takes a deep breath to energize herself enough to grab her dream journal.

> New memory of Mom. A dream, but it was her. First memory I ever had, I think. Maybe I have had them but forgot, so I only think this is the first. Whatever. I'm tired.

Just write down what happened so I can go back to sleep. She tries to motivate herself.

Allison recounts the fading memory of the dream before it abandons her. She places the journal back in her nightstand, lays her head back down, and closes her eyes, but sleep eludes her. With each passing second that sleep strays further and further, the image of her mother grows more vivid in her mind. She does what the moment will allow; she lies in her darkened room, remembering her mother in that strange moment.

The lunch crowd in the museum's food court is sparse this weekday. The food workers stand around chatting while the few museum patrons eat with their families and friends. Off at a side table near a door marked "employees only," sits Vistrus, Raymond, and

December. They take their sweet time nibbling down one fry at a time, ensuring they don't sit, all staring at each other in a way that would look strange or raise suspicion while they talk to each other in their minds. It is nothing they haven't done countless times before, but also something that each time takes mindfulness to ensure it is done properly.

Vistrus keeps a casual eye on their surroundings as they chat: a double duty to both watch for prying eyes and ensure his museum stays in proper order.

"Her diaries say nothing beyond the game of chess." Vistrus sips his drink. "I know it connects somehow, but I am unsure as to how."

"This is starting to look like a lost cause. If we cannot figure out who the Adeirrig is, then Connor's innocence will matter not," Raymond paints the obvious.

"Then we must make sure that will not happen." Vistrus pauses, thinking about his next thought. "Connor said something to me last I saw him."

"When was this? Is he okay?" December's maternal concern shines through in his mind.

"About a week or two ago. And he was fine." Vistrus nods at her sincerity.

"What did he say?" Raymond presses.

"That this council was not the first. That we replaced something." Vistrus whispers back to their minds. "But how would he know?"

Raymond chooses his words wisely to test what Vistrus knows. "Do you think there could be truth to that?"

Vistrus sees through his ruse. "We are past the time to play games. Yes. It is true. I want to know who on The Council told him."

Raymond and December exchange glances. "I think you know more than either of you realize or are letting on," Raymond says.

"There is a place…" Vistrus begins.

"The Mind," December finishes.

Vistrus breaks his characteristic stoic face to show surprise. "Yes. I did not think anyone else knew about it."

"It may be beneath you, but with the Adeirrig about, it is not as safe as it seems." Raymond issues his warning.

Concern washes over Vistrus.

"What is wrong?" December asks, seeing Vistrus tense up.

"Last time I was in there, I left something. According to Inessa's diaries, something you gave to her."

Raymond leans forward, eagerness shining through. "What?"

"A drawing and a glove."

"Just one glove?!" His voice raises in Vistrus's head.

December stares off into her past, painted with a whimsy smile. "I haven't seen that in so many years."

Vistrus turns to December, but Raymond snaps for his attention. "Where is the other glove?!"

Vistrus shakes his head. "I only ever had one. I was unsure of its importance, but figured it was."

"More than you know. It was there at the beginning." Raymond starts.

"The beginning of what?" Vistrus's interest is piqued.

"Of us. Of Legends before we had a name. It was there when we were created. And our only connection to Pasha." Raymond lays it out on the table.

"You were the firsts?" Vistrus sits upright, an involuntary reaction to his being impressed manifesting in his posture.

December and Raymond both nod. "We were," she says to his mind. "Raymond, Pasha, and myself."

"That is the second time you mentioned that name. Who is Pasha?" Vistrus slows his nibbling, whether out of a need to extend their conversation or out of awe, he is not sure.

"He was with us. He was an alchemist. Our entire village, and the villages beyond, were ravaged by a deadly plague. We were infected. On death's door." December recalls the night. "But Pasha gave us hope. All we needed was to trust him. We had no choice. As we heard our families and friends being carted off to be burned, we made a potion. While listening to the cries of our loved ones, we played alchemist. What did we know? We were desperate."

"What happened?" A long-dormant curiosity awakens in Vistrus.

Raymond takes over. "We mixed it and drank. The pain was indescribable. Even our transitions afterward weren't as bad."

"And Pasha?" Vistrus inquires.

"We fell into a deep state. I remember thinking as I was fading that it failed. That we were dead," Raymond continues.

"But we weren't," December chimes in on cue. "We woke to sounds and pains of them poking us. But we looked so disfigured from our usual selves, and we were so drugged, we did not move. They thought we were dead."

Raymond adds, "They said to burn the bodies. And they left us, I suppose, to come back and burn us later. We summoned what strength we could and left."

"And Pasha?" Vistrus tries to remind them.

"Gone." Raymond says one word that sends chills down Vistrus's spine. "Sure, we feel he is still alive and have heard of sightings in one form or another."

"But?" Vistrus says for Raymond.

"But we have not run into him since. At least, not that we know of." December takes over.

"How can you be sure he is still alive?" Vistrus tries to piece all of this together with the glove and the parchment.

"Because we are," Raymond says in a cryptic fashion.

December shakes her head. "There is an amulet and another glove somewhere. They were the first vials."

Vistrus finally catches up. "And you do not know which one belongs to whom."

Both December and Raymond nod at his realization.

"We want control of our lives. Nothing more. Our lives are in his hands, and we wish for them to be in ours." A sadness coats her voice in his head. "Our glove is not safe in our hands. If he knows where we are, then he can get to it. You must keep it safe."

Vistrus nods. "I shall move it to a safer location."

"Please. Its safety ensures ours," Decembers pleads.

The night air has a welcoming warmth to it as spring settles in. A subtle warmth that hints at a hot summer but lingers on the newness of itself, providing a comfortable feeling that Connor has long needed since leaving his home to survive in the woods. A suburban version of *Into the Wild* he has played out longer than he had hoped he would need to. But he finds himself emerging from the preserves on more nights than he ever imagined he would. Not that Connor ever imagined a need to live in the woods.

He turns down the isolated stretch of Dempster Street, walking toward the same strip mall lot he has made a regular stay of since hiding, the Jewel Osco being the primary way point for his staples. He scans the streets for anything he deems suspicious but realizes that since his actions are more suspicious than anything he sees around him, he can't grasp any reason anyone would be anything but ordinary. His convoluted thinking causes him to miss the car parked at the corner of a side street in the other direction from which he turned. A car parked there with a man eating a dipped Italian beef, topped with hot giardiniera; a man named Max Espinoza.

Max watches Connor stroll down the street in weather almost too warm to wear a zip-up hoodie, even if it is unzipped. He watches as Connor scans the walkways ahead of him, occasionally looking back over his shoulders but missing anything mundane that could be suspicious. Something as mundane and ordinary as a man in a tracksuit, hood to match, jogging at a pace to stay behind Connor.

Max has no problem recollecting that same track-suit from the first time he trailed Connor. Chance? Coincidence? It is a relatively flat path on which he can jog. And this area does not lack for joggers, even if it is a little late to see the usual slew of joggers. Max postulates more on the jogger. Maybe he works nights, and this is his night off. Or that he prefers the silence that night provides. Perhaps he finds the temperatures of the day a little unbearable for such activities. For every reason Max concludes there is nothing to worry about, he keeps the image of the broad-shouldered man and tracksuit in his head in case his reasonings are flawed.

Max watches Connor walk off, almost out of sight, before turning into the parking lot that leads to Jewel Osco. He finishes his beef, turns on his lights, starts the car, and drives into the parking lot to keep a watchful eye out for Connor, ensuring his safety for another night. Max laughs at himself, thinking about his current mindset and beliefs versus a few years ago and the path of redemption he walks.

A path with no end in sight. But he will walk it as long as he can. Though, there is an itch in his mind that wonders how long he will have to be walking this path, or what the final act will be that earns a final redemption, wiping his slate clean and allowing him to move on from the sins of his past. All he knows is that until that time comes, he will do what needs done, and in this case, it is to ensure Connor is safe.

Max knows the police are looking for Connor. A lifestyle that pulled him to a dark place not terribly long ago. He believes in Connor's innocence, and bringing an innocent man into the police station for no other reason than he knows they are looking for him shares no road with redemption, but doing the lawfully good thing does not always equal karmic balance. To solidify Connor's innocence and prove that he hasn't been keeping a protective eye on a murderous fugitive, Max will need to find out where Connor is hiding and, if he can, take a look while he is not there.

Thoughts that plague him as he sits in his car, eating. Thoughts that run through his mind over and over until the tracksuit crosses Dempster and heads toward the street he is parked on. Max watches as this man jogs in his direction. Max watches as he approaches, not slowing down, but turns his head to smile and wave at Max. It was a seemingly polite gesture that came off as anything but, given the time of night and the frequency and timing.

Now Max must also consider the possibility that Connor is being followed by more than just himself as he formulates a plan to find Connor's hiding spot while keeping any other potential tails away from it.

The posters of everything from industrial to post-punk to heavy metal, and all genres in between, plastering Allison's walls do nothing to help comfort her aching heart as she lies staring at them. She has lost count of the days and weeks since she last saw Connor. While spring is slowly creeping into the air, starting an early nudge to push out all that is winter, she feels no sense of renewal, rebirth, or any associations with the coming season.

Her stare turns to the ceiling. Pale, flat, and lifeless, much like her at the moment. She knows wallowing in self-pity with her arms behind her head, resting on her black pillow on a black comforter covering the pink sheets underneath is a pretty on-the-nose picture of bottled-up emotions. Something in that thought plants a fleeting smile on her. But as fast as it came, it left. Ah, the momentariness of a fleeting smile—comfort in small doses. Or, at least, that is what she tells herself. But wallow as she may try, a ringing doorbell disrupts her attempt at post-teenage moodiness.

"Dad! Can you get that, please?!" Allison shouts, not moving from her prone position.

She does not hear his feet step from wherever he is toward the door, nor does he respond with a fatherly remark. Nothing at all. Nothing deters the person at the door as the doorbell rings out again.

"DAD!" she screams, pushing the limits of her tiny-framed lungs.

Again, no response in any form to indicate he heard her.

She takes a deep breath, hoping the old adage is correct. If she ignores it, it will go away.

Again, the doorbell chimes, proving her wrong.

She forces herself out of bed. "COMING!"

She trudges downstairs and sees a familiar silhouette through the curtain over the front door window.

Opening the door, she greets her friend, "Bri. Unexpected surprise."

"Thought I'd stop by. Just an FYI, his car isn't in the driveway," Bri says, entering the house, holding a white, three-inch binder dotted with tabs on the top and side.

"What?" Allison asks.

"I heard you yell. I don't think your dad's home right now," Bri clarifies, following Allison into the kitchen.

"Eh, must be working. Always working on something." Resentment creeps out in her voice. She grabs two glasses from the cabinet, gesturing one in Bri's direction. "Water, soda, wine, whiskey?"

"Water today. Thanks," Bri says, sitting at the table.

Allison fills the cups with ice from the door dispenser before filling them with water. "What brings you by today? Your turn to tell me Connor isn't coming home?"

Bri shakes her head. "Nope. Done with pity parties. They aren't fun anymore."

Allison huffs at her own expense. "Truth."

"I need help with this." Bri opens the binder on the table.

Allison finishes filling the glasses with water and sits next to her friend. "What is this mess?"

"Wedding stuff." Bri beams.

Allison can't contain a laugh. "You think *I'm* the best person to help you with this? Didn't I try to convince you to make out with me not too long ago?"

"Well, that you did, but you're my only friend, besides Duncan, who's still alive," Bri states her opening arguments.

Allison cocks her head. "Not the best way to win my help."

"How about that besides Duncan, who made this monstrosity," she gestures to the binder, "you know me better than anyone else does … for given reasons. And I could really use your help." With those last words, Bri abandons all pretense, revealing the truth buried in her reasoning.

"So…" Allison pushes down her urge to scream, "what exactly is this thing?"

"Choices. Duncan knows what to do, but there are still small choices. These are them—the small choices." Brianna's finger taps the page. "I have to make the final decisions on all the choices he's narrowed down. What remains in this binder is everything he's worked on, and now, it's up to me… well… us."

"And this is actually some sort of help … what he did?" Allison asks in earnest.

"Huuuge. This is choices between A and B, not A, B, all the way through triple Z."

Allison nods her head. "Gotcha. Well, let's dig in, I guess."

"I guess?" Bri catches the reluctance in her voice.

"I didn't mean it like that. I meant it like, then we should dig in." Allison tries to clarify, but she knows the only person she is fooling here is herself.

"Look, we're friends, yes?" Bri starts. Allison nods. "Well, this is what friends do. They help each other. Do you want to do this or not? I'd rather not do it alone, which is why I came here. That and I thought it'd be fun to hang out, but if you'd rather go back to your room and stare at your posters or whatever you were doing before you finally answered the door, I can leave."

Allison holds back a laugh. "Damn, girl. Laying the smackdown a little?"

"Well, it called for it. So?"

Allison nods. "I'm in."

Allison says she's in, but while they sort through narrowing down the choices between white Stargazer or Longiflorium lilies and cornflower blue tables runners or table clothes, all with a smile plastered on her face the whole time, the only thing she can think about is her past. How in the hallway at school, Connor was abruptly dismissive on the phone or how, after getting expelled from college, he never called her on the drive home. All Allison can concentrate on is her doubts and insecurities. The lingering notion that Connor will never love Allison the way Duncan loves Bri because of her feelings for Bri. A messed-up, mixed-up web of emotions that, with each thought, entangles Allison more and more as she watches any chance of envisioned happiness drift further and further away.

Before she can tread too long in the drowning seas of her emotions, Vistrus strides through the front door, making a b-line for the basement.

"Hey, Dad!" Allison greets him.

"Hi, love. Sorry, I cannot talk right now." His words fade behind the closing basement door.

Bri turns to Allison. "That was weird."

"Weird, indeed," Allison agrees. "He's got something on his mind."

"Or a bee up his butt." Bri laughs.

Allison can't help herself but to laugh at the thought though she tries unsuccessfully to stop herself.

"There she is," Bri points to Allison's smile, "enjoying a moment. Nice, right?"

Allison nods. "Well, whatever bug my dad has flying around inside his ass, it certainly has him focused. Speaking of focused, I think Duncan may have accidentally, or unintentionally, over-complicated it."

"Explain." Bri gets up to refill their waters.

"Weddings aren't about the day. Forget the Hollywood fairy tales beaten into you by movies, commercials, and every animated kid's movie ever released. Weddings are a celebration, a party. A crap load of people coming together and being happy that two people found someone in this world that makes them want to be something better. I don't know a lot, but I know this. In twenty years, no one will remember the color of the tablecloths or if the flowers were Stargazer or Longitudinal lilies."

"Longiflorium."

"Whatever. What people will remember is how they danced until their feet hurt. They'll remember how they looked at their loved ones and realized the same thing you and Duncan already know, or they'll reaffirm those feelings with the one they've already committed to. They'll remember the food was great or the food sucked. Not that the dish was chicken cordon bleu instead of chicken Kiev." Allison stops for a moment, realizing that her possibility of having this day seems further and further out of reach than it did with each word before, if only because of the ever-growing tumultuousness of her relationship with Connor. "But I know that. People will remember the smiles on your faces, the laughs they shared over flubbed vows, and the good times you all had and thinking about the good times you all will have. Weddings are not about the dress. They are about the moment, the optimistic eye looking toward the future. Nobody sits at a wedding reception looking toward the part of the vows that mention the bad, the sickness, the ugly times. No one looks to the tumultutuity of the future." Allison stops, hit by the utter hypocrisy of her words. "Or, at least, they shouldn't, and neither should you."

Brianna sits, stunned at the wisdom pouring out with Allison's words.

"So, Al, how do you think we should handle the rest of this?"

"I have ideas. Flip a coin, drink if we're wrong." Allison shrugs at her suggestion.

"Drink if we're right?" Bri adds.

"So, drink? I can do that."

"Just kidding, but I like the coin. Or just randomly point and accept."

"Even easier."

The dark shadows over Allison lift a little as she shares a few laughs with Bri, simplifying the choices narrowed down by Duncan. Even as her mood lifts, a stabbing feeling tells her that happiness and contentment will never be friends to comfort her on lonely nights. She keeps a smile on her face, trying in desperation to hold on to whatever positivity she can because she knows at the end of the day, while Bri gets to go home to Duncan, Allison will be alone without so much the ability to say goodnight to the other one she loves.

The tires halt in his driveway, and he turns the keys, taking them out of the ignition. Vistrus grabs the parchment and glove off the passenger seat as he exits his car. He shuts the door and heads straight for the door. Entering the house, he hears Allison and Brianna in the kitchen. They cannot see what he holds, so he heads straight for the basement, hoping to avoid an interaction.

"Hey, Dad!" Allison shouts from the kitchen. He notices more chipperness in her tone than usual, almost forced.

"Hi, love. Sorry, I cannot talk right now," he finishes as he closes the basement door behind him, locking it before descending the stairs. *I hate hiding things.* He thinks about all he has had to keep from her, hoping it does not negatively affect her, but he has worries on his hands that are larger than himself. Of course, his daughter, her life and issues should never be penultimate to anything else in his life, but somehow, he has inadvertently pushed her aside for a crusade that bears eerie similarities to what Connor went through his senior year of high school. Vistrus's slacking in his adulting duties can impact him as much as Connor's pursuit of finding Jack almost halted all progress he had made. Now, in the thick of Inessa's clues and coded messages, all he can do is hope whatever consequences come to light are those from which he can recover.

Sliding the harpsichord out of the way so he can move the rug covering the floor safe, Vistrus wonders how many times he will have to move such an old, fragile piece of parchment. The glove seems to have gained no frailty over the years but worries him no less. He ponders the ways that he can secure the portrait of the Grey Fairy without compromising the safety of the one portrayed. He deposits the parchment and glove and locks the safe before replacing the rug and harpsichord.

Sighing in relief, he falls into his listening chair, though no music plays. He sits, trying to relax while pondering the future of his family, the town, The Council, and The Nation. All of which rests on protecting an old parchment one foot below his feet.

He stares at a framed, colored portrayal of Mozart, Bach, and Beethoven playing poker, a musician's rendition of dogs playing poker. But it always had a sophisticated sense of humor to Vistrus. The artist's depiction belongs in a museum, but the content is a fun mix of classical and contemporary. Something Vistrus always prided himself on being. But as he stares at the piece of art, an idea germinates in his head. An idea that might just secure the safety of the parchment and protect the identity of the Grey Fairy, all while hiding in plain sight. An idea so simple, he is only slightly surprised it had not already been done.

As this idea plants its roots firmly in his mind, he drifts to sleep surrounded by the company of his instruments.

Crouched behind the hedges lining the outside of the kitchen windows, Connor peeks into Allison's house. Watching Allison and Brianna flip through a white, three-inch binder filled with what he assumes are wedding designs.

He wants to knock on the window and say hello. His heart pounds from being so close to Allison, yet unable to hold her. He wants nothing more than to hold her and tell her how much he misses her, but he fears for her safety—for everyone's safety. Staying crouched as the sound of tires come to rest in the driveway, he takes a deep breath to silence what he can, knowing full well the sensitivity of Mr. Petrovsky's hearing. The hurried steps rushing from car to door put Connor's fear of being caught to rest. The front door slams as Vistrus enters his house. Connor hears awkward greetings as Vistrus heads away from the kitchen.

Connor watches them through the window as long as his heart will allow him. The ache of being so close yet so far churns his stomach until he can't stand it anymore. The smile on Allison's face offers solace from his little peeping indiscretion. A glimmer of hope in his weary world.

Sneaking out from behind the bushes and starting off down the road, he sees someone at the end of the block turn the corner, out of sight. Not an unusual sight to see in a subdivision, but still something doesn't sit well with him. He has no time to linger on that thought as a parked car flashes its lights at him a few times. Connor stops, freezing in place, unsure if approaching the suspiciously parked car would be the safest move in these uncertain times. After an extended moment of standing statue-like on the sidewalk, he continues, pretending he did not see the lights. After a few steps, the car flashes its lights one time. Connor keeps his sights straight ahead as the window rolls down.

"DeSalvo," the familiar voice calls out. A voice that stops him in his tracks. A voice Connor recognizes—Max Espinoza, former West Haven police officer and Legend killer. Not the person Connor wants to encounter on a dimly lit street while running from the law and trying to prove his innocence, but here he is. Unsure whether he should fight or flight. The boy who has seen more first-hand death in his days than most see in a lifetime screams for him to run as fast as he can. The Legend in him who whispers about being In because of his age and his cunning and his gripe and his paw tells him to trust his strength and his abilities. Deciding to listen to the latter, unsure if wisdom or naïveté guides him, he steps to the open window.

"Let me see your hands," Connor whispers back.

"Fair enough," Max agrees, placing his hands on the door. "You're being followed."

Seeing no one else as he looks around, Connor replies, "Yeah, by you."

"No, not by me. Well, yes, by me. But by someone else. I am not here to cause problems," Max begins making his point.

"That's a first." Connor snips.

"A well-deserved jab. Fine. I'll take it. But I've been following you…"

Connor throws up his hands. "Wait. You've been following me?! You've been following me, and you're flashing your lights at me like some dick from a cloak-and-dagger film to tell me I'm being followed?" His whispers raise in volume.

"Yes, but not to tell you I'm following you. That someone else is as well," Max refines his statement.

"If you're talking about the pale woman, I already know."

Max raises his brows at Connor's words. "The pale woman? No. A man. Always in a tracksuit."

"Tracksuit? What? What man? Why? How?" Connor spits out, unable to form his thoughts.

"For me, it started out of chance. Happenstance one night. I know you're innocent. Well, ninety percent sure you are, but I don't know why you were set up. Not wanting to possibly stir the pot, I decided not to say anything. So, I followed you from Jewel to the preserve. There was someone else, too, but I thought it was coincidence."

"And?"

"Nothing much else yet. I can't prove your innocence. Not yet at least, but I'm working on proving it beyond a reasonable doubt to everyone else. Anyway, I kept following you, and the same passerby kept appearing. Too much of a coincidence is no longer a coincidence."

"Keep going."

"He was here tonight. You're not safe."

"No one knows where I hide. Not this tracksuit guy, not the pale lady. No one, except maybe you."

Max shakes his head. "I know nothing about this pale lady, so I can't say nothin' about her. Though I've never followed you into the woods. But I know it's in there somewhere. So does he, whoever he is. You need to find a new hideout."

Connor nods, knowing Max could be right. He thumbs through a list of places in his mind that might work, but they all come back to the same spot, his current spot.

"I'll need time, but I'll find a new spot."

"Sooner than later. I don't know who this man is or why he's following you, but he is. And if he finds out, I don't know what will happen."

"Why are you doing this? After all you've done to destroy my family, my friends, our lives, why should I believe you? Why shouldn't I give the police something to arrest me for and kill you right here?" Connor knows his threats are nothing more than bark, but he can't think of a better way to phrase his anger right now.

"You saw me at the end. The hair, the teeth … I am like you. But unlike you, I hated myself. I wanted to destroy all I could about me that I didn't like or didn't understand."

"You owned a gun. You could have saved a few lives by taking yours." Connor's words sting harshly, even for him. A compassionate side of him wishes he could take back those words while the angry side has no regrets. But one of the many lessons his father taught him growing up was that anger may not have regrets in the moment; it has many in the future. "What's your point? Searching for redemption and a happy ending? You won't find that here."

"I might not. I know that. But I have to try. Redemption isn't about happy endings. It's about setting things right." Max moves his hands from the window finally. "Look, you have every right to hate me and you should, but it doesn't mean I'm wrong now. Then, sure. A hundred percent. Now, I don't think I am. Just be careful, Mr. DeSalvo. There are many people who will depend on you, and keeping you safe is the only thing I can do to ensure any lives I've ruined won't be ruined further."

Connor shakes his head. "This all sounds like nonsense. You're not making any sense."

"I know what nonsense means. And while it may sound that way to you now, it will make sense. Are you and Vistrus not working toward making you a bigger part of The Nation?" Max offers a clue.

"Look, I don't know how you know that or what you think that means, but I won't be part of anything unless I can fix this mess. Plus, don't you know no one gives you something for nothing?"

"I already took more than I can repay. Fixing this is all I'm trying to help you do in what way I can. And right now, that's telling you someone is following you. So, do something about it."

Max rolls up his windows and drives off, leaving Connor standing there, trying to comprehend everything he heard and the entirety of what it might mean.

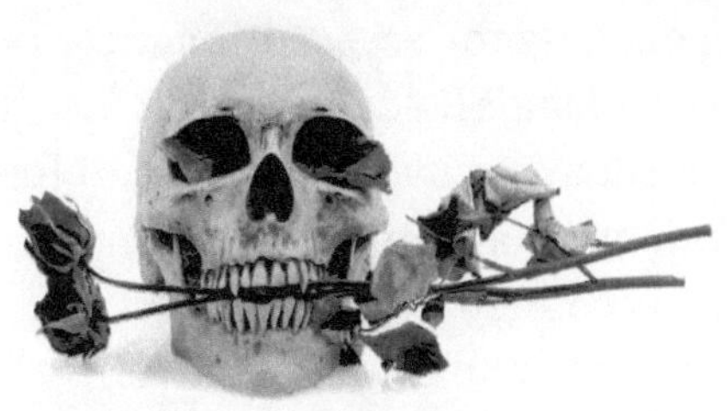

CHAPTER 11

"Do not confuse ethics for morals."
~V. Petrovsky~

Raymond Chandler puts the last touches of his mop to the Maine West Haven High School cafeteria floor for the day. The otherwise empty cafeteria rests, waiting for the students to fill its seats once more tomorrow. Relishing in the rare, quiet moment, Raymond stands, surveying his work, ensuring it is done for the day. He smiles, knowing the small things, like cleaning the floors, help maintain the veil of normalcy in an otherwise abnormal world.

As he shuts the cafeteria lights off, the door creaks open. Raymond turns to see Connor DeSalvo standing there, looking rather ill. Before Connor says anything, Raymond chimes into his mind. "Why are you here? It is not safe."

Connor does not answer back, opting instead for cautious steps toward the school janitor.

As Connor steps closer, Raymond can see he looks ill. "Are you feeling okay? You're very pale."

Again, Connor says nothing. He only glances at Raymond's hands holding the mop upright in its bucket. Staying silent, he moves his gaze to Raymond's neck.

"Connor," Raymond's voice rings out in his head. "Do you need help?"

Connor turns his attention to Raymond's stare. "I know."

Raymond keeps still, trying to assess the situation before him. "You know what?"

Connor squints his eyes, trying to read Raymond's thoughts. "An amulet and gloves. I know."

Before Raymond can respond, he notices Connor shift his disposition from knowing with a brow that meets in the middle to more curious, wide-eyed wonderment.

"I think I know," Connor adjusts his statement.

Raymond stands shaking his head. "Poor boy. I am not sure what some necklace and glove have to do with anything. Why don't you go back to your ... hideaway and get some rest?"

Connor and Raymond turn their attention to the quiet halls beyond and the approaching footsteps. Turning back to Raymond, Connor nods and exits through the lunch line doors, going backward through the lunch process.

Raymond watches him disappear to where December finishes her end-of-day cleaning duties but is pulled back from thoughts starting to wander by another voice sounding behind him.

"Sir," a voice grabs Raymond's attention, "did you see a man in a red tracksuit with a white stripe walk by?"

Raymond turns to see Max Espinoza standing before him. He does not respond with internal chimes or thoughts, only shaking his head no.

Frustration simmers on Max's face. "I know you can talk. I don't know how, but I know you can." He waits for Raymond to spill his secret, but he does not. "Fine. Then listen. I know you can do that. You know who I am and what I've done. But I stand here now, trying to do what's right. Connor is in trouble, and this tracksuit guy I am looking for has been following Connor."

Max pauses again, hoping for a response that does not come.

"I have warned Connor, but I do not know if he heeded it. This man. I can never remember his face. The details always change each time I see him. I was an officer of the law. Details were what I remembered. I can't explain it further. Does this make sense?"

Yes. Raymond understands Max's desperate words but telling him he does will open the door to a whole can of worms, whose explanation is better left for later or never. Leaving Raymond only one response, he shakes his head no for a second time.

Max holds back his frustration, now evident in a pulsating forehead vein. "Thank you for your time." Max forces out a smile before exiting the cafeteria.

Raymond turns to where December finishes her duties to see her watching them from the doorway between the lunch line and cafeteria.

"What was that all about?" December chimes to Raymond.

"I'll explain later. What did Connor say?" Raymond's curiosity about the previous encounter takes priority.

December shakes her head. "Only person to pass my way was a new gym teacher, I presume."

"New teacher? What did they look like?" Raymond quizzes her.

"Red tracksuit. Big guy." December fills in her answers.

A realization hits Raymond like a ton of red flannel bricks—an Adeirrig was in their presence, and he knows about their beginnings.

"Which way did he go?" Raymond demands.

December points through the doors she came through. "He's long gone, Raymond. Passed through without so much as a word."

"That was the Adeirrig." Raymond says, starting off to try to catch up.

Decembers joins chase behind him. "Could it be he?"

Entering the food line, they rush out the entrance doors into the hallway, finding it empty. Not a sound picks up in their ears.

Raymond turns to her. "I don't know. There's no telling how many came after us, or if some new Legend has formed. A Legend without a society."

December peers down the hallways, hoping the tracksuit man comes back through, but he does not. Both are left standing empty-handed.

Allison sorts through her CD and vinyl collection, boxing up various albums from a multitude of different bands and artists. She keeps the vinyl standing up, using the CDs to fill in the empty space in the box. She fills it with everything from The Ramones to NWA to Skinny Puppy to Static-X, and everything between and beyond. A relaxation and calm wash over her as she closes the over-stuffed box. She sits with her hand on the box, letting it rest for a moment as she breathes in and out, letting whatever thoughts are in her mind wander around to find a resting spot.

After a moment of silence and a calming peace she has not felt in a long time, she opens another box, this time a gift box, and begins sorting through her jewelry. She sorts out all her necklaces into a smaller box that fits inside the gift box and does the same for her earrings and bracelets. All except for the pair of onyx-crusted pentacle earrings Connor gave her for her eighteenth birthday. She replaces the ones she wears with these and sets the ones she took out in the box with her others. After she packs all her jewelry into the boxes, she rests her hands on top of it, taking a deeper breath than before. The wandering thoughts in her head calm down for the first time since she can remember. A feeling of serenity settles on her, and it is a feeling she never wants to let go of. She sets both boxes next to a roll of tape and wrapping paper before lying down in bed.

Allison realizes, as she sorts through her belongings, that they are only things. Material items that can be given away and, if needed, replaced. They are nothing worth holding onto with some sort of obsessive desire. A phrase enters her mind she has heard many times on the news growing up, spoken by victims who lost their homes to tornados and floods—they are only things. And things they may be. Things she no longer finds the joy in she once did. But she knows others who might find joy in them as she used to. To her, that is worth something in a time when nothing else feels worthwhile.

She rests her head on her pillow and, for the first time since she was old enough to remember, she falls asleep without trouble or without the liquid aid in her flask.

A beautiful, lush field, filled with green grass and various colored flowers spans as far as the eye can see. In the middle of its vast endlessness stands Allison. The sky overhead is a perfect blue, with cotton candy clouds and flocks of birds singing in unison as they fly overhead. No other people are in sight.

Allison looks around, smiling, calling out for anyone to hear her, but no one responds. Her joy turns to disappointment in the lonely isolation amidst the beauteous scene. The blue sky above fades to gray as the cotton candy clouds spread over the open spaces. The birds scatter in silence, leaving no other living thing in sight. She looks down at her feet. The flowers that started as lush among the green grass are wilted, surrounded by dead, brown grass. The dirt beneath kicks up in a soft wind. As her eyes look beyond the withered circle, she sees the flora die out as fast as she looks at it, in all directions. The dirt whips up in an ever-growing wind, blurring out the sky above. Allison wants to run, wants to leave this place, but her feet stay planted. She looks down and sees her feet have become one with the earth, planting her in this spot.

She starts calling out for help, hoping someone in the vast field that stood empty before the dirt kicked up is now around to hear her. No response comes. The more she screams out, the more dirt whips in fury, obscuring her vision more and more.

Growing tired and desperate, she lets out one last scream that shatters the distant clouds, clearing her vision and the skies. Though everything around remains dead, a woman in her thirties, pale, beautiful, and reminiscent of Allison, stands one hundred and fifty-one feet away.

"Mommy?!" Allison cries out.

The woman stands, staring at Allison.

"What did you do?" the woman shouts back.

"I didn't do anything!" Allison cries.

"Then why is it like this? Why do you field the blame?"

"I don't understand." Allison tries to move, but her feet are literally planted firmly in the ground.

"Look at me," the woman says this, and Allison looks her in the eye. As she does, the woman is no longer one hundred and fifty-one feet away. Now, she is mere inches in front of Allison.

"Mom!" Tears stream down Allison's face.

Inessa puts a hand on Allison's cheek. "My dear Allison. How I've missed you. Watching you grow from far away. It's nice to be with you." She pulls her hand away. "There's so much I never got a chance to show you. Would you like to see?"

Allison nods, tears clouding her vision. "Yes."

Inessa gestures behind her. They no longer stand in a wilted field but find themselves in an alley behind a run-down building, watching Legends in full form fight hordes of Normals, all equipped with various weapons from baseball bats and knives to automatic weapons and flame-throwers. She notices that among the battling Legends in full form are Connor and Brianna. A Legend whose form she has never seen before but whose face holds an air of familiarity also fights. She watches as the Legend lands a blow, then fades from sight like a mist from a spray bottle, only to reform behind the opponent. The Legend appears skinless while whole, covered only in muscles and veins that crawl around the body, never staying in place. Allison watches with her mother as fight after fight morph into one another while the dumpster nearby them fills with the bodies of the fight that morphed away.

"There is no peace here," Inessa warns. "Look."

Allison turns back. The scene shows bustling downtown Chicago Michigan Avenue, with people watching news clips on televisions in department store windows showing the violence of mob attacks against Legends playing out right behind them. The spectators do nothing to stop the violence in the streets, opting to keep their eyes glued to the television safely behind glass.

Allison turns back to her mother. "Why are you showing me this? I thought you'd show me motherly things, like movie nights we never had." Allison stares, unable to cry at the carnage playing out.

"I cannot show you what never was, only what will be." Inessa turns to Allison, a sad smile on her face accompanied by sorrowful eyes.

"Then show me something else," Allison pleads.

They turn from each other and are standing in the auditorium at Maine West Haven High School. The seats are packed with people of all ages. At the podium stands Vistrus, Scarlett, Brianna, and Connor. Behind them the stage sits empty, save for a banner reading gibberish.

Allison turns to her mother. "I don't understand. What am I looking at?"

Inessa puts a finger on her cheek and, before turning her daughter's head back to the scene, says, "Look again."

This time the audience is filled with a mix of people, half in Normal form, half in Legendary form. She turns her attention to the stage and sees her father in full form. His nose withered away, leaving only the socket, and his lips are thinned and cracked, framing his toothless grin, save two protruding fangs on top. Hair that was once full and jet black has thinned and lost all color. Overgrown muscles, accented with pulsating, varicose veins, replace his normally lithe frame, to which his torn clothes cling to in hopes of keeping him covered. Next to him stands Scarlett, still as Scarlett can be. Brianna, however, smiles as she catches her eyeball in her hand as it pops out of her head. Nothing frightening or unusual to Bri. Just another transition filled with rotting body parts and sloughing skin. Exposed skull and balding hair adorn her head. Her jaw sits agape, holding onto her face for fear the next breeze could knock it away, and her left arm lays at her side, but there is a sense of hope in her remaining eye that belies the grotesqueness of her appearance.

Connor stands, towering over the girls. His hair has thinned but lengthened. His muscles dwarf those of Vistrus but share the same varicose, which show through patches of hair covering his body in some spots where his clothes can no longer conceal. Connor's face sports fangs, though he retains the rest of his teeth.

Allison watches as the people in the audience who are not in Legendary form sit, unfazed by the appearance of those around them.

Inessa whispers, "There is peace here."

Without turning to her mother, she responds, "Where am I?"

Inessa does not respond, causing Allison to look at her. "Where am I?" she repeats.

Inessa's only response is a slow shake of her head.

"I don't understand. Help me understand," Allison pleads.

"I cannot help you no more than I tried in life. Figure out your place, and you will find your answer," Inessa offers what she can.

"That literally offers me no help."

As Allison finishes her words, the world around her is ripped away, and she finds herself back in the lush field as it was when this began, Inessa by her side.

"I love you," Inessa says as the world fades to black.

Allison opens her eyes but does not sit up. She makes no move to her nightstand to grab her journal and jot down the fading details of her dream. She lies, staring at the ceiling.

"Screw it," she whispers to herself as thoughts of her mother fade once again from her mind. She closes her eyes and drifts back to sleep.

Max Espinoza grabs a set of lock picks from his glove box before locking his car, forgoing the alarm beep, trusting he knows how to lock the door himself. Leaving his car behind in the forest preserve lot, with his police placard left over from his years in the department on display to prevent tickets or towing, he starts off toward where he has approximated Connor's hideout.

In this evening's foray to find Connor, early evening light shines through the loose canopy of trees above the forest preserve trail. Max skulks along, keeping a watchful eye out for Connor or the man in the tracksuit. A few nature lovers returning to their vehicles walk or ride bicycles past him as the remaining open hours countdown to minutes.

Nothing seems unusual, and previous searches for where Connor is fighting to prove his innocence have turned up fruitless. But he has been narrowing down the search and possible location, hoping tonight is the night to find his hideout. Reminders of his past sins haunt him as he thinks of what he might find if he finds Connor's spot. But those thoughts don't have too long to stew in his mind's cauldron. Down the trail, around a bend of trees, he spies a glimmer of light off the reflective stripes on a red tracksuit. Hoping to hide under the cover of darkness and foliage, Max ducks behind a few large bushes, waiting for him to pass.

Max remains calm as the red tracksuit-wearing man passes, seemingly unaware of Max's presence. After making sure the mystery man is out of sight, he emerges from the bushes, continuing his search.

After a few more minutes of walking on the path, Max approaches a public restroom. The trails have been abandoned of all pedestrians, and most forest animals have hidden away for the evening. But the restroom door opens, pausing Max in mid-step. He watches as Connor emerges from the restroom and turns away from Max, unaware of his presence. Moving closer to the side of the trail to hide under the cover of trees, Max follows Connor for a while. In an effort to hide any unwanted noise, he tries to keep in step with young DeSalvo. His attempts prove successful, watching as Connor turns the key to the padlock on an abandoned maintenance shack, entering it.

Max takes caution in each step, moving closer and closer to the shack, trying to hear and sneak a peek as to what is inside. Stepping one step too close, Connor hushes himself, creaking open the door to spy outside. Max ducks behind a tree and tosses a rock, hoping to distract Connor.

Looking to where the rock fell and satisfied the noises were nothing more than woodland creatures, Connor closes the door and resumes whatever he was doing in his shack.

Max's waiting and holding watch outside the shack proves more fruitful when Connor leaves his makeshift abode and locks up. His heart starts racing at the anticipation of what awaits him in the shack, no longer worried about his past digressions. Once Connor is long past earshot, Max pulls out his picks and gets to work. A short moment later, Max finds himself inside a space transformed into a think tank fit for government conspiracy theorists. The walls are covered in scraps of paper, scrawled with the names of various dead relatives, friends, and family friends. Others are names of those who have been killed by Jack and Allison. Still, others are words related to Connor's grandfather's murder and keywords that Max recognizes from his notebook. They all have strings of yarn attached, leading from one card to the next, a veritable spiderweb of clues all leading to one card with the word "Who?"

Max can't hold back a smile, looking around at the setup, knowing that in all his mistakes, he never made the one of killing Connor, the young man who holds such promise for the future. He takes a step, nudging something with his foot. Looking down at what he kicked, he sees the notebook stolen from his basement so long ago. He picks it up, flipping through the pages of notes describing, in code, the torture inflicted upon the residents of this town he so badly wanted to deny being like. Reaching the end of his notes, he sees Connor has taken to jotting down new notes, trying to piece together everything he can remember seeing, reading, and talking about over the last three years, and how anyone could think he might be responsible. Max reads the latest notes Connor scribbled about him and his thoughts on redemption for such actions.

I'm not sure forgiveness is in the cards. How would I forgive the man who took away my family? But he's helping now and that can't be discounted. His warning... should I take it seriously or is he still the man he was before? Is this some elaborate scheme to lull us all into some false sense of security, only to have him and some new crony start killing us off one by one again? Put it up when I get back.

Max sets down the notebook, leaving it open to this page while he searches for a writing implement. It only takes a moment to find a ten-cent pen lying on his makeshift bed. He adds to Connor's notes.

You may never forgive me, and that is something I have to live with. You may never trust me, and that is understand-able. But if there is ever a moment to try to earn it back, it is now. I found your place and, while looking, I saw the same man in the red tracksuit not too far from here. I do not know who he is or why he is always around when I am watching out for you, but, as I said, you are no longer safe here. If I found you, so will he. Take caution and stay safe.

Max leaves the notebook open on Connor's bed, ensuring he finds it and locks up behind him. All he can do is hope Connor heeds his warning.

The smell of bacon, eggs, pancakes, and freshly brewing coffee carries Allison out of bed and into the kitchen. She grabs a coffee cup, half filling it with cream and sugar before mixing it all with steaming hot coffee. She snatches a fresh strip of bacon off the paper towel next to the pan, crunching down on it.

Setting her coffee on the table before plopping down on a chair, she asks, "What's the occasion?" Not waiting for a response, she adds, "Bacon's pretty good."

Vistrus chuckles. "No occasion. Only pretty good?"

"Mmhm." She eyes her father. "Well, who am I to reason why? I mean, it's good. It's bacon. You know what they say?"

Vistrus turns to her, curiosity piqued. "What do they say?"

"Bacon is like se—" she catches herself, morphing the last letter into a new word, "—pizza."

"Bacon is like sepizza?"

Allison doubles down on her change-up by pairing it with a bad Italian accent, "Bacon is like sa pizza. Even bad a pizza is a good."

"Interesting," her father responds. "I always thought pizza was like sex in that regard."

"How would I know?" She turns her palms toward the ceiling while shrugging.

Vistrus plates up the eggs, pancakes, and bacon for them and joins her at the table.

"I am your father, not some bumbling fool. You are an adult, and I would not expect you to not be doing adult things."

"Your coffee," she says, extending her neck in its direction, hoping that changes the subject.

He gets up to grab his coffee.

"Toss me a few extra strips?" she asks.

Sitting back down, he tosses a few extra on top of her plate. "That said, I know I have not been the most attentive father lately," finally confessing his reasoning for the three-course breakfast. "I have had to take care of much business within The Nation."

Allison waves a piece of bacon, dismissing his reason. "It's fine, Dad. Some things are bigger than me. Larger than I? Me small, things big. Whatever. Some things are more important than others."

Vistrus smiles. "I am glad you can understand that. The problems in The Nation extend far beyond West Haven. I am your father first, and I think that I may have been putting you second."

Allison waves it off again. "As I said, some things."

Vistrus furrows his brow, unsure if she understands his intentions or still feels as if she is inferior to his other responsibilities. "You know you are number one? I may have been distracted about things, but those were all to keep The Nation safe. That includes you."

"Does it? I mean, I don't understand," she says, tossing half a piece of bacon on top of her still-uneaten pancakes. She shovels scrambled eggs into her mouth. "Who cares about any of this? I don't. I don't care that you tell me I'm some freak." Vistrus restrains his urge to correct her on the use of the word freak, not wanting to interrupt her train of thought. "I have no reason to think about it. I don't see it and don't feel it. The world around me sure doesn't see it." She shovels butter-covered pancakes into her mouth. "But you have planted these thoughts in my head. These thoughts that tell me I'm diseased.

These thoughts that tell me I can't be who I am meant to be because the world around me won't accept it. Our neighbors, our friends who aren't freaks wouldn't, won't understand."

She continues shoveling forkfuls of egg, pancake, and bacon into her mouth as she speaks. "I don't care. I want to live what life I have as me. I want to walk around outside looking like whatever the hell I look like and not worry about what people think. And before you chime in with, 'People will always judge,' I don't care about that. I mean, that people won't accept me will make me feel unsafe for no other reason than they don't like the way I was born. There is nothing I can do about any of it, but I watch you fight the good fight or whatever and ignore the trees, only seeing the forest. And it doesn't matter because as you said, people will always think and judge, and if they always think and judge, then there will always be those who act upon those thoughts and judgments, and the world will never be safe for me or our kind, and that is why I don't care."

Vistrus sits stunned, unsure how to respond.

"This is the point where you say something parental," she says, hinting at his next move.

He takes a deep breath before speaking. "The world will always try to beat you down. It does not matter if you are a Legend or a Normal. It does not matter what you look like, where you come from, or who you are."

"Then what does matter, Dad?" Allison interrupts.

"What does matter is how you respond to what happens around you. What matters is remembering that the rich and poor alike fight their own demons." He sees a question rise to the surface in Allison. "Metaphorical demons. Not real ones. What matters is the popular kid in high school had her issues that ran deep, as did the rest of them. Every person you see on the street, happy, sad, angry, joyful, or any other emotion, is fighting some personal battle against something we know nothing about. The angry woman yelling at the poor cashier has deeper problems than the wound at hand. Her outburst most likely has more to do with something beyond the checkout line than not. But we do not see that. We only see what we can, and what we see triggers what we are still dealing with. What we smell, what we hear, touch, too."

"Wanna throw taste in there?" Allison jokes.

"I am sure taste can trigger as well. But the thing is … is how we deal with the world around us. Learning to live in a world that seems to want to do nothing more than make sure we do not survive is how we make our mark. How we live our lives is the legacy we leave behind, and the fact that we survive is proof to the world that we have learned to live in it." He chews his food, letting his words sink in before he continues. "So be angry. Be upset that the world is what it is. But channel that and do something with it. Otherwise, it will win."

Allison sits, trying to absorb all the life wisdom he threw at her, but something in his words missed the connection. Something in his silence after the speech rings hollow in her ears. They sit, eating the rest of breakfast in silence, wondering what the other is thinking and if their words made any meaningful impact.

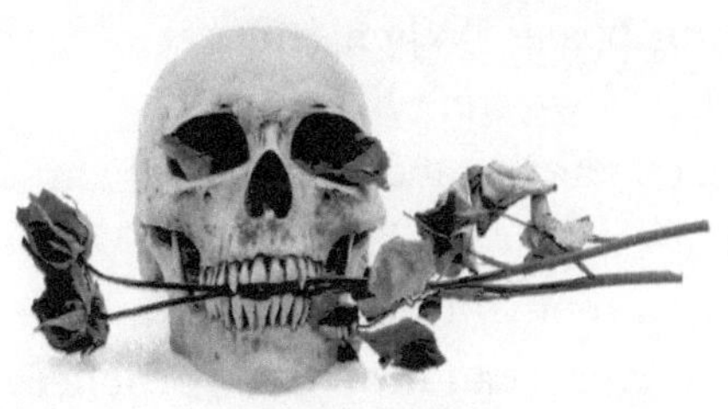

CHAPTER 12

*"Ethics knows that adultery is, like, wrong.
Morals wouldn't, like, you know, do it."*
~B. Waldgrave~

Eleanor and Vistrus sit, eating breakfast in the same greasy spoon he once sat in with Tracy. They pick at the shared pile of pancakes between them while enjoying scrambled eggs, bacon, and sausage, washing it down with glasses of orange juice.

Vistrus chomps down on a sausage link, eyeing the news playing out on a television behind Eleanor, before saying, "I do not think it is dead."

Eleanor looks down at the plate of sausage and bacon. "I'm pretty sure it is, sonny. Otherwise, there's a pig out there right pissed at an inept butcher."

Vistrus shakes his head at her attempt at humor, washing it away with a sip of his juice. "You are dealing with things, so I will not comment on that attempt at a joke."

Eleanor nods, the lightweight of her words stands in pleasant contrast to the loss she deals with on an ongoing basis. "When you get old, you say things. Sometimes we can't help it."

"Be that as it may, both you and I are far past old for Normal standards." Vistrus eyes the news clip again, waiting a moment before lowering his voice beyond what Normals can hear. "The prophecy."

Eleanor hunches down in her seat, playing into the newfound cloak-and-dagger feeling coating their conversation. "Of course, it's not dead," she begins, also in a volume low enough to avoid a Normal's prying ears. "Prophecies cannot die. They only get delayed a little longer."

Vistrus points his fork at her and shakes his head before stabbing some eggs. "Be it as it may, I believe the delay might be over. Or ending."

Eleanor perks up in her seat, her interest piqued. "What makes you say that?"

"Trust is earned, and you have earned mine, Eleanor." Vistrus hesitates.

"But?"

"But while we may be speaking in volumes low enough to stay out of Normals' ears, there might be others who are In, in here." Vistrus turns in his seat, pretending to stretch his back as he scans the restaurant for anyone listening in.

"Then why bring it up here, Mr. Petrovsky?" Eleanor points her fork at him in a mock-manner before stabbing her pancake and dipping it in syrup.

Vistrus uses his knife to point at a wall-mounted television behind Eleanor. "Because of that."

The screen hosts a graphic of the World Health Organization next to a talking head. The subtitles scroll across the bottom.

"In the battle between family entertainment and health care, it seems health care has won. The fight over the vacant land on the border of West Haven and Chicago has gone to the World Health Organization. While the Six Flags organization wanted that land as a possible location for opening a second Chicagoland attraction, they have raised the white flag. In a statement to the press, Six Flags has said, '[that] after careful consideration, now is not the right time to build a new park. But,' they added, 'we will continue to monitor our situation and build when the time is appropriate.' This brings a months-long debate to an end, with the WHO making its decision between Chicago, Sacramento, Albany, and Milwaukee. Chicago it is. They'll get all the Chicago-style dogs they can…"

Eleanor turns from the television, keeping her voice quiet enough that any Normals won't be able to eavesdrop on their conversation. "To understand the significance of the prophecy, one must understand the significance of the Legends, how the science plays into it, how the Fairies split, and why bringing them back together holds such promise." Bright light from out the window reflects off a passing car, catching her attention to the vibrant colors shining through the freshly fallen rain. The hue of the world after a rain always, even after all these years, brings her back to simpler times. Times she can smile at, remembering that while gone, once made her happy. And that, in itself, still makes her happy. "But even if the prophecies don't manifest down to the last detail, it doesn't mean they were wrong. Only different." She scans the patron and staff, seeing nothing out of the ordinary. "But you are correct. Let's not do this here." Vistrus nods in agreement.

Allison sits on the forest floor, next to the nondescript patch of dirt comprising Scarlett's temporary grave. The afternoon sun shines warmth down on an already warm day, drying up what remains from the earlier showers. She sits, listening to squirrels scream at each other as they run from tree to tree. On the far side of the clearing, she watches a raccoon who stayed out too late scurry off into the woods. Her thoughts continue racing, even in the solitude of the forest clearing. No smile crosses her as she watches the furry creatures scamper about. She sits, observing them with a scientific curiosity. Thoughts of what life must be like for racoons. The dangers of forest predators and the constant hunt for food, while dogging those scary, roaring metal monsters that stick to the hard ground. She imagines the constant state of fright they must be in, but at the end of the day, they have huge families that look out for them. Videos on social media are always filled with families of racoons, never just one, unless it's a pet. A part of her wishes she had that family. A part of her knows she did have that family, but things have changed, if only for an extended moment—a drastically extended moment. But the lack of comradery and belonging eats at her a little more with each passing day. A little more that makes her think wild animals may have the advantage on this thing we call life.

As the racoon fades from view behind the curtain of trees, her thoughts return to the present, to the best friend forever buried below the ground next to her. Now, she hopes Scarlett is still next to her. She does not relish the thought of sitting on top of her best friend.

"I don't get it, Scar. I could really use you right now." She breathes, wondering if any of her words are being heard. "Tonight is the party. You should be there. Connor should be there. I don't understand anymore. Bri was everything I hated… Here I go again, complaining about the same things as before. It's not Bri, it's me. I know. It's not having you. It's not having Connor. He still is in hiding. Still running because the world thinks he's guilty. We know. We know he's not. But the world 'thinks,' and don't we all run from what the world thinks?" Allison looks around, huffing at the irony in her words. "I have to run to work, do my thing there before the engagement party. Another thing I don't understand. What's the point of an engagement party? Yeah, to celebrate two people's happiness, but isn't that what the wedding shower is for? Is this a wedding shower? Are they the same thing? Am I overthinking it? Whatever. I wanted to stop by and say I miss you. Tell you that whatever happens, I want you to know that you were always the only one who got it. The only one who understood me. My dad says you won't be like this forever, but boy, this sure feels like forever. Hell, I'm saying things like, but boy. I wanted out of this town so much. I wanted so much more … for both of us. I thought we'd rule the world."

She stops for a moment to think about everything. "I thought a lot of things. I guess I was wrong." Allison stands up, staring down at Scarlett's resting place. "I love you, Scar. I am sorry you got stuck with a friend like me."

Allison turns around and walks away without looking back. She walks away without seeing the dirt above Scarlett shift a little.

"I am taking the Waldgrave girl and her fiancée out tonight to celebrate their engagement. Even in uncertain times, we must continue to celebrate those occasions that are important to us, if for nothing more than to live as normal a life as possible," Vistrus says, checking his watch before starting a vinyl record on the living room player.

Eleanor shakes her head. "I'll never understand certain things about you, Vistrus."

He sets the needle on the record and turns to her. "What things? There are many things."

Eleanor shifts in her seat on the couch. "Your new-found love for using as many words as possible, for one. Second, why you still call people by their surname? Society has long moved past calling someone 'son of.' Her name is Brianna."

Vistrus sits in his red wingback chair. "Proper speech is important."

Before he can amend his statement, Eleanor chimes in with a jab. "Proper speech changes as society evolves. Is that why you refuse to use contractions?"

"Smashing words together has never sat comfortably with me. It is why I do not like words like croisandwich or ginormous. It is a sandwich with a croissant for bread. We do not say ryewich or whole grainwich. It was nothing more than a sophomoric marketing gimmick. And the other is … well… They are words spoken by people who do not know words like gargantuan exist. Otherwise, it is only time until a ginormous croisandwich becomes a gicroiwich, which is literally nothing. Though it may become something." Vistrus winces, having said the combined words.

"A bit pretentious of you, my dear." Eleanor calls out his behavior. "Though making up that word, I now see where your daughter gets it."

Vistrus cracks a wry smile. "A little pretense never hurt anyone." He checks his watch again. "But to the point of finishing our meal early, what about the prophecy?"

Eleanor nods, acknowledging the need for an explanation. "You know the genetics behind us. Why we are who we are. Even if you don't remember the specifics, you know the general idea. You know it's in the genes."

Vistrus nods. "This is all very elementary, my dear Watsanor." He chuckles at his joke.

Eleanor nods again, trying to hold back an amused laugh. "Well, young man, once upon a time, the fairies were similar in their Legendary state. Much like Sylvia Waldgrave, they had thick skin resembling bark, vine-like hair, all that jazz. But something happened, and some fairies changed. Over time, the groups split into light and dark fairies, then the light fairies began calling themselves ghosts. Though, they stayed within the same Society."

Vistrus nods, knowing all this, but proceeds to interrupt. "Because of their translucent skin that disappears in Legendary form."

Eleanor nods. "And what The Nation now recognizes as ghosts were once fairies."

Vistrus grabs a cigar and matchbook from the humidor. "But ghosts are few. Only rarer are the Clochnawa."

"And why they never received a separate society. Because while their physical symptoms may have changed, their genetics did not."

"Do you know the event that split them?" Vistrus asks on the previous point.

"Do I know? I was there." A sorrowful smile crosses her face.

"It was 1600. I was traveling the world, sorting out a few things. I found myself drawn to the stories I heard about Francisco Pizarro and his adventures in a land he called Peru. Now, I hadn't known what to expect; it's not like we had the internet back then to check things out," Eleanor starts.

"I know. I was born well before the internet and mass communication," Vistrus reminds her.

"Of course, of course." She waves off her mistake. "So, I'm there. All by my lonesome and thinking about a few things. I had been there for a short while, maybe a few weeks, and had made a few friends in The Nation. Though, back then, it was called something else."

A much younger Eleanor strolls through a valley of small, rolling hills with two new friends by her side. Green grass and flowers decorate the valley floor and fluffy clouds roam overhead. The mountains lining the valley begin rumbling, disrupting the serenity of the day and interrupting their laughter and chatter. As smoke rises from Huaynaputina's peak, terror and panic set in.

The smoke thickens, and the roar of the volcano deafens them. One of Eleanor's companions transitions into full fairy form with bark-covered skin, gray eyes, and long, vine-like hair. The other follows suit, though Eleanor remains in her Normal state. They run toward the mountains and the eruption. One of the fairies tries to yell something to Eleanor, but she cannot hear her. Unfamiliar with the landscape, she follows, hoping to live through this ordeal.

As they near the end of the valley and the mountain base, lava spews into the sky, darkening the world around them. The lead fairy waves them her way. Eleanor follows as they trek up the mountain base, leaping from shelf to shelf as lava and ash fall around them. As the heat intensifies, becoming stifling, the lead fairy ducks into a cave. A rumble sends them tumbling to the ground as waves of heat fill the cavern. Through the cave entrance, they see lava flowing all around, creeping into their cave. Ash chokes out most of the light. The heat rises, pushing them further in the caverns. Sweat pours from them, evaporating as quickly as it came. The sound-dampening effects of the cave allow them to hear each other as long as they scream.

"How is running into the erupting volcano safe?!" Eleanor shouts, gesturing at the lava crawling toward them.

"Imaraykuchus mana imamanta manchachikuq!" the fairy says, smiling as she waves them farther into the cave.

Eleanor turns to another fairy. "What did she say?!"

Yelling above the rising volume, even in the dampened cave, the other fairy translates, "Because it's safe!"

"This is safe?!" Eleanor gestures around her.

The translator shrugs. "So she says!"

"So, it seems she was correct," Vistrus interjects.

"But she almost wasn't. This was no run-of-the-mill volcanic eruption. This ended up being one of the largest eruptions in modern history," she informs him. "And since liquid flows to the lowest point first, and these caves went up, it was a safer bet than trying to outrun a lava flow."

"How did this event split the fairies? I do not understand."

"It's coming."

Eleanor and her fairy companions back deeper into the cavern until they hit a wall. The heat levels off but borders on unbearable. Eleanor feels dehydration setting in. Her thirst rises as the lava creeps closer and closer, trying to climb the slight incline to them in some primordial hunger to eat any living thing in its path.

While Eleanor stares at the inching lava, a shout emanates behind her. "Kay patamanta!" The fairy points to a raised ledge they can crowd onto to keep safe. They all hop up as lava and ash continue spewing forth from the mountain, rumble after rumble, threatening to cave in this haven and bury them forever. At the peak of the volcanic rumble and lava spewing forth, something whistles from the volcano. A high-pitched, grating noise followed by a burst of light so bright, it lights the interior of the cave as bright as day, even through the ash veil curtaining the entrance.

As quickly as the light flashes, it fades, leaving them in utter darkness, engulfed in heat and ever rising lava. Their eyes are unable to adjust to the darkness, momentarily blinded by the incident outside. After countless moments that seem to span forever, their eyes begin adjusting to the darkness. The heat remains suffocating, and Eleanor now feels faint, but the rumbling dies down and the ash now floats, filling the air as it begins to settle.

Eleanor looks at her new friends. Neither are in their Normal state, but whatever state they are in looks nothing like their Legendary state. Their skin no longer boasts the trademark bark-like texture known in the Legendary community; it is now translucent. Eleanor's gaze concentrates on the veins and arteries and the blood flowing through them. Beyond the circulatory system, Eleanor watches the muscle structure contract and relax. As they writhe on the ledge floor, the muscles, veins, and arteries become more translucent with each passing moment until they disappear completely.

Eleanor's eyes go big as she watches her friends fade out. She reaches toward them, touching their invisible bodies. She fumbles around as she tries to comprehend the moment. The ground below is still deadly hot from the cooling lava, and she feels the need to stay put as she does not want to burn off her feet.

"What caused the flash of light?" Vistrus asks.

"Whatever it was is lost to the annals of time. Though, some have speculated it was a release of high concentrations of uranium heated by the eruption. The effects were much farther reaching than just the two in the cave with me. All fairies in the immediate surrounding area became the new type. The farther out from the center of the event, fewer and fewer changed. But it had a worldwide reach."

Vistrus lights his cigar, waving the match around to douse it. "How will the Grey Fairy reunite them? Science…"

Before Vistrus can finish his sentence, Eleanor interrupts with a laugh. "This isn't some children's tale where they magically combine to form some super race or completely form some new Legend. There is no combining them. Only uniting them."

"But the prophecy. Prophecies are…" Vistrus puffs on his cigar while finding his words, but again Eleanor interrupts his unfinished thought.

"Nostradamus made vague predictions that could apply to many things. But over time, the most memorable events that could be applied were applied. Making his guesses look like he could tell the future. Never mistake a faulty correlation for truth. Prophecies are reworded or changed slightly with each translation. That way, we read into them what we want. We find ways to make them come true. Most predictions and prophecies are nothing more than self-fulfilling." Eleanor pauses, letting it sink in for the old Legend, but she continues before he has a chance to speak. "But what does this have to do with the World Health Organization building a new research facility on the outskirts of West Haven and Chicago?"

Vistrus exhales a cloud of smoke, his brow trying to meet over the bridge of his nose as he concentrates on his thought. "Something Max Espinoza said about a coming storm and us being in the center. But what I do not understand is what the Grey Fairy has to do with the prophecy if nothing physical will change. Why have any of this prophecy at all? What is the point?"

Eleanor straightens up a bit, the sudden need to feel more attentive taking over. "Just because nothing physical changes doesn't mean nothing has. Just as prophecies take time to come to be, the results of the prophecies can take time as well. Also, I never said *nothing* physical will change. I do not know what will or will not happen. But more importantly, this storm

Max speaks of… what does it have to do with the new WHO center?"

Vistrus shakes his head. "That, I have no idea."

The white table clothes and red-cushioned chairs of this upscale Italian restaurant accent the Rat Pack jazz playing softly over the speakers. In the center of the table, bread sits in a couple of linen-lined baskets, while a bottle of olive oil waits to be poured onto the stack of dipping plates. A small table next to them holds a small mountain of wrapped gifts.

Duncan, Brianna, Vistrus, Eleanor, and a few of Duncan's old crew who managed to escape the clutches of Ashby dig into the bread with hungry appetites. Vistrus exchanges a few hushed words with the server while gesturing at the table. The waiter nods his head, making similar gestures before Vistrus pats his arm, sending him on his way.

Duncan rises from his seat and steps over to Vistrus. "Mr. Petrovsky…"

Before he can continue, Vistrus holds up his hand, stopping him. "We are all adults now. At least, I am pretty sure we are. You may call me Vistrus."

Duncan swallows, uncomfortable with his new station among this crowd. "V… Vistrus." He shakes his head as Mr. Petrovsky's first name becomes comfortable on his tongue. "I don't know how to thank you. This is all too much."

Vistrus waves it off. "You have proven yourself to everyone here as a valuable ally, as well. Consider this a small token of thanks."

Duncan understands when not saying anything can speak volumes above any words. With a smile, he nods his head and returns to his seat.

He kisses Brianna on the cheek before pulling his chair to the table.

"Mr. Petrovsky, isn't Al coming?" Bri gestures to an empty chair.

Before Vistrus can respond, Allison's voice sounds from behind Brianna. "Sorry I'm late. Had everything but a card." She places the two now-wrapped boxes from her room on the gift table. Allison takes the empty seat next to Duncan and leans toward him. "I think you'll dig what I gave you. I don't have much money, but they're cool."

Duncan eyes the size of the boxes, venturing an educated guess as to what's inside and smirks. "I always trust your taste."

The server returns to the table, holding three wine bottles: one Cabernet, one Sauvignon Blanc, one White Zinfandel. He exchanges a few words while displaying the bottles for Vistrus, who samples and confirms the Cabernet with an approving nod. He gestures to Bri and Duncan to taste the other two.

Duncan and Bri both sit as the server pours taste testers into their glasses. Bri sits, unsure what to do, but Duncan knows what to do. He shows Bri how to swirl, observe the legs, sniff, sip, and swoosh. She follows suit before they both swallow and shrug. "Tastes like grapes to me," she jokes, causing the server to offer up a well-rehearsed laugh.

"Shall I pour you a glass, then?" the server asks.

Duncan nods, tapping her glass. The server goes around pouring glasses for everyone before talking more with Vistrus.

Before sipping her wine, Allison shoots a look to her father, silently requesting permission to drink in public, though her twenty-first is still a few away. He scrunches his face, offering a quick couple of nods, a signal that if she won't tell, he won't tell.

Allison sips her White Zinfandel, leaning toward Bri. "I hope you like what I gave you. It's a bit different from your normal choices, but I think you'll make them work."

Brianna smiles. "Can't wait to see what it is." She notices that while everyone around soaks in the joyousness of the occasion, Allison seems to be coated in a fog of sadness. "You okay?"

Allison forces out a smile. "Yeah. Just kinda sad … and happy."

"I get the happy, but why the sad?" Brianna grabs her wine glass, taking a sip.

Allison looks around at the conversations, the laughter, the optimism everyone here seems to share. "It's ending."

"What's ending?" Bri misses the meaning Allison drops.

"This." Allison gestures around her. "Once you're married, things change."

"No, they won't. Why would they? Where's this coming from?" Brianna drinks more of her wine.

Allison knows why it will change and holds the answer to Brianna's question but does not reveal it. "I could be wrong. I'm happy for you both." Again, she forces out a smile. "It's just… we're grown up, aren't we?"

Brianna turns to Duncan and flashes him a smile. She looks at everyone gathered here today before turning back to Allison. "We sure are. And our circle is growing. Duncan's friends are pretty cool. Like, different versions of Duncan." She leans closer to Allison. "They look up to him, ya know. Like he's their leader. It's kinda sweet."

Both girls glance at Duncan, then to his friends before giving hearty belly laughs at the thought of it all.

"I'm glad you are here, Allison. It means a lot to me."

Allison smiles again, though this time she does not force it.

The server returns with a few starters, followed by another server carrying a few more. They place the plates around the table and confirm everything is well before taking their leave.

As everyone starts filling their plates with appetizers, Bri stands, holding out her wineglass. For a moment, she looks around the restaurant at the other patrons but brushes off whatever she might be thinking, then turns back to her friends. "Things in West Haven have been … not normal for the past few years. I mean, in high school I thought I had it made. Then I got reacquainted with old friends." She gestures to Allison. "She and Scarlett reminded me of who I really am … and the potential of who I may become." Bri pauses, searching for a smooth segue but can't find one. "We have lost loved ones. Many loved ones. Mom, to begin." She holds back tears. "Jack and his parents." She gestures to Eleanor. "Connor's parents and grandfather." She turns to Duncan's friends, "and made new friends. Unexpected friends." She turns to Duncan. "And the most unexpected loves flourished when everything else around seemed to be … well, not flourishing. While Allison and Scarlett may have reminded me of my potential, Duncan will be the one by my side as we walk through this … wild ride and become what our potential holds." She pauses for a moment, not so much to let that sink in but to go over it in her head to make sure it made sense. After satisfaction sets in, she continues, "For Scarlett and Connor, who couldn't be here tonight." She pauses again, unsure if elaboration is needed before deciding against it. "And Mr. Petrovsky, who has been a father to more of us than he ever dreamed of … or probably wanted to be. But he did. And we wouldn't be here tonight if not for you. So, Mr. P, thank you for everything."

Vistrus raises his glass to her toast, and everyone follows his lead. "To the future Mr. and Mrs. Duncan Elias. As Old Blue Eyes once said, the best is yet to come." He pauses to let that sink in. "I heard something once a long time ago from a great man I knew as James, and today I share it with you." He stops to make sure he remembers it correctly. "May you both live as long as you want and never want as long as you live." He raises his glass up and finishes his toast with,

"Vashe Zdorov'ye," bringing it in for a sip. Everyone else cheers and sips their glasses.

Allison tries to enjoy the festivities and food, laughing at jokes and smiling out of courtesy, but she can't bring herself to find the happiness for the engaged couple that the others seem to share. Allison only thinks about those who cannot be here tonight. She concentrates on everything this gathering is supposed to set aside, all the worldly concerns that eat away at the back of their minds and the wearing down by the daily grind. Her thoughts linger on those concerns instead of enjoying the moment and the evening for what they are before returning to her harsh reality. But she cannot. She can only stew in the worst of it, thinking about Connor and Scarlett.

The fading sun casts shadows through the forest preserve's canopy. Each shifting branch that dances with the shadows keeps Connor on high alert. A normally unjustified feeling to have on an otherwise uneventful evening. But justified they may be, remembering the warning Max offered about being followed.

He carries an unopened box of chocolate fudge Pop Tarts®, his little treat this evening. While his time in the woods has given him the knowledge to discern between an animal traipsing around or someone sneaking behind him, he is uncertain of the sound he heard from outside his shack.

He ducks behind a large tree, using the cloak of night to further stay hidden. His hand slips into his pocket and turns on his cell phone. While he can't remember if he disabled his GPS, he feels that having access to it might come in handy, especially if his hiding spot has been compromised.

He peers around the tree, trying to glimpse who or what made that sound. A second later, and the white stripe on a red tracksuit reflects the moonlight. Connor watches this man who's been following him skulk around the outside of the shack. Trying the door and finding it locked, the stranger tries peering in through cracks in the wood planks holding it together but fails from the interior adjustments Connor has made that block any prying voyeur.

Ducking behind the tree, Connor pulls out his cell phone and hides the light emanating from the screen as he dims the screen brightness, turns the volume off and the camera on.

He records the man as he tries a few unsuccessful attempts to enter the shack before turning away. While Connor cannot make out a face in the darkness, he captures a good physical size description.

Leaving the shack in the opposite direction of Connor, the man resigns his attempts, at least for the night. Connor follows with caution, keeping a safe distance from the man in the red tracksuit while continuing to record him.

As the sound of distant cars becomes less distant, the man slows down and stops. Connor, too, stops and takes cover behind a tree. He records the man as the sight before his eyes is something he has never witnessed before. While in his transitions and the transitions he has witnessed, the Legends clothes stay the same, albeit a bit more distressed. This man in the tracksuit is some Legend Connor has never heard of or been told about. He watches as the red tracksuit morphs into something more flowy. The man, too, changes his physical form from a lumberjack of a man to a more petite frame. In the low light, Connor cannot see what this new form looks like, if it is male, female, Normal, or Legend, but his eyes do not deceive him. He is watching the man and his clothes change into someone entirely new.

As the new form finishes taking shape, and it and the new clothes walk off, Connor keeps the camera trained on them until they are out of sight. He turns off his camera and shuts off his phone, pocketing it.

Thoughts fill his mind on his walk back to his makeshift home. He needs to figure out how to get this video to Vistrus or someone on The Council. Self-disappointment sets in, realizing Max was right—this place has been officially compromised, and he must hunt for somewhere new to hide unless the video somehow proves his innocence. All things he can contemplate while he decides what stays here and what will go with him as he searches for a new hiding place.

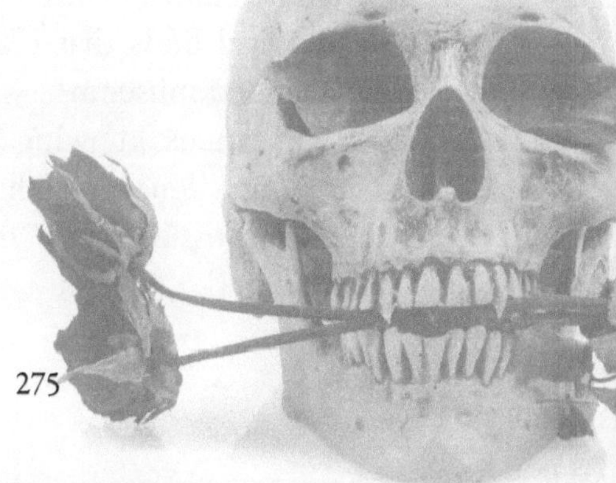

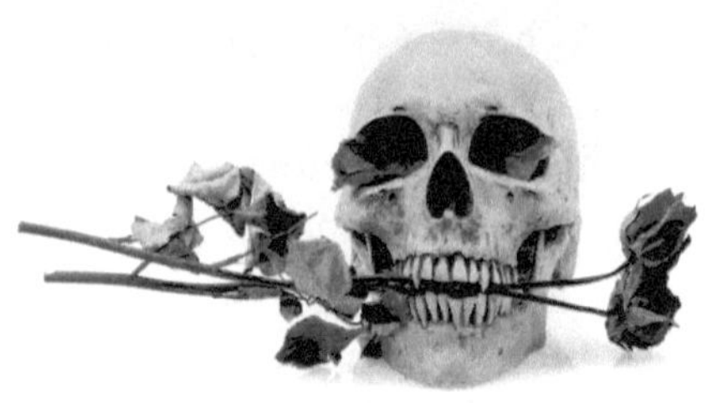

CHAPTER 13

*"Never mistake cries for help
for cries for attention."*
~N. DeSalvo~

"There is something you need to see." Vistrus keeps his words brief, leading Eleanor down the halls of The West Haven Museum of Natural History and Art.

Eleanor shakes her head at the vagueness of his words. "There are many things left in this world to see. If you're going to make such a statement, narrowing it down might help."

Vistrus huffs. "Of all the things you have seen, you have seen nothing like this."

"I don't think there are many mummy exhibits or archaeological finds that I haven't seen, dearie. I do love me a good museum."

Vistrus smiles, knowing he has something better in store. The silent walk through the long corridor to the "Employees Only" door builds curiosity in Eleanor's mind.

"I am not sure why we are here so late. Couldn't this have waited until morning?" Eleanor ponders out loud.

Vistrus checks his watch. "Your age is showing. Ten o'clock is not that late."

"Well, what is?" she asks again, entering through the "Employees Only" door Vistrus holds open for her.

"Midnight, two a.m. That is late. But I have always said do not stay out past two. Nothing good can happen then." Vistrus smiles. "That is what I tell Allison, anyhow."

"Where are we going? What is so special?" Eleanor's curiosity mixes with frustration.

"It is something you will have to see to believe." He shuts the door behind him, trying to minimize the noise. "Follow me."

"Where are we going? The vault?" She looks around back halls as the number of side rooms dwindles until they are in a long stretch of hallway. "Vistrus, this isn't fun. What is so important?"

"There is something you should have. Something you need, I believe. Something that may have to do with Inessa, as well."

"Now, I'm getting worried."

They approach a door at the end of the hall. The sign reads, "Vault Storage." In smaller letters underneath that, "Old Exhibits Only."

"So, we are going into the vault." Eleanor smiles.

Vistrus shakes his head. "Not exactly."

He leads her through the storeroom. "While reading her journals, she mentioned the game of chess. More than a few occasions. It stuck with me, but never clicked until I chatted with the sentinels."

"What did they say?"

"They mentioned the word Easpag. It's an old Gaeilge name for…"

"…Bishop," Eleanor finishes his sentence.

He nods. "Yes. Does that mean anything to you?"

Eleanor hides the feelings welling up at the mention of the word. Unlike The Council, she does not want to place blame on anyone prior to an investigation. "No," she hesitates. Not wanting to throw fuel on the smoldering kindling of a fire, she refrains from mentioning her old flame.

Vistrus continues, "There is an idea that all the events of the past few years are somehow connected to that chess piece and to what I am about to show you."

They come to a stop at the back wall of the room. He inserts his finger into the hole housing the switch and presses it. The wall shifts, pulling Eleanor's attention from her thoughts for a moment.

"Well, let's see it."

"Follow me." Vistrus starts walking down the blackened hall as he shuts the door behind them. "But the symbol, five-pointed star. One for each society— Poe, Frye, Kipling, Tennyson, Coleridge."

"Correct," Eleanor confirms.

"Where does that leave the Adeirrig?"

Eleanor stops walking. Thoughts cloud her mind with possibilities. None of which she wants to think about too much right now, and none she wants to think might be true. "I don't know, Vistrus. But we will figure out how this all fits together."

She continues a few more steps, only to have Vistrus stop them at the hall's dead-end.

"I showed this room to Nick. I think he and I may be the only living people to know of its existence. Inessa wrote about it in her diaries." Vistrus presses the secret latch, opening the door.

Turning on the lights, he reveals the walls of serpentine marble, showing Eleanor what he suspects was an old council chamber. She surveys the room, finding it empty.

"It's empty. What am I supposed to do with this information? This room is what you dragged me here to show?" She looks around again, thinking she may have missed something. "What's going on, Vistrus?"

"This is where I first found it, Eleanor. In this room." He motions to the room.

"What is this place?"

Vistrus paces in front of her. "I thought, and Nick thought I might be correct, that this was a council chamber."

Eleanor shakes her head. "They never used this room."

Vistrus stops pacing, pointing a finger at her. "That is my point. What we thought was the first council may have been the second."

"How?"

"I am working on the definitive. But this is where I found it."

"Found what exactly?" Eleanor raises an eyebrow.

Vistrus turns to leave. "That is our next stop."

Vistrus and Eleanor pull into his driveway. He notices the disbelief on her face. "I could not have given it to you here. It would not have made sense."

They exit the car and head inside.

"But you could have brought it with you. Given it to me at the museum," Eleanor chides.

Vistrus shakes his head. "I did not want it leaving the house in anyone else's hands. Hands are bad." Shaking his head again, he finishes, "All within my hands."

He unlocks the door, and they head inside.

"I still don't understand all this," she admits. "And have grown a tad worried about you, my dear."

His eyebrows raise as he nods in short bursts. "It will all make sense. No worries. The Grey Fairy. It was a prophecy we thought was gone with their deaths." Eleanor nods in agreement, allowing Vistrus to continue. "What if I told you that might not be true? Not all is lost."

Eleanor plants her wrist on his forehead, checking his temperature. "Vistrus, we already had this conversation. Bring it around already."

Swatting away her hand, he heads toward the basement, motioning for her to follow. "I know who the Grey Fairy is. We all do. We just do not realize it."

Eleanor stops again, putting her hand to her chest. "While I may be Legend, I am old. Do not say such things. You could have given me a heart attack."

Vistrus turns back with a wiry gaze. "No, I could not. No heart attack. Cannot happen. Come on."

Once downstairs, he shifts around the harpsichord and rug covering the safe door, and Eleanor sits on a chair. A few moments later, he rises with the parchment in his hand.

"That looks old," observes Eleanor.

Vistrus looks down at the parchment. "It is. Older than you realize. Not older than you or I, I do not think, but old. It was given to Inessa before she passed."

"Vistrus, more words have left your mouth in the past few months than the previous centuries of life. If this is some sort of act, we are alone." Eleanor urges. "To put the cherry on the sundae, you're scaring me a little."

Vistrus scans the room with jittery eyes. "Are we ever really alone? Can we be certain? Not certain, not an act. No one listens to crazy without proof." His hand holding the parchment inches up a little.

"Is that…?" She nods at it.

"Proof. It is." He moves to hand it to her but holds off. "It will not make sense. You will find yourself asking how. Asking how and saying wow. But I am piecing it all together."

"I've seen a lot in my day, young man. I do not think there is anything you can tell me that will have me saying, 'how.'"

"Saying wow and asking how." His free hand waves a finger. "The devil is in the details."

"Mr. Petrovsky." The schoolteacher's sternness of Eleanor's words grabs his attention.

Vistrus tilts his head in a moment of doubting her words, giving her a small smile. "Here." He hands her the paper, and, while awaiting her reaction, grabs an empty picture frame leaning against the wall. He sets it down beside her chair. "I figured if it is framed, the significance of it will not matter. Anyone who sees it will think it is a simple portrait."

She looks at the drawing sketched out on the old parchment. Before she can search for what to say, her mouth opens. "Wow!" Then a thought grasps her, and before she can stop herself, she mutters, "How?"

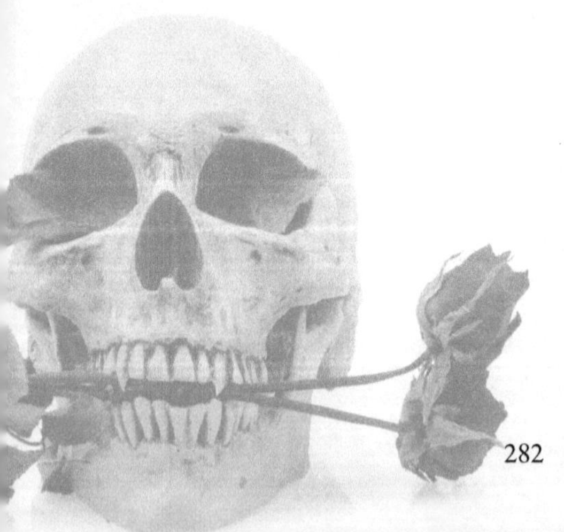

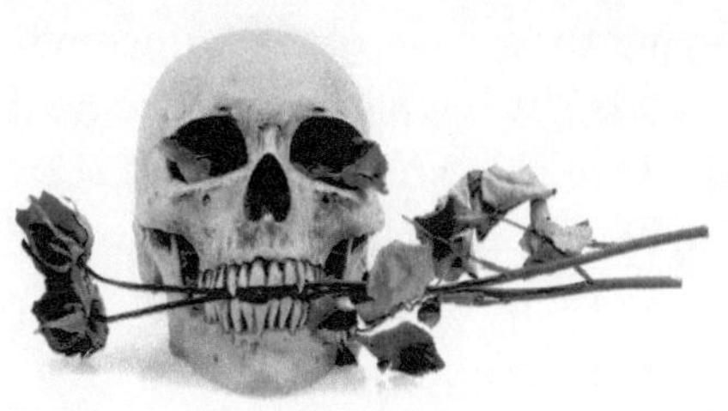

CHAPTER 14

Allison sits at a table in The Cheesecake Factory, checking her phone over and over like it should have rung or alerted her to a text already. She scans the restaurant from her seat but falls back, dejected. Her sad eyes do nothing to deter the server from making friendly conversation into an attempt at ordering an appetizer.

"Love those earrings. Black pentacles… very goth chic, honey."

Allison rubs her earrings. "Thanks. A gift from my boyfriend a few years back."

"Sounds like a keeper to me. Avocado egg rolls while you wait? A martini to calm the nerves?"

Allison gives the server a cursory smile. She shakes her head. "He should have been here thirty minutes ago. I'm so sorry."

Trying to ease her obvious uncomfortableness, the server adds, "It happens. I'm sure he'll be here soon, sweetie. Probably stuck in traffic."

The comfortable lie did little to lighten her mood, but she nods anyway in a show of appreciation. "You know, that martini sounds good."

"Which one would you like?"

Allison shrugs. "I don't know the menu that well. Give me your favorite, as long as it has alcohol."

The server gives an "everything will be okay" smile and walks away.

The screen on her phone lights up as she unlocks it. Still no missed calls, texts, or voicemails of any sort. She dials her father's number.

The rings go by unanswered. His voicemail picks up as the server returns with her martini. "Hey, Dad. It's Allison, your daughter. We had reservations tonight. You know, for my birthday. I hope you're all right and all, but … call me back. I'd like to see someone I know tonight."

The server returns holding a pale green martini rimmed with a light brown-looking salt. "I got you a cucumber martini. Had the bartender add some extra vodka." He offers a warm smile. "Who says getting schwasty can't look classy?"

Allison looks at the martini. "Thanks. Looks delicious." She runs her finger over the rim, then licking it off, tries to figure out what it is.

"Celery salt, dear. Goes with the cucumber flavor."

"Thanks." She turns from her martini to the server. "I'll take the check. I don't think he's coming."

"Date stood you up? He doesn't know what he's missing." The server attempts to bolster her spirit.

Shaking her head, she answers, "Dad. Supposed to celebrate my birthday. The big two- one."

The server searches for something to say. "Well, I might not be your dad, honey, but no one should have to pay for drinks on their birthday. I got this."

"You don't know me. You shouldn't have to pay for it."

"Pay?" A small laugh escapes the server. "No, honey. I'm gonna tell the manager you didn't like it. No biggie."

Allison offers her first sincere smile of the evening. "Much appreciated. I guess I will take those egg rolls. No wait. The blue cheese and buffalo chicken doodads."

"Coming right up. Happy birthday."

Her attention turns toward the television at the bar playing out the nightly news after some sporting event ended. The reporter smiles, reading the teleprompter. The restaurant television's muted volume forces Allison to read the subtitles about the ongoing search for Connor DeSalvo and his possible involvement in the murder of Nick DeSalvo. "Welcome to your local evening news on this day, February 5, 2021." Without breaking a beat, the reporter flows into the continuing saga. "With no success in finding the whereabouts of Connor DeSalvo, still wanted in connection with the murder of Nick DeSalvo, police are once again turning to the public. A reward of one thousand dollars is being offered for any information that leads directly to him. Anyone with information should call their local police department. And now a word from our sponsors."

At the conclusion of that segment, she sucks down half the martini, turning from the television to the surrounding patrons, refusing to see if the news denigrates her love even further than before.

Pulling out her phone again, she dials Scarlett, knowing the voicemail will be answering. "Hey, Scar. Just wanted to hear your voice. It's my birthday today, and it's not going so well. Just thought your voice would provide a little pacifyering or pacifercation or whatever it's called. Soothing. Damn, half a martini and I'm feeling it. Anyway, I hope you're healing up okay. Sure could use the company right 'bout now. Love ya, girl."

After ten minutes of watching others enjoy time with friends and loved ones, the buffalo sauce and blue cheese chicken doodads arrive. She enjoys them along with one more, different- flavored martini, hoping against hope that her father will arrive. In the end, after finishing the appetizer, she pays the bill, leaving a generous tip to make up for the free drinks.

Vistrus sits in his home office, surrounded by Inessa's diaries, drowning in the sea of entries and coded information she left for him. The drawn shades taped shut to the walls block out the passage of time. The only light source in the room emanates from his desk lamp.

He flips between three passages open before him in three different journals. Muttering to himself as his focus bounces back and forth, he misses the call buzzing on his cell phone next to him. Perhaps had he not been so focused, he would have paid attention and seen his daughter's name on the screen. Had he answered, he would have been given a stern reminder that today is not a regular day; today is her birthday. But he does not answer and does not get the reminder. He does not get to be with his only daughter on this, her twenty-first birthday.

Instead, his brain makes connections he previously had missed, overlooked, or otherwise hadn't seen. "The Body" mentioned numerous times throughout her earlier writings, especially when still back in Russia, had become "The Council." Vistrus cannot fathom how he missed what now seems like such a simple connection. But that is the way. All things seem obvious once the dots have been connected. Once the bigger picture comes into focus, all the little things that seemed out of place before now find where they belong. Still, he can't help wondering why the change in name. He wonders why Inessa, his love, his wife, his soulmate, never told him about The Body or its transition into The Council.

He sits pondering the meaning of a name, thinking about what The Great Bard said of a rose and being just as sweet under any other name. But why the change, he wonders. Change occurs with purpose, either for or against. A thought crosses his mind, thinking back to what he and Eleanor spoke about in the diner. That things within The Nation change, if only so history and those seeking out the mysteries of the world do not see the same thing for too long a period. But the timing seems a little suspect to him. Why, though, he cannot quite place.

What is the point? What is the point? What is the point? He thinks to himself over and over, searching for the reason this was done.

He eyes the third passage, the last one when Inessa wrote of the murders. His eyebrow raises as a theory strikes him. *The Body used the serpentine walls of The Mind for their chambers… make sense now. But how were they related to the change in name and the five murders she was sent to secretly investigate?* That thought lingers for longer than he feels comfortable with.

After a half-hour more contemplating the matter at hand, an urge hits that he must relieve. He closes the diaries, scanning his home office for prying eyes or any ears that the walls may have grown. A silly paranoia, he's sure, but it is not a chance he will take. He closes the diaries and locks the door behind him while he excuses himself to the restroom.

Eleanor sits on the old couch in her living room, holding the unrolled parchment in one hand and twirling her locket in the other. The hand on her locket rubs it over and over while she contemplates the meaning of the drawn impossibility. The evening light shines through the windows, casting moving shadows from the windblown branches outside. Jazz standards play softly on her stereo, but even with the music, she senses something.

She pauses the twirl of her locket, rolling up the parchment. Her ears concentrate on the sounds around them. She cannot pick up a heartbeat or breathing but hears rustling right outside her door. She whips her gaze in that direction to see if she can catch a glimpse of what it might be before it scurries off, but no whip was needed.

Outside the front door window stands Bishop. While there is a smile on his face, Eleanor does not buy the friendly attire it wears. Something inside her tells her that there's more to this visit than a friendly hello. Perhaps it is the years of him harboring unrequited feelings for her, or maybe it's a woman's intuition. Either way, she answers the door with her proverbial guard up. Still holding onto the parchment but the locket tucked back into her shirt, she greets him.

"What can I do for you this evening?" She keeps it polite but uninviting.

Bishop glances down at the parchment in her hand. Before he can speak, his gaze fixes on the paper for longer than he would like. Catching himself locked in the stare, he shakes himself back to the question at hand. "In the neighborhood. Thought I'd stop by."

"Why?" Eleanor drops the nicety, opting for curtness.

Bishop sighs. "Even after all these years, my feelings have not diminished. Though that's not why I am here."

"Then why mention it?" She pushes back.

"To remind you that you don't have to be alone." He glances down at the parchment again.

"Hmmm," she says, leaving the fault in his words alone for the moment. "Who says I'm alone? I'm an old woman, Bishop. I have friends and family. Romantic flights of fancy are not priorities for me. I'm too old to pursue such youthful endeavors."

He gestures to the parchment. "Youthful pursuit or not, it looks like someone fancies you. A gift, I presume?"

She shakes her head. "Not for me. For someone else."

"I see." He steps back from the entryway. "Well, I didn't mean to dampen your evening. Only to check in on your well-being. Sorry if that makes me a bad person."

She shakes her head, amused at his wording. "Of all the things that make you a bad person, checking in on someone's well-being is not one of them. Checking in under the pretense of something else is another matter."

His hands turn up in admitted discovery. "May I come in then? Talk?"

Shaking her head, she lets him down. "Perhaps another night, Bishop. I have things to tend to."

A nod shows his defeat. "Well, then. Goodnight, Eleanor."

She closes the door as he turns to walk away. Watching him enter his car and drive off, she can't help but wonder what his intentions were. Though, the parchment she taps against the door while deep in thought gives her a vague idea.

Washing his hands, Vistrus stares at himself in the bathroom mirror, wondering how he has fallen so far from where his thoughts on The Council and The Nation stood only a few years ago. It does not take him long to run through the slew of murders affecting him, his daughter, his friends, fellow council members, and his community, to realize the lack of action taken eventually takes its toll on those affected. His eyes, weighed heavy with sadness, stare into his soul, searching for the answers to the questions he has yet to ask. He stares, trying to find the answer as to how he could have been so blind and for so long—wondering what could have been done before to prevent the casualties or *if* anything could have been done.

His stare turns from the man in the mirror to the mirror itself: the oval shape and brushed nickel frame. He looks around the room, searching his memories of happier times, of times when he and Inessa were happy. He remembers times when she was alive, but happiness can be an elusive companion. He turns back to stare at his reflection, but a memory hits. A time when she tore the mirror off the wall. A time when he thought she was worse than ever, but he now thinks she may have been clearer than ever. He takes the mirror off the wall, leaning it against the wall opposite the sink. He exits to his bedroom just through the door and calls Eleanor from his land line.

"Eleanor. I have to do something, and I think you will want to see it."

He pauses, listening to her response.

"If that is so, then there is no time like now. Come over."

The gray clouds overhead signal the coming rain. A portent not lost on Inessa, even as she mutters to herself, walking through the side streets of West Haven. The occasional car passing by sends her eyes jumping about for anyone else who might now be in the area. She counts on her fingers over and over the numbers one through five while thinking about some thought she cannot process—stuck in a loop she cannot escape.

Approaching the street corner, her eyes peer up at the sign that reads "N. Oketo Ave," keeping mental track of her location while wandering aimlessly. Walking past the sign, the empty park swings catch her eye, providing a nice place to stop and rest for a moment.

Sitting on it, she kicks her legs out enough to rock the swing a little. Soft motions calm her as the gray clouds creep closer overhead. A distant thunder rumbles her way, but she remains seated, swaying back and forth. She watches the storm clouds creep over the white clouds, covering them in a signal of the impending rain. Still, she smiles at the world around her. Looking out at the giant field fitted with three small baseball diamonds, built especially for little league games. Even the tennis courts have been refurbished—one having been modified for pickleball. Images of a growing Allison playing on the swings, slides, and trappings of the park play out in her mind as she chats with imaginary moms, all of whom watch their children play.

Another roll of thunder brings in the start of the rain, snapping Inessa from her thoughts. Her sway is thrown off balance, not by the distant lightning crawling closer but by

Eleanor standing a few feet away. Inessa looks around the park for any other persons she may have missed while daydreaming about her daughter but finds it is only the two of them. She notices the pale tint of Eleanor's face and a sallowness to her that does not seem correct.

"Eleanor, why are you out in this weather? You don't look so good. You look like the weather. A bit off."

"I feel fine. Maybe a little under the weather, so to speak. Though the same could be asked of you." Eleanor steps toward her, also scanning for other people. "Why don't we go inside? We're getting all wet."

Inessa nods. "I don't mind the rain. I'll dry off, eventually. Always do. That's the thing about water."

Eleanor walks toward the doors leading into the park's indoor basketball court and game night concession stand. "You might not mind, but I do."

They find the doors are locked, leaving them outside. Eleanor turns to Inessa. "Well, I guess wet it is."

"You'll dry. I promise. Water has a funny way of seeping into places we don't want it to. Hard to get out once it's in … but we dry, and everything is as it was. Eventually…" Inessa loses her train of thought.

Eleanor hugs the building, staying under the awning to avoid the rain. Inessa stands away from the doors, enjoying the summer shower. She again notices Eleanor's complexion and fading color. "You sure you're all right?"

"I've lived a long time. I'll be fine. Always am. Are you sure you're holding up okay?"

Inessa steps toward Eleanor. "Things are wrong. I know, I know, it's always the same old song from Inessa. But it's there."

Eleanor leans in. "What's there?"

"The Body. The Mind." Inessa double taps her temple. *"I know the why behind why The Body is no more. I know the answers to it all. But nobody listens. Nobody sees what comes from angles. They only look ahead and to the sides."*

Eleanor's smile fades upon hearing Inessa's words.

Lightning strikes overhead, blinding Inessa for a split second. But a second is all it took for Eleanor's pale face to be replaced by someone else entirely.

"You?!" Inessa chokes out the solitary word.

The man standing before her is not Eleanor. His lumberjack frame imposes itself, hovering over Inessa's rain-soaked form.

"So, this is where it all ends?" Inessa knows the inevitable is at hand.

"All you had to do was look the other way. Keep your report simple and move on. Those back home wouldn't have known." The threat inlaid into his words shines like diamonds.

"They don't. They never did. I never wanted to put anyone in danger." Her pleas ring true but on uncaring ears. *"No one here knows. We don't have to do this. I won't tell a soul."*

"Perhaps not now. But I know the weight you carry, Inessa. I can see it eating away at you."

Inessa backs away, trying to find a safe path to run in the rain to escape.

The rain turns into a downpour as lightning brightens the sky in short flashes.

The man closes in on her, grabbing her by the neck before she can react.

"*You have no idea the lengths we go for love.*" *The threat of his words implants on her with a gentle squeeze of her neck to remind her that he has control.*

"*To keep our loved ones safe, I know exactly how far I'd go.*" *She knows the words she speaks and the battle she faces, knowing she cannot win. She stares into the man's eyes, searching for a glimmer of hope that this will not end the way she knows it will, but finds nothing. The rain beats down harder than moments before. She pulls out a small, uncorked 21-gram vial and holds it up so he can see it. She stares at the man as he tosses looks bordering on disbelief between her and the vial, unwilling to respond. Moments seem like hours as the mania grows in the man's eyes. Inessa does nothing to stop what's next. Instead, turning her thoughts inward toward her husband and infant daughter. Succumbing to what she knows is next, she asks, "And for whose love is it that you go through these lengths?"*

A menacing smile crosses his face as lightning flashes again. A booming thunder shakes the surrounding buildings, masking the sound of the lumberjack man snapping Inessa's neck.

After watching the last light of life fade from her eyes, he calls her name to make sure death carried her off. "Inessa." No response. "Inessa, you there?" He pats her cheek with his free hand, but still no response. Even the falling rain does not cause her to blink. Satisfied she has no life left in her, he drops the body, leaving her and the 21-gram vial to lie as they fall.

"You think the answer to all our questions lies behind your bathroom mirror?" Eleanor's voice shines with doubt.

Vistrus turns to her. "Yes. I wanted you here. I wanted you to hear. Hear the wall. Hear it fall. See it when it first comes out. The truth. The truth. The truth behind the wall."

Eleanor shakes her head; doubt covers her words. "And what if there is no truth behind the wall, Vistrus?"

Vistrus points to the patchwork half-blended and painted over. "It's there. I swear. She must have put it there."

"Vistrus." Eleanor's head hangs low, the meter of his speech reminds her of Inessa close to her death. Fear plants itself in her that Vistrus may hold a similar fate. "I will witness this … disaster. But if nothing turns up … we get you some help." She trails off, seeing the desperation in his eyes. Taking a deep breath, she finishes. "Let's dig in."

Vistrus punches a hole in the wall. Nothing too aggressive, screaming of unresolved anger issues or past teen angst. But strong enough to break the drywall without needing to hit it again.

"Hammers, Vistrus. They make hammers," Eleanor jests.

Vistrus nods. "And Legends do not need hammers."

"You could have hit a pipe."

"No. No pipe. Was not there when I patched it up after Inessa made a mess."

A sad smile crosses her face as she mutters. "And history repeats itself."

Vistrus pulls away the drywall, revealing the entire area he patched up shy of two decades ago.

He steps back, examining the work, but there is nothing out of the ordinary behind the drywall.

Eleanor lays a hand on his shoulder. "It's all right, Vistrus. Sometimes even the best of us can be wrong. We all make mistakes."

Vistrus pulls away, shaking his head. "No mistake. It is here. Somewhere. It has to be. The answer to it all, behind the wall."

Eleanor sweeps an upturned palm at the wall. "Look at it, Vistrus. There's nothing there. Nothing but studs and dust … and pipes are somewhere I'm sure. Nothing now but a wall that needs fixing."

"No. No. I remember. I remember her. She would not have done something for nothing. Everything had purpose. Every purpose in its place."

He peers inside the hole, looking left and right.

"Come on. Why would she have hidden something in a wall when the answers were written down?" Eleanor postulates.

"Protect the family," he offers, still trying to see inside the drywall down behind the sink. "It was always about protecting family. Her family."

Eleanor grabs his shoulder to pull him back, but he resists.

"It is here. It has to be." Determination drips off every word as he crawls into the cabinet under the sink to tear the drywall down toward the floor.

Eleanor steps back, tears form as she witnesses her friend's apparent nervous breakdown. "Vistrus, stop! There's nothing there! It won't do you any good to need to remodel your bathroom for nothing!"

Vistrus does not listen, continuing to tear away piece after piece, throwing it behind him onto the floor like a madman frantically searching a closet or chest.

"Come on, Vistrus. Let me make you a nice cup of tea. Or perhaps buy you a beer. Doesn't that sound nice?"

Vistrus tears away one more piece, leaving only half a foot of drywall left standing under the sink. The sound stops. No more drywall flung near her feet. Only breathing. A soft chuckle escapes him, and he emerges.

Closing the under-sink cabinet, he collapsed against it. Clutched against his chest is the diary. The final number in Inessa's journals, and, if he is correct, the answer to all their questions.

He looks up at her, a soft smile trying to repress itself as his hands clench harder around the diary. His face relaxes; the wiry look of growing insanity dissolves away, leaving the Vistrus that Eleanor has come to know and care about. "Inessa was not crazy, Eleanor. She did not know what else to do. It was always about protecting her loved ones—her family."

Eleanor nods. "What now?"

Looking down at the book, he smiles. "We get our answers."

The spine cracks as he opens the book. Dust of years past poofs off the pages as he begins reading.

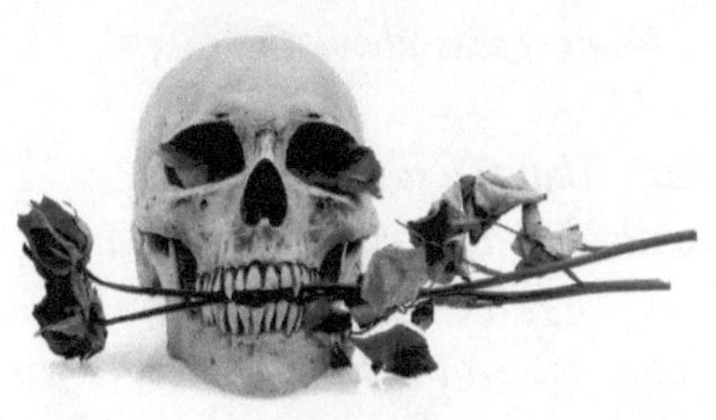

CHAPTER 15

"But is anybody listening?"
~S. Waldgrave~

James McAllister dons a worried smile, standing next to his wife Hillary as she lays covered in sweat, screaming on a hospital bed. At the foot of the bed, Dr. Wong sits on a short stool, head buried between her legs, trying to give updates above her shouts. Behind him, Eleanor and Nick hold hands, watching their grandchild come into the world.

"I can't do this!" Hillary shouts, ignoring the sweat-soaked hair strewn down her face.

James smiles and pats her hand. "You've got this, Hill. Nothing new, right?"

She shoots daggers at him with her eyes. "You try it!"

Eleanor moves to Hillary's side, opposite James. She grabs her other hand. "Breath in. Forget him. Men may try to help. But sometimes…"

Hillary turns her attention to Eleanor. "Yeah, some-times!" she screams as another contraction hits.

Dr. Wong peeks above the sheets. "Almost there! One more push!"

"That's what you said ten pushes ago!" Hillary chastises.

"Breathe in," Eleanor reminds, patting her hand.

"Push!" Dr. Wong urges.

A loud, visceral scream emanates from deep within Hillary, giving one final push, squeezing James's hand to the point he tries to pry her fingers off him.

"There you go, Mrs. McAllister. A beautiful baby girl," Dr. Wong says, standing and turning to tend to the newborn.

Hillary collapses on the bed, huffing in attempts to regain control of herself.

Eleanor sits by Hillary as Nick pulls James aside.

"James," Nick begins, bringing the tone to a more serious note. "We've talked about this moment."

"I know," comes James's solemn response. He stares at a small infant, nestled in a car seat in the corner of the room, oblivious to the world around him. "It still doesn't feel right."

"I understand. This is a situation no parent ever wants to find themselves in. But it is for everyone's protection. You know that no one will be safe if anyone finds out."

"I can't wrap my head around it, though. Who in the world would want to do such a thing?" James's naiveté shines through in his words. "A parent should be in his child's life."

"And you will be. This is what we've been preparing for these past nine months," Nick attempts to reassure him.

"It won't be the same. Hillary won't be the one to help when life gets tough. When she grows up and needs a woman's advice, it won't be from Hills. When she's old enough to understand the dangers of life, of being a Legend, the wisdom won't be from me."

"It may not come out of your mouth, but it will be your advice," Nick offers solace.

"Death is a cruel mistress for an occasion such as this. Can't we give it time?" James pleads.

"Give it time?" Nick asks, unsure of James's direction.

"We have spent the last nine months prepping for one sacrifice. And that time has been amazing, and we've had wonderful friends and family to help us through, but..." James can't bear to finish his thought.

Nick picks up his words. "But to do it, actually go through with it, without any consolation is too much to bear?"

James turns to Hillary as Dr. Wong hands her the newborn child. He watches Hillary coddle and whisper to their daughter. A sad smile crosses her as she caresses the young one's forehead. She strokes the infant's bright red hair, holding back mixed tears of joy and sadness.

"We are already dealing with those who think we are monsters, Nick. Must we be the monsters they think we are? A couple of years. Just a few, and then we will do as we must." James turns to Nick. "But look at her." He ensures Nick sees the maternal joy and sadness painted on Hillary's face. "We can't be the ones to do to ourselves what others are already trying to do. At least not so soon."

Nick takes a moment to respond, weighing all the possible options, variables, and outcomes on his mind. He watches Eleanor and Hillary make googly eyes at the baby in an attempt to conjure a smile. He turns to the infant sleeping in the car seat. His chest weighs heavier with each breath as he comes to a temporary decision.

"What has The Council decided? I had to be kept out of all decisions, Nick. This has not been the joyous nine months I pretended they were. These should have been wonderful times." Desperation clings to James's words.

Nick watches the hospital door crack open, and a hand reaches through the door. Both James and Nick watch as that hand grabs the car seat handle, pulling the sleeping infant out of the room while Hillary attends to the new child. He turns his attention back to James.

"I never told them. They know of fables, myths, legends beyond Legends, and prophecies, but they did not need to know about this," Nick reveals his nine-month secret.

"You kept this from them for nine months? What about all those times I was told to leave?" James asks, concern rising in his voice.

"I told them I was concerned about your position on The Council. They fought against me every chance they could. You are well-liked, but that doesn't mean I trust them with this."

"You tried to get me removed from The Council over this?!" James covers his exasperation so Hillary does not hear.

Nick laughs. "No. You needed time to tend to Hillary and make sure she was tended to. I gave that to you in a way that would raise no suspicion. All's well, James."

"If The Council doesn't know, then what is the big deal? Why even plan this?"

"You know as well as I that there are those that will kill over this. That is something we will not let happen."

"But so soon?" James pleads one last time.

Nick concedes, "It won't be easy knowing the inevitable. Always being on watch and making sure no harm comes will not be wine and roses all hours of every day."

James smiles. "No, it won't. With everything we're already doing, the consolation of extra time is worth the price."

"I hope so," Nick responds, as they both turn to watch their wives nurture the newborn life.

"Let me at least say hello to my child before I have to say goodbye."

The consciousness of the waking world tugs at the veil of sleep, weighing down Scarlett. Her closed eyes pull deeper into dreaming, fighting off the return to reality. Her ears still listen to the words spoken in her dream, playing out for her like an old movie. The visions dancing in her brain dissolve as consciousness tightens its grip.

As sleep fades away, Scarlett can feel something moist and gritty pressing on her face. An unfamiliar sensation she attributes to still being asleep, but it doesn't fade as she moves more and more toward waking. She goes to move her arm but finds resistance and that she cannot move.

Confusion sets in as memories of her attack flash behind her closed eyes. Images of her pale-faced cousin telling her his paleness is nothing but allergies. She remembers something peculiar about him she could not place her finger on. Only that while he looked and sounded like Connor, she did not wholly believe her eyes. Whether it was the idiosyncrasies of his mannerisms, the inflection in his words, or something else, she sensed something was not right. The next memory flashes, showing his hair-covered face with varicose veins pulsating and blood and muscles so massive, even the strongest bodybuilder would be intimidated.

She begins wiggling around, still unable to open her eyes but freeing her arms a little more than before. Still unable to wipe her face, she tries to scream, but the indescribable taste of this moist grit falling into her mouth puts an immediate stop to that. Panic starts overtaking her, realizing she has no idea how she ended up here, if anyone knows where she's at or knows to go looking. Darkness sets back in, making her wonder if what she feels may be some transition into the afterlife. Unable to keep her thoughts at bay, she remembers Connor walking away from her as she leaned against her parents' tombstones, bleeding out and trying desperately to call for help. She tries sitting up, making only minimal progress, pressing her arms harder against the force holding her down, making more leeway. She continues struggling as panic digs deeper, and the air becomes scarce.

Finally, making enough room to move her arms to her face, she begins moving the grit away from her head, pushing it toward where her arms were. She controls her breathing as a tingling sensation warms her body. She can hear the faint sounds of owls hooting their woes. For a moment, she thinks she can even feel the pitter-patter of tiny creatures skittering about. She relaxes further as the warm tingle increases, focusing on the task at hand, pushing all thoughts of how she ended up here aside. She stops moving to bask in the warmth and peace she feels overcoming her.

Her entire body starts stinging with the pins-and-needles sensation accompanied by having a foot fall asleep. She does not feel the awkwardness of having to balance on a foot that hurts with each step. No, her entire body feels the pain of an asleep foot amplified a thousand times over. The air around her grows thin as the pain starts to numb her. Fading back into sleep, she knows this must be the end.

But the hooting owls and pitter-patter still ring through her ears, and a moment of resolution shoots through her being. The tingling pain of a million needles jabbing at her awakens her, and she pushes with all her strength against the grit and grime holding her down. She presses against the ground as she sits up, using every ounce of muscle she has, making it all break away until she feels it all fall away.

A breeze brushes her hair as cool air fills her lungs. She wipes her eyes clean, opens them, and stands to find herself in a shallow hole in a small clearing surrounded by trees. The moonlight provides little illumination from behind its thicket of clouds. She sees no one but hears the owls hoot. Over and over, they sing their warning to keep a distance. As her eyes start to adjust to the darkness, she can see many pairs of glowing eyes hiding behind nearby trees.

"Hello?" she calls out to them. Her voice sounds a little more smokey than she remembers. Perhaps a side effect of death or just from having not spoken in who knows how long.

She watches the eyes shift and float around in the darkness as if hovering close to the ground. They turn to each other, then back toward her. Curious about this new being.

"Hello? Can you…?" The unfamiliar, new timbre of Scarlett's voice stops her from speaking.

Though her words did not go unheard. She watches the floating eyes emerge from the darkness as a nursery of raccoons scurry toward her.

She gasps at the sight, unsure if she should be in awe or fear of the creatures. They stop about halfway to her. She counts five raccoons as they begin chittering with each other but make no further advances.

Scarlett scans her surroundings for anything else that might provide answers to where she is, hearing only the who-who-whooing of the owls.

"Do you understand me? I don't know what happened. Please," she begs the raccoons.

They silence their chatter and crawl toward her before hissing and scattering back toward the darkened forest.

She sits back down, alone once again in a three-foot hole, thinking about what comes next as the reality of the world sets in. She must get home, but before she can rise, fatigue wins, pulling her back to sleep once more.

The elevator door opens. The dark hallway leading to where The Council meets sends a nervous chill through Connor. As he creeps toward them, his ears pick up the sound of a newscast playing in their chamber.

"Welcome to your local evening news on this day, February 5, 2021." Without breaking a beat, the reporter flows into the continuing saga. "With no success in finding the whereabouts of Connor DeSalvo, still wanted for questioning in the murder of Nick DeSalvo, police are once again turning to the public. A reward of one thousand dollars is being offered for any information that leads directly to him. Anyone with information should call their local police department. And now a word from our sponsors."

One Council member clicks off the television from the remote control. They all turn to each other, unaware that Connor stands in the doorway.

"A thousand dollars? Maybe I should turn *myself* in?" He finishes with a soft chuckle as the members turn toward his direction.

"So, you're turning yourself in, then?" a gruff voice adds to the broken silence.

Connor shakes his head. "Just the opposite."

"Time's up, Mr. DeSalvo. No running away this time," a different voice adds.

Connor smirks. "I think we know I can run away if needed. But I have proof."

"I think you misheard me. Time's up. We don't care about your proof. We care about resolution."

An approaching voice chimes in behind Connor. One that is immediately recognizable as Vistrus's. "They may not care about proof, but I do."

"But Vistrus—" a voice starts before being cut off.

"—You walked away from us. Remember?" The gruff voice leaves no room for sympathy.

Vistrus nods. "I may have. There are things in this world that are more important than sitting around a table in a dark basement, contemplating the philosophical consequences of potential action and inaction, debating the existential meaning of it all."

A third voice chimes in as he stands. As the light hits him, it is the same man who helped Brianna when she needed it. "That is an oversimplification of what we do, and you know it."

Vistrus steps into the room. The glare in his eye pierces them, keeping them silent while he paces. "Is it? In all our years, what have we accomplished?" Before any Council members can interject, he continues, "Nothing. We remain silent on any issue that deals with Normals. We protect ourselves and our secrecy at all costs, including covering up murders as tragic accidents. We condone lying to the public as long as it benefits ourselves, and where has that led us?" He eyes each member, ensuring they are still listening. "In the past three years, I have lost ... we have lost members of The Nation. Members who were family to me. And beside me now stands a man who was on his way to becoming a member of this Council. A member who would have much to contribute if it were not for the practice of silencing anything that is not easy ... anything that might paint ourselves in a bad light. So, you say it is too late for him, but I want to hear what he has to say because, given the option between his opinion on this matter and yours, I have come to learn that his is far more valuable. I do not enjoy speaking in tirades, but your inability to see past your noses in times like these infuriates me to no end."

The Council sits in stunned silence. All words that they possess to form some sort of rebuttal have fled their minds, leaving them utterly flabbergasted.

Vistrus turns to Connor. "Before all this, The Council and I spoke on more than one occasion about you replacing your father's seat. Do you remember our conversations?" Connor nods. "In the past, I have prepped future members by letting them sit in on meetings, help with investigations in our society, and the like. But times are different now. You did not have that chance."

A Council member squeaks out a thought. "He still may not."

A guttural growl rumbles from Vistrus, silencing the member. Turning back to Connor, he adds, "You said you had proof?"

Silence falls over the chamber while Connor digs his cell phone out of his pocket. "Here, I have video." He hits play, showing it to Vistrus. As he watches the video, seeing the man shift into someone new, his eyes widen with realization. The video ends, leaving Vistrus slack-jawed at his lack of piecing together the clues Inessa left behind.

Vistrus turns back to The Council. "While Inessa was alive, she … talked in riddles. Always mentioning a 'they' and a 'he.' I never knew what she meant. I never pieced together certain clues. She was not mad. There was never a descent into insanity. She was protecting her family. The murders she was sent to investigate were never meant to be solved, only silenced. And since that time, you have been ensuring that silence be kept. Why? I do not know."

The man from the Tennyson Society stands. "There has never been some cover-up. This is ludicrous, Vistrus."

The Poe Society stands. "I think the time has come for The Council to find a different member of the Coleridge Society to represent us."

Before anyone else can join in, Vistrus dashes to him, transitioning into full Legend form in under a second. "There will be no other. Why I never saw the truth in her words, I do not know. Why my wife felt safer keeping secrets than letting me in, I will never know. But I do know this. This young man will walk free. I will take care of the news outlets and police." Taking a few steps back from the Councilman, Vistrus motions to Connor and himself. "You never knew what came before us. You are all ignorant of The Council that we replaced. We were nothing to The Nation. A figure piece to stave off uncertainty about what we spent a century covering up. And lives have paid the price for it." Vistrus shakes his head, surprised by all the years he failed to see the truth. "We will walk out of here without incident, and all will be well. And when the time comes for Connor DeSalvo to sit on The Council, it will be with none of you. That is not a threat. So do what you will to try to save yourselves and your precious seats in this Nation of ours. But you are not captains and never will be. At the most, we are crewmen. More likely rats. Do not drown on a sinking ship."

A Council member squeaks out, "You cannot simply walk out of here."

Growling his words, he says, "Try me. If a Normal's life, if this Legend's life," he gestures to Connor, "means nothing to you, then why should yours mean anything to me?"

"You'd kill us all?" the member says before swallowing hard.

"Would not be the first time I have eliminated Council members." He sneers.

"Then how does that make you any better than us?" the Council member continues pushes Vistrus's patience.

"Because what I do is for the benefit of all mankind. What you do only benefits those who are like-minded as yourselves."

The Councilmen sit stunned at the truths laid out before them.

Vistrus turns from the members and toward Connor. "Come. We have your name to clear."

Connor adds, "And a girl to see."

Vistrus keeps his voice soft as they walk. "It might take a few days for the news to clear you."

"Does that mean I still need to hide?" Connor sighs.

Vistrus slowly shakes his head. "I shall inform our contact in the police department and start taking care of everything tonight. You will be safe. The court of public opinion is a different matter."

The doors open as Vistrus presses the call button. They step inside, waiting on the doors to close, peering down the hall to what remains of The Council. As the elevator lifts, a thought comes to Connor.

"Mr. Petrovsky…" Connor starts.

"Vistrus. You have earned it."

"Vistrus…" He gestures beyond the elevator doors to the council chamber. "If they are crewmen or rats on some sinking ship, then who's the captain?"

An impressed smile blooms but dies quickly. Vistrus has no concrete answer but responds with soft-spoken words. "I think it is time we find out."

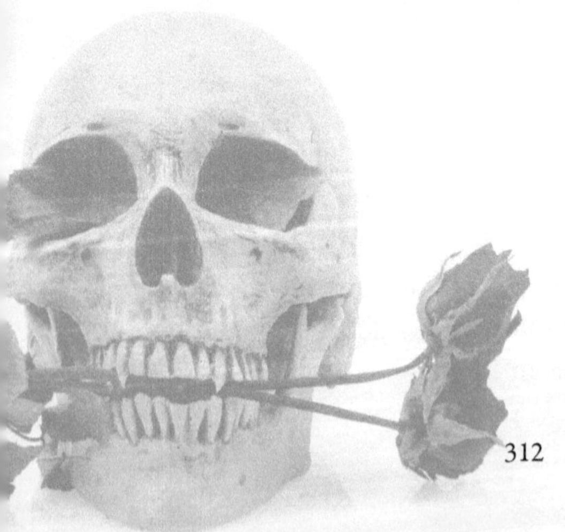

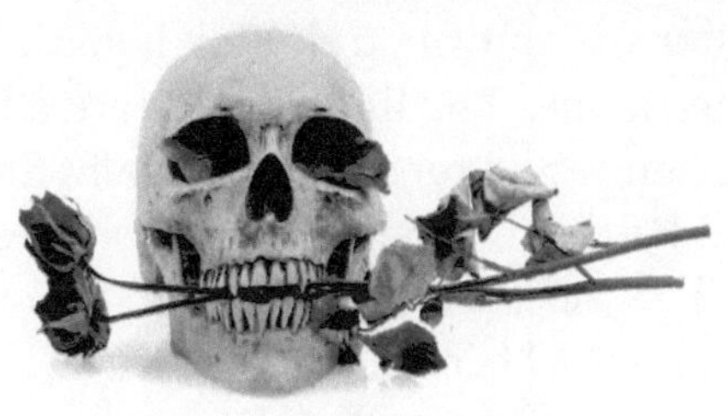

CHAPTER 16

*"Most people are too afraid to listen. The truth
can be hard to hear."*
~T. DeSalvo~

Scarlett exits the forest preserve, taking hesitant steps down the road. Cars blare by her, the sound of the engines and road noise drowning out everything else, including the thoughts in her head. She looks down as the light from the full moon and passing headlights proves too much for her eyes. Each passing car roars louder and louder, the lights more blinding as she walks to her home.

The surroundings are familiar. She knows what streets she is on, and the storefronts are all the same, but something is different. The contrast of the world seems stronger, though the colors are less saturated as her eyes adjust to the car lights, street lamps, and moonlight. She walks the sidewalks, jumping as big rig trucks pass, pondering if this is some strange afterlife or just another night in West Haven.

After making the trek back home, she stands outside her home. The lights inside are off, and Connor is not home. She turns the handle to find the door is locked. Patting down her pockets, she realizes that she either lost the key digging herself out of the grave or whoever buried her must have taken it. Then a memory of Allison surfaces, telling her about a dream she had where Allison buried Scarlett. She remembers Allison not liking this dream, trying to brush it off as if it was not something worth putting time into. But to Scarlett, who else would have buried her the way she was buried? Who else would have known to do such a thing?

The pocket pat down she gave herself revealed no cell phone either. She wants to make it to Allison's, but Grandma Eleanor is closer, so she heads there. This time, lights are on inside the house, and her smiling Grandma answers the door.

"Scarlett! Come in, come in!" Eleanor ushers her grandchild inside. "Sit, sit. You must be starving." She leads Scarlett to the kitchen to sit at the table. After making Scarlett sit, she grabs a glass of water and some cookies from a cookie jar. "Eat, child." She wraps her arms around her after placing the food and water down. "I am over the moon that you are here."

Scarlett looks around the room before turning her attention to the plate of creme cookies piled high. Her gaze turns to her grandmother, still deciding what to say.

Eleanor looks Scarlett over. "Once you eat, you can take a nice, long shower."

"I woke up," is all Scarlett manages. She takes a sip, testing the water. The feel of it on her tongue makes her realize how thirsty she is, causing her to guzzle the whole glass.

"Eat," Eleanor repeats, pointing at the plate.

Scarlett takes a bite and smiles. Her hunger overtakes her, and she starts stuffing cookie after cookie in her mouth.

After letting Scarlett wolf down a few cookies, she asks, "Do you remember anything?"

Scarlett nods but does not let up on shoveling cookies into her gullet.

"Do you feel okay enough to tell me?" Eleanor urges.

Without swallowing, Scarlett lets crumbs fall as she speaks. "I was at the cemetery, visiting Mom and Dad." She tries to catch some crumbs that evade capture. "Connor came by. He seemed off. Like he wasn't all there. Distracted." She swallows the last of the cookies she was chewing and starts on a new one in a much more civilized manner. "He said something, then attacked me."

Eleanor butts in. "Do you remember what he said?"

Scarlett shakes her head. "The next thing I remember, I'm lying against their tombstones, and he's walking away. But as he walked away, something happened. It might have been the sun, my fading sight, a combination, I don't know."

Eleanor remains calm. "What did you see, dear?"

Scarlett slows down, trying to recall the moment correctly. "He changed. As he walked away. Like maybe the light flared off him or something. I don't know, but it looked like he became someone else."

"What did this someone else look like? Can you describe him?" Eleanor urges.

"Big, burly. Like one of the loggers you see on that weird sports channel." She sees Eleanor is a bit lost. "Those sports where the guys in flannel see who can chop wood the fastest." Scarlett watches as Eleanor catches on. "Grams, Connor wouldn't kill anyone, especially family. Would he?"

"There seems to be a lot of people asking that question lately," Eleanor lets slip. "But Connor cannot do what you described." The distance in Eleanor's voice plants a question in Scarlett.

Scarlett looks up from staring at the dwindling plate of cookies. "Do you know someone who can?"

Eleanor brings herself back to the moment with a huff. "Let's get you washed up, my dear." She takes the remaining cookies and places them back in the jar, sneaking one for herself. "You know where the towels are. Take your time, Scarlett."

Scarlett stands and turns to head to the bathroom. "What happened after? Why was I buried?"

"Shower. I'll explain everything once you freshen up." Eleanor dismisses her with a smile.

Scarlett shuffles down the hall to the shower. Entering the bathroom, she turns on the light and looks into the mirror. She stumbles back, stunned by what she sees. Copper-red hair no longer graces her head. No. Now, medium brown locks frame her face—nothing too light that could be mistaken for a dirty blonde and nothing too dark that could be thought black. Her face sports no freckles. Nothing to denote her signature Irish ancestry. She knows not all Irish women have freckles but, thanks in part to Brianna, she has come to appreciate the feature she once despised. She presses her fingers into her face, wiping away the dirt to find the freckles underneath, but none are there to find.

"It's still me," she says, turning to look herself in the eye. But the face staring back is not hers. Her eyes are no longer the pale blue that have always stared back in the mirror. Now they are dark brown, almost black irises. She stares, unsure what to think of the unwanted makeover, unsure how to react to something so strange. After a few more minutes of inspecting herself in the mirror and getting acquainted with her new features, she turns on the shower to clean up. Having come to terms, at least momentarily, with the new her, her thoughts turn to the awaiting conversation with Grandma about why she isn't dead and how she came back.

Allison's mother's diaries cover her bed. She sits in the middle of them, trying to absorb all her mother wrote, re-reading entries she's read a thousand times before. Searching for something new. Searching for something that can give her some clue she can use to better understand the life of hers that has gotten so far away.

Flipping through one journal, she scans an entry mentioning the piano and a lithograph from their wedding that hangs above the piano in their new home. Allison checks the date of the entry. This home her mother wrote about is her home, but she has never seen such a picture before. The only picture Allison remembers above the piano is of her mother. That way, Vistrus can look upon her when he plays in the living room. But the entry also mentions what the safekeeping of the picture provides for them all.

Allison smirks at the futility of safekeeping, but it makes her wonder what could be behind them. She continues reading the following entry. Her mother talks of their 21-grams and needing hers kept safe if something should happen. *So?* Allison wonders. *What did happen? Perhaps the wall behind the picture will hold a clue.*

Allison closes all the diaries around her. She stacks them in neat piles in chronological order of when they were written. She places them in her father's office, back on the bookshelves. A wanting to make everything perfect for later settles into her.

"Grams! Am I dead?!" Scarlett shouts in a tone almost far too casual for the words spoken, towel-drying her hair after a long shower. She wipes the condensation off the mirror, awaiting Grandma Eleanor's response. Tugging on her hair and pulling down her bottom eyelid, as if to find some dye or contact that can be removed to reveal the traits she's come to know, Scarlett finds they are still no longer there.

"Grams?!" she shouts again, exiting the bathroom, wrapped in a towel.

The kitchen table has been cleaned and restocked with fresh glasses filled with ice and a pitcher of lemonade sits in the center. Scarlett notices a picture frame facing away, sitting against the wall next to the table.

"Lemonade, Grams?" Scarlett takes a seat.

Eleanor closes the freezer door, holding a bag of shortbread cookies. "Thought you might like more. I made these for you when you first entered the Waiting."

"The what-ing?" She snatches a cookie out of the bag. "Frozen cookies?"

Eleanor nods, gesturing for Scarlett to try one. "The things Ken and Tracy never taught you and Connor. Freezer cookies are the best cookies. And they last ages longer." She grabs one for herself and bites off a piece. "The Waiting. It's a period of convalescence. A Normal would already be dead, as would a Legend if their 21-grams weren't in a vial. We never know how long it may last. So, I grabbed you some clean clothes, charged your cell phone, and cleaned the house. Something nice for you after such a traumatic experience."

Scarlett's attention is focused more on the cookie than her grandmother's words. A lack of focus, not unseen by Eleanor.

"And so, the giant mushroom grows from your head, preventing the forest nymphs from entering and possessing your healing corpse."

Scarlett is still enjoying the cookies too much to pay attention.

"Then the six-foot-tall elf made his way through the candy cane forest and swirly gumdrops."

The last words finally catch Scarlett's attention. "Gumdrops? I'm sorry, these cookies are fire, Grams."

Eleanor nods in unsure acceptance of the compliment. "I hope 'fire' is a good thing. Good enough to not pay attention to me when you asked a question."

"I didn't know I was still so hungry." She finishes the cookie and swipes her hands together a few times to get off any clinging crumbs. "You have my full attention now. Mushrooms, candy canes, and gumdrops."

Shaking her head, Eleanor chuckles as she grabs the frame, keeping the picture hidden from Scarlett. "No mushrooms, candy canes, or gumdrops. Just know that no, you aren't dead and are, in fact, very much alive. Albeit a beautiful brunette now instead of a ravishing redhead."

Scarlett scrunches her face, still uncomfortable with the new look. She pours herself a glass of lemonade and takes a big sip before pulling the cup away in surprise. Wincing, she coughs. "Grandma Eleanor!"

Laughing, Eleanor shrugs. "Trust me. You'll need a good drink."

"I thought this was lemonade!" Scarlett says, still shocked.

"It is," Eleanor confirms. "Just with some added vodka."

"That's no longer lemonade; it's a screwdriver."

"Ah poh-tay-toe, poh-tah-toe."

"More like potato, fermented potato."

Both ladies chuckle as Scarlett pours her grandmother a glass. They both clink in a silent cheer and sip to what's next.

Scarlett's pointed finger gestures to the picture frame. "What's that?"

"The Grey Fairy was a prophecy. The second child born to a Legend would unite the Normals and Legends. It was a whole vague prophecy that was supposed to manifest."

Scarlett searches the depths of her mind for something that brings this around. She nods as something clicks. "I think I remember. Something about Aunt Tracy. Why they were killed."

Eleanor nods, relinquishing a sad smile at the thought. "Well, the reason they were killed is that someone may have been trying to stop the prophecy. A prophecy that had already happened about twenty-one years earlier."

"I don't understand."

"We weren't sure when it happened. No one wanted to risk taking any chances. We had to do something to keep everyone safe. There was no way to know if you were the first or only a coincidence."

"The first what? I don't understand what's going on."

Eleanor takes a deep breath, searching for the right words to say. "We needed proof. Proof that you were the one. But no one wanted to chance it. It looks like we were right."

"I'm what, Grams? What are you talking about?"

Eleanor turns the frame around to reveal Scarlett's face drawn on the charcoal portrait.

"What does a drawing of me have to do with anything? Are you okay?"

Nodding, she continues, "You are the Grey Fairy. There is a reason you have been protected for so long. They've been watching you from a distance for all these years. To protect you, your parents, and … well, there is something else."

"Something else besides the ludicrousness of this whole situation? Besides the Grey Fairy, the rising from the dead like some David Blaine illusion, and some secret, nameless protectors watching me from a distance? Sound like stalkers to me." Scarlett sips her drink.

"Yes," Eleanor starts. "But you didn't rise from the dead because you weren't dead. And your protectors are not nameless. You've known them for years. Raymond and December."

Scarlett lets out a bellowing laugh. "Yeah. Some story you got there, Grams. The school janitor and lunch lady are really superheroes on a mission to protect me cause I'm just that important. I mean telepathy is one thing, but this… come on, Grams."

Eleanor takes a deep breath, hoping Scarlett's thoughts calm down.

But Scarlett continues laughing at the absurdity of the whole situation. She shakes her head, downing the screwdriver. "You're right. I did need this. There's no way you're not losing it right now. Someone approaches you with some charcoal thing and is like, 'Hey, she's the one,' and you accept this as truth?"

"I still haven't told you the last thing, Scarlett."

"Oh, I'm sorry, Grams. Yeah, what's this one last thing? Cause being told I have school employee protectors who have been watching me and my parents—" She catches her words, and they stop her like a concrete wall stops a speeding truck. "My parents?"

Inhaling, Eleanor picks her next words carefully. "That's what I was getting at. They are still alive. They've been watching you grow and live, but they had to stay away to keep you safe. To keep your sister safe."

Scarlett waves her arms, stopping the conversation. "Woah, woah, woah. So, not only are you telling me that I'm some weird chosen one but that my parents never really died, and I also have a long-lost sister I never knew about. Why? Why tell me all this? Why be like, 'Hey, glad you woke up from some buried-alive experiment, but yeah you also have a sibling and parents who abandoned you'? No, people don't do that. Not without good reason."

Eleanor's eyes turn toward the portrait. "This piece of art is over one hundred years old. There's no way it is only a coincidence."

"My parents abandoned me because of a piece of paper? Some portrait that was drawn decades ago that bears a resemblance to me? What kind of parents did I have?!" Scarlett pours another screwdriver and gulps half of it.

"It's not like that, young lady. Legends can't carry more than one child—"

"Oh, I remember. Our lady hormones don't like it. Mr. Petrovsky told us all about it after the crazy cop and his wife killed them." Scarlett shakes her head, regressing back to denial of it all. "Some town we live in!"

"Well, they weren't the first to have a second child. Hillary and James were."

"And I'm the second child? And you believe all this because some person tells you that my parents are still alive and guess what, I also have a sister?!" Scarlett finishes her glass of vodka and lemonade.

Eleanor mutters to herself, "I knew this wasn't the best way to handle things." She turns to her grand-daughter. "Think back to all the times you were at the cemetery, talking to your parents. What was always the same?"

Scarlett thinks for a moment but shakes her head. "They were always dead. Their tombstones were always in the same spot." She shrugs. "I don't know what you are looking for."

"Was there not always a groundskeeper nearby? Someone always tending to the area not too far from where you were speaking?"

Scarlett thinks back to her visits. A groundskeeper forms in her memory. Someone raking leaves or bent over near other tombstones, polishing them. A funeral director stands not too far off … someone who looks extraordinarily similar to the maintenance man.

"I went about the same time in the week. It was probably the same schedule he had. Cleaning and maintaining that section."

"Every time you were there?"

The situation that crashed and sped up again comes to another grinding halt as Scarlett realizes the coincidences that can't be denied.

Eleanor continues. "Think about the last time you were there. When you were attacked. Where was he then?"

Scarlett tries to remember, racking her brain for some image of him. "He wasn't." Her eyes go wide. "Was he the guy who attacked me? Did the groundskeeper try to kill me?!"

"He's your father. He's been keeping an eye on you, listening to everything you told them all these years."

"Why?! Why would you do this?!"

"To keep everyone safe. To keep The Nation secret and protected, and to wait for a time when you were old enough to find out."

Scarlett grows angry. "And for half my friends and family to die! This is all their fault. All your fault!"

Eleanor grabs Scarlett's hands to calm her down. "It's no one's fault except those who killed. We were waiting for you to transition. We were waiting for you to find out your true self until we laid all this on you. But things happened."

"Understatement of the century."

"Perhaps. But you have to understand. Your safety. The safety of The Nation rests on this secret."

"I don't think we can keep this a secret much longer. People have already died for this stupid prophecy."

Eleanor resigns to Scarlett's words. "You're right. I think someone may already suspect you, and we all are in greater danger than we thought."

Scarlett shakes her head at the ludicrousness of the situation. "I can't deal with this right now. I have to go see Allison and let her know I'm fine, alive, whatever. We'll talk after."

Scarlett rises, downing the glass of alcoholic lemonade, and huffs out the door.

Eleanor sits, making no effort to further add fuel to the young Legend's fire. "Wait until your parents get to say hi," she whispers to herself, watching Scarlett run down the driveway.

CHAPTER 17

"Or that the words they hear are a reflection of themselves."

~J. McAllister~

A hammer smashes against the wall where the picture of her mother, Inessa, hung moments ago as Allison tries to ignore the nightly news playing out on the television. A small hole reveals a shelf built into the drywall, holding two vials. She grabs them both, examining them for some sign of which one might be hers. Her eyes scan the couch for the remote control. She cares not about listening to the news talk about the decline of the world in a most cheerful fashion. She turns back to the two-inch tall vials containing swirling smoke inside. Both are glass and unlabeled, stopped with plain cork. Even the bottoms are seemingly plain. The only difference is one is etched with the number one and the other etched with the number twenty-two. Assuming they are nothing more than lot numbers, she takes a guess at which might be hers. *What's the worst that could happen?* she thinks.

Before she can uncork the vial, her attention is drawn to the television as she hears the blonde reporter in a blue dress speak her boyfriend's name. She glances at the graphic, a picture of him taken during a baseball game with the words "Suspect in the murder of Nick DeSalvo." "In the ever-developing story of the murder of West Haven's own, Nick DeSalvo…" Allison grabs the remote, shutting off the television before being forced to listen to more slander, then tosses it back on the couch.

The ringtone of her cell phone jabs at her ear, trying to pull her away from this moment. She checks the caller ID to see Bri's name. A sad smile sprouts, then fades. She rejects the call and turns her phone off before slipping it back into her pocket.

Uncorking the vial numbered twenty-two, she returns to her interrupted thought, *Let's find out.*

The smoke escapes, dissipating into the air. Allison looks herself over, feeling no different from a moment ago. *I hope that was it.* She thinks to herself. *I don't want to mess with Dad's.* Placing the cork back on the empty vial, she places them both back on the shelf. She hangs her mother's picture back to cover the hole and stares at her, wondering what she would think now if she saw her doing this. She wonders what sort of life Inessa had planned for them before it all went wrong. Allison stares into the pictured woman's melancholy eyes, hoping they eventually found peace before looking at the six wavy lines in the background, pondering their purpose. Giving up that train of thought, she looks down, noticing bits of drywall dust coating the top of the piano.

Not wanting to leave a mess, she grabs some paper towels and cleaner from the kitchen and wipes up the mess. Before putting the cleaner back, she looks over the area. Happy with her work, she throws out the paper towels and puts the cleaning solution away.

"Hey Al, thanks for burying me. Long time no talk," Scarlett rehearses what she wants to say while she walks to Allison's. "That won't do." She shakes her head. "Hey. I just wanted to say thanks for saving my life. Sorry I … stayed dead so long. Who the hell says that?" Scarlett quickens her pace. "Al, how do you like the new hair? New hair?" Scarlett laughs at herself. "So, the 'rents are alive and well. How you doin'? I'm some stupid prophecy, fancy a drink?" She laughs at her words. "What is wrong with me? I look like a looney talking to myself. Plus, it's Allison. Not like we haven't spent time apart… We have… I think." She grunts, clearing her mind as her pace quickens to a jog for about half a block before her stamina drains her. She stops, struggling for breath but finding it.

After a few moments of panting on the street corner like someone in the middle of hardcore marathon training, she turns her head, catching a news segment playing on a television through a store window. There are no subtitles for her to read and no volume to listen to, but the graphic on display next to the blonde reporter in a blue dress raises an alarm. It is a picture of Connor DeSalvo taken during a baseball game, and under the picture are the words, "Suspect in the murder of Nick DeSalvo." Watching the news clip a moment longer, a red circle with a diagonal line through it is laid over him.

"What the hell is going on? Connor? Grandpa Nick?" she whispers, watching as the news segment changes to reports of a land grab dispute between Six Flags and the World Health Organization. "Oh, a new Six Flags would be cool," she says, momentarily forgetting her cousin is being sought after by the cops in one capacity or another. Her attention turns back to her trek to Allison's.

She thought a personal appearance would be the proper way to greet her friend, but now she wonders if a phone call preparing her would be an easier way to settle in. Dialing Allison's number, she continues her walk, but voicemail picks up before it even rings. She hangs up, favoring the personal appearance approach after all.

Allison closes the bathroom door behind her, leaving it unlocked. She places her iPod and dock on the sink counter, plugging it in and turning it on. Searching her library, she stops at a song before enabling the repeat function. She turns on the bathwater, finding a comfortable temperature.

While the water runs, she heads to her bedroom, grabbing the dream journal and pen from her nightstand. As she goes to leave, a thought interrupts her. She pulls her cell phone from her pocket, thinking about the missed call from Bri. For a small moment, she holds the phone, contemplating turning it on to see if Bri left a text or voicemail. A pain wrings her stomach, sending a wave of nausea at the thought of the screen shining to life and not finding either of those things. She rubs the phone like it's a small pet who has lived past its prime before placing it face down on the nightstand. Turning to leave, she looks back at the phone, trying to convince herself that there is something there for her, if only she'll trust herself. But she does not. She leaves it there, exiting and passing by the linen closet, grabbing a clean towel.

Back in the bathroom, she plugs the drain, letting the tub fill up a bit as she undresses.

Carefully folding all her clothes, she stacks them neatly on the closed toilet lid, putting down her jeans first, then her shirt, bra, underwear, and socks. Straightening them, she ensures they are picture-perfect before placing the folded towel on top. She opens the cabinet, grabbing the pack of snap-in-half razors used for straight blades. Taking one from the pack of five, she snaps it and replaces the rest in the cabinet, closing the door. She holds her hand over the corner, making sure the magnet that keeps the sink cabinet shut does not loosen. She sets the blade on the corner edge of the tub.

Allison looks around the bathroom one last time, making sure everything is in its place. Satisfied, she steps into the tub, lowering herself. The only thing she wears are the black onyx earrings Connor gave her for her eighteenth birthday. She lays her head against the back of the tub as the rushing water fills around her. She rubs her fingers on her earrings in some hope that their reminder will stop her from what she has planned next.

The moonlight provides minimal coverage this night for Connor to sneak up to Allison's house, but it is a chance he feels he must take. These last few months have not been easy on Allison and him. He has avoided her calls out of a need to keep her safe and him away from anyone who might be tracking him. An endlessly repeated cycle he wants to end.

He scans the surrounding area, looking for anyone who might be following but sees no one. Feeling safe in his position, he knocks on the door. Bending his ear to listen for footsteps, he hears no movement inside. He tries the doorbell, but still, no footsteps stir within. Wanting to talk with her, he tries the front door, but it is locked. He skulks around past sliding patio doors to the back door, finding it also locked.

He pulls out his cell phone and turns it on, hid-ingas much out of sight as he can while the phone loads up. After it does, and making sure the GPS is turned off, he dials Allison.

He stands, anxious for her to pick up and hear her voice. But the only voice he will hear is her voicemail.

"Hey, baby. I know I've been less than stellar as of late, again. I had to, but it's almost over. With everything going on, I had to keep everyone safe. Like your father said, find a place no one will find me. But that's the thing. I was found. Followed. But that's not why I called. I wanted to call to tell you I have proof. I cleared my name. Well, your dad helped a lot.

"Baby, I've listened to your voicemails. I have heard them and listened to them. Memorized them. Most nights, hearing the sound of your voice is the only way I can fall asleep. The thought of putting all this behind me and holding you in my arms again is the only thing that gets me through the nights and keeps me going. I wish I could have told you all of this in person. And I know I will soon. I wish I could've told you how I felt sooner and why I had to wait until now. I wish it could have been sooner.

"Allison, I love you. I know I have not always been the best of boyfriends, but I have always loved you. More so with each day and the time apart has certainly made my heart grow fonder. I don't know where you are, but please know that I love you and can't wait until we can be with each other and not worry about anything but what we can do to make up for lost time. Call me. I love you, Al."

Connor hangs up the phone but leaves it on. If Vistrus cleared his name, as he said he would, turning it off would no longer be a safety measure.

CHAPTER 17

I am not sure what I am supposed to say.
I've read that this is what people do.
They leave notes. So, I'm leaving a note. I
don't know who will get this read this. If
someone does, I guess I should say something. That's the rub, though, in order
to say something you have to know something. And I don't know anymore. I don't
know what to think. I don't know how
to do it. This thing called life beats us
down. It tells us we can't be ourselves. It
tells us we must hide who we are because
people only understand what looks like
them, what talks like them. People don't
want giant freaks roaming the streets.
Well, as said freak, I am not sure I can
hide. I am not sure we should hide. I
am not sure about everything, anything,
whatever. I do this not because I am mad
at anyone or hate anyone. I think I let
go of my hate when I admitted my feelings. I am not doing this because of her. I
am sorry, though. I am sorry, Con, about
putting you in the middle of it. I am
sorry I didn't better understand your side
when college was hard. I am sorry I didn't
give you your space.

I am sorry, Scarlett, that you had to deal with my shit for all these years and are left with no one to deal with yours. And I am especially sorry about that. That is my fault. I got Jack killed. I don't know if you ~~knew~~ know that or not. I was having a day and had one too many from my handy flask. What a joke picking that thing up was. Never should have done that. But I can't undo it. I can't bring Jack back. I can't unsay what I said in the hallway. I can't make Mrs. Espinoza unhear what I said. I can't make Jack undead, not dead. Whatever. I can't go back in time and bring him back. I can't love Connor as I need to. I can't understand the why of everything happening. I have tried and tried to read through Mom's diaries, trying to understand why she didn't tell someone. Trying to understand what she felt so unspeakable that ~~is~~ was safer for everyone that she pretend to decline, speaking in cryptic riddles. I have always loved you, Connor. I have only ever loved you, but my mind betrays my feelings, and I can't be what everyone needs.

I can't be what or who I need to be. I wish I could. I wish I could be happy. I wish I ~~could~~ can understand what it all means. I wish I could walk outside and be confident in who I am. I wish I could believe in the disease and the Societies and The Nation and the ridiculousness that everyone seems to be buying into. That we are all ... or at least I am a vampire, or whatever we are supposed to call ourselves. What a strange thing to be so confused over. We spent our entire lives being told they aren't real, then one day it's surprise; not only are they real, but I'm one of them. That's a hard pill to swallow ... oh, I get that phrase now. Doesn't matter. I feel like either I abandoned everyone or everyone's abandoned me, and I can't do this on my own. I can't, and I'm sorry. Maybe had things been different. I don't know what or how, but different. Somehow. Someway. So many little things that could have and should have been different. If those all added up, perhaps, it wouldn't be like this. It wouldn't have ended this way. All the little things ... ha.

It's never one thing that leads to this. It's a hundred things. Well, many things. Maybe not a hundred. Maybe more. I never counted them all. But they happened. All of them, building and snowballing to roll down that hill and push me here. I wish I could have been what everyone needed me to be. I wish I could

have been what I needed me to be. I wish
I could have loved myself the way I loved
you all. I do love you all and will see you
on the other side.

Love always,

This Vampire Named Allison Petrovsky

Allison places the journal on the floor next to the tub, resting the pen on top. Turning off the water, she lays her head back against the wall, sliding down into the water. She rests for a moment before surfacing to grab the razor blade off the tub ledge. Her heart beats steadily as she holds the blade in her hand. She stops for a moment to listen to the lyrics being sung through a small speaker about death. An old Megadeth song titled "A Tout Le Monde" has been playing on repeat since she closed the bathroom door. Over and over she listens to the lyrics, holding the razor in her hand.

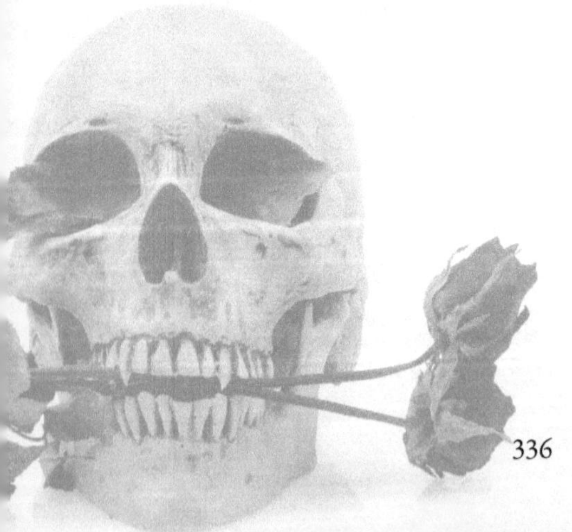

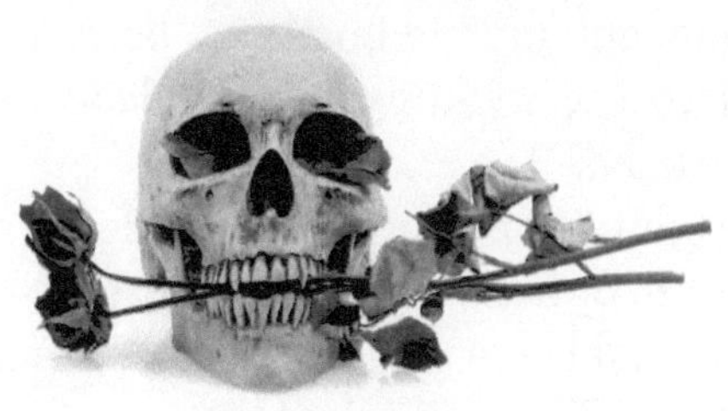

CHAPTER 18

"Silence can kill."

~H. McAllister~

Brianna and Duncan sit in her living room, drinking beer and watching the nightly news play out as they go over a coffee table full of wedding details. She turns to him. "I can't believe we're actually watching the news. I feel like such a grown-up."

Duncan smiles, shaking his head. "It's all the small things, isn't it?"

Her brow furrows. "What's that supposed to mean?"

Upon hearing her almost accusatory tone, a chuckle escapes him. "It means, we're planning our wedding. Not in general, but literally right now, but it's the news that makes you feel grown-up. I think it's adorable."

She turns to the binder and papers scattered in front of them. "This makes sense. You don't make me feel old or whatever. Watching the news does."

Duncan sips his bottle of beer, and then holds it out to the wedding plans. "Babe, do you realize what we did?"

Bri thinks for a moment but doesn't want to strain her brain, opting to shake her head. "Nope. What?"

"We planned a wedding. We're done."

"Done? That can't be right."

"Okay, not done done. We still have to tour the chosen halls, taste food and cakes. But all the big decisions are done." He sips his beer.

"Almost all the big decisions. We still need a date."

"Truth. We never picked one."

"I was thinking a fall wedding. I know New Year's Eve or Day has always been the hot choice, but winter is … well … cold." Bri shrugs, taking a drink of her beer.

"Halloween," Duncan offers.

"Halloween?" Bri seems confused.

"It's a holiday where people dress up in costumes."

Bri playfully slaps him on the arm. "I know what Halloween is. I am not sure why you think that's a good idea."

He sets down his beer, ready to get serious when the news cuts to a picture of Connor taken during a baseball game with the words "Suspect in the murder of Nick DeSalvo" below it. A blonde reporter in a blue dress speaks, "Connor DeSalvo. In the ever-developing story of the murder of West Haven's own Nick DeSalvo, the aforementioned Connor DeSalvo has been the center of this investigation. And it seems there has finally been a break … and a twist … in the case." A red circle with a diagonal line through it pops up over the picture. "And the twist is good news for Connor DeSalvo. New evidence exonerates him from any pending charges, clearing his name..."

The rest of the words fade from their ears as Bri picks up her phone, dialing Allison. Before the phone can ring enough to go to voicemail, the call is rejected, sending it straight there.

"Al! I can only assume you saw the news and are already on the phone making googly sounds at each other. In case you weren't though and have no idea what I'm talking about, Connor is cleared. Innocent. Free. Whatever. Call your man, come over here. Celebrate!" She hangs up the phone, an ear-to-ear smile on her.

Duncan hugs her. "This is great news. I never thought he did it."

"Me neither."

"I also never thought the media or cops would stop until they had a fall guy."

She pulls in the hug tighter for a moment before releasing. "Not every situation turns out horribly."

A one-sided smile irks out as he huffs. "Apparently so. Glad I can be wrong."

Before they can return to discussing the date of their wedding, a knock at the door further interrupts them.

"Coming!" Bri chimes. As she opens the door, she starts babbling away, unaware of who stands there. "Al, I just called you. Did you hear?"

But as the door fully opens, she does not see Allison or Connor. Neither does she see Vistrus nor Eleanor. No. All the joy on her face drains away upon seeing the face of the man who was responsible for killing Connor's parents, Ken and Tracy. The man who helped orchestrate the death of Jack Taylor and his parents. Officer Max Espinoza. Badge number 51. The man who was given a chance to leave town has dared show his face again, and, of all places, at the home in which he and his now deceased wife killed Sylvia Waldgrave, Bri's mother.

Before Max has a chance to part his lips to speak, a shrill, panicked, horrifying scream emanates from Bri, "Dunca—!!" Her cry for help cuts off as three teeth fall out from her mouth, blood trickling with them.

While seated only ten or so feet from the door, Duncan jumps over to her as if he had never left her side. He sees the panic and terror on her face, the blood dripping from her mouth, and hair starting to fall off in chunks. Eyeing the man at the door, Duncan drapes his arm around her, walking her away from Max and back toward the couch.

"I know who you are. You are not welcome here," Duncan warns.

Max puts up his hands to show he means no harm this time around. "I am not here to fight."

"Just to cause panic and mayhem? I've seen your kind before. You lord your power over those you consider lesser. You think that because you were granted some modicum of authority, you can use it to make up for all the insecurities you feel about how Mommy never hugged you enough or Daddy didn't say he loved you ever by taking it out on everyone else. Exacting some sort of revenge for your child-hood trauma." While talking, he rubs Bri's arms and shoulders, trying to calm her down while keeping an eye on Max. Turning to her, he adds, "It'll be okay, love. I am here."

His words do nothing to calm her. Her receding lips and withering nose add to her anxiety and panic. Bri sits, hyperventilating on the couch as her skin sags off the bones and face sinks farther in with each passing moment.

Max still stands in the doorway, arms up. "I have made mistakes. Mistakes is the wrong word. I have made wrong choices. Done bad, horrible, terrible things. I did not know what I'd done. And yes, I am responsible for her mother's death. I was told never to return."

Bri turns to him, left eyeball starting to pop out of its socket. "Then why rethurn?" Her words slur as her jaw slackens in its socket.

"Because of what I've learned. I wanted to come sooner. I wanted to tell everyone. Safety in numbers for you and to be sure what I told you wasn't false. Wasn't some rumor to make you think I was trying to deceive you. I have news. Big, terrible news."

Max dares step past the doorway and into the house. Duncan shoots him an evil eye. Heeded, he stops one step inside.

Bri tries calming her breathing a little, but her transition continues. Her eye hangs out of the socket as skin rots away, exposing bone. She goes to speak, but her jaw won't function. Only inarticulate grunts sound forth.

Duncan shakes in anger, turning back to Max. "Why? What is so important that you need to be here? Haven't you caused enough pain?"

Max searches for his words before speaking. "I have caused tremendous suffering. I can never make that up. I understand I am beyond redemption. But haven't you watched the news?"

Before Max can continue, Duncan interrupts, "The news? You came here to discuss the news?!" Growing angrier, he snaps back, "Yes, lovely weather we're having. Such a great time for grilling and botchi ball!"

"No. The battle between the new thrill park and the World Health Organization. It's not what it seems."

Duncan holds his words back, still trying to calm Brianna down, who seems to be holding steady at this point in her transition. Though not calm, she holds herself better than before. Duncan nods to her hanging eye. "Can you see okay, baby?"

She shrugs, bobbing her head side to side, and shakes a hand as her non-verbal answer. Before Duncan can get too far off track, she tilts her chin back to Max. "Whaaa…" is all she manages to say.

Max dares take another step inside. This time, he meets no resistance. "All right, sir. When I took part in those … unspeakable acts, I took notes. I performed tests. As did others."

"Who? What others?" Duncan insists.

Max shakes his head. "Never got their names. I was told who to answer to, what to do, and all that was paid with empty promises. I was never going to be cured. I was never going to rid myself of the thing I hated."

Duncan shoves a hand toward him, stopping him. "No pity parties. What's your point?"

Max continues, "I thought that what I was part of was some localized cell. Something that went nowhere. A group of people who didn't like what they saw in others and I in myself."

"But?" Duncan adds.

"But I was wrong. It is so much bigger than I ever imagined. It's bigger than West Haven, bigger than Chicagoland, and all of Illinois. You can't think that this small town houses all the Legends there are, do you?" Max pauses to give them a moment to think about that, but not to respond. "This is larger than all the United States. It's worldwide. The Nation, the Societies, all of it." Max takes a breath. "I was never told. I was never given information when I did those things. I had to work my way back into their ranks. Pretend to be this thing that I once was and not hated so I could learn. So, I could see the scope of it all."

Duncan tries to keep this all straight in his mind. "What does this have to do with some new medical center?"

"The World Health Organization is a research facility. The CDC. All those cities the news mentioned were possible homes for the next center. They are all hubs for The Nation—surrounding towns with councils and Legends and people deciding who would be their next test subjects."

Duncan shakes his head in disbelief. "No way. The CDC is good. The World Health Organization would not secretly experiment on people."

"No. They wouldn't. Not the organizations as we know them, but someone inside is."

"Who?" Duncan asks.

A voice new to this conversation pipes in from outside the entryway. "Apparently, that's what we need to find out." Connor flashes a friendly hello smile to everyone. Seeing Bri, he walks to her, sitting on the opposite side of Duncan. "I need you to breathe slowly. Think happy thoughts. Even if those thoughts are ripping off this guy's head. Happy thoughts. Slow breaths." Connor looks around, searching. "Where's Al?"

Duncan nods at Connor. "Been tryin'. This guy's nuts for coming here, spewing all this nonsense." He stops for a beat before realizing there is still one unanswered question. "She's not here. Thought she was with you. Good news and all."

"Might be workin'." He turns to Max, hiking a thumb his way. "But what he says is worth a listen. I've seen some things while I was hiding. Things that make a little more sense, hearing him now." Connor turns to Bri. "It's great to see you again, Bri. Let's see what we can do to grow your beautiful hair back." Connor rises from the couch and heads to the kitchen.

Max clears his throat, grabbing their attention. "The cure was never the final phase. They want to wipe out every last one of us. We need to stop them."

"Hhhhhh," is Bri's attempt at conversation.

Duncan chimes in, "How?"

"Find the man in charge of it all. Cut off the head of the snake, so to speak."

From the kitchen, Connor adds, "But who is that? How many Legends are left in West Haven to go against an army?"

Duncan shrugs one shoulder. "An army of humans. I think a few of you guys in full form stand a good chance."

Connor shakes a drink in the kitchen, speaking over the noise. "Do we know who this person is leading this assault?"

Max steps further inside. "Is there *anyone* you trust? A Legend who might be able to help answer that?"

Duncan turns to Connor, shrugging. "I ain't got no one in my family."

Connor turns to Bri, who still sits in her Legendary state. Her lower jaw still missing and eyeball hanging there, though something about her seems calmer than before. She holds up a peace sign.

"Peace?" Duncan says, confused.

Shaking her head, she turns the sign around.

"Two?" Connor takes a guess.

Shaking her head again, she tries to speak. "Eeeee." Bri grunts in frustration and concentrates on the word. As she does, her lower jaw regrows the bone and attached muscles. "V."

Excited tears well in her eye and eye socket. The other eye falls off as a new one grows in its place.

"Vishtrus." She slurs as the muscles tighten. "Vistrus."

Connor takes out his cell and dials his number, but it goes to voicemail. "Nope."

They all think for a moment. "I could call Grams?"

There are smiles all around as he dials her up. "Grandma. Hey, we're all at Bri's." A moment for him to listen. "Yeah. Sylvia's daughter." He listens again. "Yeah, we're here. Can you come over? It's pretty important." He listens to her words. "Love you, too. See you soon."

He sits next to Bri again, opposite Duncan. "You're looking better."

"It doeshn't … doesn't hurt anymore. Talking … is harder, though," she admits.

Max holds up a finger, adding, "Members of the Tennyson Society experience that sometimes. You'll be fine in a bit."

A sad nod confirms his words. "Truth. But, like my now less-than-perfect skin, something might not be quite as right as it was before I transitioned."

"Again, those will lessen and end."

"How do you know all this?" Duncan asks. "From your time killing them?"

Max shutters at his words. "After. When I went back. The things I saw…"

"He's not wrong, though." Bri's words sound more confident in their pronunciation. Her rotting skin reforming. "The Councilmen guy told me some of this when I first, idk, flipped out, transitioned, or whatever." Bri looks at them, staring at her as she transitions back to her normal self. "What? Why's everyone staring?"

Everyone shakes their heads, waving hands, and mutters words in their defense.

"Fine. What-ever," Bri resigns. "But now that I can talk again, I tried calling Allison to tell her the good news that you've been, like, proven innocent, but it went to voicemail. Figured she was already doing sexy phone time with you."

Connor scratches his neck. "Sexy phone time?"

"Yeah, you know." Bri switches between imitating Connor and Allison. "'Oh, baby, it's been so long.' 'Oh, yeah, soooo long, Con.'"

Everyone lets out a well-needed laugh.

"Stop. I get it." Connor's laughter continues. "But no. I stopped by her house and left a message as well."

"Two messages and no pickup?" Bri ponders.

"Maybe she left her phone in the backroom?" Duncan offers a simple solution.

The talking seems to be working to calm Bri. Her skin has fully recovered from the transition, and her jaw and eye are formed again. All with no new imperfections for her to later dwell on.

"After we figure this all out, I'll stop by her work. Surprise her. I could really use some time with her."

Duncan raises his eyebrows twice. "Yeah, you could."

"Not what I meant, but yeah, that too." Connor chuckles his admittance.

The front door opens with a knock. Eleanor walks in holding the framed charcoal portrait of Scarlett she presented to her.

"And she comes bearing gifts," Bri jokes.

Before Eleanor can answer, Max steps toward her, hand extended to greet her. "You must be Eleanor?"

Eleanor looks him up and down, shaking his hand with noticed hesitation. Pulling away a little too quickly, she looks down at the portrait. "This is for

Scarlett. Sorry, dear. When you said to come over, I figured she was here."

"Nope. Don't know where she is," Connor says.

Bri turns to Eleanor. "She's not dead anymore?!"

Connor loses his breath for a moment. "What?! Scarlett died?!"

Eleanor sets the portrait down before turning to her grandchild. "So much you did not know. All is well, child. Scarlett is alive and well. She went to see that tiny girl, Allison."

Bri, Duncan, and Connor all turn to each other, nodding in agreement that Allison and Scarlett must be somewhere, doing something.

Connor turns back to his grandmother. "So, she didn't die?"

Eleanor shakes her head. "No. She was in the Waiting. I'll explain later. What did you all need?"

Max speaks up. "There is something happening in West Haven."

Eleanor nods. "Yes. Stuff you've been a big part of."

"I see you know who I am." Max's words are not filled with confidence, but another reminder that redemption is beyond his reach.

"After what you've done, I don't think there's many Legends around here that haven't committed your description to memory." The ice over Eleanor's words chills him.

"Deserved," Max admits.

Connor steps to the matriarch. "Grams, there's something bigger going on. The WHO is building a new facility and if Max is right, it will make the last few years seem like a cakewalk."

His words grab her attention with a steel grip. She turns to Max. "Fine. What is it that this old lady can do?"

"Rumor has it Nick was not the head of The Council. You were," Max cuts to the chase.

Eleanor smiles at a rumor she hasn't heard in decades. "I've heard that before. I always find it amusing that no matter the situation, it always comes back to that old adage."

"What old adage?" Bri chimes in.

"That behind every man in charge is a woman who makes the decisions," Duncan answers.

"One of many takes on that, but yes." Eleanor nods in his direction. "Knowing things and being in charge are not the same. I know things. But anyone who's lived as long as I does."

Max interjects, "Well? What do you know?"

"Oh, sweetie. Had you asked me a few days ago, I'd've said not nearly as much as I do today." She offers up a smile. "My dearly departed was begin-ning to think that maybe The Council was not all that they seemed. He thinks … thought some of them were not…" She stops mid-thought, unsure what is safe to say in front of this killer of Legends, road to redemption or not. She reorganizes her thoughts. "If Connor is right and the last few years are only a glimpse of what's to come, then we need to know why and why now."

"He says The Nation is bigger than West Haven, that it's worldwide." Connor starts pacing.

A delightful laugh escapes Eleanor. "Of course, it is. Do you think I was born here? My darlings, I've lived all over. Under different names. Spoken different languages. West Haven is not unique." Gesturing to Max, she adds, "Is that what this man led you to believe?"

All three of the young adults turn to each other, unsure how to respond. Max tries to clarify. "When I said worldwide, I meant the experiments. The new research facility is the latest. The newest tech, and it will be the closest they come to wiping us off the map."

Eleanor takes in the gravity of the situation, finding a chair to sit on. The suffocating silence of the moment surrounds them. Each turns to the other for some unspoken answer. Eleanor turns to the portrait of Scarlett, the Grey Fairy. A thought ember smolders in her mind, connecting the timing of it all. She rubs the amulet hiding under her blouse, thinking of how the puzzle pieces all fit together.

"We have a prophecy," Eleanor starts.

"The one that died with my parents?" Connor continues pacing, thinking about her words.

"Yes. Then there are the murders and the experiments, and the reason Nick thought The Council was not all they seemed to be," she adds to the pot.

"How does this all fit together?" Bri asks with a raised hand.

Eleanor gives Max a once-over, debating if the next words she wants to speak are words she can trust him with. After a good moment of deliberation, she decides that since he has been here this long with no incident, it is safe for now. "If my source is right, then it all connects to the murders that Inessa Petrovsky was sent to investigate."

"But what connects them?" Max asks the million-dollar question.

"If Vistrus's theory is correct…" Eleanor begins, but a frenzied knock at the door interrupts her.

Eleanor, still being the closest to the door, opens it to find Bishop standing there.

Bri sees past Eleanor to the lumberjack-sized man in red flannel she does not recognize. "Who are you?" she calls to him. "What do you want?"

Bishop moves past Eleanor into the home. Max tries to control his emotions, but Connor sees something in his eyes. A primal response that he has felt before. Noticing Max start to transition, Connor works his emotions to the edge, controlling what he can so his strength will be there when he needs it.

"Eleanor, I followed you here," Bishop starts, ignoring Bri's words. "It's not safe. Connor is still wanted by the police." He points at Max. "And this man killed Ken and Tracy."

Eleanor's head tilts, knowing a hidden agenda hides behind false concerns.

"Connor's been cleared, Bishop. Max may be another matter, but neither of those is why you are here."

Duncan, Bri, Connor, and Max all tense up. The words spoken by their elder do anything but ease their minds. This causes Connor's senses to heighten. He picks up noises outside the house—soft, creeping footsteps making their way around back. Connor waves a subtle hand at Max, grabbing his attention. He points to his ear, so Max knows to listen. Connor mouths the words, "Hear that?" Max listens for a moment, nodding that he does.

Bishop steps toward Eleanor, giving her his best puppy dog eyes. Though she does not allow him to speak, she adds, "This isn't about me or Nick. It's about you."

With those words, Bishop's puppy dog eyes squint into a glare. Connor sits beside Bri, whispering in her ear. "You feel like you can control yourself if you need to?"

Bri turns to him, not wanting whatever is about to transpire to happen in her house. "I'm not sure. It's still a bit rough."

Connor taps Duncan. "Tell her something nice."

"Like what?" Duncan searches for specifics.

"Give her something to be confident about," Connor suggests, turning back to his grandmother and Bishop.

Bishop huffs. "In some way, it's always been about me."

Eleanor shakes her head, wagging a finger at him. "About you and the Body, the Mind, and Inessa." Her disbelief fades away. "How could you have done this to my family?"

Those words stop Bishop dead in his tracks. Connor also hears the tiptoeing outside halt. An eerie silence descends as everyone waits for some sort of response from somewhere.

"It wasn't supposed to be like this!" Bishop's demeanor shifts. His shouted words trigger an exposed ambush as two blond men break through windows into Bri's house. Bishop grabs Eleanor by the arm, causing Connor to transition into full Legend form, unleashing a painful, guttural scream as he does. Never has Connor gone from Normal to Legend so fast, a process his body is still not acclimated to. The warning scream pulls Bishop's attention from Eleanor, allowing her to pull free from his grip. Bishop swats at Connor, sending him to the floor.

Bri stands to intervene, but one of the blond men grabs her, forcing her back to the couch. The jolt and surrounding commotion send her full-spiral back into her transition—eyeball bulging, jaw hanging slack, skin rotting, nose withered, and hair thinned. Duncan darts between his fiancée and the blond man. Max sees this and steps toward them, his muscles growing hypertrophic and patchy hair growing over his arms and hands. The blond man pulls a long knife from his boot, lunging at Duncan, but Max pushes him out of the way, taking the hit. The knife plunges deep into the upper right-hand side of Max's abdomen, penetrating the other side. Falling to the ground, Max reaches his thickened, claw-like nails out, gripping the blond man by the neck and sinking them in. He pulls the knife from Max, and blood pours from both sides of the wound. Max wastes no time ripping through the man's neck, sending his gurgling, dying body to the ground.

Standing back up, Connor rushes Bishop. Grappling the old man, Connor takes him to the ground. He raises his fist, ready to drop hammer strikes onto Bishop's face, when his skin turns to bark, protecting him from the blows. This does not stop Connor from doing what he can to protect those who remain of his family. Clawing and striking over and over, Connor recognizes the futility of his actions. Connor rises off Bishop but keeps his guard on him, and the second blond man side tackles Connor.

Eleanor pulls the man off him with strength beyond both her years and physique. She looks down at Connor, outstretching a hand to help him up, allowing Bishop the opportunity to scurry out the door.

Duncan wipes himself off as he stands, squatting next to the man who saved his life, trying to stop the bleeding.

Bri, seeing the other blond man kip up off the floor, rushes toward him. Spotting her old jawbone and eye lying next to the overturned table, she grabs them. The blond man reaches into his boots, pulling out a similar long knife to the one that the other man had. Bri sees this and yells, throwing her old eyeball at him, pegging him above his right eye.

"Did you just throw an eyeball at me!?" he shouts, pointing the knife at her.

Bri shouts again, swinging the jawbone his way, knocking the knife from his hand.

As she closes the gap, he pulls out a smaller knife, swiping at her and lopping off a chunk of her arm. She does not react to the blow, instead stiff-arming his face and sending him to the floor. She jumps on top of him, whacking him over and over in the face with the detached jaw. As the teeth tear into him over and over like some primitive melee weapon rending flash from an enemy, she accosts him, "How dare you, like, action-movie-jump through my windows, which I now need to replace, and try to kill the man I love!"

As she speaks, her slack jaw grows stronger and her eye recedes into its socket. "My home is not to be used as some slaughterhouse, got it?!" Her blows fall on dead ears. The blond man no longer tries to defend himself. "My friends and my family are not targets for your crazy ass … whatever! Leave my Duncan alone!!!" With one final blow, her detached jawbone snaps in half on what was previously a face and now looks like a ribeye steak over pounded by a meat mallet.

Duncan grabs Bri, pulling him off the dead man. "Baby, I'm all right. Max saved me."

Bri stops, fully back in her Normal state. With tears streaming down her face, she collapses in his arms.

Connor runs to Max, crouching beside him. "Where's your vial?"

Max shakes his head.

Connor rephrases, "Where's your 21-grams?"

Again, Max shakes his head.

"Why do you keep doing that?! I need to know you have it so we can save you." Connor gives him a gentle shake.

Max's words are weak. "I don't have one. Never knew how to preserve them."

Eleanor, hearing his words, steps over to them. "I do not know you, only what you did." She kneels beside him, opposite Connor. She turns to her grandson. "I got this, child." Connor nods and walks to Duncan and Bri. Eleanor turns back to Max. "Your actions here saved a Normal. I thank you for that, but I cannot say I am sad to see you go. Perhaps, now, you shall find peace." Seeing the life fade fast from Max's eyes, she closes them for him and sits, waiting for his end.

Connor stands next to Duncan, who still holds Bri. "Duncan, is there anything I can do?"

Duncan shakes his head. "I got her. She'll be okay."

Connor nods, pulling out his cell phone. He sees Allison has not returned his call. "Grams, Allison…"

Eleanor nods. "Go. Find her. Tell her you're free. Be with her. I can take care of this mess."

Connor nods, making one last check with Duncan before heading out the door, finding Bishop long gone.

Bri continues crying into Duncan's shoulder for a while longer. The sounds of chaos and battle have quieted, and Max has passed on.

Eleanor stands, surveying the scene, hoping there's a way she can salvage Bri's home. She heads to the kitchen and dials a number. All Duncan and Bri can hear is Eleanor say they need a full carpet cleaning service and possible remodel at her address … and that tomorrow is too late.

Pulling away from Duncan and drying her tears on his shirt, she looks at him. "Halloween sounds perfect."

Connor's Mustang pulls into the record store parking lot. The lights are still on, but the open sign has been turned off. Exiting his car, all seems quiet and after the night's events, silence does not sit well with him. He tries the door, but it is already locked. Spying movement near the back, he knocks on the window. The figure moves from behind the aisle toward the window, but it is not Allison. Connor waves, offering a friendly smile.

"We're closed!" the clerk shouts through the glass.

"I'm looking for Allison. Is she still here?" Connor replies.

The clerk shakes his head. "Didn't work today. Sorry, bro." With his final words, the clerk returns to his closing duties.

Connor stands outside the record store, a lone soul in the parking lot. Pulling out his cell, he dials Allison, again going straight to voicemail. Not knowing why she wouldn't answer, he tries his cousin. One ring, and she answers. Before he can say anything, he starts running toward his car, hanging up without saying a word.

Scarlett feels an eerie silence surrounding the Petrovsky residence as she steps up the driveway. She notices the missing feeling of anticipated liveliness that she always feels when approaching a friend's house. Those little ideas that flutter into her mind of what they might be doing inside as she approaches the door—what chair Mr. Petrovsky is sitting in or what Allison is listening to on her stereo. Nothing floats through her mind, and it does not sit pretty with her. She slows her steps as she approaches the door, wondering to herself if this newfound dread somehow relates to having been dead, or if it is something else. She ponders if it is some unspoken anxiety about Allison seeing her with brown hair and eyes and a freckle-less face.

Standing at the door, she tries shaking off her anxiety. The house is vacant of joyous laughter echoing through the door or lights shining from lamps, telling the outside world there is life inside.

An intrusive thought enters her head as she peeks into the house, trying to see something that alleviates her fears. A thought that, perhaps, is trying to calm her down and tell her that everything will be all right. She has this idea that she is in some strange musical; at this moment, it is more *Sweeney Todd* than *Sound of Music,* but either way, the humor in that is something she pushes down. *This is not the time for this nonsense.* No footstep approaches or whispers from the kitchen. No sounds that settle. She hears nothing when she listens. Not a faint sound from a violin string. These are definitely not a few of her favorite things.

She knocks and straightens her clothes as if waiting for a cute boy to answer the door for a date. The silent moments that follow do nothing to quell her fears or tell her they are unfounded.

She knocks again. With still no answer, she realizes that while her fears still might be remnants of the Waiting, some foundation begins solidifying for them. She bends her ear to the door and listens, but nothing.

Knocking again, Scarlett calls out, "Allison!" Still nothing. The concrete foundation holding up her fears further cures. "Come on, Al! This isn't funny!"

With still no answer, she tries the door. Locked. She pats her pockets as if she might have a key but comes up short. She looks around as if her one time breaking and entering might somehow provide insight, but again, nothing.

An idea simmers that the back of the house is the answer. Perhaps Allison decided to chill outside and soak in the beauty of the suburban life. A thought that sends a chuckle to her throat, only to die there. Shaking her head, she heads around back.

No one. No half-pint of a woman sitting, napping, drinking from her flask. Vistrus does not strum some obscure instrument in beautiful song while the smell of cigar smoke fills the air. Nothing.

She looks up at Allison's window. Her lights are off. Maybe she is taking a nap, just in her bed and not outside.

Scarlett tries the sliding glass door, finding it unlocked. Even the wood stick used to keep it from opening sits off to the side. Peeking her head inside, she calls out, "Anybody home?"

Scarlett steps in after no one answers. If nothing else, she locks the patio door behind her. Vistrus will be happy about that—if he ever realizes the door was left unlocked. A noise catches her ear, faint and not so distant. Coarse, gritty singing over beautiful and melancholy guitar. Music while Allison showers. Explains why no one answered the door.

All of Scarlett's fears crumble on the budding foundation. Simple answer for a simple question. Music while showering makes it hard to hear. Though, as Scarlett makes her way upstairs, she hears the song end, and the start of the next song is eerily similar to the one that just ended. As the words come to the refrain and the sound becomes clearer, she realizes it is the same song … and that she does not hear the shower running.

"Allison! I've got some things to tell you. You're not gonna believe it." But Allison does not respond, even as Scarlett stops outside the bathroom door.

She knocks, hoping not to startle Al, but still there is no answer. Scarlett listens to the words sung through the speakers of life, loss, and moving on. "Come on, Al. Open up."

The lack of response sends Scarlett's heart into her throat. "I'm coming in."

Opening the door, the humidity from a hot shower does not smack against her. No foggy mirror or condensed water on a ceiling when the fan wasn't turned on. She turns to greet a friend, warning against seeing her in her birthday suit, but stumbles back against the door before she can speak. The red-tinted water surrounding her best friend re-solidifies the foundation beneath the fears felt outside. Tears start streaming down her face as she rushes to Allison, shaking her to wake up. Allison does not respond. Glints of steel catch Scarlett's eye. First to the onyx-crusted pentacle earrings she kept in, then to the razor blade set on the corner of the tub against the wall. In a frantic haze, she pulls Allison's arms out of the water and checks her wrists—across and down. Scarlett pushes out all thoughts of why Allison wanted to do this and thinks about what she can do at this moment. Without realizing she still holds her best friend's arm in her hand, she wipes the tears from her face with Allison's hand as if it were a rag.

The thought of what she did sends her stomach churning and her to the toilet. She lifts the lid in time to lean over the toilet and revisit the cookies at her grandmother's house. Wiping her mouth, this time with her shirt, she looks back at her friend, but more food works its way up and out. Wiping her mouth again on her shirt, she grabs the towel from the ring beside the sink and gets an idea.

Grabbing Allison's wrists, she uses the sink towel and the bath towels as tourniquets, though the bleeding has already stopped. She drags her friend out of the tub, wrapping her in a towel. She rests Allison against the side of the tub and calls Mr. Petrovsky on her cell phone.

"Come on! Come on! Come on! Answer!" Scarlett shouts to the universe.

"Hello?"

"Mr. Petrovsky! It's Scarlett."

"Are you okay?"

Scarlett takes a breath, deliberating her next words. "It's Allison. Come home, now."

The definitiveness in her voice, the resolve in her words, left no room for interpretation for Vistrus. "On my way."

Scarlett drops the phone, not bothering to hang up, and grabs Allison, rocking her back and forth. "Allison, come on. Hang in there. Allison!"

She holds her friend, fighting down the urge to revisit what might still be left in her stomach. She rocks back and forth, listening over and over to "A Tout Le Monde" on repeat.

Her mind tries to understand the events. Perhaps she never woke up and is still in the Waiting. Her mind tries to convince her this is all just a dream, surreal and vivid, but false, nonetheless—that Allison is not dead, and this is Scarlett's personal hell for some evil deeds committed over the past few years. For no just and benevolent God would do such a thing to her, and surely would not allow such a kind, albeit feisty, soul such as Allison to do this to herself.

Scarlett's phone rings. Seeing "Connor" on the caller ID, she answers before it can ring again. "It's Al. Get to her house, now." She hangs up with no further explanation needed.

The thoughts, rationalizations, and possibilities play out over and over, overlapping one another, growing larger and flooding her mind with each passing moment. Tears streak down her face, blurring her vision, but she does not wipe the tears, lest she let go of her best friend. Scarlett stays rocking, holding Allison in this bathroom-turned-hell while the outside world fills with sounds of chirping birds, kids laughing and playing, and teenagers falling in love. But in here, in this bathroom in the Petrovsky house, all has ended for Allison and, at least for the moment, for Scarlett as well.

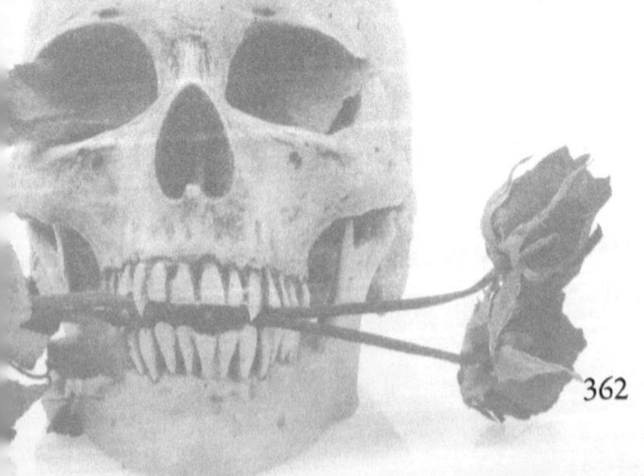

BOOK CLUB QUESTIONS

1. What would you consider the overall theme or themes of this book?

2. Are these themes similar to the themes from the other books in this series?

3. Do you think things would be different for Allison if she were a Normal?

4. Is ignorance bliss or just an excuse to ignore issues people don't want to or aren't ready to deal with?

5. Why do you think Vistrus accepts his nature so willingly but also believes that the myths within The Nation can't be true?

6. Who is your favorite character and why?

7. Why do you think the author chose realism in a fantasy novel instead of tried-and-true tropes relating to the undead and supernatural?

8. Who is your least favorite character and why?

9. Does the fact that this series is rooted in science make it any more believable than traditional fantasy?

10. If you've read the three preceding books, which is your favorite so far and why?

ABOUT AUTHOR

Nick Savage originally hails from the Chicagoland area but currently resides in the greater Orlando area with his wife and two cats. Besides being an award-winning and Amazon best-selling author, he is also an avid video game nerd, artist, and musician.

Other books by Nick Savage:

Other books in *The West Haven Undead* series:
Us Of Legendary Gods
So We Stay Hidden
The West Haven Undead

The Fairlane Incidents

The Fortunate Finn Fairlane
The Fragile Finn Fairlane
Finn Fairlane: The Complete Package
Coming Soon:
World Whore, D

Also featured in the anthology
Once Upon a Brothers Grimm (AMR Publishing)
Summer of '87: A Rock Anthology
(Venom Studioz Publishing)

More books from 4 Horsemen Publications

Paranormal & Urban Fantasy

Amanda Fasciano
Waking Up Dead
Dead Vessel
Dead Show
Dead Revelations
Dead Carnage

Beau Lake
The Beast Beside Me
The Beast Within Me
Taming the Beast: Novella
The Beast After Me
Charming the Beast: Novella
The Beast Like Me

Chelsea Burton Dunn
By Moonlight
Moon Bound
White Moon
New Moon Rising

J.M. Paquette
Call Me Forth
Invite Me In
Keep Me Close

Kait Disney-Leugers
Antique Magic
Blood Magic
I Heart Magic

Lyra R. Saenz
Prelude
Sonata
Scherzo
Ragtime Swing
Midnight Cumbia
Sea Song de la Corsaire
Falsetto in the Woods: Novella
The Devil's Trill

Megan Mackie
The Finder of the Lucky Devil
The Saint Liars
The Devil's Day
The Digital Mage

Paige Lavoie
I'm in Love with Mothman
I'm Engaged with Mothman

Robert J. Lewis
Shadow Guardian and the Three Bears
Shadow Guardian and the Big Bad Wolf
Shadow Guardian Boys That Went Woof

Valerie Willis
Cedric: The Demonic Knight
Romasanta: Father of Werewolves

The Oracle: Keeper of the
Gaea's Gate
Artemis: Eye of Gaea
King Incubus: A New Reign

Rebirth
Judgment
Death

SciFi

**BRANDON HILL &
TERENCE PEGASUS**
Between the Devil and the Dark
Wrath & Redemption

PC NOTTINGHAM
Mummified Moon
Severed Squadron

C.K. WESTBROOK
The Shooting
The Collision
The Judgment
The Aftermath

T.S. SIMONS
Project Hemisphere
The Space Between
Infinity
Circle of Protection
Sessrúmnir
The 45th Parallel
Orenda

NICK SAVAGE
Us of Legendary Gods
So We Stay Hidden
The West Haven Undead
A Vampire Named Allison

TY CARLSON
The Bench
The Favorite
The Shadowless
Convergence of Gods

**DISCOVER MORE AT
4HORSEMENPUBLICATIONS.COM**

www.ingramcontent.com/pod-product-compliance
Lightning Source LLC
Chambersburg PA
CBHW021415310726
48971CB00005B/1343